NEW STORIES
FROM THE SOUTH

The Year's Best, 2006

NEW STORIES
FROM THE SOUTH

The Year's Best, 2006

Selected from U.S. magazines by
ALLAN GURGANUS with KATHY PORIES

with an introduction by Allan Gurganus

Algonquin Books of Chapel Hill

Published by
ALGONQUIN BOOKS OF CHAPEL HILL
Post Office Box 2225
Chapel Hill, North Carolina 27515-2225

a division of
WORKMAN PUBLISHING
225 Varick Street
New York, New York 10014

ISSN 0897-9073
ISBN 1-56512-531-2

CONTENTS

Allan Gurganus

INTRODUCTION: THE REBELLION CONTINUES, AT LEAST IN THE SOUTHERN SHORT STORY

Battle Notes While Choosing 2006's *New Stories from the South*

"God created Man because He loved to hear stories."
—African proverb

What Northern academics pathologize as "Southern Gothic," native North Carolinians call "the Yankees retired next door."

New Stories from the Upper Middle West and Michigan Peninsula? There is no such thing. Why not? Surely citizens up there pay property tax six months earlier than do most Southerners. True, they have less. They have less racial strife, being mainly one unchallenged race (ex-Swedes?). Such prairie-dwellers probably never once considered marrying even their most attractive first-cousin. But, face it, the only region of the U.S. ever to declare war on every other region of the nation won—if not that great gray fib of secession, then most of the recuperating country's truest stories.

Southerners respect a joke, having been cast too long as the Hick in all Traveling Salesman tales. Flannery O'Connor, asked why Southern writers specialize in portraying freaks, answered with some pride, "Because we're still able to recognize one." Often at family reunions.

Feared for playing breakneck Bear Bryant hardball, Southerners remain championship grudge-bearers. That's excellent training for staying the world-class rememberers we are. It's an odd recipe, but the proof is in the stories. Take our itch for feuds and duels. Mix in our family pride over . . . well, over our family pride. Add history, acreage, the witch's brew of slavery, start—then really lose—a war, stir with 20-20 memory: flavor to taste. Hang over a hickory fire. Then age it good.

I'm sure that other regions—stretching West to Easterly—take better care of their picket fences. Certainly their small-town papers devote fewer column inches to property-line disputes leading to the use of contested fence posts as cudgels. More orderly record-keeping might go on in those distant lands of conifers and frostbite. But as for their impenitent brilliant lying? As for their in-depth knowledge of codes, tricks, sacraments, and livestock? As for their feeding fat into the blue campfire called Fiction?

Naw.

Every year, just as farm couples "put up" their canning, a fresh crop of short stories—Southerly forged and salt-sweat-cured— appears upon the table of some brave jurist south of Maryland.

That judge for these past two decades has been Shannon Ravenel. A cofounder of Algonquin Books, in 1985 she conceived *New Stories from the South*. Editing *Best American Stories* helped get her into Olympic trim for the tough regional squeeze play to come.

Imagine the countless Southern sagas Ravenel has weathered: all those tea parties, all those breakdowns. That's enough Spanish moss to crochet into a life-sized replica of King Kong. Having braved so many pages, this editor deserves her own Purple Heart, plus a Sunday school perfect-attendance pin made of beaten gold encrusted with emeralds.

Ravenel still smiles when discussing the Short Story and its Dixon-under-Mason tropical health. She notes the regional tradition of reliving local lives through short stories. Now that tobacco has been debunked, maybe the Short Story is our most addicting export.

Last year, she passed along the right of choosing; a series of guest writers will now do that. I said an impulsive *Yes* to going first. I soon understood the depth of Ms. Ravenel's labor. She had steadily perused over a hundred magazines and journals for twenty years straight. How would I hold up? In judging this Big Top gathering of living talent, I feared I might start groaning at each new stack of stories. These were left, like ransom-noted orphans, on my doorstep. A year is a long stretch when every inch of it comes covered with narrative.

But the quality, the press of a whole new generation coming into full voice, began to stir, then soothe and excite me. I end my term by feeling downright Mayoral. Fact is, I've started cornering people at parties, not with my *own* stories, but with those I've found. That's as unattractive as showing photos of your grand-children to strangers trapped beside you on some form of public transport.

Even so, there sure are a lot of Southerners writing (Southern) stories, are there not?

For the first time since college, enforced reading became a daily way of life. During airplane rides endless as my one to Easter Island, I kept a heavy lapful of tales. Like some new father toting diaper bags everywhere, I now carried three huge white envelopes. They were marked "YES!," "MAYBE?," "NO WAY!" At first, the middle one stayed fattest. But soon, protein migrated upward into the slim if rock-hard affirmative. Carbs sunk most stories of their own weight toward "NO."

At times I grew irksome: pulling for others' thwarted tries at this most difficult form. But, on finding the raw ore of a brand-new talent, elation came and stayed. These New Kids on the Block sometimes turned out to be even older and grayer than I—department heads at South something State University. But I bragged about them anyway. They were "new" to me.

Though New York publishing still treats the Short Story as a harelipped stepchild always tagging along behind that heiress called the Novel, the Story continues as our literature's truest Cinderella. Some scholars credit Edgar Allan Poe with the form's invention. Since Poe grew up in Richmond, any card-carrying Southerner might claim the Story, like jazz itself, as an essential Southerly–U.S. contribution to world culture.

But even in the most highly colored and eventful of regions, little is harder than writing a memorable short story. One thousand strategies go into telling a single tale. Each blueprint must be hidden under the breathing immediacy of a narrator's urgent "I." Each third-person overview must find the perfect fulcrum between convenient all-knowingness and the immediacy of human surprise.

Being vocal music, stories consist wholly of what singers call "exposed notes." Meaning: If you go sharp, everybody's likely to hear. Novels are more forgiving; chapters can vary in quality. They can be assembled so a weaker unit gets propped between its betters. But, poemlike, everything in a short story must count, show. The tale has to ride its own gyre while withholding its true method. There can be no dossier "background" for a character, all must emerge as essential visible action. In a story, narrative lift underwrites itself like the encouraging wind of Kitty Hawk hoisting the Wrights' cranky mixture of bamboo, varnished muslin, and combustion.

Not all the hundreds of entries I read were dazzling, alas. Not even Orville and Wilbur and the Army Air Corps could have got some off the ground.

But for every great country-and-western songline ("All my exes live in Texas"), we'll wade through jukebox oil-spills of moonlight, highways, sobby Mommas left praying at kitchen tables.

As folks who recognize a freak on first sight, maybe we'd benefit most by studying the "MAYBE?" pile and that giant mound, "NO WAY!" Even the worst Southern story can evince a certain clanking energy. Indeed, its very country-girl force sometimes proves a story's own undoing.

Some tales I read recalled those jalopies Junior Johnson once fixed up: pace cars for white lightning, transport meant to pass unnoted along country roads swarming with Federal moonshine-hunters. Rusted if artful Dodges, they let the shell of a terrapin hide the guts of a rocket. Sometimes the outside of a story could look mighty sleek, but under its hood, I'd find just one twisted oxidized rubber band.

Like the Bible parables that oftentimes inspire them, Southern stories can come front-loaded with tag-line lessons. Others are so nostalgic for our cotton-picking past, they resemble the cutesy Mall Art you've seen while trying not to.

Such plaques show three small farm-girls, bonnets in profile and with matching gingham granny-dresses, herding a row of pretty geese about the girls' same height. (Now, on farms I knew in Eastern North Carolina, geese would have fought all children's sticks and guidance. Geese that size attack kids so little! But not in "art.")

The narrative equivalent? Yarns about farm life written by kids from suburban Charlotte. Imaginary pastorals result, "faux" native. The tone is ersatz agrarian, usually naïve, often condescending toward its own uneducated players. Educated Southerners who create *Dukes of Hazzard* clichés for Northern export constitute our region's Uncle Toms.

Their stories are in love with comic place-names. Such tales tend to open with "The First Time I Ever Gigged Frogs with Ray-Bob . . ." or "The Night Sherman Burned It . . ." Recycled are cute routines long ago discounted by any writer disciplined and restless.

(And here we have a family secret that needs saying plain, folks: Bad Southern Lit is like Bad Southern Oysters—nothing will make you sicker when it's "off." Just as nothing can ever taste better than sea-salty raw oysters on the half-shell when fresh, when real.)

The geese-herder idylls of farm and NASCAR life are some-times written by earnest boys who prepped at Woodberry Forest, bright girls from Ashley Hall. (Where are their honest tales about failure at golf, about recent weight gains preventing a debut? Are these not Southern stories?) Though their own first names are Tyler or Taylor, their tales somehow always star honky-tonk heroines with double-barreled-monikers ("Luta-Chloe"). In this realm, nasty highway wrecks are weekday occurrences; young-bloods sport police records complex as their tattoos; small towns are tyrannized by a political boss named Boss Something, often accompanied by his still-virginal-looking daughter named Missy or Sissy or Blanche. (She will be in love with a bad, yet handsome, poor boy whose Dad works for Boss—a boy named Chance, Skeeter, Junior, Cherokee, or J.T., B.C. Possibly Moose.)

In goose-girl goober fiction, brand names of cars and guns, plus the word *Wal-Mart,* are considered unaccountably hilarious. (To me, Wal-Mart runs the opposite of funny. Just ask its clerks, working forty hours a week for paltry wages, healthcare often unaffordable.)

No comic romp with *Wal-Mart* in its title made our final cut. By my count, there were six.

Here, let me try combining elements from the scores of such best-if-used-before-this-date stories encountered in over a hundred journals. These were stories I purged as unqualified for eyes as good as yours.

> That ev'nin the hogs ate MeeMaw and PeePaw (leaving nothin' but what we'd later find stuck way down in their boots, God love 'em) was the self-same chilly midnight that Miss Maybelle Pettibone high-dived off the tip of the Holiday Inn's new water feature out on U.S. 70 Business, the ver' same night that her worst student ever, "Dumbo" DeWitte Dufrayne, 38, busted free of the State Nut-House for Criminally Insane Men in Milledgeville to hitchhike back our way, with a forty-five-caliber something crammed under his belt, come a-lookin' Miss Maybelle, the "old-maid school teacher" who had taught DeWitte how to French kiss the same night she flunked him in Vocational Arithmetic. T'was Miss Maybelle that

doomed "Dumbo" (so he told the poor fool Mormon boys that'd picked him up thumbing home to kill her) to a life of petite crime, an extended period of sexual confusion (especially in that no-holds-barred Nut-House for other Insane Men) and—math-wise—to his short-changed lifetime of not being able to even carry the one.

Actually, that sounds more promising than I intended. But then the Southerly ingredients themselves effervesce to the point of making every lab-experimenter feel a latent Dr. Frankenstein. Assemble the parts. Jump back. "It's alive!"

Ingredients include: comic overexaggeration, lethally arbitrary phonetic spelling, the rope burn of village interaction, impending gun violence crudely foreshadowed, the thrill and tickle of pan-generational sex, plus a traffic-pile-up run-on-sentence construction lacking any Faulknerian suspension-bridge engineering.

So, fellow reader and fellow sufferer, you see what I have spared you? But you will also note that, even in obvious comic parody, the Southern Story boasts a cheesy sorta potency.

Now, don't it?

In choosing the best of this year's *New Stories from the South*, I first sought Energy and Heart. I hunted a Point of View previously unknown to me. All twenty took risks with traditional forms and unregulated emotions. All went after themes so ancient they became fully new again, warranty extended. Sometimes hilarious, these tales could head south fast toward a heartbreak almost voluntary. Hopeful as third marriages without the option of a pre-nup, each attempted something difficult sung in a whole new key. All featured either black or white people, upwardly mobile or downwardly mobile-homed. But every character still crazily believed in love and some sort of future.

Certain stories I considered early on proved immaculately "finished," but they felt finally airless, foregone. I'd rather see some wiry person take a huge and nervy leap at a mountainside than watch some Olympic pole-vaulter clear a shoebox. I want to encourage not just immaculate upholstery, but broad jumps into the great unknown.

The main elements I stalked were Wide-Open Sympathy and a Living Wit—two traits in very, very short supply during Second Bush's second term.

In the end, each of the tales could not, I think, have been written by or about anybody anywhere else.

The Southern sense of humor has been subjected to many singularly unfunny books. Likewise flattened: our humid sexuality, our religious strictures. But somehow the presence and value of animals in our literature slipped right through Academia's barn door. Southern artists—including the inventor of our gingham goose-girls frieze—often show beasts and people in uneasy coexistence. I'll always love Twain's professional jumping frog and Faulkner's untamable "Spotted Horses."

In trying to herd the geese and cats of this year's stories, I soon saw I was repopulating Noah's Ark. Maybe we've reached a point in our exasperating history when people find it harder to identify with people. In today's fiction, animals no longer serve as mere mascots. Now they more readily assume "human" traits. The stories featured ideal hunting dogs, rattlesnakes needing milking, mordant and playful porpoises. Aesop's view is again borne out: Creaturely behavior echoes, then subverts our own. If animals can be shown as moral, what does that say about our species' beastly foolishness?

Humanity's long ecological carelessness has begun polluting *us*. We hear it in our breathing; we see it jeopardize our children's very concentration. We finally start feeling a new, half-religious regard for our fellow victims, the nontalkers.

Everybody knows how miners once took canaries into unlit shafts. Birds gave early proof of men's failing oxygen. In bitumen darkness, surrounded by workers so dependent on them, did canaries sing?

Today—aboveground in plain daylight—animals are our sacrificial stand-ins. They suffer before we do the consequences of man-made oil spills, Chernobyl-sized disasters, steady human encroachment. Our fellow beasts keep offering a terrible narrative lesson, one understood perhaps too late. They've assumed a new role in our dreams and fiction. The animals whose welfare our earliest ancestor was charged with protecting now make us feel—even as we lose them—more akin. More akin to each other. And far more like every beast we've ever beaten, ever eaten.

Critics wonder why the crankiest region ever to insist on being called "hospitable" should come out ahead in both subject matter and the sheer number of liars willing to shovel that rich mulch of wishing. (This is the Junior Chamber of Commerce part of our show, folks. All of you from Maine and the Upper Middle West, go back to recaulking your storm windows and writing in your diaries about today's ice storms.)

But, admit it, any precinct that counts among its fibbing truth-tellers Flannery O'Connor, Tennessee Williams, James Agee, Eudora Welty, and William Faulkner, just for starters, has surely been slipping Jack Daniel's into its baby formula for a long while now.

Pound for pound, any betting person who still reads must consider Faulkner the greatest American novelist of the twentieth century; Tennessee Williams remains by far our nation's greatest playwright, ever; and surely Flannery O'Connor ranks among our essential short-story writers. Is this not the Triple Crown? (You might add Jasper Johns as a painter from South Carolina . . . but, no, today I will stick with Literature only. Why rub it in?) Picked out of a police lineup on Saturday night in downtown Memphis, Faulkner, Williams, and O'Connor would appear unlikely immortals. But that's how it works in the South, that's how it always works with Immortality.

These giants' impact on the literature of Central and South America might be easily understood; but a few years back I saw a strong production of *The Glass Menagerie* in Lapland. Who can tell us how these disparate oddball Southerners managed it?

They did so with very few fencing consonants, but much imagination. They took advantage of isolation and its unmonitored miles of narrative spillway. They appropriated epic amounts of human experience into their feudal vision and fireball humor. Their embattled senses gave them purchase, then dominion. They won by knowing Losers best.

Somehow we all now feel ourselves to be the walking family albums of these artists' fictional characters. Joe Christmas, Blanche DuBois, Ruby Turpin, are now so at one with our own secret aspirations, they're mortised into our very heart-walls.

Thirty years ago, extinction was predicted for the Southern accent. Everybody, we were told, would soon sound like that fellow nightly manning the CBS anchor desk. Our twang and all its Texas Pete would be crushed under the Styrofoam of Mid-Atlantic speech.

And yet, just yesterday, I discovered I still can't understand my own car mechanic. Not till he tallies my latest bill by underlining the crucial digit a third time, then pointing repeatedly from that high-dollar amount to my lumpy little wallet.

"Oh," I say.

There yet remains something uniquely Southern—both in tone and perspective. I'm glad. It persists with a redheaded Scotch-Irish cussedness. A wise Supreme Court Justice defined *Obscene* as something you only know when up-close you really, really see it. And somehow, "Southernerness" makes you recognize it—even as it morphs through dissimilar stories. The narratives here continue to speak with stronger opinions than are strictly needed. Why do they hurry past mere reason? In order to entertain us. They each claim and patent an accent that rests aslant, astride, atop something still richly conducive to the spinning out, to the care and feeding, of another goodly Tale.

• • •

What finally is the *use* of fiction, Southern or otherwise? Why should such stories matter, except as tonight's means of escape? Surely, with our nation at war, amid the shameless display of Washington's worst corruption since the nineteenth century, we should expect our questing literature to do a bit more than distract us from our desperate age.

Eudora Welty was living in Jackson, Mississippi, in 1963, the night racists executed Civil Rights leader Medgar Evers. Welty's family home stood less than four miles from the driveway where Evers died. It's not impossible that one of our leading short-story writers heard the blast that killed this innocent man.

A Northern friend soon learned the news by radio and at once phoned Welty. She asked, "What are you going to *do* about it, Eudora Welty? Sit down there with your mouth shut?" The great storyteller responded by doing most everything that we writers can: She *wrote* about it. First she crafted (overnight, it is said) her prophetic story "Where Is the Voice Coming From?" a startling attempt to understand one murderous Klansman's real motives. According to publishing legend, the *New Yorker* stopped its presses to fit Welty's meditation into the very next issue. Her story leapt whole out of contemporary sadness to become what Ezra Pound called "the news that stays news."

Two years later, she wrote her essay "Must the Novelist Crusade?" The title itself bespeaks a sort of confusion, grief, embarrassment, the frustration we feel in confronting public events past our control, crimes impervious to our finest aesthetic principles.

Welty explains, "Great fiction shows us not how to conduct our behavior but how to feel. Eventually, it may show us how to face our feelings and face our actions and to have new inklings about what they mean."

But the only writing that matters, including Miss Welty's own, always fixes on ethics: How our tenderer concerns for others either change their lives and ours or—as usual—cannot. The crucible of moral choice, offered dramatically on the page, inspires our best and questioning feelings.

What can I do to save another person? For whom am I responsible? Are compassion and truth-telling their own essential everyday crusades? Are any of my tries at decency barely enough?

Fiction's form of education gives us privileged glimpses into others' struggles. That makes our art a relentless call to action, empathy.

The best stories I read this year hold in common a singular (and therefore various) sense of voice, a fear of violence alongside an attraction to it, a sinking understanding that families are both the only thing we have and, of all things on earth, the hardest to endure. In many of these tales, the hope for true love is many marriages along. And yet such wild faith in "the right one, next time" stubbornly endures.

The creators of *New Stories*—unlike my ticky-tack composite about the flirtatious old-maid schoolteacher and her innumerate convict-stalker—have made their characters round and dense and fully packed with contradictions. And yet there is always, in Southern writing, the playing with, to, and against "type." (Faulkner and Williams and O'Connor did their own miraculous turns at re-creating the sexually thwarted unmarried intellectual lady: See "Joanna Burden" of Faulkner's *Light in August* and "Hannah Jelkes" in Williams's *Night of the Iguana* and "Joy-Hulga" of O'Connor's "Good Country People.")

Fiction still finds blissful material in the old agony of occasions gone wrong, botched loves. And Southern fiction is additionally required to treat the ongoing pain of racial inequity. The extensive hydraulics we have leveed around this very central quicksand helped elevate our fiction up toward the universal. "The history of the world is the history, not of individuals, but of groups, not of nations but of races. . . . He who ignores or seeks to override the race idea in human history ignores and overrides the central thought of all history." So wrote W. E. B. Du Bois back in 18 and 97. And no major Southern writer has ever imperiled himself by squarely facing this epic issue. It's been the making of many a great book and person.

Finally, along with the double-bind betrayals of races living in close quarters for centuries, we readers and writers of the South still feel—beneath everything—the pull of homeplace (burned), of farmland (lost to the Bank).

Our family plot? It's only rented now in eighth-acre eroded tracts. "The land, Katie Scarlett" is today largely an offstage goad, trigger, and hymn. The family farm has been reduced to a single designer hunting dog cohabiting some tiny studio apartment in Atlanta. This neurotic creature, trained to betray other creatures to men with guns, is now trotted out only twice daily and then on a leash. But the poor hound still seems vigilant in its bloodlust, if only now for squirrels in public parks.

Such longing for our homeplace lost is something we share with the ex-Confederacy's newest residents: Mexican-Americans and Cuban-Americans. They also remember leaving not hovels nor mere houses, but haciendas—preferably ones with Corinthian columns, presumably formed of adobe.

Tara is now spelled *Tierra*.

The South has for many years been whispered about as the backward Sibling of American regions. That's gratitude for you!

We know things. We have seen so much. But somehow, in the age of factoids and e-mail, we, overlooked, remain in possession of a choir of cross-racial voices all dedicated to eloquent Telling at full blast.

In early April of 1865, a piece of paper—much-revised and eventually perfectly written—was presented to the boss of Northern Forces. One Reb leader sat down and signed his name. In doing so, he admitted we had finally surrendered.

But from that very hour, the unlucky side vowed to gain at least the struggle's story rights. Having lost, we made of losing the one way to know. We made defeat our merit.

"Stories only happen to people who can tell them," one Confederate widow confided.

Since Appomattox, a trillion other Southern pages have been committed—also much-revised, even perfected. And since that April, our region's prose has sung most everything except surrender.

True, we lost once, big-time.

But our concession prize? The stories.

Having got those in the settlement, we really are funnier and darker and shrewder—bigger—than the ones who still believe that they, at least, are smarter. We have been blessed with a language all our own; it encompasses those jazz-rich minority languages that make our region major. Race woes and that old rugged cross called Religion have left us as ornery as eloquent. We've been given bumper crops of younger hearts, just wising up, just coming into their new, truer versions of the ancient tale.

We have outlived the forgetters, my talkative brothers and sisters.

At last, we win and win and win. We have finally become what time will tell.

NEW STORIES
FROM THE SOUTH

The Year's Best, 2006

Tony Earley

YARD ART

(from *Tin House*)

She lived south of Nashville, in a big house in Brentwood bought with the royalties from a bad country song. When her husband, the singer of the song, moved out, he took the furniture with him, out of spite, and stored it in six large units at a place on Nolensville Road. She kind of liked the house without furniture—she had acres of parquet floor on which, after a few glasses of wine, she liked to slide in her sock feet—but one of the toilets downstairs ran constantly, which drove her crazy. She could hear it all over the house, even when she covered her head with a pillow. The plumber she called was a singer, of all things—*Arlen Jones, the High Lonesome Plumber,* that's what his ad said in the Yellow Pages—and it was the High Lonesome Plumber who now sat backwards astride her noisy toilet, working on something inside the tank while she leaned against the doorjamb and watched.

The plumber's pants had not slid down the way one frankly expected a plumber's pants to, but when he leaned over the tank, his golf shirt slid up his back, and she found herself staring at the thin column of curly, gray hair that had migrated north of his belt. She looked at her wine glass and set it down on the counter. She had no idea why she had called a plumber who wanted to be a singer instead of a plumber who just wanted to be a plumber, because—for the moment, anyway—she hated all singers and thought that the

I

world would be a better place if somebody invented some kind of bomb to drop on Nashville that would kill all the singers without hurting anybody else. Well, maybe not all the singers. Maybe just the hat acts. That's what all Nashville needed—a hat-act bomb. Her soon-to-be ex-husband, the furniture thief, was a hat act.

The plumber slid off of the seat, got down on one knee, and twisted the valve open. They listened. Once the tank filled, the water stopped running and did not start up again. Her house was cavernous. He stood and looked at her.

"It was just a seal," he said.

"A seal?" she said, thinking suddenly of ice, of some man in a fur parka looking through binoculars.

He blinked a couple of times, then grinned. "They're bad this time of year," he said. "Them seals."

She covered her face with her hands. Her cheeks were hot. Too much merlot. She wondered if her lips were purple.

The plumber sat down on the toilet and began putting his tools into a canvas bag. He looked up at her and smiled again.

"I'm so stupid," she said.

His brow dipped once, but he didn't stop smiling. "Don't say that," he said. "No reason you should know anything about seals." He jerked his head at the tank. "That kind, anyway."

She wanted to change the subject and asked, "Why do you call yourself 'the high lonesome plumber'?" even though she already knew the answer. Singers.

Ordinarily, when a woman asked the plumber that question in, say, a bathroom in a little house in North or East Nashville, or in one of the karaoke bars on Dickerson Road, he would say, "Well, darlin', it's because sometimes I'm high, and sometimes I'm lonesome." But here, in Brentwood, in this big house, to this expensive woman, he could hear in his head how wrong it would be to say it. He didn't even know why she had called him. Nobody down this way ever called him. Even the plumbers down here were snobs. He said, "Oh, it's because I sing a little bit. Bluegrass mostly. Some karaoke. I'm a high tenor. You know, like Bill Monroe."

"Oh," she said.

The plumber zipped the tool bag, but made no move to stand. Here it comes, she thought.

He said, "Cammie Carson. Aren't you . . ."

"Mrs. Keith Carson?"

He nodded.

"That's me. That's me for now, anyway. I mean, it'll still be me, I guess, but we're getting divorced."

"I read about that."

She had until recently been a regular in magazine and newspaper gossip columns, as in "Cammie and Keith Call It Quits." Now she wasn't anybody important. She shrugged, slapped her hands on her thighs, picked up her wine glass.

"That song was quite a hit," he said. "How long was it number one?"

"Eleven weeks."

The plumber whistled. "Eleven weeks," he said.

The house grew large and quiet around them, and she found herself wishing he hadn't fixed the toilet.

"Well," said the plumber.

"But it's a *stupid* song," she blurted out. "'I Keep My Hat in My Truck.' I mean, what kind of song is that?"

"I wasn't planning on singing it."

"Good. When Keith wrote that song, we didn't even *have* a truck."

They paused for a moment, listening to the song play inside their heads.

"I don't care where he keeps his damn hat," she said.

"Alright then," said the plumber, standing up. "If you don't care where he keeps his hat, I don't care where he keeps his hat. That's just the way it'll be."

She turned, walked into the hallway, and motioned for him to follow. "Right this way," she said. "I keep my pocketbook in the kitchen."

The plumber thought that maybe he had been in larger houses, but knew for certain that this was the largest *empty* house he had ever set foot in. They crossed a living room that had a floor big enough to hold a basketball court, with a cathedral ceiling high enough for, well, a cathedral. They did not talk in the living room. Ahead of them, down a long hallway, lay the kitchen. On top of an island in the middle of the floor sat what the plumber at first thought was a rock, but turned out to be, as he drew closer, a small squatty statue of an old man and an old woman, roughly carved out of a piece of limestone. The old couple sat squarely beneath a recessed spotlight.

"What's that?" he asked. "Did you get it in Mexico or somewhere?"

"That," she said, "is Millie and Joe. They're the reason I don't have any furniture."

"How'd that work?"

"Well, when we split, Keith said we had to sell it, and I told him there was no way in hell. Then one thing led to another, I lost my temper, and he got the furniture. And he didn't even want it, the jerk. He *stored* it."

The plumber leaned over and stared closely at Millie and Joe. "I believe I would've rather had the furniture."

"Have you ever heard of William Edmondson?"

The plumber shook his head.

"He was a sculptor, from Nashville, and he was the first black man to have a solo show at the Museum of Modern Art, back in the late thirties. He did this."

"Huh."

"He was a genius," she said.

"Okay."

"What don't you like about it?"

"I didn't say I didn't like it," the plumber said, "but it looks to me like he could have done some more carving on it. This thing just barely seems carved out at all."

"That's the whole point," she said. "I mean, look at those two. You can tell they've been married forever, that they can't imagine waking up without the other one lying right there, but, like you say, they hardly seem carved out at all." She reached out and touched Millie's face with a finger. "Edmondson could do the grandest things with the smallest gestures. I don't know. I just think that's wonderful."

The plumber walked around the island and looked at the statue from the back, then returned to where he had started. The old couple sat with their hands on their knees, their shoulders touching, and smiled as if they had just eaten a particularly satisfying meal.

"I don't know nothing about art," he said, "but they *seem* happy."

"They are happy. And they make me happy. After that damn song went number one, Keith and I bought a whole lot of stuff, and spent a whole *lot* of money, but this is the only thing we ever bought that meant anything at all to me. I keep it here because that spotlight is the brightest light in the house."

The plumber placed both hands on the counter and turned and stared at her. She thought he looked as if he were in the middle of realizing something important. She imagined he was beginning to understand the gorgeous incongruity of William Edmondson's primitive modernism.

"What's it worth?" he asked.

"Mr. Jones. Be ashamed. I know your mama raised you better than that."

"Well," said the plumber, "all I can say is, Mama tried."

"Well, she didn't try hard enough, apparently," she said, hoping that she had sounded light, but realizing that she hadn't. She almost told him what it cost, by way of apology, but caught herself in time. Millie and Joe had cost $108,000. Telling him would have made her afraid.

The plumber stared into space for a moment, then swallowed. A blush appeared from beneath his shirt collar and rapidly rose up his face. "You know what?" he said. "I know where one of these things is."

•••

The next morning, in the plumber's truck, she stared at the red bandana tied around her right wrist (it matched the one tied Dale Evans–style around her throat) and just felt like crying. She had become, at age twenty-eight, the kind of silly Brentwood house-wife who dressed up for plumbers. She could not believe she had tried on more than one outfit.

The plumber made her sad, too. He wore a starched white shirt and jeans with creases pressed down the front. A Windbreaker zipped halfway. Tasseled loafers. Date clothes. His truck, not the work truck he had driven yesterday but what she realized now was his *good* truck, had been freshly vacuumed and smelled like pine trees growing in a field of cigarette butts. God, she thought, we deserve each other.

"I've been thinking about what you said yesterday," he said. "About how that Edmondson man did big things with small ges-tures. You know, Hank Williams wrote songs like that."

"Huh," she said.

"The only thing I know much about, besides plumbing, is music, and I had to put what you said into music terms to understand it. But it makes sense."

The plumber glanced at her. "I made you a tape," he said. "I hope you don't mind."

Please, God, she thought, not a tape. Once Keith's single took off, he hadn't been able to go to the men's room at Houston's without bringing back somebody's demo. Now they were coming after her.

He pointed at a cassette sticking out of the dash. "Push that in," he said.

The song was "I'm So Lonesome I Could Cry." The sound was muddy, and the plumber had tuned his guitar sharp, but he had a high, clear, actually pretty, voice. She wondered how many times he had sung the song into his tape recorder before he was satisfied with it. When the tape got to the part about the silence of a falling star, he tapped waltz time on the steering wheel and softly sang high harmony along with the melody.

When the song finished, they sat and listened to the tape hiss. The plumber pushed the eject button. She knew this was the part where she was supposed to say, God, that was in*cred*ible, can you send some copies over, I know some people, they're going to want to hear this, *this* is going to blow their minds. But the sad fact was that she didn't really know anybody, except Keith, and the plumber was thirty years too old. She said, "That's a gorgeous song."

The plumber nodded.

She could tell by the look on his face that she had disappointed him, so she added, "You have a nice voice."

"Well, thank you," he said.

"I really don't know anybody," she said. "And they probably wouldn't talk to me if I did."

"That's not why I played it for you," he said. "I know there's not much demand in the industry for fifty-six-year-old bluegrass singers. My ex-wife reminds me of that every time she gets a chance."

"Oh. How long were you married?"

"Twenty-seven years."

"What happened?"

"Too much karaoke, I guess, is the short answer. Too much singing. Too much drinking. Too many women. Too much fighting about drinking and women. Singing don't seem to be a good thing for marriage."

"Singing isn't the problem."

"You're right about that, I suppose. What about you? How did you hook up with Keith Carson?"

"Believe it or not, we were high school sweethearts. We went to Cookeville High School in Cookeville, Tennessee. We started dating sophomore year."

"Now that I think about it, I believe I might've read that somewhere."

She wanted to ask the plumber what magazines he subscribed to, but didn't. "Then we went to MTSU together. I studied nursing and Keith studied music."

"You a nurse?"

"Nurse-practitioner. I was a midwife. After we graduated, I worked at Baptist, and Keith did some bartending, and went to songwriter nights, and open mic nights, and hung around on Music Row. Then he got a deal at Sony. And then, as you know, the song hit." She thought the phrase sounded ominous, like an automobile accident, but decided that was appropriate.

"So, tell me," the plumber said, "what were you like in high school?"

She didn't like his tone and shook her head. This wasn't going to turn into a date.

"Then what was Keith like?"

"Well, for one thing, he was a band nerd, he played the trumpet, although now he's got God knows how many publicists trying to keep that hushed up. It's that whole 'Garth Brooks was a decathlete' thing. Apparently you can't be a band nerd and keep your hat in the truck."

"Huh," the plumber said. "Band nerd. What else?"

"What else," she said. "Okay, when we were in high school, after Keith got his driver's license, he would come over to my house real early on Saturday mornings, and my parents would give him my car keys, and he would drive my car to his house and wash it. And I would stay in bed and pretend to be asleep until he brought it back. Every Saturday morning he did that. And he did it all winter long, no matter how cold it was."

"That sounds kinda sweet."

"It was sweet." She touched the tip of her nose with an index finger and stared into space until the plumber began to wonder if she had forgotten what they were talking about. "A long time ago," she said, finally, "a long, *long* time ago, Keith Lee Carson of Cookeville, Tennessee, was a very nice boy."

That morning, while settling on the bandanas, the chinos, the denim shirt, the leather jacket, and hiking boots she now wore, she had begun to worry that the plumber might take her off somewhere and kill her. She had tried to dismiss the thought as paranoid—when Keith left he seemed to take all the crazies in Nashville with him—but when she saw the plumber's truck pull through the gate, she scrawled his name on a Post-it Note and stuck it to the mirror in the bathroom where he had fixed the toilet. She was fine on the interstate coming north—the plumber seemed normal enough, slightly sleazy in the way most of the divorced men she knew were, but, other than that, okay—but once they exited onto Dickerson Road, she started to worry again. The motels they passed had bars on the office windows and signs advertising hourly rates. She saw a prostitute leaning through the window of a parked car. A man with a bright red face and vivid, stricken eyes staggered across all four lanes of traffic. She began to picture that pretty Greek reporter from Channel Four doing a live report from in front of the woods where somebody—deer hunters, probably—had found her partially clothed body.

"It wasn't always like this," the plumber said.

"What?"

"Dickerson Road. It wasn't always like this. It's always been working class, don't get me wrong, but you didn't used to see all the whores and crackheads and shit like you do now."

"Oh."

"I wouldn't have brought you over here, but this is where the statue is."

She tried to smile in a manner she hoped made her look brave and game, a formidable person, but in the distance behind the reporter she could see police tape strung through the trees. "Oh well," she said. "I'm glad I dressed for adventure."

The plumber stopped his truck in front of an abandoned bungalow in a sad neighborhood south of Dickerson Road. The windows of the house were boarded up, and somebody had spray-painted obscenities and what she assumed to be gang graffiti, or satanic symbols, on the plywood. Briars and broom sedge and young trees grew waist-deep in the small portion of the yard that hadn't been overrun by a marauding privet hedge. The plumber looked around carefully, studied his mirrors, then gunned the truck up over the curb, through the yard, and around the back of the house, where he stopped it out of sight of the street and cut the engine. "Okay," he said. "Here we are."

She tried to remain calm, but had to concentrate very hard to keep from seeing what lay inside the police tape. Then the plumber reached over, opened the glove compartment, and pulled out a shiny, black handgun. She recoiled as if he had magically produced a rat, or a hissing snake. She yanked and yanked on the door handle, but her door would not open. When he touched her on the arm, she pushed herself as far back into the corner as the door would allow her to go and stared wildly at the plumber.

"Oh Lord," he said. "Oh Lord. I'm sorry." He flipped the pistol in his hand until the butt pointed toward her. "Here. You take it. You can carry it. Oh darlin', I am so sorry."

She looked down at the proffered pistol, and then up at his face. He looked as if he were about to burst into tears. Please don't cry, she thought.

"Darlin', I didn't mean to scare you, honest to God. But we just ain't in the best neighborhood right now, that's all. I promise. I got a permit."

Without taking her eyes off of the plumber's face, she slowly began to shake her head. "No," she said. "You keep it. I'm alright. I'm fine now."

"You sure?"

"I'm sure. You can stop calling me darlin'."

The plumber smiled a little. "Okay," he said. "Good. I'm sorry about that. I guess I should've told you, I keep my *gun* in the truck."

She didn't laugh. He reached back toward his armrest and pushed a button. She heard the door behind her unlock. He stayed in the truck while she sat on the bumper with her hands on her knees and concentrated on breathing. He didn't open his door until she stood up.

"Tell me where I am," she said. Now that she had convinced herself she wasn't in danger, the adrenaline still coursing through her body made her feel powerful, strong, a cop at a crime scene, not a corpse. She wanted to ask questions, get to the bottom of things.

"This house here used to belong to Mrs. Louise Twitty. She was a black woman who used to keep me when I was little. Her mama helped raise my mama, and she helped raise me. I rode the school bus here every afternoon until I got old enough to stay at home by myself."

"What happened to her?"

"She died seven or eight years ago. Fell and broke her hip. Almost starved to death before anybody came to check on her. Died in the hospital."

"That's a sad story."

"It is," he said. "It is a sad story. She was a good woman and deserved better."

"And she had an Edmondson?"

The plumber nodded.

"I ain't going in that house," she said. "You can forget about that."

"It ain't in the house. It's back there." The plumber pointed with his chin toward the far corner of the backyard, which, if anything, was more overgrown than the front. "It ain't going to be easy to find, but that's where it is."

She followed him into a small thicket of briars and honeysuckle. He tried to mash the briars down with his feet to clear a path for her. "I had no idea it had grown up like this," he said. "This has all gone to hell. Miss Louise would pitch a fit if she could see this." When they neared the back of the lot, the plumber slowed and leaned over and began to look around on the ground, as if he were searching for the tracks of an animal. "It's right around here somewhere," he said. "Unless somebody else figured out what it was and beat us to it."

"Look," she called out, but realizing as she called out that she was pointing at an irregularly shaped piece of limestone, and not a statue.

"That's good," he said. "We're getting there. Gene was standing in the middle of a circle of rocks."

"Gene?"

"Gene was her husband. It's a statue of him. He was killed at Pearl Harbor and she had a statue made. Look around and see if you can see some more rocks."

"There's one," she said. "And there's another one."

"Okay," he said. "Okay. Now we're right on top of him. There ought to be some seashells."

"Seashells?"

"Miss Louise put seashells inside the circle, around Gene, since he was killed in the navy. Every time anybody she knew went to the beach, she always asked them to bring her back some shells. We used to bring her back a sand bucket full from Gulf Shores every year."

She dragged at the honeysuckle and briars with the toe of her boot until, beneath a layer of old leaves and dead vines and briar stems, she saw the white, scalloped back of a seashell. She felt a cold puff of adrenaline squeeze through her scalp and vanish into the air. When she reached down to pick up the seashell, a piece of briar she had been holding back with her foot snapped forward and latched itself onto the back of her hand. "Ow," she said, jerking her hand away. "Shit."

"Careful," said the plumber. "You alright?"

"Yes, dammit," she said, sucking at the back of her hand. "There's a seashell."

The plumber held his palm flat in front of him and moved it in a circular motion, as if waxing the hood of a car, or divining the area for spirits. "There was a circle of rocks here about five yards across," he said. "And inside the rocks was a layer of seashells. And in the middle of the seashells was Gene."

"Can you remember when Gene was killed?"

"Lord, darlin', I ain't that old. I wasn't born until forty-six. And I can't remember anything about coming here until, say fifty or fifty-one. What I do remember is Miss Louise wearing me out with a switch one time for setting foot inside the circle. She didn't allow nobody inside the circle."

"What were you doing inside the circle?"

"Some other little kid dared me to run in and rub Gene's head. Miss Louise used to keep a whole bunch of us little kids, whites and blacks, while our parents worked. When I was real little, before I started school, I don't guess I could even tell the difference between white and black. Them little black boys were the first friends I ever had. We run around all over the yard together. And I loved Miss Louise like she was my third granny."

"What happened?"

"Well, after we grew up some, I wound up fistfighting just about every one of them ol' boys. Some of them two or three times. We didn't go to the same schools, of course, but after we got on up in high school, we used to drive around on Friday nights looking for each other. And when we found each other, buddy, look out."

"Do you ever see them now?"

"Oh, I see them around some. We speak and all. They turned out alright. I think most of their kids, though, is on crack."

"You got any kids?"

"I got a daughter."

"Is she on crack?" She asked the question before she had time to consider its politeness and discard it.

"No," said the plumber. "She's not. Her specialty is eating Krispy Kreme doughnuts and having illegitimate children. Hey, I think I found something."

The plumber kicked at a clump of honeysuckle, and she heard the dull thud of his shoe striking something solid and hard. He stomped the briars down as best he could, and reached over and jerked at the honeysuckle with his hands. When the vines came away, a small face appeared suddenly between his legs. She leaned over and gasped and clasped her hands together in front of her chin.

"There he is," the plumber said. "Gene."

"Oh God," she said. "Let me see. Let me see."

The plumber knelt down and pulled away the vines still clinging to the statue.

What she saw at first was what she wanted to see, an undiscovered statue by William Edmondson, the Edmondson she had planned to steal and display in her house in Brentwood. It took a moment for her to see the cracked and rotting cast-concrete figure actually standing there. Yard art.

"It's not an Edmondson," she said.

"It's not?" said the plumber. "Sure it is. See, he's a sailor. Look, he's wearing a little sailor hat."

She shook her head.

"And look at the suit. Look at the kerchief. And the yoke on his shirt. He's wearing a sailor suit. Gene was a sailor."

"Listen, Arlen," she said. "It's not an Edmondson. It's made out of concrete. It's a replica of the sailor on the Cracker Jacks box."

The plumber sat still for a moment. "Cracker Jacks," he said. "Cracker Jacks."

"Miss Louise always said he was looking up at the sky. She said he was looking at the planes and knew he wasn't coming home. She said she could tell that he was thinking about her. But it's the Cracker Jacks guy."

"That makes me want to cry," she said.

"You know, when I was a little fellow, I thought Miss Louise was already as old as dirt. But she couldn't have been, what, thirty-five years old? She was still a young woman, but she never married nobody else. I never heard of her even looking at nobody else."

The face of the statue had worn almost completely away, and what was left was scarred with lichens. Gene stared up in what seemed to her a rigor of anguish. Gene had known he wasn't coming home, but his final thoughts had not been of his wife back in Nashville. He had thought instead of burning oil, or water pouring into the twisted steel room in which he found himself trapped. She could see it in his face. She felt her eyes fill with tears and turned away. Miss Louise had not commissioned a statue from William Edmondson, an old man whom God had ordered to carve figures in stone, later anointed a genius by the likes of Edward Steichen;

Miss Louise had gone instead to a gravel lot scattered over with birdbaths and garden benches and fat cherubs, and selected a replica of the Cracker Jacks sailor from a line of identical figures.

She had considered Miss Louise's story romantic, even mythic, when it contained an undiscovered Edmondson, but now it seemed small and ordinary and so simply and terribly *sad*. There was no other word for it. Had the little dog been included in the price? What had Miss Louise done with the *dog*? She pressed the heels of her hands into her eyes. She cried for Miss Louise and her cheap statue, and because Keith Carson's money had made her the worst kind of snob. She cried because a long time ago she had loved a boy who had washed her car even though his hands ached in the cold, but now that boy was dead, as surely as the girl who had loved him. She knew then that she would sell her house and buy a smaller one. She would go back to work and pull babies screaming into the world. She would donate her Edmondson to a museum. Her name would never again appear in a national publication. She would marry a man who would stay with her until she died, a man who would select a stone for her grave from a line of identical stones. His grief, though remarkable to him, would be ordinary. Her shoulders began to shake. If that's all there was to hope for, why couldn't she accept it as enough? Why couldn't anybody?

She heard the plumber stand up. "Well," he said. "Fuck."

Tony Earley is the author of three books: *Here We Are in Paradise*, a collection of short stories; the novel *Jim the Boy*; and the personal essay collection *Somehow Form a Family*. He is the winner of a National Magazine Award, and his fiction and nonfiction have appeared in the *New Yorker*, *Harper's*, *Esquire*, the *Oxford American*, *Tin House*, and other magazines. He lives in Nashville, Tennessee, with his wife and daughter, where he is the Samuel Milton Fleming Associate Professor of English at Vanderbilt University.

VANDERBILT UNIVERSITY

*T*he genesis of this story started when my wife, Sarah, and I saw a
   show of William Edmondson's sculpture, shortly after we moved to
Nashville, nine years ago, and fell in love with his work. Because Edmondson
apparently made a great deal of art, and most of it is thought to be unac-
counted for, some people in Nashville still believe there's a chance—somewhat slim at this point, but still a chance—that an undiscovered piece of
it is going to turn up. I, for instance, became convinced that there was a
lost Edmondson in the crawl space underneath my house. When I crawled
underneath my house—ostensibly to insulate it—all I found was an old door-
knob (which I put into another story). Eventually I wrote a story, not very
good, about two people who find an Edmondson. Then I wrote a story about
two people who look for an Edmondson, but find something else—a situation
I more or less knew firsthand.

Cary Holladay

THE BURNING

(from *Fugue*)

Waugh's Ford, Virginia
Beside the Rapid Anne River
January 29, 1745

The woman is burning alive. As the fire eats her skin and muscles and nerves, her screams shake the rocks. She is chained by the neck to a metal loop attached to an iron stake driven into stone, and heavy ropes around her waist hold her fast. Her arms are tied behind her, the wrists lashed together. Her skin flakes to ash, peels away from her body, and rises in pieces around her. Beside her, the river boils and churns from recent rains. It's bound to flood. Families who live by the river will gather their things tonight and move to higher ground, to the woods.

The woman, Rose, is a slave. She murdered her master, Peter Ryburn, by poisoning milk and serving it to him. Rose has had a trial in the Court of Oyer and Terminer, where she was found guilty and ordered drawn upon a hurdle to the place of execution and there to be burnt.

While the preparations were made, Rose was held six days in the gaol. Last night, Ryburn's son William and nephew Robert stopped there and paid the keeper to go away while they raped and scourged the woman. She meets her death bruised and lacerated, with a broken arm.

Had the men who bound her and lit the fire—William and his cousin Robert among them—anticipated the volume of her screams, they would have gagged her. They did grant her the kindness of a blindfold. Her shrieks rise and swell. The heads of the men and women gathered at the river are bells, and Rose's cries are the clapper. Children cover their ears with their hands and run off. No men went to work at the gold mine this morning nor the coal mine, though some of the planters stayed home to work their sodden fields and tend their animals, and they too hear the cries. In time, settlers all the way in the Blue Ridge Mountains, thirty miles to the west, will claim they heard the woman die.

The fire takes the woman fast. William stands with Robert as close as they dare, the fire too loud for them to talk. The slave woman is a live crouching thing, her skin blackening, blood and hair exuding their own particular stench as she roasts, her limbs changing position as the smoke lifts and blows. Within the fire, tethered to the stake, she moves in a slow crawl as if stalking or hunting. She works an arm free and claws at the blindfold, casts it from her face so that it sails beyond the circle of fire and catches William full on the cheek. He staggers, cursing, flinging the blazing cloth away, searing his fingers and palm. Through the smoke and his own pain, he sees Robert scoop a rock from the ground and hurl it toward the woman.

William is the one who will go and report to Dame Ryburn— Eileen—his father's young bride, only recently arrived from Ireland, in Virginia barely four months and now eight months gone in pregnancy, that the execution has been accomplished. He dreads this chore. Eileen will ask for details. Beautiful, she nonetheless possesses the most expressionless face he has ever seen on a woman, and the most insatiable curiosity. You should have been there yourself, he will tell her if she presses him too much. He is surprised by how deeply the sight of the execution has troubled him. Eileen will remember forever whatever he tells her, with the same satisfaction with which she examines the jewels William's father gave her, treasures to be scrutinized and set back in their nests of velvet, inside a teakwood box, rings and bracelets that once belonged to the first Mrs. Ryburn, mother of William, a woman so much older than Eileen and dead so long that Eileen has admitted confusing her with her own mother, has pictured her own mother wearing these adornments, though her mother, dead too, was poor and owned no jewelry at all.

When the woman is reduced to an immobile form, like melted statuary, the rain begins. It falls on her smoking body, quelling the last flames, sizzling on the stones. The rain drives the people off, farmers and women, miners, blacks who came for their own reasons — curiosity or mourning — to watch her die, an Indian or two or three, for they have not entirely vanished as they are said to have done, only retreated to the darkest places of the forest, which they share with deer and bear and elk.

Rose is a knot on the boulders, a piece of bone showing through her charred leg. In death, she has twisted, woven herself into a mat of her own leather and marrow and hair.

William's face burns with a wretched heat and so does his hand, the fingers and palm that touched the blindfold the woman threw at him. How she writhed beneath him last night, while his cousin held her down. Now the running of the farm is up to William, in this time of damnable flood, and William is not the farmer his father was.

William turns away from the river and fetches his tethered horse. Robert has already ridden away. William will ride home to the Ryburn plantation with its three hundred acres, sixty slaves, and the splendid brick house his father built, the house he shares with his wife and this young stepmother. He will enter the room where Eileen pours tea from a porcelain pot, hiding her condition beneath rugs and robes, the room airless from the fire she insists on day and night, believing it will drive off the fevers she fears in this strange new country. William will tell her that the slave woman is dead, and she will sip her tea and look out the window at the rain falling on the bare branches of trees and the flooded pastures, the forests of tulip poplar and the gouged red clay embankments where the rain has washed away chunks of soil, carrying with it horses, cows, and sheep and the unfortunate dwelling or two, and there will begin a long war between William and Eileen over the management of the farm. In the house, and even while drifting away from the burning, the Ryburns' slaves whisper among themselves that Eileen's baby will be born dead or deformed, a devil, but the infant that will come cannonballing out from between Eileen's legs the morning after Rose's death will be in fact superbly healthy, just small and premature, a posthumous son.

William and his wife have not been blessed. His wife, Martha, has not been able to bear a child, and now she is past fifty. She is older than William, who is forty-seven, and far older than eighteen-year-old Eileen.

As William mounts his horse and turns away from the river toward the road, children play with the wooden hurdle upon which Rose was dragged. They climb upon it, crashing and shrieking, and take turns pulling each other, for the object is, after all, a sledge, and it will be saved by the county officials for use again. William wonders if the King will be notified of the events of the poisoning and the execution. It's the sort of thing his wife Martha might take upon herself, regarding the King as she does with a sense of duty so profound that she writes letters to him on all kinds of Orange County matters, of crops and livestock and weather, even politics, though William has tried to discourage her. She pours into the letters the attention she would have given their children, had they produced any. He should know of this, she will say, meaning the King, and she'll disappear into her chamber. Hours later, William will find her with a thick stack of cream vellum stationery, filled with her beautiful hand, letters ready to go to England. She's a loyal subject, ever proving her obeisance, whereas William for his part has begun to question whether the colonies might not be better off with self-government.

William's horse stops in the road and whickers. William slaps

his legs against its sides. Rain smacks his face. His burned hand
is too sore to hold the reins. The horse behaves strangely, circling
slowly, turning in the road as if performing a maneuver that circus
animals are said to do, preparing for some elaborate equine flight
or trick. William cries a sharp command, flaps the reins, and kicks
the horse's side, but the animal turns back to the river, faces the
execution place, pauses, then gallops toward it.

William has owned horses all his life, but he didn't know one
could spring from stillness to such speed in an instant. He loses
his balance, slips from the saddle, shouting, then falls from the
horse to the road, so hard he wonders if he has cracked his spine.
Luckily, he fell clear of the horse; he wonders if the creature meant
to throw and drag him.

William sits up with difficulty, feeling every moment of his age:
the burned face and hand, the bruised spine, the sharp dental flares
that signal the onset of one of the toothaches that have plagued
him in recent years. By nightfall, he'll be tying his jaws up in a
huge handkerchief and searching his wife's cupboards for lauda-
num.

The crowd is taking its time dispersing, people talking among
themselves. Does no one see him dazed, here in the muddy road?
He jerks himself to his knees and stands, dizzy. The shouting children, the bucking sledge on its rope, blur before him. Here comes
his horse, ambling, returning to him, docile yet with lightning
in her eyes. Nothing to do but catch the bridle and climb again
upon her back. He thinks the children are laughing at him, that
the women bending their heads toward each other and the groups
of men knotting and unknotting as they leave the riverfront are
finding fault with him and his family.

"Damn you," he says, unsteady on his horse's back. "Damn
you."

A child mocks him, mimes his fall—that is how William inter-
prets the youngster's swaying gait—and he leans from the saddle
and cuffs the boy's impudent, startled face, sending him sprawl-
ing in the muck. The boy's mother screeches at William, and he

takes off at a trot, then a canter, the horse's long strides familiar beneath him.

He can still smell the woman Rose and the fire, even through the rain. He needs a bath to wash her from his skin.

Rose took her secret with her: what she used in the milk. Trial and torture did not pry it from her, nor the Ryburn men taking turns in what for William was a surprisingly pleasurable assault; his cousin Robert kept his head enough to spit some questions at the woman, but she did not speak to them, just fought with demonic strength even after Robert broke her arm above the elbow so that it flapped and dangled. That was the only time she cried out.

Arsenic, people say, for arsenic can be found on every farm and in any apothecary's shop, and there are druggists in Orange and Stevensburg. Hemlock, perhaps, or some roots and herbs known only to Africans, mixed in darkness and cursed in a savage tongue.

But it was powdered, dried foxglove that stopped Peter Ryburn's heart. That was what Rose used, and some of the other slaves know it, the blacks having discovered the concoction in a corner of the cabin where she lived alone, an arrangement created by Peter Ryburn the better to spend time with her. A little brown flower, a little dust, and a man's heart slows and halts. The milk was tart, but that might have been because of something the cow ate, or an effect of the flood, changing the taste of the water that the cattle drank from river and streams. Peter Ryburn, aged seventy-three: hale and strong. Everyone knew his was not a natural death, and the doctors agreed it was murder. He reeled from the table clutching his chest, his starched white napkin falling from his lap. William had leaped from the table to steady him, but Peter was dead before he fell to the floor. They had been arguing, father and son, over which crops to plant in which fields, while Eileen looked from one to the other with the only real expression of pleasure William had ever observed on her face, as if she were glad to see William at odds with his father.

All day, the day of the burning, Rose's remains lie on the stone. From high places in hills and trees, the buzzards come, dropping down to wait at the riverside until the body cools from its fierce heat to a pleasant warmth. Despite the char and ash, there is still nutrition in the deeper parts, savory to the creatures that can make a meal from carcass and offal. These morsels they reach with beaks and tongues, flapping their wings as they jostle and balance on the boulders. Tonight, men will come with burlap and wrap what's left of her. They'll bury her in the woods unmarked, white men, for they are keeping charge of her and they don't want her grave to be a witching place for other slaves who would do as she has done.

When the birds have eaten their fill and raised their huge wings to the sky, what remains among the tossed bones is a small white stone, the size of a grape, translucent and containing a frozen human form, as if fire can freeze and preserve: Peter Ryburn's last child, a loop of flesh with a discernible head, its legs a fishtail curved within the sac. The iron stake, Rose's stake, will be pried out of the stone by slaves in the night and, for years, will inspire plans of revenge.

Eileen will hear of the treachery of William's horse from others, as if she has an ear in the wind. That will please her, William knows, that he was thrown, humbled, that he was hurled into the mud. He and Eileen are rivals for reasons he doesn't understand. She doesn't care about Rose, just the burning. The horse and its small mystery, the puzzle of its turning, circling with William helpless and furious on its back, its headlong rush to the river, leaving him behind, then its diffident return to its injured rider: Eileen will love that image, turning it over and over in her mind as she warms herself at the fire, as she suckles her baby, the weight of new motherhood melting away despite the toddies and rich, buttered shortbreads she enjoys. The servants cosset her, silent, turning the blankets back, swinging the bedwarmer between the cold sheets. She has no fear of them, pays them hardly any mind. They hated her husband, but so did she. She'll have the new baby to entertain her and the image of William in the red mud, and such information about the execution as she decides to cherish.

William knows Eileen heard Rose's screams, even in her rooms with the thick walls. His hand and face throb where the blindfold hit him. He trots home dully, hysteria building in his heart. He wants only silence and warmth. Peter Ryburn was buried three days ago, on Sunday, after services. The night before the burial, William and Robert sat up in the hallway of the great house with the old man's corpse, the cousins side by side on a bench beside the coffin. It made a sound, the body did. Deep in the night, a sound, not the crude farting and moaning and sighing that the dead are known to make, and which William has heard before — having sat up with his mother's corpse years earlier — but a spoken phrase, a few syllables that William in his drunkenness could not make out, which the corpse would not repeat despite his entreaties. Peter Ryburn was dead when they laid him out and dead when they put him in the ground, but for a moment during those hours in between, he spoke. Robert heard it too and wept, seizing the old man's shoulders, while William slumped back on the bench. It was so like his father, to have the last word. Then: sealed lips. Coins on the eyes. Gold, from the mine Peter Ryburn owns, the mine that William's wife has described shyly in letters to the King. William believed his father spoke, as his soul crossed over, in a language known only to the dead. Robert, devoted nephew, sobbed out his sorrow into the whiskey and tilted the bottle to the old man's open mouth to revive him. The liquor went down. Robert poured till the bottle was empty, and still the liquor never came up from the old man's mouth, and Robert cried out with hope, but William knew all along he was dead as a stone.

Eileen says to make use of the woman's cabin, there is no reason it cannot be occupied by several of the others. So William directs the slaves to clean it out. The blacks balk. William and Eileen stand before the cabin while the slaves study the ground, drawing their feet through the dirt. A fine mist falls.

"It built on a rattlesnake nest," a woman says at last. "We stay away from it."

"That's ridiculous," William cries. It hurts to speak, the bad tooth radiating needles of pain through his jaw.

"She build it her own self," the woman says, an old granny with eyes gone icy from cataracts. "You can hear them snakes sometime. They's hundreds of 'em."

Eileen stands straight and slim, as if she has not borne a child only days before. "Tear it down," she tells William.

He hates for the slaves to see her making decisions about the running of the place, this young woman, while he stands with his face swathed and swollen, his body hurting all over from his fall from the horse. But tear the cabin down they do, once he gives the order. It's a sturdy cabin, though small. Three black men knock it down, and William asks later if they saw snakes.

"Yessir," they say, but they weren't bit. A whole nest of snakes is still deep in the ground, they say, *boilin' there,* they say, only a conjure woman would build there.

"All right. Burn the wood," William says. "Burn the ground, so that if any snakes are there, they'll die." His order goes unheeded. The wood remains unburnt in a messy heap, grim and wintry. Is it then that the unraveling begins, with the slaves' disobedience while William slouches miserably in his chair in the comfortable, enormous house, waiting for an abscess to burst in his mouth? Eileen hearkens to the slaves' stories, their excuses: that fire will bring the snakes out to take over, to multiply and swarm. Their fears have alarmed her.

The cabin remains a wreck of timbers. If snakes weren't there already, it's an invitation to them now. William holds his jaws with his hands until he can't bear it any longer and summons a doctor to pull the tooth. The long bloody root, ivory and red in the doctor's extractor, is his reward, that and the thick, bitter gush of pus into his mouth.

•••

And my husband and his cousin had congress with the condemned woman, Your Majesty, in her cell in the gaol, the night prior to her execution. I saw, for I followed them. I have learned to walk quietly, and I do not need a lantern.

Did you not call us your loyal old dominion? As you would deem an old friend. My loyal Old Dominion.

By the time the flood recedes and the snow falls, William is sick. He blames the woman, Rose, for the sores that rise on his genitals and thighs. Fever plagues him, only to subside and then assail him again, so that he acquires a new habit: he climbs out of his bed at night to go outside in the snow and stretch out full length, clad only in his nightshirt, the heat of his body melting through the crust, down through a pillowy drift of snow so that in the morning, when he creeps indoors again, his human form shows his household where he lay.

Beneath the heavy snow, the earth is packed with water and ice. The river runs high, ice gathering at its shores in sheets and slush. It runs too fast this year to freeze. Those who would cut blocks of ice for summertime will have to wait.

Summer has never seemed so far off.

William asks his cousin Robert if he too is afflicted, but Robert says no.

Why would one man contract the disease and the other be spared? William remembers the gaol cell, its cold dirt floor, the smell of mice and damp, the strenuous climbing and conquering of Rose's limbs. He had been with slaves before, young women whose bodies attracted him, but that was long ago, and he had not forced them. It was a game then, and they were willing. He wonders if the sickness has been in his body for a while. No, it was Rose. He's certain. The woman, the sores: she wished the illness upon him. Is it possible his father gave her the disease, and she poisoned him out of anger?

Lying in the snow at night, aflame with fever, William turns face down until at last the fever cools. He has never known a season of so much rain and snow, and there are still months of winter ahead. The sound of the surging river is always with him, even when he's in his chamber with the draperies drawn and a pillow over his head.

He consults with his doctor and swallows bitter blue pills recommended for the malady. The medicine makes his gorge rise. He takes the vial of pills out one night and buries it in the ground, digging deep beneath the snow, and afterward, sweating and thirsty, he wonders why he bothered. The sores multiply on his body. His mouth isn't healing, either. The empty socket of his tooth runs with serum and stays tender, tasting foul, the edges ragged. He mixes warm water with salt, honey, and alum and gulps it, swishing it around his mouth, and that helps a little bit. Skin flakes from his burnt face and hand.

Sunshine and fresh eggs. His father swore by sunshine and fresh eggs, the keys to health. William directs the cook to serve him eggs at every meal. The sky remains heavy, the air colder day by day. Yet he has never seen such magnificent shades of gray as the clouds during these weeks, pewter and silver, dawn and afternoon and dusk, nor does he recall the last time he thought the sky was beautiful.

He melts the snow at night with his heat and sweat, packs it into his mouth and around his scrotum, beneath the fabric of his nightshirt and robe. Eileen loves the snow. She makes the cook prepare a dish with sugar and cream. William can't eat enough of this dessert. Snow cream and eggs are making him fat. All day he looks forward to his bed of snow. Even that doesn't cool him enough. Fresh snow falling at night brings him a relief that borders on joy. It covers him, but it doesn't last. If there is moonlight and if he looks up toward the multitude of windows in the house, he might glimpse a gleaming candle and, above it, his wife's face gazing down on him.

During the day, his dogs sniff the hollows where he lay, spaces where he melted through the snowdrifts all the way to the grass. All his life, he has had a horror of illness, of weakness. He has scorned those who are frail, the lame and the infirm. When he was younger, he could throw off sickness.

"You're getting old," his cousin Robert says.

"You're nearly as old," William answers.

To look at the two of them, William has to admit, you would no longer know they were separated by only four years. Yet these are modern times. Men live longer than they once did. William's thoughts are too disordered for him to determine how to regain youth and health.

He was a young man once, courting Martha, who became his wife. Hide and seek in the garden that is now covered with mounds of snow. William's fever burns hotter than any heat of summer. Even in summer, down in the garden, there were cool spaces, shadows, dew under the boxwoods even in afternoon, and a trellis covered with blue ivy where Martha used to wait for him, stifling her laughter, jumping out to surprise him, even frighten him.

Martha: a scurrying sound in her room, at her papers and letters all day. He is married to a sound. The ivy in the garden smelled like an old, lost world, she used to say, a sweet old place, the smell of memory. She would pluck an ivy leaf and twirl it beneath his nose.

One night he awakes outside in panic, convinced all of his stock are dead. He bolts from his bed of snow and rushes into his house, calling out for his wife, but it's Eileen who appears on the steps with a candle in her hands, her hair carefully arranged, a velvet dressing gown belted at her waist.

"The animals," he gasps. "Are they dead?" He can't remember when he has last seen a sheep or a hog, a horse or a cow. The snow must have killed them weeks ago.

"They're fine," she says.

"You or my wife saw to them, then," he says stupidly, "or the Negroes."

Eileen goes to the heavy front door and pushes it closed. There is finality in her movement, as if by closing the door, she wins their long, undeclared battle, but it's hard for William to concentrate. He's troubled by a memory—the recollection of the stake, Rose's stake. "It was iron," he says, "so it didn't burn."

"What are you talking about?" Eileen asks.

"We should get that stake," William says. "Somebody should go get it. It must not become a talisman for slaves, a thing of witch-craft and," he flounders, the sweat beading on his face, "a thing of evil. I'll dress and go get it."

"William," Eileen says. "You must go to bed. The stake was pulled up long ago. It doesn't matter."

"But it does," he says, near tears.

"After a while, it'll be just an old piece of metal," she says, "and nobody will remember what it was. It'll be used for something else, or melted down, or lost."

He is getting old. He will not live as long as his father did.

"Where's my wife?" he asks.

"In her chamber, I suppose," Eileen says.

She stands aside, this woman Eileen, this stranger his father married, so William can climb the stairs. Sweat courses down his cheeks, and the stairs are steep and hard to mount, as if he's push-ing his way through snowfall on a mountain. He has not thought about his wife in days. Is that her room, that closed doorway at the end of the hall?

He turns the knob, but the door is locked. He kicks it so the hinges crack from the frame, and he shoves the door open. There sits an old woman in lace cap and nightdress, frozen with horror in her chair at a writing table, surrounded by stacks of paper. In her hand is a dripping stick of red wax. Her gaze travels from his face to the broken door and back again.

"What are you doing?" William demands.

"Sealing my letter," Martha answers. The wax is bloodred and sweet-smelling. She blows out the flame on the taper and presses a brass implement into the daub of wax.

"Who are you writing to?" William asks.

"The King," Martha says. She lifts the letter to her lips and blows on the seal. "I'm writing to the King. You knew that. There's so much to tell him. Tonight I've written him about the horses in this country, how they're descended from those on shipwrecks and those brought by early explorers. I explained how they grow so strong here and are well suited to the work of farms and mines."

William reaches out and takes the letter from her hands. He touches the wax, which is soft enough to show the print of his fingertip. "Where did you get this?"

"The paper or the wax? I order the paper from a shop in Philadelphia. The wax and ink I've had since we were married. My mother gave them to me in great supply. Don't you remember?"

"Do you think the King cares about your letters?"

"I do," Martha says. "He's concerned about the colony. The people. He should know what's happening here."

William turns the letter over, reads the King's name in his wife's elegant script, "Who will deliver it for you?"

"I'll find someone traveling to a port city," she says, "who will take it to a ship's captain. I've done this many times."

"But he doesn't answer. The King."

"William, you're very ill," Martha says. "No matter what I say, you won't believe me."

Martha makes William lie down on the couch in her chamber, and she fans the sweat from his face with a folded sheet of paper. Her heart, startled to triple its normal beat by William's kicking in her door, has only just begun to return to normal. She takes a deep breath as William settles himself on her couch, his thick shoes leaving marks on the gray silk upholstery.

"That woman," he says, "is killing me."

"Eileen?" Martha asks, for she hates the younger woman, the smug one, who is now the mistress of the house, mother of the heir. Martha has expected that her husband would fall in love with Eileen, that he would divorce her, that she would be packed out of the house to live a pauper's life. Ever since Eileen's arrival, and with greater urgency since Old Ryburn's death, Martha has been saving money in a leather bag.

"Not Eileen. Rose," he says.

"No," she says. "Rose is dead."

Martha fans William's cheeks, the pores open and perspiring still. After a while, he falls asleep.

Yes, William wronged the woman Rose, but Martha must try to save him. She has watched him all these weeks since the execution, and she has hardened her heart against him, but she was with him in the days of the twirling ivy, when they were young.

He wakes in his fever and says, "Wife," then sleeps again. All night, Martha sits up on her couch with his head on her lap. This person is a ruined stranger.

Toward daybreak she dozes, then wakes to find his arms wrapped around her waist. Laboriously, she moves him aside and stands up stiffly, as if her legs are uneven. She takes a clean sheet of paper and writes, *Downriver, there is a rock in the water. Only when the rock is visible is it safe to ford the river. The place is called Raccoon Ford because of the abundance of those animals in the area, their meat is poor but their pelts are warm; hunters prize the tails as decorations for their caps. Raccoons may be readily tamed and kept as pets.*

She puts the letter aside. Should there not be an expedition to explore the wild land to the West, across the mountains and beyond? She will write and suggest it.

But first she must tend to her husband. She orders a basin of hot water brought to her, and soap. She orders her servant to remove her husband's clothing. Snow is falling outside, and the basin steams up the windows of her chamber. She'll have to concentrate and work very hard to save her husband. Winter has been so long, and she must bring everything together in her mind, all that she knows of the poison and the business in the gaol and the burning. She herself had argued, albeit only in her head, for bullets or hanging, or even exile to the West. Why burning? Barbaric. She wrote about all of it to the King, who answered with his familiar silence.

William's skin is thick and yellow. While Martha bathes him, he sleeps on, his head sometimes jerking as if he would wake. The sores on his groin and privates exude heat. She has guessed they were there, but these are worse than she'd expected, a rampant, livid consequence of his visit to the gaol. For a moment, her heart fails her. She dries his skin with a cloth, covers him with soft blankets, and curls herself around him, stroking his head.

Her father-in-law, old Ryburn, had drunk the milk with deep swallows, smacking his lips as he set down the glass. He and William had been arguing about some matter concerning the farm. Old Ryburn rose from the table and took one, two strides toward the door, where a tradesman waited to see him, then gave a guttural cry. With one hand he gripped his throat, with the other he reached high, as if grasping for something. The woman, Rose, turned her head from her place at the sideboard, where she was stacking plates. Turned her head so that out of the corner of her eye, she saw him fall. Such a pretty shape Rose's cheek made, with her chin tucked into her shoulder, her face all eyelashes and stillness.

"The milk," Ryburn gasped. "Rose?"

It was William who caught Rose even as she tried to run, and Martha who sprang toward Old Ryburn, catching him as he fell. Eileen remained in her chair, a buttered scone in her hand. Didn't she finish it, lifting the pastry to her lips and nibbling amid the commotion? Gooseberry jam was on the table that day, and clotted cream, and oranges from the tropics.

Old Ryburn used to find hangings and beheadings such merry affairs. Martha has heard of his courtship of Eileen. On a visit to Ireland, his homeland, he had learned of an execution to be held in a far county, and he took the young beauty to it, with her father and brothers for company. The convict was a man who had killed his neighbor in a dispute over a hog. The scaffolding was so high, Eileen had reported to her new family, that she had to hold her hand over her eyes against the sun. There was the drop of the trap and a brief wriggling of legs, a motion that disturbed her far less than if a gnat had flown into her eye, and then the man hung limp. Eileen had declared herself disappointed. They had come so far for that. Why was she not moved by the spectacle when, all around her, the crowd displayed such fury and satisfaction? There was no turning back from Old Ryburn then. She had already agreed to marry him, was already carrying his child. Together, they would make the crossing to Virginia. When she arrived, her pregnancy was evident to everyone, not just to Martha. The day of the hanging, old Ryburn had bought his wife-to-be a length of lace from a peddler and a tray of cherry tarts, yet even then, Martha is certain, Eileen was bored, going home in the bumpy wagon, smoothing the lace out on her lap, scolding her brothers for dripping cherry juice on their shirts.

Martha knows that Old Ryburn drank the entire glass of milk that Rose brought to him, but somehow in her memory, the glass tips over from Ryburn's hand, and milk spills all over the table, a thick puddle spreading to the edges and dripping onto the floor, a white lake. Old Ryburn. He was some kin by marriage to Eileen's mother. Now Eileen is his widow, and William is bound to take care of her and her brat forever.

And Eileen is the one who killed him. Martha knows this as surely as if she'd heard Eileen order the slave woman: *Give me some foxglove.* Eileen must have mixed it with crushed vanilla beans and sugar, then returned the compound to Rose saying, *Put this in my husband's milk when next he orders it; it is to strengthen him.*

Yet during her trial and even at the stake, Rose, the slave, did not betray Eileen. Martha, with her husband sleeping heavily in her lap, considers the fact briefly as Eileen's infant wails down the hall in its nursery. The child's nurse, one of Rose's daughters, will tend to it. Eileen might have murmured a promise, or what Rose must have taken for a promise, when she accepted the compound from her mistress's hands, *I'll take an interest in the welfare of your children.* If Rose had accused her mistress in the courtroom, or from the stake, who would have believed her? Rose must have known that.

Martha rolls her husband from her lap so that he slumps on the bed, snoring. Her relief that he's here in her chamber, instead of sleeping outside in the snow, is inexpressible. She goes to her window, parts the curtains, and looks out at the night. The land-scape presents an odd reversal. As if the world is upside down, the snow glows like sky. These weeks since Rose's execution, Martha has assessed the particulars of the woman's final moments. William told her very little. He arrived home from the execution in a frenzy, his face scorched, his clothes muddied and torn. She had to work to get the story of Rose's death, from various neighbors. *No, Rose* said at her trial, when asked if she had murdered her master. *No, I didn't kill him.* Martha has heard that much. Yet surely Rose knew what substance was in the compound that Eileen gave her. Rose, not Eileen, was the one who put the powder, brown and innocent as cinnamon, in Old Ryburn's milk. Rose knew. Yet she didn't tell.

A wolf howls, and Martha lets the curtain drop from her hands. She loves to hear the wolves at night, to know they are near, and herself safe in the thick walls of her house. She has seen the bloody heads brought in for bounties at the courthouse, knows the val-ues: forty pounds of tobacco for the head of a young wolf, seventy for an old. Orange County stretches to the gigantic lakes of the North, all the way to Canada, and westward farther than she can imagine.

How many millions of wolves live within that land? Martha writes to the King. *The balance here is delicate, between the land and those who would tame it. We plow, we farm, we herd and build.*

She pauses. The King doesn't know what it's like, living here, when that balance could tip at any moment. In fifty years, this place could return entirely to savages and woods and darkness. She writes, *Do not wait. Come now. Come and visit your Old Dominion in its struggling youth, its early days from which it might rise to glory.*

The King will never come. He'll read her letter with impatience, holding it away from his weak eyes, wondering why this one subject, some old woman out in the wilderness, writes to him so eagerly, as if he would concern himself with wolves, as if he would know how it is to be alone, your only consolation a few pieces of gold in a leather sack, saved against widowhood or eviction from your home. He cannot know, does not care, that she and her husband and their family and slaves and neighbors keep a fragile foothold. *Indians and floods,* she writes, *and crop failures and our own hatreds and greeds, Your Majesty, these threaten us, yet this is the finest country.*

Beside her, William moans in his dreams. Martha writes, *My husband's cheek has healed badly from the burning blindfold the woman threw at him. It hurts him even when he sleeps.*

———————

Cary Holladay's newest collection, *The Quick Change Artist,* is coming in fall 2006. She is the author of a novel, *Mercury,* and two collections of short stories, *The People Down South* and *The Palace of Wasted Footsteps.* Her work appears in recent issues of *Epoch,* the *Florida Review, Gulf Coast, New Letters,* the *Southern Review, New Stories from the South: The Year's Best, 2005,* and *Shenandoah.* Stories are forthcoming in the *Georgia Review* and the *Idaho Review.* Her awards include a fellowship from the National Endowment for the Arts and an O. Henry Prize. A native of Virginia, Holladay is married to the writer John Bensko. They teach in the creative writing program at the University of Memphis.

*"*The Burning*" is part of a series of stories that I'm writing about Orange County and Culpeper County, Virginia. The story is based on an actual trial that took place in 1745. Accused of poisoning her master, a slave woman was tried, sentenced to death, and burned at a stake beside what was then called the Rapid Anne River. Orange County was wild*

frontier country at that time. My family's homeplace, on my father's side, lies within sight of this beautiful river, which is now known as the Rapidan.

I imagined incidents before and after the execution. I wondered about the effect of the deaths on the community, on the survivors of the dead man and the dead woman, and on everybody who would keep telling the story.

Wendell Berry

MIKE

(from *The Sewanee Review*)

After my parents were married in 1933, they lived for three years with my father's parents, Marce and Dorie Catlett, on the Catlett home place near Port William. My mother and my grandmother Catlett did not fit well into the same house. Because of that, and I suppose for the sake of convenience, my parents in 1936 moved themselves, my younger brother Henry, and me to a small rental house in Hargrave, the county seat, where my father had his law practice.

And then in 1939, when I was five years old, my father bought us a house of our own. It was a stuccoed brick bungalow that had previously served as a funeral home. It stood near the center of town and next door to a large garage. After we had moved in — there being six of us now, since the births of my two sisters — my parents improved the house by the addition of a basement to accommodate a furnace, and by the installation of radiators and modern bathroom and kitchen appliances.

My brother and I were thus provided with spectacles of work that fascinated us, and also with a long-term supply of large boxes and shipping crates. The crate that had contained the bathtub I remember as especially fertile with visions of what it might be reconstructed into. These visions evidently occasioned some strife between Henry and me. The man who installed our bathroom assured me many years later that he had seen me hit Henry on the head with a ball-peen hammer.

One day, while Henry and I were engaged in our controversial attempt to realize our unrealizable dreams of making something of the clutter in our backyard, a man suddenly came around the corner of the house carrying a dog. The dog was a nearly-grown pup, an English setter, white with black ears and eye patches and a large black spot in front of his tail. The man, as we would later learn, was Mike Brightleaf.

Mr. Brightleaf said, "Andy and Henry, you boys look a here. This is a pup for your daddy."

He set the big pup carefully down and gave him a pat. And then, with a fine self-assurance or a fine confidence in the pup or both, he said, "Call him Mike."

We called, "Here Mike!" and Mike came to us and the man left.

Mike, as we must have known even as young as we were, came from the greater world beyond Hargrave, the world of fields and woods that our father had never ceased to belong to and would belong to devotedly all his life. Mike was doomed like our father to town life, but was also like our father never to be reconciled to the town.

Along one side of our property our father built a long narrow pen that we called the dog lot, and he supplied it with a nice, white-painted doghouse. The fence was made of forty-seven-inch woven wire with two barbed wires at the top. These advantages did not impress Mike in the least. He did not wish to live in the nice doghouse, and he would not do so unless chained to it. As for the tall fence, he would go up it as one would climb a ladder, gather himself at the top, and leap to freedom. Our father stretched a third strand of barbed wire inside the posts, making what would have been for a man a considerable obstacle, and Mike paid it no mind at all.

As a result, since our father apparently was reluctant to keep him tied, Mike had the run of the town. For want of anything better to do, he dedicated himself to being where we children were and going where we went. I have found two photographs of him, taken by our mother. In both, characteristically, he is with some of us children, accepting of hugs and pats, submissive, it seems, to his own kindness and our thoughtless affection, but with the look also of a creature dedicated to a higher purpose, aware of his lowly servitude.

One day our father found Henry and me trying to fit Mike with a harness we had contrived from an old mule bridle. We were going to hitch him to our wagon.

Our father said, "Andy, Henry, don't do that, boys. You'll cow him."

I had never heard the word *cow* used in that way before, and it affected me strongly. The word still denotes, to me, Mike's meek submission to indignity and my father's evident conviction that *nothing* should be cowed.

Mike intended to go everywhere we went and he usually did, but he understood his limits when he met them. One Sunday morning we children and our mother had started our walk to church. Mike was trailing quietly behind, hoping to be unnoticed, but our mother looked back and saw him. She said sympathetically, "Mike, go back home." And Mike turned sadly around and went back.

He was well-known in our town, for he was a good-looking dog and he moved with the style of his breeding and calling. But his most remarkable public performance was his singing to the fire whistle. Every day, back then, the fire whistle blew precisely at noon. The fire whistle was actually a siren whose sound built to an almost intolerable whoop and then diminished in a long wail. When that happened, Mike always threw up his head and howled, whether in pain or appreciation it was impossible to tell. One day he followed us to school, and then at noon into the little cafeteria beneath the gymnasium. I don't believe I knew he was there until the fire whistle let go and he began to howl. The sound, in that small and supposedly civil enclosure, was utterly barbarous and shocking. I felt some pressure to be embarrassed but I was deeply pleased. Who else belonged to so rare an animal?

But Mike knew well that his deliverer was my father. He might spend a lot of time idling about in town or playing with children, but he was a dog with a high vocation, and he knew what it was. He knew too that my father fully shared it. Mike loved us all in the honorable and admirable way of a dog, but his love for my father was too dedicated to be adequately described as doglike. I think he regarded his partnership with my father as the business of his life, as it was also his overtopping joy.

My father was a man of passions. I don't think he did much of anything except passionately. When he was removed from his passions, as in some public or social situations, he would be quiet, remote, uncomfortable, and unhappy. I think he was sometimes constrained by a sense of the disproportion between the force of his thoughts and the demands of polite conversation. He loved serious talk and the sort of conversation that is incited by pleasure. He loved hilarity. But he had little to offer in the way of small talk, and he always seemed to me to be uncomfortable or embarrassed when it was required of him.

He was passionate about the law. He loved its argumentative logic, its principles and methods, its discriminating language. He was capable of working at it ardently and for long hours. His sentences, written or spoken, whatever the circumstances, were concise, exact, grammatically correct, and powerful in their syntax. He did not speak without thinking, and he meant what he said.

He used such sentences when instructing and reprimanding us children. We were not always on his mind, I am sure, but when we were he applied himself to fatherhood as he did to everything else. When we were sick or troubled he could be as tender and sympathetic as our mother. At other times, disgruntled or fearing for us as his knowledge of the world prompted him to do, he could be peremptory, demanding, impatient, and in various ways intimidating. I was always trying to keep some secret from him, and he had an uncanny way of knowing your secrets. He had a way of knowing your thoughts, and this came from sympathy. It could only have come from sympathy, but it took me a long time to know that.

I have always been a slow thinker, and he was fast. He could add, subtract, and figure averages in his head with remarkable speed. He would count a flock of sheep like this: one, five, seven, twelve, sixteen, nineteen, twenty-four . . . One day when he had done this and arrived promptly at the correct number, a hundred and fifty or so, he turned and looked at me for my number. I was still counting. "Honey," he said with instant exasperation, "are you counting by *twos*?" That was exactly what I was doing, and in my slowness I had had to start over two or three times.

He was passionate about farming. He could not voluntarily have quit farming any more than he could voluntarily have quit breathing. He spent great love and excitement in buying rundown farms, stopping the washes, restoring the pastures, renewing the fences and buildings, and making other improvements. He performed this process of regeneration seven times in his life, eventually selling six of the farms, but he kept one, and in addition he kept and improved over many years the home place where he was born and raised. He hired out most of the work, of course, but he worked himself too, and he watched and instructed indefatigably. He would drive out to see to things in the morning before he went to the office, and again after he left the office in the afternoon. He took days off to devote to farming. He would be out looking at things, salting his cattle and sheep, walking or driving his car through the fields, every Sunday afternoon. In the days before tractors he would be on hand to take the lines when there were young mules to break. He did the dehorning, castrating, and other veterinary jobs. All the time he could spare from his law practice he gave to the farms. Because of his work for an agricultural cooperative, he would frequently have to make a trip to Washington or some other distant place. Sometimes, returning from one of those trips in the middle of the night, he would go to the home place or one of the others and drive through the fields before going home to bed.

Of farming, he told me, "It's like a woman. It'll keep you awake at night." He loved everything about it. He loved the look and feel and smell of the land and the shape of it underfoot. He loved the light on it and the weather over it. He loved the economics of it. As characteristic of him as anything else were pages of yellow legal pads covered with columns of numbers written in ink in his swift hand, where he figured the outgoes and the incomes of his farming.

When he went to the farms, he would often take Mike with him. He would hurry home from the office, change his clothes, and hurry out again. Going to his car, he would raise the trunk lid. "Here, Mike! Get in!" And Mike would leap into the trunk and lie down. My father would close the trunk, leaving the latch unengaged so Mike would have air.

If there were farm jobs to be done, Mike would just go along, running free in the open country, hunting on his own. But, if it was hunting season, my father might bring along his shotgun in its tattered canvas case. The gun was a pump-action Remington twenty-gauge, for in those days my father had excellent eyes and he was a good shot.

In those days too the tall coarse grass known as fescue had not yet been introduced here. That grass and the coming of rotary mowing machines have made the good old bobwhite a rare bird in this country now. The improved pastures in Mike's time were in bluegrass, and a lot of fields would be weedy in the fall. There was plenty of good bird cover and as a result plenty of birds. My father would know where the coveys were, and he and Mike would go to seek them out.

And here they came into their glory, and here I need to imagine them and see them again in my mind's eye, now that I am getting old and have come to understand my father perhaps as well as I am ever going to. For right at the heart of his passions for his family, for the law, and for farming, all consequential passions with practical aims and ends, was this other passion for bird hunting with a good dog, which had no practical end but was the enactment of his great love of country, of life, of his own life, for their own sake.

When he stepped out in his eager long strides, with Mike let loose in front of him, he was walking free on the undivided and priceless world itself. And Mike went out from him in a motion fluid and swift and strong, less running than flying, and he would find the birds.

Once he had learned his trade, Mike was a nearly perfect dog, giving a satisfaction that was nearly complete. I never heard my father complain of him. He understood that little pump gun in my father's hands as if it were a book of instructions, and he did what he was supposed to do.

He was remarkable in another way. He would retrieve, and to reward him my father started feeding him the heads of the birds when he brought them back. Before long, Mike got the idea. From then on, he ate the head of the downed bird where he found it and brought back the headless carcass.

From time to time during my father's life as a bird hunter, which had its summit during Mike's life, he would go somewhere down south on a hunting trip, usually with one other hunter. I know about these trips only from a handful of stories, all of which had to do in one way or another with the prowess of my father's great dog.

In Hargrave we lived across the street from Dr. Gib Holston, who was the town's only professed atheist. He had the further distinctions of a glass eye and a reputation for violence. Once, in the days of his youth, a man had insulted him, and Dr. Holston had killed the offender by shooting him from a train window. Most of our fellow citizens who used profanity might properly have been said to cuss, for they used it thoughtlessly as a sort of rhetoric of emphasis, but Dr. Holston *cursed,* with blasphemy aforethought and with the intention of offending anyone inclined to be offended.

He was a small man, about five feet tall, but strongly built and without fat to the end of his days. He thought of himself as outrageous, and so of course he was, and he enjoyed his outrageousness. He was a strange neighbor for my good mother, a woman of faith, who obliged him by finding him on all points as outrageous as he wished to be. She, with conscientious good manners, and my father, with a ceremoniousness always slightly tainted with satire, called him Dr. Holston. The rest of us called him Doc or, when we wished to distinguish him from other doctors, Dr. Gib.

Doc, then, was one of my father's clients, which sometimes required them to make a little business trip together, and at least once they went together on a hunting trip. Why my father would have put up with him to that extent I am not sure. Perhaps, as a man of my grandparents' generation, Doc knew and remembered things that my father was interested in hearing; he always liked his older clients and enjoyed listening to them. But mostly, I believe, he put up with Doc because Doc amused him. It amused him that when they went somewhere together, Doc insisted on sitting by himself in the back seat of the car. It amused him to see in the rearview mirror that when Doc dozed off, sitting back there bolt upright by himself, his glass eye stayed open. Once, when my father advised him that a neighbor of ours, a very aristocratic and haughty old lady, had been "dropped" in a certain town that they visited, Doc said, "Goddamn her, I wish she had dropped on through!" That amused my father as if it had been the gift of divine charity itself, and he was therefore *obliged* to be fully amused. The one story that came of their hunting together is about my father's amusement.

They had come to their hunting place, uncased and loaded their guns, and turned Mike loose. The place was rich in birds, and Mike soon began finding them, working beautifully in cooperation with my father, as he always did, and my father was shooting well as *he* always did. But this story begins with my father's growing awareness and worry that Doc was not shooting well.

There is a good possibility, in my opinion, that Doc by then was not capable of shooting well. I have been on hunts with him myself, and I never saw him hit anything. He had bought a twelve-gauge Browning automatic, which he pointed hither and yon without regard to the company. You had to watch him. I think he bought that gun because he couldn't see well enough to shoot well. It was an expensive gun, which counted with him, and that it was automatic impressed him inordinately. He had the primitive technological faith that such a weapon simply could not help compensating for his deficiency. He had paid a lot of money for this marvelous gun that would enact his mere wish to hit the birds as they rose. If you can't shoot well, you must shoot a lot. And so when he heard the birds rise, he merely pointed the gun in their direction and emptied it: *Boomboomboom!* And of course he was missing.

And of course he was eventually furious. He vented his fury by stomping about and cursing roundly everything in sight. He invited God to damn the innocent birds who were flying too fast and scattering too widely to be easily shot, and his expensive shotgun which was guilty only of missing what it had not been aimed at, and the cover which was too brushy, and the landscape which was too ridgy and broken, and the day which was too cloudy. My father, who instantly appreciated the absurdity of Doc's cosmic wrath, took the liberty of laughing. He then, being a reasonable man, recognized the tactlessness of his laughter, which doubled his amusement, and he laughed more. Doc thereupon included my father in his condemnation, and then, to perfect his retribution, he included Mike who, off in the distance, was again beautifully quartering the ground. This so fulfilled my father with amusement that he was no longer able to stand. As we used to say here, his tickle-box had turned completely over. He subsided onto the ground and lay there on his back among the weeds, laughing, in danger, he said, of wetting his pants. He was pretty certain too that Doc was going to shoot him, and he was duly afraid, which somehow amused him even more, and he could not stop laughing.

How they leveled that situation out and recovered from it,

I don't know. But they did, and my father, to his further great amusement, survived.

In the general course of my father's life Doc, I suppose, was a digression, an indulgence perhaps, certainly a fascination of a sort, and a source of stories. His friendship with Billy Finn was another matter. Between the two of them was a deep affection that lasted all their lives. On my father's side, I know, this affection was weighted by an abiding compassion. Billy Finn was a sweet man who sometmes drank to excess, and perhaps for sufficient reason. He had suffered much in his marriage to an unappeasable woman, "Mizriz Fannie Frankle Finn," as my father enjoyed calling her behind her back. To the unhappy marriage of Mr. and Mrs. Finn had been added the death, early in World War II, of their son, their only child. The shadow of shared grief, cast over the marriage, had made it maybe even more permanent than its vows. Mr. Finn was bound to Mrs. Finn by his pity for her suffering, so like his own; he suffering in addition, as she made sure, his inability to pity her enough. Life for Mr. Finn, especially after the death of his son, was pretty much an uphill trudge. I think his friendship with my father was a necessary solace to him to the end of his life, near which he said to a member of the clergy visiting him in the nursing home: "Hell, preacher? You can't tell me nothing about Hell. I've lived with a damned Frankle *for forty-nine years!*"

When my father would go away on one of his bird-hunting trips, his companion almost invariably would be Mr. Finn. Mr. Finn loved bird dogs, and he always had one or two. The dogs always were virtually guaranteed to be good ones, and nearly always they disappointed him. He was not a good hand with a dog, perhaps because he had experienced too much frustration and disappointment in other things. He was impatient with his dogs, fussed at them too much, frightened them, confused them, and hollered at them. He was a noisy hunter, his utterances tending to be both excessive and obsessive, and this added substantially to my father's fund of amusement and of stories, but also to his fund of sorrow, for Billy Finn was a sad man, and my father was never forgetful of that.

On one of their hunting trips down south, as a companion to Mike, Mr. Finn took a lovely pointer bitch he called Gladys, a dog on the smallish side, delicately made, extremely sensitive and shy—precisely the wrong kind of dog for him.

When the dogs were released, Mike sniffed the wind and sprang into his work. Gladys, more aware of the strangeness of the new terrain than of its promise, hung back.

"Go on, Gladys!" Mr. Finn said. But, instead of ranging ahead with Mike, Gladys followed Mr. Finn, intimidated still by the new country, embarrassed by her timidity, knowing what was expected of her, and already fearful of Mr. Finn's judgment.

"Gladys!" he said. "Go on!"

And then, raising his voice and pointing forward, he said, "Damn you, Gladys, go on! *Go on!*"

That of course ended any possibility that Gladys was going to hunt, for after that she needed to be forgiven. She stuck even closer to Mr. Finn, fawning whenever he looked at her, hoping for forgiveness. And of course, in his humiliation, it never occurred to him to forgive her.

They hunted through the morning, Mr. Finn alternately apologizing for Gladys and berating her. His embarrassment about his dog eventually caused my father to become embarrassed about *his* dog. For, in spite of Mr. Finn's relentless fuming and muttering, they were having a fairly successful hunt. Mike was soaring through the cover in grand style and coming to point with rigorous exactitude. And, the better it was, the worse it was. The better Mike performed, the more disgrace piled upon poor Gladys, the more embarrassed Mr. Finn became, and the more he fumed and muttered, the more my father was punished by the excellence of Mike.

"Oh, Lord, it was awful," my father would say later, laughing at the memory of his anguished amusement and his failure to think of anything at all to say.

And it got worse.

Sometime early in the afternoon Mr. Finn's suffering grew greater than he could bear. He turned upon Gladys, who was still following him, and said half crying, "Gladys, damn you to Hell! I raised you from a pup, I've sheltered you, I've fed you, I've loved you like a child, and now you've let me down, you thankless bitch!" He then aimed a murderous kick at her, which she easily evaded and fled from him until she was out of sight.

My father would gladly have ended the day there and then if he could have thought of a painless or even a polite way to do it. But he could think of no way. They hunted on.

But now Mr. Finn was the one who needed forgiveness, and Gladys did not return to forgive him. He began to suffer the torments of the guilty and unforgiven, of shame for himself and fear for his dog. He began to imagine all the bad things that might happen to her, unprotected as she was and in a strange country. She might remain lost forever. She might get caught in somebody's steel trap. Some lousy bastard might find her wandering and steal her. She would be hungry and cold.

My father, being guilty of nothing except the good work of his own dog, was somewhat calmer. He thought Gladys would not go far and would be all right, and he sought to reassure his friend. But Mr. Finn could not be comforted. From his earlier mutterings of imprecation he changed now to mutterings of self-reproach and worry.

As evening came on, they completed their long circle back to the car, and Gladys was still nowhere in sight. Mr. Finn had been calling her for the last mile or so. For a long time they waited while Mr. Finn called and called, his voice sounding more pleading, anxious, and forlorn as the day darkened. They were tired and they were getting cold.

Nearby there was a culvert that let a small stream pass under the road. The culvert was dry at that time of the year, and it would be a shelter.

"Billy," my father said, "lay your coat in that culvert. It's not going to rain. She'll find it and sleep there. We'll come back in the morning and get her."

The only available comfort was in that advice, and Mr. Finn took it. He emptied his hunting coat, folded it to make a bed, and laid it in the culvert. They went back to their hotel to their suppers, their beds, and an unhappy night for Mr. Finn.

The next day was Sunday. On their hunting trips my father and Mr. Finn scrupulously attended church on Sunday. That morning they shaved, put on their churchgoing clothes, ate breakfast, and then hurried out into the country where they had lost Gladys and Mr. Finn had left his coat.

Aside from ordering his breakfast, Mr. Finn had said not a word. But now as they drove through the bright morning that still was dark to him, he uttered a sort of prayer: "Lord, I hope she made it back."

My father, who was driving, reached across and patted him on the shoulder. "She'll be there," he said.

She was there. When they climbed the fence to look, she was lying in the culvert on Mr. Finn's coat, a picture of repentance and faithfulness that stabbed him to the heart. He knelt on the concrete beside her. Her petted her, praised her, thanked her, and called her his good and beautiful Gladys, for she was at that moment all the world to him. And then he gathered her up in his arms, went to the fence, and started to climb over. It was a tall fence, fairly new with a barbed wire at the top, a considerable challenge to any man climbing it in a suit, let alone a man climbing it in a suit and carrying a dog. He got one leg over and was coming with the other when he lost his balance and fell, one cuff of his pants catching on a barb. And so he hung, upside down, with Gladys frantic and struggling in his arms.

My father would tell that story suffering with laughter, and then he would look down and shake his head. It was sadder than it was funny, but it was certainly funny, and what was a mere man to do?

•••

I loved to hear my father tell those stories and others like them, and I can still see the visions they made me see when I was a boy. But now I love better to try to imagine the days, for which there are no stories, when Mike and my father hunted by themselves at home. On those days they passed beyond the margins of my father's working life and his many worries. Though they might have been hunting on a farm that my father owned, they passed beyond the confines even of farming. They entered into a kind of freedom and a kind of perfection. I am thinking now with wonder of the convergence, like two birds crossing as they rise, of a passionate man and a gifted, elated, hard-hunting dog, and this in a country deeply loved and known, from many of the heights of which the man could see on its hill in the distance the house where he was born. And it would be in the brisk, fine weather of the year's decline when every creature is glad to be alive.

My father would have been in his early forties then, young still in all his energy and ability, his body light with thought and implicit motion even when he stood at rest. He and Mike would pass through a whole afternoon or a whole day in the same excitement, the same eagerness for the hidden birds and for the country that lay ahead.

Thinking of him in those days, I can't help wishing that I had known him then as a contemporary and friend, rather than as his son. As his son, I was to see him clearly only in looking back. He was obscured to me by his anxious parenthood, his fears for me, and by my own uneasy responses.

And yet I remember standing with him one day, when I was maybe eight or nine years old, on the top of a ridge in a weedy field. We were on the back of the farm we called the Crayton place. Beyond us, Mike was working with the beautiful motion that came of speed and grace together. My father held his gun in the crook of his left arm, at ease. He was in the mood that made him most comfortable to be with, enjoying himself completely, and with his entire intention allowing me to see what he saw.

Mike came to point, a forefoot lifted, his body tense from the end of his nose to the tip of his tail with a transfiguring alertness. Without looking at me, without looking away from the dog, my father allowed his right hand to reach down and find my shoulder and lie there.

"It comes over him like a sickness," he said.

Like lovesickness, I think he meant, and even then I somehow understood. He was talking about a love, paramount if not transcendent, by which Mike was altogether moved, which he felt in his bones and could not resist.

And now of course I know that he was speaking from sympathy. He was talking also about himself, about his love, not only for the birds yet hidden and still somewhere beyond the end of Mike's nose, but for the country itself, his life in it, and the great beauty that sustained it then and always.

It was lovesickness, recognized in the dog because he knew it more fully in himself, that held him still, his hand on my shoulder, in that moment before we started forward to walk up the birds.

Mike, I think, was my father's one superlative dog, and his noontime just happened to coincide with my father's. It did not last long. After Mike there were other dogs, but my father did not exult in them as he had in Mike. And he had less time for them. Griefs and responsibilities came upon him. His life as a hunter gradually subsided, and in his later years I don't think he much wished for it or often remembered it.

It may be that those summit years made the measure of the later ones, revealing them as anticlimactic and somewhat sad. The years with Mike may have established a zenith of performance and companionship that he could not hope, and even did not wish, to see equaled.

I don't know exactly when Mike died. He lived long enough to become Old Mike to us all. And then the day arrived when we came down to breakfast and our mother told us, "I wouldn't go out there if I were you. Your daddy's burying his dog." And we could see him with a shovel down in the far end of the garden, digging the grave.

That was all I knew about the burial of Mike until one day, near the end of his own life, when my father told me a little more: "I had almost covered him up, when it occurred to me that I hadn't said anything. I needed to say something. And so I uncovered his head. I said, 'Blessings on you, Mike. We'll hunt the birds of Paradise.'"

Wendell Berry was born in 1934. He is a native of the small Kentucky community where he lives with his wife Tanya and their children and grandchildren. His most recent books are *Hannah Coulter* **(a novel),** *Given* **(poems), and** *The Way of Ignorance* **(essays). He is self-employed and an unpaid consultant to a number of agribusiness corporations.**

The story "Mike" is founded on several scraps of memory and hearsay that have been lively in my mind since I was a child. But the scraps did not of themselves make a story. To make a story I put the scraps at the service of imagination, or vice versa, hoping nonetheless that the story might tell me more than I already knew of a certain kind of man living in a country like my own in the early 1940s. It is fortunate, and a pleasure to know, that my story can take up life and room in the imaginations of other people.

Kevin Wilson

TUNNELING TO THE CENTER OF THE EARTH

(from *The Frostproof Review*)

First of all, we were never tunneling to the center of the earth. I mean, we're not stupid. We knew we couldn't get to it with the equipment we had. The psychiatrist that mom and dad hired to talk to me is responsible for the whole Journey to the Center of the Earth thing because, to him, what we were actually doing wasn't as exciting. In fact, I don't think he ever fully understood what it was we were doing. I don't think we really understood it either. We were just digging.

It started last summer. The three of us, Hunter, Amy and myself, had just graduated from college with meaningless degrees, things like Gender Studies and Canadian History and Morse code. We had devoted our academic careers to things that lacked applicability to the real world. We never really thought about it when we were in school, reading about Gender and Canadians and Samuel Morse. We never realized that we were supposed to be preparing ourselves for a future life, a self-sustainable life with jobs and family cars and magazine subscriptions. We just really wanted to know about Gender and Canadians and Morse code. And so I think it was that kind of disconnection from what we were expected to do that made us get out the shovels. It's the only reason I can figure.

We had just been sitting around in my room at my parents'

house since graduation. We still wore our graduation caps, would twirl the tassel like a strand of hair as we watched TV or played cards or smoked cheap pot that Amy's brother sold us. My mother would leave the want ads outside the door of my room and that's where I left them. Pretty soon they started toppling over, scattering on the floor, and she eventually got rid of them. "Maybe you could teach Morse code to kids at the elementary school," she told me one morning as we ate breakfast. And sure, I would have loved to teach kids Morse code, to tap my finger onto their tiny palms and explain the words being formed on their hands. But schools don't have that kind of money, can hardly afford to teach real languages like Spanish and French.

Besides, no one really wants to learn Morse code anymore. They only want to know how to say two things: "I love you" and "SOS". They want to know a romantic code and then tap it out on their lover's naked body and spend the night a little less lonely. So at parties I was always tapping out the same things, showing drunk people the correct timing, the pauses necessary to say the words, but even then it didn't matter. These people would tap whatever they wanted, correct or not, and their lover would be happy. And if they were in a situation where they actually had to resort to using Morse code for help, well, they were not going to get it. They were going to die.

None of us came up with the idea on our own that morning. It just sort of hit us all simultaneously. You spend enough time with people, you start to think in sync with them, and at this moment we all just thought the same thing. *We should dig, get underground.* So we did.

We went to the garage and grabbed all the shovels and digging tools we could find. Hunter took the post-hole digger, for the initial opening, plus another shovel once we got started. I had a new shovel, with a perfect, unblemished silver blade and a lacquered handle. I also took one of those shovels with the pointed blade, to break through the rocks or tree roots that we'd likely come across.

Amy wore two garden spades on her hips like a gunslinger, for the intricate digging and shaping along the sides of the hole. She also filled one of her pockets with spoons from the kitchen, just in case.

We stepped outside the garage with purpose, weighed down with our tools, and walked into the backyard. My mother was washing dishes in the kitchen and slid open the window. "What are you kids doing?" she asked us. I told her that we were going to dig a hole. She asked us to stay away from her tulip garden and we did, picked a spot in the far corner of the yard and started digging.

We worked day and night that first week, burrowing down a good twelve feet into the earth, expanding the hole so that all three of us would fit at the same time. We took our lunch breaks back on the surface, where my mother would bring us sandwiches and chips and lemonade. We liked to lay on our stomachs and eat our food, staring down at the hole we'd made. We'd gotten down far enough that we were touching earth that probably hadn't felt the glaze of sunlight in hundreds of years. When we were digging one time, Amy took a big handful of dirt and held it close to her face, took deep breaths of it. "It smells like a museum," she said, "like something from the past."

My father came over one afternoon and knelt over the hole, careful not to set his knee down in the torn-up earth. "Son, your mom asked me to tell you that if you are going to keep digging this"—he searched for a word—"hole, well then you're going to have to do something about all this dirt."

I asked him if we could just spread it out evenly through the backyard, maybe heighten the ground by a few inches, but he said no.

"You see, son, we have all this grass and plant life in the backyard and if you just throw a blanket of dirt over all that, you're going to kill it all. No, you're just going to have to figure out a way to get this stuff out of here."

We used Amy's truck to haul the dirt out. We did it at night, once the lights all went out in the houses of our subdivision. We loaded the dirt onto a plastic tarp in the bed of her truck and drove down to the lake. Amy would back the truck right up to the edge of the water and we would pull up the tarp like a magic trick, yank and yank until the dirt was gone. The surface of the water would bubble as the earth drifted down, worked itself in with the silt and debris at the bottom of the lake. By the fifth week there was a report in the paper that the water level had risen even though there had been no rain in twelve days. And the water was somehow, according to one of the sources in the article, "dirtier than usual." That's how much dirt we were hollowing out of the ground.

One night, Hunter woke up thrashing in his sleeping bag, rolling from side to side dangerously near the mouth of the hole. When we finally got him awake, he told us that he'd dug too far in his dream, had felt the earth give easily under his shovel and that fire had come out of the cracks, spilling around his feet.

"We can't keep digging down," he told us. "We'll find mole people or molten lava or some underground ocean."

"Or China," Amy offered. "We'll come up in China. That would be embarrassing."

Hunter nodded in agreement. "There is nothing good down there," he said.

So we went sideways.

We started expanding, tunneling further and further underneath our town. We dug random patterns that looped in on themselves and spread from one edge of the town to the other. We dug tunnels high enough to let us walk upright, quickly turning into tiny pinpoints, so small we had to wedge ourselves through to keep going, the earth scattering in pieces as we moved. We never worried about cave-ins or getting lost. We were young and felt invincible. You never think about dying when you're twenty-two and drunk-driving or bungee-jumping or digging ill-designed tunnels underneath your parents' house. It never occurs to you. Under the surface, the air was cool and slightly damp and we felt like we were moving through a haze, a dream world that held no possibility for pain or disaster. And then we had a few near misses, some small cave-ins, and pain and possible death seemed slightly more possible. So we started building structures, wood and metal supports that Hunter built from his recollection of a documentary on the first subway system. The supports looked suspicious, creaking and shoddy, but they worked, reinforced the walls of the tunnels and kept us safe. After that, we just kept moving, up and down, left or right.

Eventually, we added rooms that served as the heart for all the tunnels, the source for all these paths to come and go from. We made them wide and high and eventually started sleeping in them at night, when we couldn't dig anymore. My mother gave us food weekly, dropped bags of groceries into the hole in the backyard where one of us would go pick them up. "Here's your snacks honey," she would tell me as she dropped the groceries down the hole. I wore sunglasses to protect my eyes from the light that shined down on me. I was covered in dirt, under my fingernails and behind my ears. My mother was not pleased. "Honey, do you think that maybe it's the drugs that are making you do this?" I reached for another bag of groceries and shrugged. "I don't know," I told her. "I don't think so." I didn't know how to tell her that I was actually happy for the first time since college had ended. I had a purpose. I had to dig. I don't think she would have understood even if I had told her.

We found time capsules that had been forgotten and never dug up. The canisters were rusted and sealed tight, holding memories that had waited for years to remind, but we knew nothing of their significance. Amy made up stories for each memento, giving new pasts to the objects we found before we sealed the capsules again. We always put them close to the surface, poking out of the ground slightly, where someone might notice the glint of sunlight reflecting off the silver canister.

We found a surprising number of jars filled with money. Old people must have buried them and then forgotten where they were. They were stuffed full of moldy tens and twenties, folded and wrapped in rubber bands, the jars sealed tight with paraffin wax. We found Styrofoam McDonald's containers and metal poles that had sunk into the ground and been forgotten. We found animal bones and human bones, and the still-decomposing body of Jasper Cooley, a drunk who had disappeared a few months ago. We couldn't find any signs of why he died, and the clothes he was wearing were nice, even covered in dirt and bugs. Amy had found him, scraping her shovel against the rubber soles of his shoes until she finally realized what they were. Hunter and I worked carefully to fully remove him, mindful of the decomposition that was taking place. Finally, we carried him in a sheet of plastic all the way back to one of the rooms. We propped him up against the wall until we could think of what to do about him. Hunter wanted to take him aboveground, leave him where someone could find him and give him a proper burial. "He's properly buried right now, Hunter," Amy said. "For all intents and purposes, he is buried." But Hunter did not like this answer and so Amy and I had to dig a grave in the floor of the room, digging deeper into the ground. We had a ceremony and said a prayer and felt somehow better.

We ate sandwiches and listened to the faint noise of people and cars and machinery aboveground. We had portals all over town, tiny, obscured openings in the earth, which we could pop out of if we ever wanted. But we never did, spent all our time underground, digging more tunnels, coming out only in the middle of the night to dump the dirt in the lake. We were trying to hollow out a new world under the earth, to fill up the one above us.

Our shovels bit into the earth until they disintegrated, finally wore down to the wooden handle. We used the money from the sealed jars to buy new ones, pure titanium that my father got from the hardware store. He lowered them down to me one night, telling me, "these are the best they got. Good, dependable shovels." I took each one he handed down and bundled them together as well as I could. He also handed down boxes of batteries, and more flashlights, candles, and lanterns. "Mom and me aren't quite sure what you're doing down there," he whispered to me, stooped low over the hole. "We hope it's nothing we've done, but we just want you to be happy. So, if you have to be underground to be happy, that's fine with us." His hand came down through the hole and I shook it. Finally, we both walked away in the same direction, his feet above me as we moved.

At night, when our day of digging was over, we would gather in one of the main rooms and eat our dinner. We talked about our days, where we had dug, and what kind of soil we'd encountered. We loved to talk about dirt now. We all knew the wonderful feeling of digging into a new kind of soil. There was something transforming about watching the earth change as you dug and then passing through it, feeling yourself changed in the process. We were seeing the secrets of the earth revealed in tiny increments. It was better than drugs. Though we still did the drugs. There wasn't a whole lot to do at night under the earth.

We smoked pot that Amy's brother dropped through one of the holes on the surface. We did not tell him about the tunnels though. We didn't want him and his high school friends using the tunnels as make-out spots, littering them with empty beer cans and used condoms. We just said it was our new drop spot, and he was too bored to care much beyond that. At nights, we rolled joints and made shadow puppets on the walls with a spotlight. Hunter could recreate *Apocalypse Now* in its entirety with only his two bare hands, twisting and flexing in the light, while Amy and I watched the shadows of his hands against the wall. He would make the bald head of Marlon Brando with his hands curved into a dome while he murmured, "the horror . . . the horror." We felt like cavemen, discovering all the various ways we could amuse ourselves. When we finally went to sleep, we dreamed of tunnels, endless, perfect structures that led us to some unknown place that we knew was heaven. Amy, the Gender Studies major, kept saying that there were Freudian theories based on these kinds of dreams, a fixed system of symbols that signified repressed sexual urges. Eventually, she succeeded in making Hunter incredibly anxious about his relationship with his mother, but I really think that sometimes a tunnel is just a tunnel.

We had nearly burrowed beneath the entire town; there was nowhere left to go. Hunter was tunneling one afternoon with Amy close behind him with her garden shovels, smoothing the passages. He hit something with his shovel, which he assumed to be rock. He traded off for the other shovel he had, the sharp, pointed one and tried to work his way around. After an hour, he realized the rock spread out for at least ten feet on either side. "There's a boulder in the way," he told Amy, but kept chipping away. These kinds of things had become fun to us now.

Finally, he felt the rock give and saw light burst into the tunnel, filling up the passage. Hunter poked his head inside the hole and looked around the Corning family's basement. He'd broken through the cinder-block wall of the basement, which had been turned into a recreation room for the children. The Corning children stared back at him, the foosball table no longer in action. "Sorry," he told them. "I must have the wrong house. I'm sorry." He and Amy started backtracking, filling the tunnel back in and feeling terrible about the whole thing. That night, we all sat around in one of the main rooms and thought about how the Corning children were going to be punished tonight by their parents for destroying the wall in the basement. Their parents would stare at the opening in the wall, the repacked dirt spilling onto the carpet, and roll their eyes as the children tried to tell them about the man with the shovel digging into their basement. Actually, perhaps we didn't feel all that terrible about it. Perhaps we laughed for a long time. In all honesty, I am pretty sure that we laughed for a long time.

And then it was November and cold. We took all three of our sleeping bags and zipped them together to make one large bag to hold all of us. Covered in dirt, teeth chattering, we huddled against each other and waited for morning, or what we suspected was morning. The truth was that we had no idea for the most part. We dug until we were tired and then we slept. With both of their bodies covering my own, I felt the breath enter and leave their bodies, their hearts beating. And if there's any chance of being happier than that, filthy, cold, and almost imperceptible from the ground we slept on, I would like to know how.

But it got colder. The ground was more resistant to our shovels, and the metal blades chipped away even faster. We ran out of money and had to make do with what was left. My parents were only providing the bare essentials now; they said it was hard to support three kids, especially when only one of them was their own. I understood, did not begrudge them this fact. We were finding the limits of what we could do and even though we acknowledged the fact that we were running out of options, we had no idea what to do about it. We just kept digging.

Even though we still made new tunnels, we always seemed to find ourselves near the original hole by the end of the day. We would eat our dinner, crackers and bottles of water, and peek out to look up at the stars. A few times, we climbed all the way to the top of the hole, looked over at my parents' house, warm and well lit, and then slowly crawled back into our tunnels. Our food was nearly gone. Our tools were broken. Our bodies were tired. We knew it was time to leave but we were hesitant to say it out loud, to make it irrefutable. We scratched in the dirt with a stick, weighed the pros and the cons. Whoever wanted to leave could leave, no questions asked. In the morning, Hunter was gone, the sleeping bag less by one. Three days later, with no tunnels dug, Amy kissed me on the cheek and wriggled out of the sleeping bag and then it was just me and the entire earth below the surface. It was a little lonely.

I tried to refill the tunnels but the work was much harder than hollowing them out. I had only one shovel left, nicked and dinged and inefficient. I finally gave up and crawled back to the main room and waited for something to happen. I lit one of the few candles left and tapped on the walls of the tunnel, *di-di-di-dah-dah-dah-di-di-dit*. SOS.

A few nights later, I felt a hand on my shoulder and I pulled myself deeper into the sleeping bag, afraid of what was inside the tunnel with me. And then I heard my father speak. "Son," he said, "it's just me and your mom." I peered out of my sleeping bag and saw the bright light of a headlamp and my father's face beneath it. My mother was close behind him, holding a candle. "Your friends called us," he continued. "They wondered if you had left yet. I think they may be wanting to come back, feel like they've disappointed you." I shook my head, said that I didn't know if I was ready to leave. I couldn't imagine life aboveground, or, if I did, it seemed less tenable than what I had. "It's winter now," my father said. "It's getting cold. Less daylight." My mother then said, "It's time to come back up." They told me that they would let me live in the house with them for a while, until I could find my own place. My father had talked to a friend about getting me a job with his landscaping firm. They had contacted a psychiatrist who I could talk to. They made it seem very plausible, like a good idea. I grabbed my shovel and then took a plastic shopping bag and filled it with dirt and then, one by one, we climbed out of the hole and walked back to the house.

I don't talk to Hunter or Amy anymore, though I heard that Hunter was in Alberta, spelunking around in Castleguard Cave on some grant from the North American Society. And Amy is getting her Ph.D. in geology publishing some articles revolving around gender and mining. I'm still doing landscaping work, digging and planting and hauling. I ended up seeing the psychiatrist for a year. He said that I had been postponing my life, that hiding in the tunnels had been a way to avoid the responsibilities of the real world, an adventure under the earth. And yes, that is true. I knew that the minute we started digging. But it was more than that. I don't know what it was, but I know it was more than that.

Sometimes, when work is over and I'm gathering up the equipment and supplies, I place my hand flat against the ground and I feel the *thump, thump, thump* run through my body like Morse code. I listen for a long time to the sound of the earth and then I realize that it is just my heart, and the things it is saying are indecipherable. I dig my fingers into the freshly tilled ground, scoop up a handful of dirt, and feel happy again, happier than anything on earth, anything on top of the earth.

Kevin Wilson is a native of Winchester, Tennessee. His fiction has appeared in *Ploughshares, One Story,* the *Greensboro Review,* the *Cincinnati Review,* and elsewhere. This is his second story to be selected for *New Stories from the South.* A graduate of Vanderbilt University and the MFA program at the University of Florida, and a recipient of fellowships from the KHN Center for the Arts and the MacDowell Colony, he currently lives with his wife in Sewanee, Tennessee, where he teaches at the University of the South.

LEIGH ANNE COUCH

*T*he story of this story is simple enough. I graduated college, moved to Boston, had a nervous breakdown, moved back to Tennessee to live with my parents, tried to dig a hole to the center of the earth, and, finally, wrote this story. Unlike the mother and father in the story, my parents stopped me before I dug even a few feet into the ground, and I am grateful for that. With this story, I tried to tell my parents that it was all worth it, but they're just thankful that I have my own place to live.

J. D. Chapman

AMANUENSIS

(from *Mid-American Review*)

In December of 1917, I was sent from Europe to a hospital for tubercular vets in western North Carolina. At first it didn't seem too bad. It was quiet. The ward smelled like ammonia, good for battling the ghost-stink of coal and salt from the transport ships, and sour bodies and cordite from the front. They served us biscuits. We got free cigarettes, too, although I couldn't smoke much except right after coffee, and we got all kinds of magazines. The hospital had a librarian who would come sit beside you and ask what sort of material you might care to read. Her name was Ivy Morgan, and she was not interested in improving any of us morally or academically unless we wanted. She liked Lardner's stuff, and she passed it on to me when she'd finished with it. Same with Mencken.

Half the men there were illiterate, though, and for them there was no escape from thinking about death. The chaplain came on Sundays to bludgeon us, but otherwise they lay alone in their iron beds, hacking ganglia onto the mottled marigold sheets.

There was one fellow in there named Brown, and his wife wrote him the most God-awful sort of business. "Dear Horace," she wrote, for that's what his name was. "Dear Horace. Well, I finally done it. I got tired of waiting on your malingering and I went ahead and had Jesse shoot that hog. It's November, Horace, and we are without meat, so I know that you won't mind, or if you do, too damn bad. I have never liked that hog, as you know, and have never understood how you could let it sleep under the porch like a hound where the smell of its shit will sneak up into the house. Anyway, Jesse was over to visit, and I baked him a pie. He's been very helpful since you left for your little vacation in the mountains. I says to Jesse, 'Well, take these apple-peelings out to Horace's nasty hog.' And Jesse says, 'That ole hog is still around?' And I says, 'Well, I reckon.' And Jesse says, 'Why?' So I says, 'Jesse, that's Horace's hog, that he thinks is a pet.' And Jesse says, 'Then why ain't he here to feed it?' And I says, 'Well, I guess he ain't here to take care of a lot of basic needs.' And one thing led to another till Jesse took your Daddy's gun off the mantel and went outside and shot the hog three times between the eyes. You should of seen it, Horace. That hog just stood there with his legs apart. At first I thought it was going to charge, and I yelled at Jesse to get away, but then the hog's eyes got sort of marbly, and he started swaying back and forth like he was fixin' to dance. Then blood came out both of his nostrils like from a pump, and he sat down and coughed just like a man. Jesse butchered him up and smoked him, and you were right when you said a kitchen-fed pig tastes different. Write soon, Gladys."

I read Brown the letter, since he couldn't read himself. "Jesus," I said.

Brown sighed. "Yeah. You write her back for me?"

I said OK, but that I couldn't imagine what to say.

Brown looked at me. His skin was gray and his eyes were leaking something like poached egg. "Tell her I'm fine. Ask her how was Thanksgiving. Tell her we had yams and turkey from a can."

Half the men there got letters like that, meant to grab them by the backs of their heads and wipe their faces in something bad, but, except for crying at night, they all acted too broken to care. I myself had left for France with a fiancée and two parents and returned to just a mother. The fiancée took up with a one-legged traveling preacher named Gonzelle Brough, and my father died in a sorghum field clutching a bottle he kept hidden out there, buried. The dogs had been at him by the time mother found him, but he still smelled of whiskey. "God will forgive him," wrote my mother, "but I cannot." In other words, I didn't have much in my life to feel superior about and I didn't mind admitting it, so a lot of the boys began to ask me to read and write out their letters for them.

There were a couple of us that could string words together, or spell at least, and after a while we began to charge money and specialize. There was a fellow named Jenkins who could do wistful sweetheart pieces, and another named Rose whom I couldn't stand and who wrote pious, scripture-ridden homilies, but when the men wanted something nasty, they sent for me.

"My Dearest Prunelle," I would write. "Time hangs heavy on a man's hands here. My only consolation is that I am miles away from you, and that public health officials have forbidden either you or your family from molesting me in this eyrie. Perhaps you will be surprised to learn that I was glad to hear that you have thrown me over for Hank James. Certainly, a year ago, I would have only been angered by such news. But reflection and distance have granted me perspective and wisdom, and I now see that you are perfect for one another, whereas my recent voyage outside of our wretched town introduced me to a variety of suitable ladies more charming, gracious, and, frankly, sanitary than yourself. I am, I have learned, a particularly able lover, and would probably have caused you to damage yourself in gratitude had I ultimately married you—a fate you will now be emphatically spared. But I misspeak. I do not mean to cast too negative a light on the amative powers of your Hank. How well the whole town recalls the many hours of practice he had among the goats and sheep in his father's stockyard in anticipation of his wedding night!" And so on.

Half the time they didn't send my letters, but only paid me to hear their bitterness translated into words. They'd listen while I read them what I'd written, then ask Jenkins or Rose to retool it. They kept mine and slept with them under their pillows.

•••

In January, Ivy came by to bring me a new issue of *The Smart Set*. "Hey Jimmy," she said. "When are you going under the knife?"

They'd told me I might have to get a lobe cut out, but they hadn't told me when. "Probably before spring," I said. "They've hauled me in to get X rays twice this week. Why?"

Ivy shrugged. "No reason. I worry about you boys is all."

In search of something to do, I had fallen in love with two nurses in the ward before turning my heart toward Ivy. Both of the nurses were pretty in a hard mountain way. Their faces reminded me of fence posts. They had terrific keisters under their uniforms, but their hands were cold, and they always wanted to talk about frequency of bowel movements, so romance was thwarted. Ivy's face looks like a chewed shoe, and she doesn't seem to know that there is hair on her head. It perches up there like a possum. I guess it seems strange to fall for a woman like that, even if she is funny and smart, but a TB ward will make you do it. War will make you do it, too.

"Shit, Ivy," I said. "Don't toy with me. You know I dream of you, reading Balzac in your spinster flat. Don't tell me you're down there dreaming of me, too."

She hit me with the magazine. "Ha. Don't flatter yourself. I'm too busy fending off the bachelors of Asheville. They sit on my porch clutching their hats and moaning."

"Even in the snow?"

"Oh, especially."

"Well," I said. "I'd like to see that. If they cut me and it goes well, maybe they'll give me a weekend pass, and you can bring me down in your motorcar. Then we can drive over to see the Vanderbilts."

She touched me on the arm. "Why not?"

Then I surprised myself. "Hey, Ivy. Want to get married? In case I die instead?" She looked at my eyes. "Ha!" I said. "Ha, ha! Just kidding!"

"You asshole," she said. "If I say no, I break your heart, and if I say yes, that means I think you are going to die, and I break your heart and mine both."

"Sorry," I said. She hit me with the magazine.

Lots of the men did die. They died during the day like sputtering engines while the rest of us huddled on the other side of the ward like chickens. They died on the table, and they died at night, so you'd wake up and find them gone, their letters unfinished. Jenkins and I got up a little sideline writing wills from a book Ivy found for us. None of the men had any property to speak of, or else they wouldn't have been in that hospital, but they liked the idea, and some of them hired us to write new ones every week.

A man came and died before any of us had spoken to him or even learned his name. It was John Dix; I found it out because a letter came for him the day after he coughed himself out like a candle. "Dear Dix," it said. "I heard you made it through and are the only other one still alive. You lucky son of a bitch. I am in a hospital in England and I have no legs. They gave me extra morphine to write this. I keep a stick by my bed. When the morphine starts to wear off, sometimes I bite the stick, and sometimes I beat the mattress where my legs should be. I blame you. If you hadn't ordered us to go up and over, I might still be in France. If I live, I'm going to hire a nigger to carry me to your bedroom window, and I'm going to shoot you in the back. Love, Paul Morris."

"Dear Paul Morris," I wrote back. "As it turns out, I am dead. So fuck you. John Dix."

X rays show you what you'll look like when you've been eaten. Doctor McBride showed me mine; the bottom of my left lung looked like a floating bone. "That's the part we've got to cut out," he said. McBride is divorced and lives in a rooming house in Asheville. His body is matted with fur, and he sheds; red, bowed hairs from his hands appear on your pajamas for days after a consultation. I thought about them dropping onto my cracked ribs or floating in pooled blood in my open chest.

"Hey, Doc," I said. "Wash your hands, OK?"

He smiled. "Don't worry."

A nurse I'd never seen before shaved my chest and belly. She talked to me about her daughters while she did it, but I didn't understand much of what she said. Her hand circled over me, the boar's hair in the shaving brush swishing like a cat's tail. The soap smelled like lime. Some of it rolled down my sides and into my armpits where it dried.

They took me to a room tiled in yellow squares and had me lie on a table. McBride came in. He had on a white apron, and his sleeves were rolled up. His forearms were hammy.

"Don't worry," he said. "Think about your mother. Think about sweet corn."

They strapped me down at the wrists and ankles. A man put a glass and rubber bowl over my face and I huffed something cloying. I thought about soldiers, masked like cartoon animals. I thought about the Scots, about how gas got trapped beneath their kilts.

I didn't really sleep. I felt drunk and waterlogged, and the world came through in flashes, like frames in the funny papers. I saw the burning lights, and I heard the bone saw. Once, McBride held up a crescent of flesh glistening like a bluegill. There was pain, but I didn't feel it—it lay warm beside me.

When I came back to myself, I was in a different room. It was dusk outside, and a sweet, melancholic blue light came in the window and tinted the sheets and wall. Nobody else was there. On the table beside me was a card. I recognized the fat balloons of Rose's script, but I couldn't read it.

A Cherokee came in and mopped the room. He kept whispering to himself and glancing sideways at me. I tried to nod, but I didn't have the energy. I thought, "I'm too tired to talk, and so I won't call this man 'Chief.' Otherwise, that's probably what I'd do. I'd say, 'Hey there, Chief.' But he's probably not a chief, or else he wouldn't have to mop this place. And that would make me a bad person for teasing him. So, right now, in this one way, I'm lucky." I slept.

• • •

Brown shook me awake. "You farted," he said. "That means you gonna live, old son."

Jenkins was with him. The afternoon sun was sliding in the western windows and making them squint. They were both sitting in the cane-and-hickory wheelchairs they make us use outside the ward, and they had blankets on their laps.

"Y'all look like you're sailing to Cherbourg," I said. My chest hurt. "Ohhh," I said.

Jenkins patted me. His hair is parted in the middle and greased. He sometimes uses his fingers to shepherd strays back behind his ears. He ducks a little when he does it, and it makes him look like a woman. He did it twice. "McBride said you talked during the operation," he said. "You asked for a smoke. Ha!"

I smiled, and found that hurt, too.

Brown said, "You're a pistol, Bell," and nodded his big, gray head. "Hurry up and get better. I got a job for you. I'm divorcing Gladys. I need a good kiss-off."

I tried to look quizzical so I wouldn't have to talk, but Brown just kept bobbing his head up and down, grinning like an idiot.

Finally, Jenkins spoke. "McBride told him he could leave this month."

"I'm moving to Arizona, and I'm taking Nurse Jane with me." Brown was beaming too much to be lying. I tried to picture him making love to Nurse Jane, whispering behind the starched curtains, his brown, sawmill claws stroking the hem of her white dress. It was too much.

"Ohh," I said again.

Jenkins patted me. "We'll tell them to bring you some more morphine." They rolled out, locking wheels as they jostled for position at the door.

I waited for Ivy to come see me, but she didn't. I asked a nurse to send for the librarian, but she told me I was too weak for reading, and that I should try to sleep as much as possible. I told her I needed to read to sleep, so she gave me a Christian women's magazine called *Promised Pastures*. It was about what you'd expect:

lots of dreadful kitchen verse and essays on the dangers of various penny-ante domestic sins. There was no mention of the War, or of the readers' husbands and sons and brothers who were busy murdering other people, or the alarm this might cause God. There was one interesting "true story" about a Washington whore, but it fell apart at the end when she was rescued by some evangelists. I told the nurse I wanted a sheet of paper and a pencil so I could write *Promised Pastures* a letter of gratitude for the inspiration it gave during this dark hour.

It hurt to write. The extra breath I needed to move my hand made me cough, and that was like a bayonet in my chest, but I felt better doing something. "Dear Sirs and Madams," I wrote. "I ought to write 'Dear Angels,' because hey, that's what you are, but no doubt you would edit that out. I am writing to you about a true story I have recently read in your fine magazine, *Promised Pastures,* called 'The Fallen Dove of Foggy Bottom.' I thoroughly enjoyed it. I am not afraid to say it: although a decorated war hero and muscular Christian, I cried buckets. I have had my share of the soiled sisterhood, have laid down my pennies and taken my chances, have followed others into the breach, etc., etc., and have up till now comforted myself with the idea that 'Hey, Jesus did it, so it's good enough for me.' You see, somewhere along the line I learned that Jesus and Mary Magdalene spent time bathing one another, etc.; I know there aren't any really dirty parts in the Bible, but I figured they were just edited out (like in 'The Fallen Dove of Foggy Bottom'). I am not sure where I learned about the bathing, though my mother made us go to a Catholic church for a while when she was being sparked by a Polack, and probably it was there. Anyway, thanks for the story, as it really cleared some things up. I look forward to sharing it with the whole battalion, so that they will stop going to whores and concentrate on the godly work waiting for us in France. Bless You! Cpl. Rollo Stump."

The next day, Ivy still had not come, and I began to feel a boy's sickness down in my belly that the morphine couldn't touch. I thought about her visiting the other men. She liked Rose for some reason, and laughed at his meatless jokes. I tried to remember their conversations, picked over them for clues of an open heart. I pictured her blushing at the crude talk of my old nemeses, the rakish amputees, their virility undiminished, even concentrated, by the absence of a limb, while I hacked my own youth out in gusts.

The Cherokee came back, and I offered him two dollars to go find Ivy and bring her to come see me.

"You don't have to do that," he said. "I know her; she'll come."

Doctor McBride came and changed my dressings. "You look pretty good, considering," he said. "I kind of thought you'd die, to tell you the truth."

"What?"

"Well, you don't eat, you growl at everyone, and you don't seem to enjoy much. Guys like you die all the time."

My flesh was raw and cold where he had the bandages off. The pain was horrible, and the sight of my spoiled body was worse. "I guess I am not very cheerful," I said.

"Right," said McBride. "Try to be more cheerful. You'll be OK."

"For fuck's sake," I said.

McBride frowned. "That's a bad start."

"Look," I said. "You don't have too much to be cheery about either. You look at pus all day and we keep dying. Plus, you could get sick, too. You're the one who should readjust."

He chuckled. "A month ago, I would have agreed with you. Might have snuck you a pint of Irish if you'd begged, even if I knew it would kill you. But I'm a different man today. The world surprises you. You have to hold out."

"Hey, Doc," I said. "I've got a magazine here that's perfect for you."

Ivy finally came. I was hobbling down the hall to the bathroom to urinate standing up, the first time since the operation. I held an iron stand with little rubber wheels with my right hand and had Nurse Jane supporting me on my left. She's a horsy Presbyterian, and an enigma. "What are you doing with that yokel?" I asked her.

"Horace is sweet," she said.

"Brown's not sweet. He's a killer," I said.

"War doesn't count."

Jane and I were slowly, painfully waddling, my withered, bed-sore buttocks hanging out the back of my gown. Ivy walked up the hall toward us. She had a book in her hand. She came up to Jane and said, "I can handle him." Jane nodded, and Ivy pulled my arm over her soft shoulders.

"They tell me you've been raising some hell," she said.

"Not really," I said.

"Where are we going?"

"I have resolved to piss like a man. So, the toilet."

"Fine," she said. We inched along and I put as much weight as I could on the stand so that she would think me stronger than I was. She opened the door to the bathroom and turned on the light. I parked in front of the bowl.

"Do I stay?" she asked.

"That's up to you," I said. "I can manage."

She left me to do my business clutching the sink for support. It made me sad. It's not that I wanted her to see me, or that I thought anything might happen, but that I wanted from her the kind of easy comradeship we all had with the nurses. I wanted my shattered body out of the way. I wanted her to not even notice it.

I finished and I pulled myself in front of the sink to wash my hands. There was a mirror, but I didn't look in it. I didn't want to see that man.

"Dear Gladys," I read. "How are you? How is your paramour, Jesse Platt? Don't answer—I ask these questions rhetorically. I am already aware of the various acrobatic, carnal sins the two of you have been committing in our marriage bed. Wicked woman! Did you think that God could not see? Did you think that I was so weak I would not ask for justice? Well, a shit-storm is about to rain upon you. I have secured the services of Edwin Digby, counselor-at-law, and he has hired Baldwin-Felts agents to hide beneath the window and listen to the two of you rut. I divorce you, I divorce you, I divorce you, you harlot, you strumpet, you sow. I will soon travel to Arizona and there wed a pristine woman, a woman who does not feel the need to rub her hindquarters on every local male. I hope for you that the shame of your being legally declared a jeze-bel does not turn Jesse's walleye to younger flesh. I hope that Jesse can feed you and keep you in the shapeless sack-dresses you favor. I will no longer. Your liberated dupe, Horace Brown."

"How is it?" asked Jenkins.

"Pretty good," I said. "Kind of holy. And it doesn't sound like Brown said it."

"He didn't want it to. He said to make it sound like your stuff."

"Close enough, then. Close enough."

I didn't have the energy to write anything for Brown or anyone else. Jenkins had doubled his business, taking over my trade and buying himself fountain pens and a chess set with the extra money. I sat in my bed in the corner of the ward, reading and waiting for Ivy to free me, till one Saturday she did.

I was napping, a week-old, soup-stained *Baltimore Sun* on my patchwork chest.

"Wake up," she said. "You need a haircut. You look like a coyote."

"Ha!" I said.

She was leaning over an empty wheelchair. She had on an Easter dress and she looked good, big and soft and curvy like a divan. "Get in," she said. I did, but only after changing into my suit in the bathroom. The collar was smudged and my shoes were scuffed, but I didn't care.

"Oh, I'm the Sheik of Araby!" I sang as she pushed me through the halls.

She slapped the top of my head. "Stop that."

We drove lazily over the dusty roads into Asheville. The sun was shining; it was nearly eighty degrees. Cows and sheep and Tennessee fainting goats watched us from pastures beside the road. "Look at this," I thought. "Look at all this the War hasn't even budged." Ivy drove like a man, her fingers loose on the wheel. She handed me a peppermint and I sucked on it and smelled the mountain air. I could pull it down into my lungs and I didn't cough a bit.

"Hey, Ivy," I said. "Maybe McBride ain't crazy."

"What's that?" she said.

"I say, maybe McBride ain't crazy. Maybe the world is good."

"I guess," she said. Her hands tightened on the wheel.

In town, we ate roast chicken and fresh strawberries at a hotel. They had clouds of Negro waiters, all dressed alike in crisp white suits and conked hair. They gave good service, refilling our tea, attacking crumbs with a little silver brush. "Hey Ivy," I said. "Do the Vanderbilts come here?"

"Not hardly. Zebulon Vance used to, though."

After we finished, we sat in a swing on the porch. There was a giant chestnut tree in the front yard, and the green, burred nuts hung full and eager from the branches. I could smell the flowers of the pear trees down the road, and the sharp gin of the croquet players in the side yard. "This is the closest thing to being a human I've felt in two years," I said. "Ivy, I'm a happy man."

"I'm glad, Jimmy," she said.

"Thank you for inviting me," I said.

"I promised I would."

"What's next? I would love to stay here forever, but we've only got a few hours more."

"It's your day." She smiled. "Where you wanna go?"

"I hate to ask you on your day off, but is there a bookstore open here?"

There was not, but there was a department store with a book room. I had a wad of will-and-letter cash in my pocket, and I meant to spend as much as I could. I smelled the fresh paper and stroked the unbroken spines. I bought three novels and a book on polar exploration. The clerk wrapped them in brown paper.

We left and sat in Ivy's car. "That's all you care about, isn't it Jimmy?" she asked me.

"What?" I said.

"If I gave you the option, right now, of trading me those books for a real polar expedition, you wouldn't take it, would you?"

I thought for a minute. "No."

She looked at me full in the face for the first time that day. "Why not?"

"I don't want to die, Ivy. People who have adventures also die."

"Everyone dies, Jimmy."

"Some people hasten their death. Those people are fools. I intend to guard mine if I can."

"You're not alive now, Jimmy," she said. "You don't talk to people. You just read and read."

I shivered. "That's why you like me, Ivy. We're the same."

"No, Jimmy. That's why I understand you. But we're not the same."

"Ivy," I said. "What are you saying?"

"Jimmy, I know that you think that you have feelings for me. I know that you think you can court me and marry me. I don't know what you think that would mean, but I bet you think it would mean you lying on a mattress all day, coughing and reading, till I come home and ask you about what you read."

I blinked.

"That's not the life that I want, Jimmy. And that's the life you've already got."

"That's worse than being alone?" I asked. "I'm worse than being alone?"

"I told you before, Jimmy, that there were other men who wanted me. Do you think you're the only one who would? Everybody I see is a man, and you think you're the only one who might like me?"

"Oh, Jesus!" I said. "Not Rose!"

Ivy frowned. "No. David."

"Who?"
"McBride, Jimmy. I am marrying Dr. David McBride."

The nurses dressed us as if we were children, knifing our feet
with shoehorns and pulling our ties snug against our throats.
McBride had ordered boaters for us to wear. They were unyield-
ing, so that every man's was tight in places and loose in others,
and we were left with spotty red creases in our skin, as if we had
been wearing soup tureens. The sun was fierce and the air thick.
Ivy looked tired and hot; sweat darkened the silk of her gown in
crescents and tapering triangles. McBride's hair was wet where
it bordered his skin, and the minister kept a handkerchief in his
sleeve to wipe his face during the service. Ivy threw her daisies
into the air, and the nurses made a show of grabbing for them.
They jumped at the flowers; they sprang toward them, laughing
like flutes. Then Ivy hiked her skirt so McBride could tug down
her garter. Her skin was flushed and bruised there. McBride stood
on a hillock, a sneer on his face, and twirled the garter around
his finger. Men with pinned sleeves and trouser legs cuffed at the
knee crouched among consumptives who heaved and wheezed like
trains. McBride stretched the garter taut to shoot it like a rubber
band. He pulled it back and back till it snapped like a rifle shot and
fell at his feet and the men piled forward, slipping in the mud of
the trench and clawing and huffing like farrow to the teat.

J. D. Chapman was born and raised in southwest
Virginia, where he lives with his wife and son
and works as a schoolteacher. At the moment,
he is also a student in Hollins University's MFA
program. "Amanuensis" was his first published
story. His work has since been accepted by
Shenandoah and the *Southeast Review*.

GIULIANA CHAPMAN

*T*his story began with me pretending to be Dashiell Hammett. I set it near Asheville because my sister and brother-in-law live down there, and so did I for a few months when I was working at a fecal diagnostic laboratory built on the ashes of the asylum where Zelda Fitzgerald died.

   This is fiction, obviously, so I took liberties—using "Sheik of Araby," though it hadn't been written yet, for example. I made it all up, in other words, but when I showed it to a friend of mine who'd had TB and had lived there, she said, "I know exactly what hospital you mean."

William Harrison

MONEY WHIPPED

(from *The Texas Review*)

K nox liked movies and decided to make one. Why not? Since selling his business — the manufacture of steel cable — he had lots of cash. Apart from that he had only his cranky mother, his new wife Beezie, two houses, three cars, and a plane he hadn't learned to fly.

He thought up a good movie story — Beezie helped on it — then went about finding a screenwriter. He knew exactly what he wanted: another Texan, male, bookish but not some wimp, a guy who at least played golf, and somebody with real screen credits, not some pretender or run-of-the-mill suck-up.

It took him awhile to learn about the Writers Guild, then more time to pick names from their membership list: Texans, male, screen credits. All this began in April, but in the heat of July arrangements were finally made. A writer named Drew Gamble agreed to fly to Houston for an interview. They met in Knox's big apartment on Riverway for cocktails, planning for dinner later at Café Annie, except they drank too much and never got there.

Beezie wore a glittering blouse open to her navel, a pair of white shorts, and tennis shoes that she kicked underneath the glass coffee table. She crossed her long legs and pumped her lacquered toes ever so slightly, keeping a sensual beat to a music perhaps only she heard.

Drew, the writer, currently lived in London and possessed a great mane of blond hair. He dressed in tight, faded jeans, a gleaming white T-shirt, and an unlined and wrinkled summer sports jacket, blue, that matched his eyes. Perhaps forty, he moved and looked like a younger man because of the hair—coiffed to look wild and unruly—and struck an attitude that suggested both danger and insouciance. He looked as though he had just flown in from a war.

Knox, paunchy and darkly tanned, enthusiastic as always, showed Drew the view from the terrace with the Houston skyline spread out before them, and tried to make small talk while aching to tell his writer the plot points of their story. Beezie gazed over the rim of her glass, wearing it like a mask that hid half her face, her large brown eyes never blinking.

When they settled in the sitting room Knox began walking and gesturing with his tumbler of bourbon. "See, Drew, the Vietnamese came to Texas after the war. Refugees. They were the friendlies, of course, who had worked with our guys in Saigon. Anyway, they settled on the coast and started shrimp fishing. But the established fishermen down there resented them, so there were, like, acts of violence. Guys burning boats. A feud. One refugee got killed. All this was in the newspapers. So in our story there's this lonely vet. He was wounded in Vietnam and had some Vietnamese pals. Maybe one of them saved his life. So when the shrimp war gets nasty he throws in with the refugees. Maybe there's a love interest. Maybe an American girl, but you decide about that. By the way, you didn't happen to serve in Vietnam, did you?"

"He was too young," said Beezie from behind her glass.

Drew nodded in response.

"So that's the story," Knox said proudly "We've got more details, naturally, in the written outline."

"Sounds intriguing," said Drew.

"Also, it's got good movie visuals," Knox continued, filling his glass. "Explosions and boats on fire, all that. And maybe there's an old wise man, a refugee with a white beard, and he and this vet become pals. And the American girl is a lot like Beezie."

"You an actress?" Drew asked.

"I was a model once," she answered. "A long time ago."

They knocked back another drink. Drew soon learned that Beezie was Knox's third wife — they had married six months ago — and that most of the ideas for the movie were hers. Then Knox talked about his former business, steel cable. Aircraft companies used miles of cable in every fuselage and wing, Knox explained, and the shipping companies were also big-time buyers. He had warehouses for his cable on every continent, he told Drew, and his real estate purchases had also gone very well.

"Tell him how much you sold for," Beezie urged him.

"Nah, what's the difference? Money is only defined by what you do with it. I like to help my employees and I'm not the kind of guy who ever money-whips anybody. And some money needs to be play money, so that's where you and the movie come in. Oh, yeah, did I tell you I watched that African movie you wrote?"

"We rented the video," Beezie added.

"You've got the knack, see, Drew, for exotic settings and people, so I figure you'll do great with the refugees. Also, I checked your price and my sources tell me a writer should always get a boost from his last assignment, so how about my offer?"

"I flew to Houston because I appreciated your offer," Drew said, rattling the ice cubes in his glass. "And I accept. Where do we go from here?"

"Lordy, this is great," Knox said, and he touched Beezie's shoulder as he crossed to the bar. "I'm gonna fill up the glasses!"

"I thought I might head down to the coast for a few days," Drew ventured. "See the actual fishing fleet and talk with a few of the fishermen."

"Get right to work, eh? Great, I like it."

They drank to the movie forming in their heads, to themselves, and to the night that hovered above the city. Then they told one another about their lives, weaving omissions and lies in a pleasant inebriation. Beezie hailed from Kingsville and her good looks, she admitted, had launched her out of South Texas into a world of men with cameras. Her name was Barbara Catherine, BC, Beezie, and as he talked Knox revealed that she was thirty-two years old and that he had a daughter who was thirty-nine. Knox grew up in Dallas, he said, in a place called La Reunion, a prefab housing development on the wrong wide of the Fort Worth highway, a shantytown where his father came back from World War II and drank himself into oblivion. Knox outlined his climb to success: odd jobs, factory work, a series of cockeyed inventions that failed to get patents, then the little cable company that he bought in bankruptcy. He had borrowed money to make the down payment, then modified the machines, tooling out a process that made better cable faster.

"Tell you something, Drew," Knox went on. "For just a sport shandy —"

He stopped as Beezie gave him a look.

"For just a short span," he corrected himself, "we live on this earth. Life's precious, then it's over."

From this declaration they began to talk about what each of them believed in. Drew said he believed in the English language, beautiful women, wine with dinner, neatly trimmed fairways, and constant travel. Beezie said people, she really liked all sorts of people, she was a people person. Reciting this, smiling, not unlike the beauty pageant contestant she once was, Beezie watched Knox raise a toast in her direction.

Knox then went into a long ramble about religion. He didn't exactly believe in God, he told them, and predicted that all religion would one day be absorbed into the study of astronomy. The galaxies, he offered, will one day be seen as the miracles they are. From this he began to discuss molecular biology, clones, and the speed of light. Beezie noted that Knox hated organized religion, but was actually a very spiritual person.

Long after midnight they helped Knox to bed. He went from his bourbon haze to a deep sleep, dreaming of the empty spaces between the stars.

Later, his own snoring woke him up. After relieving himself in the bathroom he circled through the apartment. Beezie wasn't in her bed or anyplace else. The French clock tolled four times.

The terrace was empty, too, and he thought, all right, Beezie has driven our writer back to his hotel. Knox slumped in a lounge chair, fighting the suspicion that his young wife and the handsome writer had found each other too appealing. He considered driving over to the Omni and checking the hotel room, but padded through the rooms, turning on the TV then turning it off again, and finally going back to bed. Lying there awake, he heard Beezie returning after five in the morning, then listened while she took a long shower and went to her bed.

Before noon Knox was reading the newspapers and having coffee when Beezie appeared on the terrace. Before he could ask any questions she smiled and said, "God, I stayed up late! I drove Drew back to the hotel, then we sat in the car talking."

"About what?" he asked as casually as possible.

"The script. And I'm not sure if the Vietnamese refugees should, like, be in the movie. I love the idea of a lonely war veteran. He should live in a lighthouse. And this beautiful woman befriends him and, well, maybe it could be a great romantic story."

"No Vietnamese fishermen?"

"Maybe, but really a love story. But we don't have to decide right now. Drew's renting a car and driving down to the coast today. He's probably already gone. He wants to check things out before we make, like, final decisions."

Knox felt grateful that Drew had left town.

He watched Beezie spread jam on a honey bun, then wolf it down. She ate like an animal, filling her cheeks with huge bites so that her cheeks puffed out. She was still a brightness that filled him up and even if his mother didn't like her, he told himself, I do, I could forgive her anything, I adore her.

Knox's mother, Avis, lived in an old River Oaks mansion that now resembled a Mexican piñata: colored tiles set in crazy patterns on its stucco exterior, a lumpy figurine on the front lawn adorned with shards of colored glass and tile, a rooftop wearing the reindeer from last Christmas, assorted urns around the gardens, a stone sombrero filled with red hibiscus, and mismatched lawn furniture stacked up like a jungle gym alongside the driveway. Beyond a giant mimosa and within sight of those passing in the neighborhood — an otherwise elegant district of sedate homes — stood the cornfield. Avis, now eighty years old and unable to do strenuous gardening, still rolled out her own fresh tortillas and spent her days cooking and eating. She liked red-hot jalapeños and popped them down like lemon drops while listening to the old tunes of the Tijuana Brass on her boom-box CD player. Over the kitchen stove hung a framed and autographed photo of Cary Grant. Since Knox's first successful days in the cable business Avis had enjoyed her widowhood in this house, a great box of nineteen rooms resided over by a dozen cats who fed on leftover enchiladas. Her son's daily visits — usually for lunch — comprised her social life.

"My prodigy!" she always greeted him, and except for his marriage to Beezie she regarded him as a genius.

At lunch that day, watching him nibble around the edges of a taco salad, Avis asked what was wrong. Nothing, he told her, and they poked at their meal in silence.

"Something's got your appetite," she prodded him, and unable to resist he blurted out the whole story of the previous evening. This prompted her usual litany: Beezie talks like a waitress, she reads with her fingers tracing the words, she has silicone breasts, she can't enter this house, she's just after your money.

He offered all his standard justifications including Beezie's enthusiasms for the act of love, but Avis waved it all away.

"Wanta know what'll happen next?" she asked. "Beezie will concoct a trip for herself. Simple and natural sounding. Like she'll decide to visit her mother — who, by the way, hates her even more than I do. Anyway, she'll leave town and hook up with that writer. You say he wears a wig?"

"Yeah, it's gotta be a wig," Knox said, moaning.

"How old is this screenwriter?"

"Twenty years younger than I am. You think I should hire a private detective to watch him?"

"No, you'll just go crazy knowing more than you do already," Avis told him, biting into her taco.

Knox leaned on his elbow beside his plate of food. "You really think she'll manufacture a trip for herself?"

"Son, if I know you, you'll help her pack, then kiss her good-bye," said Avis.

The lunch before him looked awful, like swill with salsa.

"I'm thinking of flying up to Dallas to see my mother," Beezie informed him that evening as she painted her toenails. She occupied the middle of her giant oval bed, cotton balls wedged between each toe as she applied a coat of golden lacquer.

"You and your mother don't even speak."

"On the phone, no, because she hangs up on me," Beezie countered. "So I need to see her face to face. We need to make up. Maybe I'll take her a nice present."

"Okay, I'll go with you," Knox suggested.

"No, this is a girl thing."

"Then I'll have our pilot fly you into Love Field, so you'll be right there at her place in Highland Park."

"I was thinking of flying commercial."

"You'd rather go through two airports with all your baggage rather than fly into a private terminal?"

Beezie tried a weak smile in response.

"Tell you what," Knox said. "While you visit your mama I'll zip down to the coast and see our writer. Scout some locations with him."

At this suggestion Beezie managed only a defeated nod.

The next morning their pilot flew Beezie up to Dallas, then returned to pick up Knox and to deliver him to a sad little airport on the north side of Nueces Bay. In the meantime Knox phoned Drew, so the writer could meet him with a rented Cadillac. They drove over to Corpus Christi for dinner, talking golf, Texas food, and the movie. In Corpus they found a seafood restaurant adorned with a mural of Venus rising from the sea, then searched the menu for something that wasn't fried.

"Yesterday I ate lunch in this café over in Aransas Pass," Drew said. "Afterward I asked the waitress if they had any Rolaids or Tums. She told me, 'Honey, hell, we make our profit on Rolaids.'"

At that, they had their first real laugh together and started talking in earnest about their movie.

"The Vietnamese fishermen stay in the movie," Knox asserted.

"Sure, who says otherwise? That's what'll give the film all its depth," Drew quickly agreed.

After this Knox doubted that much had passed between Beezie and the writer—who seemed supremely professional. Yet he phoned Beezie that evening, making sure that she stayed at her mother's house in Dallas. Satisfied, then, he phoned his mother who said, no, please she didn't want to talk about her daughter-in-law, no thanks, because she couldn't form a simple declarative sentence about Beezie without using the word slut.

The next morning Knox and Drew toured Port Aransas, definitely no tourist spot. They saw rusted-out fishing boats, smelly nets piled on outworn docks, old men with leathery faces, scores of aggressive gulls, vacant lots littered with beer bottles and discarded bathroom fixtures, a creaking old ferry, and finally a squat little lighthouse—unoccupied and boarded up.

"We'll go down to city hall and find out who owns this wreck," Knox remarked, walking around it and rubbing his hands together. "We'll buy it or lease it, then refurbish it for the movie. Our wounded war veteran will live here."

Drew gave him an odd smile.

"What?" Knox asked.

"Nothing personal, but I'll always be interested in how money talks," the writer said.

"We're gonna spend, Drew, then make money," Knox promised.

They ate lunch in an establishment that was just the frame of a building: patches of screen tacked around, a sagging roof, and everything seemingly held together by neon tubing that spelled out the names of beers. Drew talked about living in London.

"I was always the quiet type. Played tennis. I was sort of formal and reserved—not like the shit kickers at the University. English major, you know. I lived and thought like a Victorian and when I went to Africa for my research on that movie I wanted to be, oh, Graham Greene or some BBC writer composing brittle dialogue for *Masterpiece Theater,* I wanted to lose my Texas drawl. Go up to Lake Windemere and take melancholy strolls on the forest pathways. But, hey, I was always a Texan—one of the nomadic Texans—and I never had enough money to be all that aristocratic. When you phoned I was thinking about giving up my flat and heading back to Blanco County. If we do this movie, though, I'll have enough in the bank to stick in London for another year and see what happens."

In the extreme midday heat they found a little movie house and sat with large tubs of popcorn watching a bad western. Later they drank beer and listed the great movies: *The Godfather, Cabaret, Casablanca.* At the docks in the late afternoon they watched the fishing boats come in, and Knox paid out a bouquet of hundred-dollar bills so they could join the crew of a professional boat for the next day's fishing. The captain, a crusty little guy who looked like he might have been a general for the Cong, told them to show up at four the next morning with their own food and drink. He pocketed Knox's money, promising to split it with his men.

That evening they filled a cooler with beer, bread, and barbeque, then ate dinner in a smoky bar and talked about women: Knox's wives and two divorced daughters, Drew's many girlfriends and his reluctance to get married: the natural disorders of sex and love.

During this Drew apologized for staying out late with Beezie.

"Nothing happened," he added quickly. "We just sat there talking too long, and I didn't know how to break it off since, well, because she's the wife of the boss and she had all these ideas about our movie. Anyway, I know it must've looked indiscreet staying out so late. And I'm sorry if you worried about it."

"Beezie told me all about it," Knox said. "We won't mention it again. Here, look, I need to give you some cash."

"What for?"

"Pay the rental car outta this," Knox instructed him, and he produced a roll of hundred dollar bills, pushing them into Drew's hands without counting them. "You'll have other expenses. Incidentals. I'll pick up our hotel, naturally, and, wait, I don't really think this is enough."

"It's more than enough," Drew assured him, and they arrived at a familiar male covenant: soldiers in a cause, everything sealed with alcohol, sincerity, and cash. They had a nightcap, then went back to their hotel to sleep.

By dawn they were out on the gulf, the engine of their boat coughing up clouds of diesel while their Vietnamese hosts chewed Red Man tobacco and spat long brown streamers into the waves. On the choppy sea in the midst of fumes and brownish saliva both Knox and Drew felt queasy but devoured their barbeque sandwiches and drank a couple of beers each before ten o'clock in the morning. The crew members sipped from Mason jars filled with clear liquid — possibly rice wine, possibly vodka — while working, chewing, and spitting.

By noon, hopelessly seasick, both Knox and Drew heaved at the rails as the boat moved through rising swells. As the crew worked the nets, hauling in shrimp, they were both too sick to watch the effort. They staggered around midship as observers, but saw little because every few minutes they hurried back to the rails.

"Keep out of way!" shouted the little captain, and they nodded grimly as they puked. They knew they were comic and pathetic as they gasped for air in the diesel fumes, then watched in horror as a crew member converted himself into a chef and turned the wheelhouse into a galley where he boiled rice for the midday meal. The electric winch sent up its high whine and the gulls circled overhead with a descant of mocking laughter.

"Why're we here?" Drew asked, trying to grin. His shirt was fouled and his beautiful hair hung down in strings.

That evening Knox spoke with Beezie on the phone. Her mother had thrown her out, so she had checked into a fancy Oak Lawn hotel.

"Lemme come down there with you guys," she pleaded.

"I'll be back in Houston tomorrow and I'll see you there," Knox told her. "I'll send the plane for you around noon."

After the phone call Knox sat thinking how he had met Beezie and how much he loved her. He had occupied a barstool in Anthony's when she appeared at his side to take his order: a little too busty for modeling anymore, sassy, and with eyes that looked as though they had just popped open in surprise. He told her that he owned his own airplane and asked if she wanted to fly to Bimini and she answered, sure, why not, let's go, and where exactly is Bimini? They didn't come back until she sported a five-carat diamond and his last name. After all, his big apartment was hollow and full of echoes. His daughters, he knew, wanted him to die and leave them more than they deserved and he felt his age, over sixty and climbing.

That evening Knox and Drew settled their stomachs with whiskey and soda. They found a roadhouse over toward Rockport with a three-piece western band playing a medley of Patsy Cline songs.

Drew was soon drunk with his arm draped over Knox's shoulders, saying, "Knox, you're the king of cable and what do you do? You decide to make a movie with a serious social message! It makes me proud to know you."

Knox, less drunk, listened and smiled. Such flattery made him uneasy and usually preceded a major hit, so he interrupted Drew's oncoming speech with another roll of hundred dollar bills.

"What I gave you wasn't enough," he said. "Remember I told you that? So here, take this."

As Knox pressed it into Drew's hands the screenwriter's protests were short. Then he leaned close and said, "We're gonna see our names on the big screen, Knox, I feel it. This movie'll happen. But it's also more than that: we're gonna be friends for a long time. You know that, too, doncha?"

Knox was experienced enough to know that some deep candor was about to take place, something confessional, something that money often pried loose. He had seen it dozens of times and never knew exactly what form it would take, yet as he watched Drew slowly pushing the money into the tight pockets of his faded jeans he felt it coming.

"Knox, my friend, remember our first night together? When you went to bed drunk? Beezie went to her room, Knox, and put on this — well, it was a little gown."

"Uh huh," Knox replied, and he topped off their whiskies.

"A gown. Transparent." Drew leaned in, lowering his voice into intimate confidence. "A little gown with flowers on it. So then she drove me back to my hotel. The Omni. You know the little gown I'm talking about?"

Knox felt his chest flutter as if he might have a heart attack, but managed a nod.

"Anyway, Knox, we didn't go directly to the hotel. I want to tell you this because you and I — well, we're friends now. So Beezie and I drove to this little park down by the river, Knox, and this little gown, well, she didn't have any panties on underneath it."

Knox wanted the writer to shut up, but the money and liquor prompted him to go on.

"Knox, I'm only a man. A mortal creature. All my life I've wanted to be a gentleman. A Victorian gentleman. All the courtesies. I do not put heavy moves on women. Never. I didn't put a move on Beezie, not so much as a signal. I also wondered if you two might do this sort of thing with others — friends or strangers or business partners. How could I know? So I was a little drunk myself that evening. And confused."

"Enough details," Knox managed.

"We've come a long way together in a short time, Knox, and

I want to feel good about us, man to man. And unless you say otherwise I consider it a one-time thing."

"Yeah, let's call it that," Knox agreed.

"Good. Fine. It's over, then, with Beezie and me," Drew said, and he finished his drink, taking a deep satisfied breath. His hair, Knox noted, was finely coiffed again, so that since their time on the gulf the writer must've worked on his hairdo.

Drew started a more jovial topic. "So if we shoot this movie, Knox, I guess you and I won't head out into the Gulf Stream again, will we? I mean, hell, let the second unit shoot the scenes out there! We've had it with shrimp fishing, right?" The writer laughed louder and longer than necessary.

"You're right about that," Knox replied, trying to smile.

They went to the parking lot and found the Cadillac. A hot and humid evening: a sticky gulf breeze and, far off, a wall of giant thunderheads rising above the horizon with soft displays of lightning.

"Let me have the car keys," Knox said.

"Sure, good idea. You drive."

As Knox accepted the car keys he took a deep breath and said, "Drew, our movie deal is cancelled. You stay here. You're fired and I don't want you in the car on the way back to the hotel."

"Hold on," said Drew. "I was just tryin' to be honest."

"We're not talking anymore. You got cash, so go away."

With this, Knox slipped inside the Cadillac and clicked the locks, shutting Drew out.

"I thought we were friends!" Drew shouted through the closed window. "I wanted to be honest with you! At least give me a ride back to the hotel so we can talk, okay?"

"Be a Victorian gentleman with somebody else's wife," Knox told him, and drove off.

Driving alone through the darkness Knox wished he still owned his business, that he was still spinning out cable. He longed for his company and his old office. I sold out for money, he told himself, and now my daughters love money, not me.

He drove as if following where the headlights led.

Maybe Beezie's the same, he said to himself. She's broken my heart and she's everything, she's what's left of me, and I can't spend the rest of my life in my mother's kitchen.

He picked up the car phone, dialed his pilot, and told him to head for the airport and to prepare to fly. Then he phoned Beezie and, amazingly, she was in her suite and seemed happy to hear from him.

"Get dressed and grab a taxi for Love Field," he said. "I'll be in the air within the hour and I need a kiss."

"Knox, thank goodness! I've been missin' you, sweetie," she responded, and he wanted to cry for joy. He'd tell her later that Drew didn't work out. He'd say he was sorry, he knew, although for what, exactly, he wasn't sure.

The movie, he decided, was stupid. I know nothing about shrimp fishing, the feud, Vietnam veterans, good writing, the Gulf of Mexico, camera angles, or acting like a producer. Pretentious.

Yet, at seventy miles an hour the night seemed to settle around him and he thought, wait, why not a movie? And no apologies for a young and beautiful new wife. Starting over suits me fine. I'll go talk to my daughters — and not to money-whip them, but to ask for their affection if they have an ounce left. And I'll say, Beezie, maybe we didn't go at this the right way, maybe we made mistakes, but who knows if we can make a movie or not? And the next screenwriter will be older than I am. Ancient.

William Harrison is the author of eight novels—five of them set in Africa—as well as three volumes of short stories, essays, and screenplays. His stories have appeared in *Esquire,* the *Paris Review, Playboy,* and *Antaeus,* and elsewhere. A Texan, he taught at the University of Arkansas for a number of years and still lives in Fayetteville.

*W*ith only one or two minor exceptions, I've always worked like a jour-
nalist, finding stories and characters in my travels, rarely turning
to autobiographical material. I met the businessman in "Money Whipped"
in Houston. I met the writer in London. Knox's mother is an invention, and
Beezie is a composite.

The short story is a mysterious thing that usually arrives whole. Unlike
the novel—often filled with baggage, leftover lint, and sad efforts to be
profound—stories can sneak up on the reader with a curiously diabolical
impact. That's why I love to read them and why writing them is so satisfying.

Erin Brooks Worley

GROVE

(from *The Gettysburg Review*)

His parents live in Florida, in a town called Frostproof. Their trailer sits at the edge of an orange grove. There is a lake behind the trailer, and motorboats tied to a wooden dock. Small fish swim at the edge of the lake, over the sand where the water is thin. If we are quiet and still, the fish swim through our fingers. The air smells like the fruit that has fallen to the ground and rotted. It smells like trapped heat.

His father owns two motorbikes. He lets us fill them with gas from the can and speed through the groves, over the bumps, laughing. His mother stands in front of the trailer, pushing her hands up and down the rough front of her skirt, worrying.

He has an accident on the second day of our visit. He's riding ahead of me and hits a root that juts out of the ground, and he falls.

When I crouch down beside him, I see that he is blinking his eyes hard, taking short breaths. He rolls away from a handlebar that is digging into his ribcage.

Oh, sugar, I say, and he tells me it's alright.

No, I say, and hold the horn down so his parents will come and help.

Don't, he says and pushes my hand away. I can walk back up. You'll scare them.

I'm sorry, I say.

You can stop apologizing, he says. I've heard it enough.

The water that comes out of the faucet in the trailer smells of sulfur. His parents say you get used to it. I pour water and ice into a clear plastic bag. His mother takes it from me, adds more ice, and gives it to her son. He lies on the couch and holds the bag to his side.

I knew those bikes were bad news, his mother says.

His father takes out a pack of cards and asks if I'd like to play. He teaches me a game. We fall into a rhythm of passing cards back and forth, turning them over with small slapping noises. His father is quiet, smiling, and smells of aftershave, though his face has thick whiskers. When I kiss him on the cheek to say good night, he says, Be careful you don't get scratched, now.

His mother is sitting on the couch, knitting. I kiss her cheek, and she says, Make sure he stays off that side.

There are nightlights in the bedroom, small bulbs behind frogs made of glass beads and wire. He is already asleep under a heavy afghan. Aren't you hot, I whisper, as I lift the sheets.

No, he says and pulls me back against his warm skin.

Does it hurt? I ask.

Only when I breathe, he says.

What's that buzzing noise, I ask.

Mosquitoes, he says. The porch light outside.

I look at the window, at the lines of yellow light between the blinds. When I focus I can see insects moving and their small shadows on the windowsill. He is asleep again, and I am still awake. I try to put one of his hands over one of my ears, but it falls away.

I wait until I hear his parents go to bed. The walls are thin wood panel, and I can hear them murmuring to each other, then silence. I take a small red flashlight from the nightstand, leave the bedroom, and walk outside. I touch the furniture in the living room, the rough afghans over the chair backs. I pick up the glossy animal figurines off the tables and cabinets, careful to put them down exactly as I found them. I turn on the bathroom light. I open the shower door and drink whiskey from my shampoo bottle. He won't smell it on my skin by morning, and so what if he does. I never asked him to leave his wife. I lean back against the cold tile wall and take just a couple shots, then I screw the top back on, yawning. Shhh, I say to myself, closing the door until it clicks into place against a magnet.

In the morning he says, I can smell it on your skin. He rolls away from me. There is sweat on my back where his chest had been. I specifically asked you not to bring liquor into my parents' house, he says.

Breakfast, I say. I can hear water running in the kitchen, voices.

He sighs. We'll take the boat out, he says.

His mother is standing near the stove, dropping doughnuts into a deep fryer. When they're golden she lifts them out with tongs and drops them in a bag of cinnamon sugar. His father touches her shoulders when he walks by, and she leans back into his touch.

I sit at the table, and his mother brings the hot doughnuts on a plate covered with a printed paper towel. He groans as he sits down. I reach over and touch his side with my fingertips. Maybe we should put some heat on that? I say.

Needs more ice, his mother says. He used to eat eight doughnuts in a sitting. Isn't that right?

That's right, he says. He won't look at me.

When I stand to clear the dishes, his mother follows me to the sink. You'll break his heart, she whispers, close to my ear.

I wonder how much she knows about me, what exactly he has told her, and I feel betrayed.

I walk into the grove to pick some oranges for juicing. There are flies and bees on the fruit that rots on the ground. The migrant workers are here for the cooler morning hours, up in the ladders in the trees, shouting back and forth in Spanish. A man throws a ripe orange down to me, and I say thank you.

The orange juice goes in a thermos that goes in a cooler that is filled with crushed ice that will melt and smell like sulfur. The doughnuts are wrapped in tin foil. The cooler sits in the bottom of the boat, under my seat. He holds a Styrofoam container filled with lake water and minnows. We've got rods leaned between the seats, and a tackle box filled with hooks and sparkly rubber worms. I don't want to push hooks through minnow heads. We fill the tank with gas from a can and start the motor.

His father helps us, untying the boat, pushing us off. As he bends over I see his hand go to his lower back. He winces then looks up at me and smiles. I want to touch him, to put my hand against his rough face and say thank you.

I put my hand through the water's warm surface, and the water lifts in walls around my wrist as the boat moves faster toward the center of the lake. He stretches, and the veins in his arms stand out like strings. There are clouds in the sky, and we cover our skin with repellent to keep the mosquitoes away. They still bite and leave hot red knots on my skin. He watches mosquitoes swell with blood on his arm before smacking them dead, and their bites don't even leave a mark. He grew up near a lake; he is immune.

The motor on the boat is loud. It seems useless to try to talk. I open the Styrofoam container and lift a minnow up in my hands. It twists, and the tiny gills stretch open, the mouth a desperate circle. I lower my hand into the water and feel it escape through my fingers. I look at him for a reaction, but he knows what I am looking for and looks away. I reach across and hold his hand. Sorry, I say.

Just stop, he says. I just want you to stop.

Your mother hates me, I say. He cuts off the motor, and the boat drifts.

We would have beautiful children, he says, staring at me. Little girls with green eyes. Boys tall like me.

Sad girls and fickle boys, I say.

When I crashed the other day, what did you think?

I thought, Oh god no.

I was lying there looking at the ground, trying to figure out what was wrong, and nothing hurt until you touched me.

Does it hurt now? I ask.

No, now it's not so bad.

There are heavy, dark trees strung with gray moss along the shore. There are the backs of trailers visible through the woods. The sun is high, and sweat drips down our necks.

We tie the boat to a dock and climb up to strip down to swimsuits. There are women lying on the dock, stretched out on faded towels, oiling their skin. They're listening to a small transistor radio tuned to an oldies station. They have silver beer cans in a bucket of ice. Hey y'all, they say, putting their hands over their faces as visors. They smile like they know us. Help yourselves, they say.

I stand beside the bucket, look at him and smile.

Just one, he says. One. No more.

We hold our cans close to our bodies and jump into the water and surface under the dock, where the water is coolest. We hang off the slick ladder and drink fast. Then I float on my back and look up at the lines of boards, towels, skin, sun. I feel numb and content. Under the water, his hand touches my waist.

Did you ever think you would be here? he asks. Meeting my parents?

No, I say. What happens when we go home?

You know that's up to you, he says.

What are y'all talking about? asks one of the women, leaning her head down over the edge.

I think we're about to have an argument, I say.

'Bout what? she asks. Her upside-down face is turning red.

If she won't stop drinking, we couldn't even have kids, he says.

That's true, I say. Pregnant women shouldn't drink.

Lord, she says. What does he want kids for?

He likes kids, I say. And his wife can't have them.

So you're one of those, she says. Huh. Well, look at you two. Ain't no good reason you can't be happy.

I am happy, I say.

Huh, she says, and twists her body back up onto the dock.

When we're done swimming, I ask for a couple more beers. He doesn't say anything when I lift them from the bucket, or even when I open them in the boat. He drinks a few sips from one can, and I drink the rest, leaning back in the boat and watching the darkening sky. The wind is cold on my damp skin, and we don't speak.

We tie the boat to the dock and wade in. I feel dizzy and de-hydrated, and when we walk into the trailer, I stumble on the carpet.

Time for a nap! I say. He puts his hands on my hips and steers me back to the bedroom.

At night he and his father go to the store, and his mother watches game shows. She looks away only to stare at me. We used to have a problem in this house, she says. I know what it's like to like drinking.

Who told you? I ask.

You just got to stop, she says. Just put it in your head to stop, then do it.

I don't want to stop.

You'll make everyone miserable.

I don't mean to.

No one ever does, she says. The boys'll be back in a second. When they come back, you should tell him you're not feeling well. Tell him you need to leave.

We sit looking at each other, only looking away when we hear their voices outside. The scraping metal sound of the porch door opening.

She says she's not feeling well, his mother says. That maybe y'all better leave early.

Is that right? his father asks.

I'm not feeling well, I say. Baby, can we go? Can we pack up the car and go?

He shakes his head. Let's try to sleep this off, he says.

I won't, I say. That won't work.

Son, if she's feeling sick, his father says. What's wrong?

I'm dizzy, I say. I feel like I'm coming down with something, and I wouldn't want you to catch it.

She's a sweetheart, his father says, looking at his mother. See?

In the car, driving home, the air is wet in the headlights. A small animal runs fast across the road. We are the only car. Have you ever, he says and turns off the headlights.

I gasp. Pitch black outside, no streetlights. No reflectors, no road. Only speed and the sound of the engine. I can see the dusky outline of him holding the wheel straight, then I can see him smiling. Enough, I say.

It's incredible, he says.

I feel as though miles go by. I put my hand on his leg. Please, I say.

He shakes his head no, but I can feel that he is trembling a little. And for minutes we sit like this in the dark.

Stop, I say. Please!

He turns the lights back on, locks his hands on the wheel, ten and two. I bite my lip and lean back in my seat.

I thought you would like that, he says.

———————

Erin Brooks Worley was raised in Gainesville, Florida. Her work has appeared in the *Gettysburg Review, Indiana Review,* and *Ninth Letter.* She earned her MFA from Syracuse University.

SABINA PIERSOL

*W*hen I wrote "Grove," it was winter in
Syracuse and I was homesick for Florida.
*I chose to base the setting on my memories of my
grandparents' home. Those memories were happy
and nostalgic, and I was surprised this story grew around them, forcing the
details to darken in accommodation.*

"Grove" was my first published story.

George Singleton

DIRECTOR'S CUT

(from *The Atlantic Monthly*)

M y father had an affair with a woman once married to an Irish Traveler—one of those guys who takes money to seal your driveway, but then skips town. The woman, a Flora Gorman, ran the Dial-a-Style beauty salon and cut my mother's hair once a month. The salon, a three-seater, must've been a front for other things, because it remained hidden way out on two-lane Pick Road, which dead-ended at a creek that fed the Savannah River. My mother had to go out of her way to the Dial-a-Style, which probably meant that she suspected my father's dalliance.

"I lived with a bouffant atop my brain from 1977 to 1979, back when it hadn't been in style for ten years," my mother told me. "You remember. Dial-a-Style my ass. Every Irish Traveler's woman down there looked like that girl on *I Dream of Jeannie*. That girl on *Gilligan's Island*. Jackie Kennedy. Whoever posed for the Mr. Bubble's box of bubble bath."

This was over the telephone. I'd not talked to my mother since taking my wife down to meet her a couple of days after our impromptu wedding ceremony, thirteen years earlier. As I've always contended, the noncommunicative nature of our relationship stemmed from Mom's unwillingness to believe that I knew nothing of Dad's affair, plus her presumption that no man named

Spillman could turn into anything but a petty and ceaseless phi-
landerer. I said into the receiver, "I remember that big sign out
front of the Dial-a-Style. Like a rotary phone where you could
turn to a pageboy, or that haircut that looked like a nuclear bomb
exploded your bangs. And then the Peter Pan look."

My wife, Raylou, turned her head toward me and squinched her
eyebrows—the international facial expression for "Who's that?"
She flipped through a gardening book too fast, as if in search of
the plot. I mouthed "Mom" and shrugged my shoulders.

"Yeah. Yeah, like any one of those women married to Irish-
Traveler scam artists knew how to cut hair. Those bitches didn't
know shit."

I calculated my mother's age. She wasn't quite old enough for
classic dementia. Maybe she suffered from a post-menopausal syndrome akin to Tourette's. Even when my father packed up and
left for New Orleans with Flora German, my mother hadn't gone
on a cussing binge. I said, "So, what's on your mind? Raylou and
I are still together, by the way, and I don't run around on her. I
quit drinking. Raylou has a slew of people across North America
and Europe who collect her face jugs. I make sculptures, welded
entirely from bolts and hex nuts. You can see them standing in a
number of cities, and I just got a commission to weld some giant
angels for Birmingham, Alabama."

"Good," my mother said. "Your father and I were married for
almost fifteen years before he took to foreign snatch. So you still
have time to become a true Spillman."

Raylou set down the book, opened the end-table drawer, and
took out a pack of Lucky Strikes that I hadn't touched in two
weeks. She held a cigarette lengthwise in her open palm, sprang
her arm like a catapult, and caught the thing in her mouth after it
had flipped a few times in midair. "What're you doing?" I asked
my wife.

My mother said, "I watched a fascinating show on the influx of
nutria and armadillos down in Louisiana, which made me think
of your fucking father, which made me think of you. Where the

hell's this Gone Ember where you live? I called Information about twenty times before the stupid man on the other end figured out I wasn't saying 'sputum,' and then I got you. Then I thought that you'd invite me up, seeing as I'm retired from teaching those goddamn little chalk-eaters. And I've changed my hair. I've convinced myself that if you look me blankly in the face and don't recognize me at first, it's because I have a new hairdo instead of that son-of-a-bitch beehive that made me look like either a linthead working the cotton mills or a punk rock singer."

I veered my eyes away from Raylou and said, "Okay. Well, okay. Can you still drive, or do you need me to come down there and get you?"

I held the phone away from my ear as my mother went into a stream-of-consciousness curse that embarrassed me. She finished by saying, "I got a van, and I got equipment. I got almost enough backers, and I got people."

I told her that I seemed to be missing something in the conversation. I said, "People for what?"

I listened as my mother exhaled smoke — something she didn't do when bringing me up alone as the only white boy within about a two-mile radius. She said, "I've spent the last twelve years studying up on it. Thank God for the invention of the VCR. We never did get a movie house within twenty miles of here, Harp. Anyway, I took a college course in the mail, and after conference calls to my professors at Southern Cal, I've finally figured out how to make a movie."

At that moment I wished that Raylou and I had a speaker-phone feature so that she could listen in. I said, "Wait. You took a film class at the University of Southern California?"

She exhaled again. I heard a Zippo click. "Southern California Junior Film College. I might have those words turned around. Some such crap. Anyway, I successfully completed the program. My major's in directing. My minor's best boy."

• • •

My mother, her hair buzz-cut a half centimeter all over, hadn't been in our house for more than five minutes when Raylou decided to pipe up. "You know," she said, "I have an idea for you. Why don't you try a documentary on Harp, here? You can do a documentary that'll be multilayered as can be. First off, you get him doing these twelve-foot angel sculptures for the city of Birmingham. Then you get his constant struggle with staying off the liquor. If some of his new friends show up and you get to interview them, I see Sundance Film Festival in your future."

I looked at my wife, and just in case she couldn't interpret my expression, I said, "I'll kill you." But what she had said was true: since I'd quit drinking, quit going to rehab, and quit going to AA meetings, the rehab participants and AA victims had taken to coming my way. Sometimes I thought they were checking up on my progress. But most of the time I suspected they felt safe at our little compound, on a twenty-acre rounded piece of granite far from liquor stores and bars. I imagined a documentary wherein my part-time helper, Bayward, went into detail about how he had tried to perform a tracheotomy on himself so that beer would shoot out his throat—which of course it wouldn't—before reaching his bloodstream. I daydreamed about Vollis, Evan, and Kumi—the Elbow Boys—trying to explain how they had discovered a questionable orthopedic surgeon down in Costa Rica who had fused their elbow joints together so that they couldn't bring a drink to their lips. I said to my mother, "You don't want to make a documentary about everyday people doing nothing. It would be boring and a waste of cellulite."

"It's *celluloid*," my mother said, taking suitcase after suitcase out of her Dodge van. "Damn. First test in history and terminology class." She looked around at the Quonset hut I used for a studio, Raylou's work shed and adjacent kiln, the clear expanse of smooth granite where nothing man-made was standing. "Not many trees around here," she said. "Wouldn't have a problem with lighting." She reached down, picked up a suitcase, and put it back in the van. "Okay. I'd say it's about time for a drink, but I won't do that.

When in Gone Ember, you know. I believe Marty would act thusly too. Marty and Francis Ford. Frank. F. F. Quentin's another story, though."

I thought that if this were a movie, my mother and I would undergo an awkward hug while Raylou looked off at the horizon. "Did you actually get taught by those directors somewhere along the line? Do you know them somehow?"

"This'll work out perfectly," my mother said. "Great idea, Raylou. Listen. I've got to be up-front on this." My mother put some of her luggage in an outbuilding, an eight-foot-square structure that, I felt certain, my wife insisted on having built as a kind of alcoholics' playhouse, for when those forced-upon-me acquaintances showed up uninvited. "I know I said 'When in Gone Ember,' but this old cinematographer could use a drink. Are you sure you quit, Harp? You're named after a by-God Irish lager, among other things."

I said, "We're fresh out. If you brought your own, fine. I won't be bothered."

Raylou grabbed two suitcases to haul into the house and said, "We've got bourbon and vodka, I think, Ms. Spillman. You come on in, and I'll fix you up."

Where? I thought. *Where's the booze?* I hadn't gone on any scavenger hunts since I'd quit, but believe me, I knew every inch of fiberglass insulation and its underside from the old days of Raylou's hiding. I said to my mother, "You were going to say something about being up-front."

We walked a straight line to the house. I didn't point out the snapping-turtle pond between Raylou's workspace and our sliding glass door, for fear that my mother, who had suicidal tendencies, might dive in.

We sat in the den. My mother looked surprisingly young for a woman nearing sixty, a woman whose only husband had run off with a jack-Irish Traveler's wife who used to operate the Dial-a-Style, a woman who must've lost all reason to live if she'd spent hard-earned retirement money on the Southern California Junior

Film College correspondence course. She'd lost weight, and she looked more wiry than I could remember. Her baldish head made her look like an older and savvy California woman involved in the movie industry.

"I'm neither ashamed nor proud of it. I was going to make a feature film about your father's running away like he did. And I was going to let the guy have it—kind of like a modern-day Job, you know. But now that I see you, Harp"—she held up a see-through square with her thumbs and index fingers, like a camera lens, I supposed—"and with Raylou's suggestion, I see how I can turn this all around."

Something sounding like an earthquake occurred in the guest bedroom, bottle shaking against bottle. I tried to envision where my wife had hidden the booze over all these dry days. Or months and years. I said, "As long as you don't need my help, do what you want. I have a thing against movies. And I'm not a theater snob. I just have a thing against actors."

Raylou came out carrying Old Crow so old that it came in one of those embossed bottles. My mother said, "You look exactly like your father when he was thirty-eight. As a matter of fact, that's when he left us. Oh, I can see all kinds of possibilities in a documentary, sort of a cross between *Fahrenheit 9/11* when it comes to showing how stupid you are—I mean your *father* was—and, oh, I don't know. Let me think back to the syllabus we had second semester." My mother did those fingers my way again. "I can see a multilayered before-and-after, then-and-now, the-acorn-doesn't-fall-far kind of movie, with a ton of voiceovers provided by yours truly."

I didn't like the sound of this, of course. It's not how I ever imagined a reunion with my odd, obsessed mother. My wife said, "The bourbon's old, but the mixer's new. What'll you have with this, Ms. Spillman?"

"I've got it! A cross between that and maybe a little-known film we saw on Rube Goldberg and his ways." To Raylou my mother said, "I'll take it straight out of the bottle, if no one is joining me. And please call me Ansel."

Raylou walked a wide half circle from my reach and handed the untapped Old Crow to my mother, a woman whose name I'd always known to be Margaret. Margie. Peggy. Peg.

My wife converted to Quakerism. She hosts her fellow parishioners in the eight-by-eight outbuilding on Sunday mornings, and asks that I tiptoe, that I don't fire up the MIG welder, that perhaps I use this time to take a long, long, quiet walk far away from our house. Raylou and her pacifists require a boatload of quiet. I brought this up when my mother—or Ansel—said that she wanted to work in seventy-two-hour cycles with one day off in between. I mentioned that we couldn't work on Sundays. "I don't have much use for Quakers," my mother said. "I'd've liked to've gone to a Quaker school, though, just to beat everybody up. You have to understand, I like *action!*"

I asked myself how long doing this documentary could take. She would watch me weld for a minute or two, and ask some questions; watch Raylou form a face jug, ask some questions; and then maybe assume that ubiquitous voiceover to rant about how her husband, my father, never had any ambitions beyond grading eggs and peaches for the South Carolina Ag Department before he ran off with a younger woman who couldn't dial but one style.

My mother said, "I really need to hire someone to run a second camera, or at least hold a boom mike." This was kind of late on that first night, and the booze didn't seem to have affected Ansel.

Raylou said, "You know, we could do this between the three of us. When you're shooting Harp, I could hold the microphone, and vice versa. On top of that, Harp and I both learned how to run a camera and do lights back in college. You don't need a rocket scientist." Raylou kept talking to a point above my head. I wasn't sure, and tried to retrace the evening backwards, but she might've excused herself to the bathroom and smoked some pot in there.

Maybe she had hit a bowl or two, probably with a ceramic pipe she'd made between face jugs, which took her thirty minutes to form and she sold for upwards of $300. Back in my more politically incorrect drinking days I might've pointed out that slow kids, too, grew up to fetch top dollar on their face jugs. I said, "I have enough to deal with right now. I'm not even sure I'm all that hip to someone's putting my mug on film. Some people out there might be looking for me, you know."

My mother didn't say "Oh, come on and humor me." She didn't say, "Well, this is a fine welcome after all these years of silence." She got up from her seat and said, "Well, this little cinematographer needs to visit the editing room to unreel a spool."

I looked at my wife when Mom got out of earshot. "You've been smoking pot again, haven't you? I can tell. Don't try to hide a high from an old drunk, Raylou."

She giggled. She said, "First off, do you think your mother's film will ever be seen by anyone? Give it a break, Harp. This might be the highlight of her life. And you want to take it away? Check your ego in the Green Room, man. And second, your mom gave me the pot, back when you were pretending to need something in the room where I had the bourbon hidden. The latest etiquette books say that smoking dope is proper and right if it's offered by an older family member. Family sharing keeps everybody from feeling uncomfortable."

I looked at my wife. I'd forgotten that her eyebrows kind of arched up like a clown's, like a McDonald's sign, like the wings on my giant welded angels, when she got stoned. I said, "I'll love you tomorrow, but I want to go on record as saying this is trouble."

My mother came back and said, "False alarm." She grabbed her bottle and sat back down. "Oops, there it is again. *Take two.*" She walked faster to the bathroom this time.

"A big mistake," I said.

I unboxed a new crate of shiny steel nuts from Southern Hex, stood back, and stared at the frame I'd built of rebar. My mother stepped in closer to me and said, "Unlike most artists, Harp Spill-man doesn't hold his thumb up to the work in progress."

I laughed and said, "Cut!" I said, "That's just stupid, Mom. Can you go back and add the commentary later? And let me know what you plan to let out of your mouth?"

Raylou lowered the boom mike to rest on our granite lawn. She said, "That *was* kind of dumb, Ansel, I hate to say."

My mother made no promises but said, "And . . . action!" — like she'd seen in the movies, I supposed. I pulled the trigger on my MIG and beaded a nut down low, and then another and another. In the distance wild dogs barked, and a flock of ducks passed over. I sensed the camera angling up toward the sky. I said, "The trick to these things is getting them heavy enough to remain sturdy, but balanced so they don't tip over while I'm working. And I want enough negative space to create the illusion that the angel is nearly airborne."

This time my mother yelled "Cut!" She said, "Okay. You weren't good at direction when you were a kid, but I let you slide, seeing as your father was to blame. But you're an adult now. Hell, you're old enough to leave your wife."

Raylou said, "Thanks."

I said, "See? I told you."

I circled the half angel, and my mother operated the camera about two inches from my face, which luckily couldn't be seen for the welder's mask. She said, "So. When your father left you for that skank gypsy, what did you think, Harp? Was that when you decided to become an artist — because your brilliant mother supported you, and helped nurture your talent, and urged you to follow your dream, even though she couldn't afford to get her hair fixed right in a proper hairdo?"

I said, "Most of that's correct. I think my mother really only wanted to see the pretty colors all swirl together while she smoked dope in secret."

My mother said, more quietly, "Yes. Yes. That'll keep an audience riveted." I pulled the trigger again. Over the hiss my mother said, "How's about that father of yours? Do you think you received your alcoholism through him genetically, or did you start drinking hard early on in life as a means of trying to forget what an asshole he was and still is?" I didn't answer. I continued working, reaching down for new nuts, standing back half crouched, trying not to think about how I would soon invest in a series of massage-therapy sessions, or at least a case of Doan's Backache Pills. My mother said, "I'll take that for a yes."

Raylou kept the mike above my head, and my mother shot for a good half hour in silence. Finally I set the MIG down and pulled up my mask to get a look at the sculpture. My mother turned off her hand-held camera. I said, "Maybe it would be a good time to go film Raylou. I'll hold the mike. You probably have enough footage that you can cut and splice together."

We went through the same format, pretty much. I held the mike, Raylou sat down at her electric wheel, and my mother said, "Raylou, do you truly believe that Harp received his alcoholism genetically, or that he began drinking at the age of thirteen because his father left a stable household in order to navigate the strange choppy waters off the Gulf of Poontang?"

I leaned the microphone up against Raylou's groundhog kiln. She started laughing. I said, "Are you intent on making an X-rated film? You need to watch your language a bit, Mom, if you ask me. I don't care what those correspondence-course directors say, even art-house movie joints have some sense of decorum, from what I hear."

"Cut," my mother said. She set the camera down on the hard rock of our acreage. "Don't y'all have any friends or anything?" She swept her arm around. "I need some people to tell me some stories, man. Y'all obviously can't do it."

She left her equipment on the ground and walked back to the house as if marching toward a spank-needy child. I said to my wife, "I told you this wouldn't work out. She was kind of nutty way back when. That kind of behavior doesn't reverse itself."

Raylou shrugged. She said, "I'm betting she won't need another twenty-four hours to understand she can't find a story here."

Those same ducks, I was pretty sure, flew back overhead in the opposite direction. My mother yelled out, "What the hell are these things?" and I looked to see that she'd almost stepped into the snapping-turtle pond.

I said, "Never mind those things. It's a long story that involves Raylou's getting too involved with rescuing animals she thinks are being tortured by biologists."

"Biotoxicologists!" Raylou called out. "Hey, now that might be—"

"Hurry up and bring the camera," my mother yelled. "Leave the microphone for now. Hey, when these things have their necks stretched out, they kind of look like . . . good God, man, talk about your *father*." She said, "I got a whole new idea. Take one, baby, take one!"

What my mother decided to shoot ended up—I'll give her this—as kind of a good idea. She took a real liking to the six snappers—now weighing in at about twenty pounds apiece, their necks able to stretch out nearly a foot—and filmed them burrowing down in the mud, gnawing on chicken necks, sticking their heads out of the water like prehistoric periscopes. My mother said, "I think I could just dub some Bartók over the film—maybe some Shostakovich—and then market this documentary to schools, so they can get their students to understand biology and music. I'll call it something like . . . damn, what're those words for a turtle's shell? One for the top and one for the bottom."

My wife said, "We have copperheads around here too. A few rattlesnakes. You'd have to go farther south to find cottonmouths. I'm thinking you could do a whole series of shorts involving, you know, God's scary creatures of the South."

I said, "We got fire ants, and the neighbor down the hill tried to smuggle in some anteaters from Central America or someplace, but they all got loose. Two of them, from what I understand, are now mounted, looking down from some confused hunter's mantel."

We sat in mesh chairs that Raylou got somewhere; they rolled up and fit in a bag. We sat in the Quonset hut, surrounded by what angels I had finished, drinking coffee. My mother and Raylou ate dry, dry homemade scones that I wouldn't touch, because I figured they'd remind me of the days of pretzels and beer. My mother said, "You know, it's really not all that bad here in Gone Ember. I don't see the hustle and bustle like where you were brought up, Harp."

My home town might've held two thousand residents. Maybe nothing is more selfish than a committed drunk become a committed recoverer, which may explain why I said, "Don't think about moving up here."

Raylou said, "Harp. That's not very nice." To my mother she said, "You can come up here any time you want."

"Hollywood East," my mother said. She rubbed at her scalp a few times, the way a kid might rub a balloon to create static. "No, I was just being polite. I'll keep my home base right there near the Dial-a-Style, so I can remember every day why I'm on this planet."

I cleared my throat. I got up, rummaged through a drawer of old washers, and found a pack of Camels I'd stashed for mornings when I felt lost without bourbon. I said, "Is your reason for being on the planet that you want to make sure everyone knows what Dad did twenty-five years ago? I mean, that first documentary you started — the one about how I looked like him, and I was destined to act like him — to be honest, I thought it was plain meanspirited. And kind of presumptuous."

Raylou got up and said that she wanted to throw a couple dozen face jugs, that she needed to chop oak for the kiln, that she'd bought a new shingle hammer she thought might work best for cracking up the old porcelain plates she used for scary teeth. I think she felt uncomfortable. I think she thought my mother and I had to have some kind of long-time-coming talk, in which my mother might admit to some shortfall in her child-rearing skills, or I might confess that I should've initiated contact years earlier, before the era of correspondence courses, when my mother had no hobbies or use for family members.

When my mother opened her mouth wide, I thought she was going to acknowledge some shortcomings on her part, or say that

she admired my overcoming the Spillman family's drinking problem. The sound that came out of her throat, though, sounded
like what happens when you use one of those trick cellophane-
and-cardboard discs that kids put in their mouths to talk like the
speech-afflicted. Or it sounded like a death rattle.

I said, "What?"

My mother pointed at her chest twice. She pointed at half a
scone—and later I would observe that outside of a cheap way of
killing yourself, scones were better used as door stops—and then
at her throat. She got up out of her chair and walked quickly to my
twelve-gallon wet-dry Shop-Vac. She made that noise some more
and stamped her feet. On her face I read—frustration? discomfort?
some kind of existential dread? Finally she eked out "Choking."

She was the one to turn on the switch. I jumped up like a good
son and tried to figure out how to perform the Heimlich maneuver without touching my mother's breasts, because, well, I had
enough nightmares.

My mother shoved the black nozzle in her mouth, tightened her
lips around the business end, and unclogged her air passage. The
image was one I knew I would never escape, even with daily visits
to a certified psychoanalyst with training in hypnosis to eradicate
Oedipus complexes. I screamed for help, but by the time Raylou
showed up, the vacuum's hose was snaking around on the floor, a
chunk of scone stuck to the plastic attachment, and I stood there
cradling my mother's abdomen from behind. Raylou said, "I knew
y'all would patch things up. I wish I had this on film. I didn't
want to say anything before, but you don't need all the cursing
and violence."

I let go of my mother. Later I would think about how most
people would thank a son for having a Shop-Vac at the ready, for
my at least attempting to heave at her diaphragm. "Lucky thing I
don't wear dentures," my mother said. She went back to her chair.
"If you end up with your teeth falling out someday, Harp, you can
blame it on your father's gummy side of the family. Maybe that's
why he ran off with Flora Gorman. It wasn't for her hair, believe

me. Maybe her having retractable teeth played a part in it. I saw it before. I saw her in the Dial-a-Style. I saw her have to apply another strip of that gum glue." My mother laughed and laughed. She reached into her pocket and pulled out a four-inch clay pipe that I supposed Raylou had given her. "Now that I think about it, your daddy's mistress looked about like those snapping turtles when it comes to smiles."

Then, like any good sniper, she left the premises. Raylou went back in the house, and I stood in my studio making a mental list of what I needed to do next. My mother packed up her van and drove straight through Gone Ember, without so much as an invitation to come see the final cut of whatever it was she had shot. I realized that in the movies I would probably have a voiceover saying "What just happened?" or "I hope to hell this is all a dream" or "This isn't good for my recovery."

I locked the door to the Quonset hut. At the snapping-turtle pond I tried not to think of my father's mistress from years ago. Inside, while my wife took orders for her face jugs over the Internet, I turned on the television. One of those cable channels was showing a *Three Stooges* marathon. Another was showing a Marx Brothers film. The Atlanta station had Laurel and Hardy, and the cartoon channel offered up Roadrunner.

Nothing seemed funny.

I turned to the Independent Film Channel. A German man and woman, their faces in close-up, talked about the good and essential symbiotic nature of termite mounds, with subtitles. I think the man tried to make some kind of connection with Schopenhauer. I turned to Animal Planet, and—God or Satan will insist that something more powerful than I had planned this all along—a man was doing a voiceover explaining the many differences between land tortoises and aquatic turtles, but declaring that both depended on sturdy plastrons and carapaces. A woman pointed out that although it's not common, snapping turtles have been known to be monogamous, and one pair stayed together more than fifteen years.

I thought about post-acute-withdrawal syndrome. I turned back to the cartoon channel.

———————

George Singleton is the author of four story collections and one novel. His stories have appeared in the *Atlantic Monthly, Harper's, Playboy, Zoetrope,* the *Georgia Review, Glimmer Train,* and several anthologies. His nonfiction has appeared in *Best Food Writing 2006* and *Dog Is My Co-Pilot.* He teaches at the South Carolina Governor's School for the Arts and Humanities and lives in Dacusville, South Carolina.

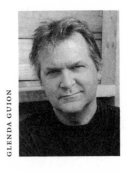

GLENDA GUION

*W*hen I sit down to start a new story I imagine two characters in an uncomfortable situation, which normally causes tension, and therefore a conflict. Over the past few years I had written a number of stories wherein the narrator's mother disappeared in one way or another, so I thought it might be time to create the mother of all mothers—a salty and obsessed woman intent on documenting what went wrong in her past in order to, perhaps wrongheadedly, afford her a better future. To grasp how a character might talk as if she were best friends with famous film directors, I had only to think about any music shop I'd ever entered, where the clerks walked around playing air guitar, sang off-key to what got piped in above, and made comments about my CD selections as if they—the clerks—were critics and/or rock stars. I'm not quite sure from where the scone/shop vac scene emanated. I don't want to know, either.

Geoff Wyss

KIDS MAKE THEIR OWN HOUSES

(from *Image*)

I never loved Rachel more than when she was talking about education. This is a woman, I tell you, who could use words like *standards* and *benchmarks* with force and clarity, as if they were more than abstract terms handed down by the state. This is a woman who could make you believe no child need be left behind. This is a woman who could run a Smart Board. You will think I am being wry. I am not. To see Rachel confidently integrating technology, bending its sleek surfaces to her will with an ease so unlike my own submissive truce with things mechanical — this, to me, was beautiful.

We were rehearsing in her basement.

"Alignment of your curriculum to state norms," she was saying, "is important for many reasons, one being the movement toward accountability we are seeing in the schools. As something to hold up and say, *Here's the knowledge my students have accomplished.* Another being that in under-resourced districts like yours" — we were to give a seminar in Birmingham, Alabama — "you should experience an immediate and measurable jump in exit test scores."

She saw a cloud flutter across my face.

"What?"

"Do we believe that? I don't think I believe that."

116

"Yes, you do." The coercive optimism of a former cheerleading coach buoyed her words. "Come on. You do believe it."

"I don't know. I'm thinking that the same exhausted teachers are going to be teaching the same illiterate kids in the same windowless schools with—what do you call them?—*tags* all over the exterior brick. I mean."

"Come on, Gary. You can do it." This was one of the pep talks I occasionally required. Rachel's confidence in what we had done—quitting our teaching jobs, setting ourselves up as educational consultants, destroying her engagement with our affair—never wavered. Mine did. I was a leaky ship torn by the winds of my own conscience, and she was the steady shore I kept tacking back to.

"Can I? Can I do it?"

"Yes, you can." She saw that I was partly playing and cracked a mischievous grin. She hated to waste time but loved to play. I should mention that Rachel was wearing brown corduroy overalls with a pair of embroidered flowers on the central chest pocket, their stems crossed sentimentally, an atypically girlish choice, but one I found affecting.

"It's a spurious and untested claim. I don't believe it."

"You have to. It's what we're saying." She added a tender expletive, and we laughed the laugh of people for whom everything has become unexpectedly new and fun. Rachel and I had worked side by side for fifteen years in the MacKinley County school system, fifteen years of teen pregnancy and overheated copy machines and self-doubt and rare human triumph. We had sat on committees where we had schemed with and against one another; we had scolded, strong-armed, and expelled students as members of the discipline board; I had passed the doorway of her classroom as she lectured about the Vietnam era while wearing a fringed vest, a gambit that became oddly touching as she aged. Rumors about the dissolution of her first marriage had trickled down to me, as to everyone else, in the faculty lounge, and, like everyone else, I had tried to detect the signs of devastation in her professional behavior. (There were none.) And then, last January, as heads of our respective departments, we were asked to attend a seminar about raising our school's ACT scores, a seminar about whose utility I was already feeling cynical when we were instructed to draw the animal that best represented our feelings about having to alter our curricula, and downright hateful by the time we received our catered lunch of pressed chicken in floury white sauce. I steadied my plastic knife and remarked that *I* could place irrelevant cartoons on an overhead projector and peddle test-taking hints in half the time and with twice the verve of the idiots running the seminar. How could these people sleep at night knowing how many other people's time they'd wasted, et cetera? Rachel vilified them for their disorganization. We continued the conversation over a cigarette outside, beneath a corrugated awning where the ash urns were. I had a set of essays waiting for me at home in which half the students would compare *The Red Badge of Courage* to one Disney movie or another. We were standing there smoking the smoke of the near-dead, smoking to kill ourselves, when we realized not only that there was an easier way, but that it was okay for us to take it. One of us, probably Rachel, said, "You know what? Let's goddamn do it," and that lone statement constituted our decision-making process. Rachel had been Teacher of the Year the previous year, I had been Teacher of the Year the year before that, and she was engaged to a middle-manager of an oilfield named Rusty, but we stood there valiantly facing a future where we would throw all that away for billing rates of four hundred dollars per hour and weekends in climateless hotel rooms with six versions of Showtime. "I'm sick of always having to tell someone where I'm going and how long I'll be there," she said, waggling the diamond solitaire on her cigarette hand. I wanted to reciprocate her sentiment, to establish a mode of discourse that wouldn't duplicate the evasions and niceties of my own failed marriage, so I said something about how all forms of responsibility are ultimately infantilizing. My point in mentioning this is to explain that we fell upon a way of speaking to each other that involved saying aloud the vaguely shocking things we had spent our adult lives muting.

Rachel came halfway across the basement in her overalls, laughing still, and put her hands on her hips in the projector's unfocused glow. I should specify that Rachel is not beautiful, not conventionally so, but I liked her physical substance and athleticism. She has the kind of sturdy jaw that reminds one of properly executed cabinetry. Her legs are legs you could trust for guidance in a hailstorm or riot. Chastened by half a life's trials, she has aligned her bodily self with the demands of the world and achieved a tempered grace. The word PERFORMANCE was projected in watery capitals across the ridged terrain of her waist.

"Do you think I really believe the schools will ever amount to anything in this shithole state? I don't even care."

It was the sexiest, most godless thing I had ever heard anyone say. I knelt to untie her clean white running shoe, and we took each other roughly on the basement floor.

But this isn't a story about how bad two people can help each other become. Or it's not only about that. It's about how you can work with someone for fifteen years, watch her eat two thousand, five hundred lunches across a sticky table, stand in line with her at the copy machine as she cuts and pastes maps of the Thirteen Colonies, urge your homeroom to vanquish her homeroom in contests involving tempera paint and butcher paper, and still barely know the first thing about her. It's about the fantastic difficulty of knowing another human, even if you're on a fast-track of revelation and abandon. I sometimes thought of my ex-wife as Rachel and I drove to Motel 6's and Super 8's along the American interstate highway system, coordinating my cigarette intake to the mile-markers as Rachel governed our windswept flight with her left wrist. My wife and I had shared a traditional view of marriage as an agreement in which both parties avoided contact with the essential nature of the other by devoting their discourse to silver patterns and the bowel movements of pets and the best time to purchase new tires for the car. In terms of Bloom's taxonomy, my understanding of my wife never advanced beyond *knowledge,* the level of rote names and dates, and I reminded myself of this every time Rachel — in this case just outside Jackson, Mississippi — plunged her hand deep into the moist recesses of her soul and pulled out something sick and wriggling.

"I'm just going to tell the truth. I hate children."

NPR was airing a segment about preteens who had started their own charities. Rachel was at pains, I could see, to locate words which would carry the weight of her feeling, and I waited as a mile's worth of orange construction cones whisked past on the left.

"The falseness of the way you have to interact with them. The lie of how you have to present yourself. The myth of innocence we create about them, when the truth is they're the most selfish and cruel people in the world. Adult lies are so much less debilitating, because you expect them."

Rachel's arm on a steering wheel is a firm and purposeful thing, given solidity by years of hefting teacher's editions and emphasizing her points on the board with stunts of chalk. I rooted unsuccessfully through the junk drawer of my own heart for sentiments to match as I watched her arm edge the wheel now clockwise, now counterclockwise. Instead, I lodged a niggling protest, something like, *Is that necessarily true, do we always lie to them?* This inspired the scornful tone she might have used for a student who kept claiming he hadn't plagiarized even as she dangled the internet original in front of his face. "Don't bullshit me, Gary."

I did lie to students, true, lied to them all the time, but my lies were lies of good cheer and good will, the kind of lies whose maintenance made me a better person and our school a better place. I could be accused of serving up a false joviality that made my students see me as a person with more faith in the goodness and greatness of the future than experience had taught me to expect, but what of that? Was it my duty to brutalize them with anecdotes of failed potential, breached trust, lives cut short by unregulated capital? If I was lying when I described the things my students might become in my letters of recommendation to colleges, the artists and engineers and curers of disease, then these were lies I needed too. Except that I didn't have students anymore. I had given them up, and with them the fleecy lies we had used to cushion each other's paths through the world, in favor of an enclosed missile of vinyl and plastic piloted by a woman of rude health toward the jagged cliffs of truth.

"I guess we could stop telling them that they'll grow an extra arm if they smoke pot, things like that. We do a certain amount of harm."

"You totally misunderstood me. I blame the *kids*."

Rachel's mouth made what, for lack of a more precise word, would have to be called a smile. We went dancing that night, that simple and exalted thing people in a civilization do, and I kissed her when they played "All of Me." But I am getting ahead of myself.

I should mention that our school, the school Rachel and I taught at before we leased our souls to a devil's trade, was located in a suburban dell founded and kept tidy by white flight. I record this fact because I wouldn't want you to think we were war-torn from disarming kids with homemade weapons lashed to their calves, from holding our breaths and scuttling past bombed-out lavatories. Our school allowed families who drove Lexuses to speak about the importance of public education while enjoying the peace of mind of not having to send their kids to a school with the kids of families who drove Hyundais. It was partly my ability to form sentences like this, laced with shards of dry humor and suppressed anger, which convinced me that I had to get out.

My principal was surprised. He was a small man, in truth a tiny man, with a swag belly and a ring of hair, who took pride in never being caught off guard, but I hadn't shown any of the advance signs teachers show when they're preparing to bail out—the stupor, the torpor, the rancor—and the agitated manner in which he drummed a gold pen a niece or nephew had given him against the palm of his left hand told me he was nonplused.

"Well, this is a complete shock, Gary. I thought we could count on you to be here at MacKinley South forever." Employing the language of betrayal was one of the ways he got people to do things for him, sit on committees and the like. I recognized it as a valid educational tool and didn't hold it against him. "For goodness' sake, you're one of our best teachers. You're what MacKinley South *means* to many of these students."

I can't evaluate whether he was right or not, but I knew at least part of his consternation came from the thought of having to place an ad in the paper and spend two or three days of his summer interviewing applicants who would show up with Fu Manchu mustaches and vestigial ponytails. I couldn't think of a way to say that I was putting my own needs before the needs of the students for the first time in fifteen years without it sounding so selfish as to seem a personal insult, so I settled for something bland and unanswerable like, *It's time for me to try something new.* Someone else could be what MacKinley South meant to the students — although, I reflected, not Rachel, because she would be coming in fifteen minutes later to tell him the same thing.

The life of an educational consultant is an incredibly easy one. I found myself buttering leisurely bagels in the noon glow of Rachel's kitchen nook. I reread novels I hadn't read since graduate school and which I had been recommending to people for twenty years, and found I didn't like them anymore; I read with new appreciation books I had spent my life publicly criticizing because my youth had prevented me from having proper sympathy for them. I was growing and improving as a human being. I prepared omelets and other high-protein foods to help us become stronger as the rest of the world grew weak. Two or three days out of seven — though usually on weekends, it must be admitted — I donned a suit and did my undemanding work, then ate dinners paid for by administrators who wanted to impress me with anecdotes about the progressivism of their districts, essentially decent but harried and needy people. But I've gotten ahead of myself again. Rachel and I were still copying computer files and enhancing text, assembling the graphs and tables of our nascent trade.

By the time our teaching checks ran out in July, I knew the lobes and fissures of Rachel's mind and body well enough to have at least passed a multiple-choice test on the subject. I hardly spent any time at my own house anymore, in part because we were so heavily involved in developing our presentation, and in part because we had agreed to consolidate our resources in the name of thrift. A certain amount of software had to be purchased, a certain amount of hardware. A certain number of three-ring binders and two-colored highlighters so teachers could annotate the attractive charts we would supply. To construct even the most vapid of presentations on the most mundane of subjects takes longer than one would suppose, but I enjoyed every minute I spent in that house with its thick evidence of another life. I discovered a glass vial of cardamom in Rachel's cupboard and a chill ran through me — I can't explain why. A small porcelain figurine of a Siamese cat on her dresser gave me a half-hour's speculation about where she had gotten it and what it might mean to her. The angle of her toaster seemed to suggest whole philosophies of living. Here was a woman who had been alone in her house for five years and built up a humid personal atmosphere of rituals and objects which I could now study in the most invasive of ways. Do you understand what I am saying? I wanted to subsume myself within another human being, disappear into the baseness and beauty of someone in a way I not only never achieved with my ex-wife, but never even dreamed of. Walking through Rachel's rooms, I finally understood my students' fascination with my private life. A teacher is both more and less than fully human, diminished into the necessities of discipline and subject matter; glimpsing the dandruff shampoo or family photos behind the public figure brings him back into the human family, where you can love or destroy him as you wish.

Rachel took one of my Celebrex and I took one of her Claritin and we went hiking.

By hiking, I don't mean humping sixty pounds of specialist gear in shades of earthy green. I mean an undemanding stroll in the woods behind her house.

"Rachel, would you call me a trivial person?"

She was intent on conquering the leafy incline we had chosen, picking our path upward through thickets of trees whose proper names I didn't know, a million board-feet of inscrutable nature. She wasn't the most attentive conversationalist in any case. I huffed after her, spacing my footfalls to land in the smudges her own steps had made in the years-old carpet of leaves.

"I worry about the angle of staples in documents. I use a single brand of pen exclusively."

Her right foot slid backward from under her, and I prevented her from falling by bracing a hand against her lower back. We continued up the rise.

"I require my socks to fit in a very particular way. I eat only one brand of cereal. Isn't there something more to life?" It was the question I meant to ask, but it filled with all kinds of pathos as I spoke it, the locution of a televangelist or a noir gangster.

"Look," she said.

At the top of the hill, which I reached with two more lunging steps, the ground disappeared into a steep ravine deep enough to take away what little breath I had left, a plunging green gorge of plant life and whizzing birds watered by a silent rill far below. I want to say there was a mystic fog hanging over the land. In part because I am afraid of heights and in part because I was shushed and humbled by the immensity of the view, I fell to one knee and took hold of Rachel's calf.

"We used to come here when we were kids," she said.

"It's amazing. I feel somehow unworthy."

"We smoked cigarettes. We practiced French kissing."

"Where did you live then?"

"Where I live now. I've been living in the same house since I was born."

I tried to absorb the full meaning of this. The ridge I knelt on had been trodden by Rachel at nine, Rachel at eleven, Rachel at fourteen. This very soil—I reached down and lovingly rummaged it—held the impress and memory of her tentative middle-school necking and furtive tobacco use, all her junior-high longings. This is where she had come to map out the life which now involved me. I felt overwhelmed by the blunt force of existence, the majesty and briefness of it.

"We used to get down to the water over there," she said, pointing to the shallowest part of the decline, a descent only a teenager flush with his own immortality would attempt. "We built dams and played with fire. Playing with fire in the woods." She giggled at this recklessly improper act, then took a seat next to me on the loamy precipice.

"I could live here," I said. "I really could."

"Right."

I don't know whether a sneer can be pretty, as in, *She sneered prettily,* but that's what I'm asking you to imagine.

"I'll rephrase. Assuming I could get six months of training in which mushrooms not to eat and how to prevent birds from pecking my eyes out when I sleep, I think I have the temperament for it. Some pastoral gene deep in my body."

"I wanted to live in L.A. after I saw *The Big Sleep* in high school. For six months I told everyone I was going to move there after graduation."

I admitted that I had signed up for the Peace Corps after watching *Pather Panchali* but balked at the last second and ended up working in my uncle's construction business.

"Ever feel guilty about that?"

We turned to face each other, our legs crossed, kneecaps touching.

"Every day."

"But you almost said no. I saw you."

"I heard somebody say once that regret is an unnecessary emotion. It made a lot of sense to me," I said.

"It made sense, but not to you."

I rocked forward and planted my hands at the top of her thighs, in the hollows where her legs met her pelvis. "Let's build a tree house out of vines and spider webs and live back here. Never come out," I proposed. I half thought we might. I started kissing her face to suggest my commitment to the idea.

"Follow me," she said, pushing me away.

She led me left along the ridge, then left again, angling back down the hill we had climbed, then followed a thin, dried-up watercourse choked with leaves that I would never have noticed on my own. After five minutes or so, she hopped down over a small waist-high falls, also dry, into a cove or grotto whose central feature was the exposed root-structure of an immense toppled tree. By immense, I mean that the tree, even on its side, was taller than I, the airy ganglia of its underside reaching well above my head like a frilly awning. The divot left by the yanked roots had been deepened and improved by human hands into a common area which held a cast-off card table, two upturned industrial buckets for seats, and various scattered implements of tinkering and chopping. The tree having fallen uphill, its cupped underside provided a tilted half-roof for the hobbit-dwelling below.

"I guess kids still come here," she said. The sad shortness of human life pierced me once more, but this purely personal reflection was swept quickly aside by the epiphany that Rachel was presenting me with the rebus-puzzle of an obscure childhood of neglect and self-reliance, and that, if I could only solve the puzzle, I would both win and save her.

On the way back to the house, Rachel fell and sprained her ankle. I was behind her, and I saw her foot sink into the hidden hole left by some digging animal, and I heard her light squeal of surprise and pain as she fell. I rushed to help her, but she was inconsolable—she believed she had broken it. I could almost see the clearing that marked the edge of her property from where we were, which heavily informed what I did next: bending down, I lifted her and carried her the quarter-mile back to the house. Several times as I crab-walked through the crowded trees or felt my kneecaps creak and twinge, I believed I would falter. But I found new strength each time by imagining that my ex-wife was watching, and by thinking about the things she would say if she were.

By September nostalgia was hitting me hard. I dreamed of booming tubas at pep rallies in the gym. I remembered with fondness the sweet flurry of uniforms into doorways as the tardy bell rang. I wondered about the academic and social fate of Cash Monet, that student with the most repeatable of names and a crippling case of acne who came to my classroom at lunch every day to discuss the arbitrary cruelty of God. I wanted to know how the English III students with whom I had read Hawthorne and Poe were doing in Mrs. Richardson's English IV class. (Were they constructing specific, arguable thesis statements? Did their body paragraphs make use of clear topic sentences? Were they proofreading carefully, making last-minute corrections in a neat hand with a black pen?) And I wanted to see who had taken my place in their affections. Part of me knew it was a bad idea—Rachel told me it was a bad idea—but I convinced her to come to a football game.

People began to recognize us in the half-dark of the parking lot, gaggles of parents hailing us in the crepuscule. I had disliked many of them, these parents, but I felt vaguely offended by this evidence that their lives had continued in my absence, that they were tripping out to sporting events with such blithe unconcern. I greeted the women in their makeup, the men in their collared shirts. But it was their unspoiled children I longed to see, and that's who mobbed me—mobbed us, I mean—when we pushed through the turnstile.

"Mr. Wilkins! Ms. Bruno!"

They gathered around us in their rap-inspired jeans and ball caps with corporate logos and told us about their grades and their friends, their ambitions and fears. Yvette Harfield, a retiring girl with oily hair from my freshman study-skills class, fixed me with a deeply needy look—the look that destines certain women to marry men who will beat them—and asked if I liked my new job. I said what she wanted me to say, that I missed MacKinley South and missed my students—which, by the way, was the truth as I said it, and is the truth now, as I write it. Michelle Boggs blushed mischievously and asked Rachel and me whether the rumors about our romantic involvement were true (someone had seen us at the grocery store together, someone else had seen me spray-washing the car as Rachel sat inside behind the streaming windows). I made a joke about Ms. Bruno's preferring taller men, which Michelle, who is six foot one, found funny. I clapped Tommy Carwell on the shoulder and gestured imperially toward the stands. "Let's go find a seat," I said, "so folks can get through."

MacKinley South was losing 21–0 by halftime, which meant everything was right with the world. The best athletes at MacKinley South don't play football anymore; they play soccer. The same shadow has fallen over schools throughout the South, and I find the shift disturbing, though perhaps beneficial to civilization. I want bone-crunching hits at high skill levels. As a man, I want my team to dominate other men's teams mentally and physically. But the students at MacKinley South don't care whether the football team wins or not. Football, for them, is less a sport than a social opportunity, and so I duly record a sample of our conversation:

"We have to compare Edna in *The Awakening* to Hester in *The Scarlet Letter.*"

"That's a great assignment. Whose class is this?"

"Miss Harper. The new lady."

"That is a *great* assignment. Why didn't I think of that? Hello, Mr. Applesmith."

"She's mean. She yelled at Mike."

"Scarlotti? I'm sure he deserved it."

"Mr. Wilkins!"

"I'm just telling you what I heard. Now that was a football play."

"I have to go find my sister."

"Peace, love, and happiness. Jason, still kissing teachers' butts for grades?"

"As if. I told Mr. Villalongo he ought to be more professional and look over the vocabulary words he's teaching before he teaches them. He had no idea how to pronounce *sang-froid*."

"Blame that on the French, not Villalongo. Hi, Mr. Becker."

"In Mrs. Ellis's class I never take out a book and I'm making a B. I read stereo equipment catalogs."

"Am I supposed to say I'm proud of you? You're corrupt, and I predict you'll be jailed for white-collar crimes."

"This team," pointing at the field. "A bunch of pussies. See you later."

"Ciao."

"Mr. Wilkins, I'm driving now."

"Now *that* was a football play. Wait, driving? What are you, nine years old?"

"I'm sixteen!"

(Here I fake-grab my heart, indicating shock at the precipitous march of time and, by implication, my own dwindling quotient of it.)

"Well, I'm turning in my license tomorrow morning. Mrs. Saint Peter, nice to see you."

"I'm a very responsible driver, silly. I've seen you squeal out of the parking lot."

"I am visiting you for the first time in four months. Don't tell me about your driving privileges. Tell me about your heart."

"Wait, what?"

"What you believe and whom you love and why the world will be better for having you in it. How's your mother?"

"In remission. The doctors are hopeful."

"Good. Very good. Do you still write poetry?"

"Sometimes."

"Good."

By the time the final horn sounded, the score was 41–7, and I felt wonderful. I had to round up Rachel from the spot under the bleachers where she was talking to Todd Tracey, a guidance counselor at MacKinley South whose integrity and heterosexuality I doubted, despite his wife and two children. I used to catch sight of Todd on the drive to work every morning as he darted past me in excess of the speed limit, fiddling with his radar detector or cell phone or climate-control knobs. But he was a meticulous worker. If he planned Red Ribbon Week, for example, you knew that the anti-drug slogans would be supported with reliable statistics and that the guest speaker he brought in would know how to make the girls cry with anecdotes about gray stillborn babies and lives lived in slavering alleys. I shook his hand with the special gusto I reserve for people I don't like.

"Todd."

"Rachel here's telling me about your new gig. Sounds sweet."

"Yeah, well." It always takes me a minute to warm back up to adult conversation, to find my way back into its ellipses and obfuscations and evasions. "It's not for the faint of heart."

"Counseling," he spat. "Fucking shit, it gets tiresome listening to kids talk about themselves all day. *Oh, mm-hm. I'm totally fascinated to know who snubbed you at the dance. Do you realize you smell like vinegar and have no interests?*" He was wearing a very nice blue oxford shirt, so nice I experienced it as an insult to me and to all other men.

"Talk to you later, Todd," Rachel said, taking me by the wrist. Only when we reached the crunching gravel of the lot again, with the stadium glow behind us, did it occur to me that I had just cashed in fifteen years of camaraderie and good will for four quarters of football. To visit again would be merely pathetic, like the students we expel who hang around by the gate after school, leaning on their mud-flecked fenders and waiting for friends or girlfriends to emerge.

Our first day-long seminar was for the Mobile District Schools. We drove down the night before and had sex in the hotel room in front of *Little House on the Prairie.* (Mary had broken her back, and Pa had to sell the farm and work in a mine to amass money for the operation. It was deliciously bad, and we acted in kind.) Rachel rehearsed her introductory remarks, then we ordered a pizza with four kinds of meat. I don't like to rehearse. The appeal I have as a speaker comes from the impression I give of spontaneous thought, of shooting from the hip and heart. Plus I was nervous, and I didn't want Rachel to see that.

We mingled with the teachers over coffee and bagels from eight thirty to nine, and then we were on. Rachel's opening bit went perfectly, exactly as it had in our hotel the night before. We were in a high school theater set up in the round for an upcoming production, and Rachel made use of the long teardrop stage with complete self-assurance, addressing the various compass-points of the audience as if her scene had been blocked out in advance by a technician with Hollywood credentials. She was wearing a red suit with a knee-length skirt, and the beauty of her calves was only enhanced by the bandage around her left ankle.

My role, during her introduction, was to look knowledgeable and click a few PowerPoint slides, but I felt the back of my neck grow cold and tight as I watched her perform. She had her part memorized. I felt betrayed by her excellence. These were the crucial first moments, when the assembled teachers would decide just how much they hated us for stealing a day from their irretrievable lives, and Rachel was going to pass them off to me attentive and optimistic, trusting against all precedent that I had something to offer that would enrich their careers. I reminded myself that insurance salesmen, lawyers, vice-principals, and politicians spoke in support of things they didn't really believe every day—I used to tell my classes that deceiving one another was how most of the human race made its living—but I still suffered a chill of horror when Rachel said, "I'll turn the mike over now to Gary Wilkins, who's going to tell you a little more about what the switch to standards-based education means."

"You're up, hotshot," she whispered as she made the hand-off.

My plan was to focus on a terrifically obese woman in the front row and let myself be guided, as I spoke, by sympathy for her daily trials. She looked heartsick and tired, with her twenty-year-old hairdo. How recently I would have been the one to whom she passed her listless doodles! How recently I would have sat beside her sketching knives and guns and implements of destruction to express my feeble outrage at our subjugation to terminology and cant! I never wanted to return to that world again, that world of chalky impotence and makeshift collegiality, so I opened my mouth and spoke, and what emerged was a rant fueled not by sympathy, but by self-preservation:

"I am truly glad that you have come here today. And I know why you have come. You have come because your principals made you" — a short pause for laughs, and then with all possible earnestness — "but also because you care about learning. You believe that learning is the purpose of life. You are the heads of social studies departments and English departments and math departments, and you teach your students to gather knowledge about the world around them. You are the heads of science departments, that word that means knowledge. You know how to set high goals and inspire your students to crest or supersede them. You are the heads of foreign language. You go home at six fifteen with stinging eyes, and you are tutoring again at seven thirty in the morning because you want what is best for the children in your care; you believe in some way having to do with tradition and endeavor and hope for the future that your life has meaning only to the extent that it serves the lives of others." A short pause here, pregnant with sentiment, the speaker wrapped in private reflection. "But what, you ask, does all this have to do with standards-based education, or SBE, as we'll be referring to it, and what does this man with unstylish eyewear and an off-the-rack suit want from me? To which I say: nothing. Nothing that you don't want yourselves, and that most of you don't already provide for your students. We will be presenting today an array of tools and techniques which may actually make your jobs easier while at the same time satisfying the State of Alabama. I'd like to begin, however, with a personality assessment activity, so if you'll kindly find the peer partner assigned to you on page seven of your spiral binder . . ."

•••

I turned out to be, if not thoroughly excellent, then at least moderately talented at consulting. Rachel said as much on more than one occasion. She had preparation on her side — and organization, and marketing skills, and a better command of recent educational research — but I projected the honesty and human realism that unified our message, that gave it a girth and fizzy essence. I flattered myself that I was the soul, as it were, in our steroidal body of lies.

So we displayed graphs of student success and then stood in line at the bank to split our criminally large remittance. We visited Dollywood to sample the local handicrafts, then wowed Sevier County Schools with a half-day on collaborative learning. And then, some time around Christmas, I fell in love with Rachel. I saw her as a woman who had made the most of a difficult marriage to a man named Galvin, and myself as the man who could wear away the shell of taciturnity which even her students remarked on, and which I had tapped against experimentally in planes, in cars, in the bed we shared, an ineffable stiff sadness that colored all she did. I was attracted to her spartan lifestyle (store-brand shampoo, no cable) and to her oddball interests (collectible thimbles, Antarctica, the history of battlefield tactics). I admired her audacity behind the wheel of a car, the centrifugal on-ramp ascents. We were both over forty, and it was time to choose someone to cling to through the hunchback years, the drug-cocktail and tomato-garden years. But I'm making it sound like I considered the issue carefully before proceeding. I did not.

We were at the funeral of Roland Burgess on perhaps the tenth or eleventh of December, a sunny day with icy, biting winds, winds that seemed somehow cruder because the sun was out. A rotten day to go into the ground. I watched old Roland's easeled flowers get dismantled by the gusts as the pallbearers placed his husk at the frosty grave's lip — Roland, the grand old man of education in our town, forty-five years as a teacher, coach, and administrator, the kind of figure who could tell students about their parents' misdeeds in those selfsame classrooms, who spent whole periods in banter and reminiscence. At the end, in his twenty-second year at MacKinley South, he was back in the classroom, teaching European history and advanced Greek to honors seniors, many of whom were now huddled around the grave in twos and threes in inadequate winterwear. Even Rachel, hung-over and vulnerable and unable to check herself, was crying. Cash Monet found us in the crowd.

"He was just teaching us about Savonarola on Friday," Cash said, weeping lightly. "I think it was Jesus's way of letting us know he was going to call him home."

This is why I liked Cash Monet. He could talk intelligently about the reverence for the carnal in Whitman's poetry and also be capable of the most piercingly beautiful faith in God.

I meant something different than Cash would have, but I said, "We must remember that he hasn't really died." Cash's face broke wide open as he nodded, and for a moment I was holding both Cash and Rachel to my breast.

When Rachel tried to start the car, I put my hand over hers on the knurl of the ignition and said, "I love you. I don't want to be separated from you."

"What—oh, wow." She started crying all over again. She sat there in the bucket seat of the new Chrysler we had bought and caught her grief, or whatever it was, in both hands.

"I've thought about it. I do."

She forced her breathing to resume its normal pattern with a concerted effort, the bridge of her nose held in a forceful pinch. The leather seat squeaked in time with her breath. The wind blew tilted human figures across our windshield.

"I can't talk about this now. Not today," she said, and her hand twisted under mine as she started the car.

Well, it's the second-oldest story in the world, I suppose. The oldest being fucking, and the second—mine—being the confounding of fucking with love. But I did love her. I succeeded in feeling for Rachel the helpless abandonment of self to the whimsi-

cal enterprise of another, and this abandonment didn't feel like a
compromise, and it didn't rankle. I remember arguing with my
ex-wife, Jean—I write her name here—over the way a nine-by-
thirteen casserole dish should be washed and holding my line like
a French infantryman. But with Rachel my ego had been washed
clean. Watching her alter my orders at drive-up windows and shaving my beard on her command helped me achieve the sort of total
selflessness that some people spend years in the lotus position
searching for. But ours was, finally, a contract of depravity, and I,
Gary Wilkins, defender in the abstract of depravity in all forms,
wasn't strong enough to honor it.

What happened next shouldn't have been difficult to predict.
Rachel took me to a Cajun restaurant and told me she was letting me go, bringing Todd Tracey on board. I'll admit I'm still
horrified by the inelegance of the scene—the menus slick with
other people's fingerprints, the tipsy accordion from the jukebox,
the admonition on the door about shirt and shoes. The fact that
the only thing visible in every direction from the asphalt parking
lot was the landlocked terrain of central Alabama. Those were her
exact words: *I'm bringing Todd on board.*

"The hell you are."

"We've been discussing changes and improvements that can be
made."

"Why aren't *we* discussing changes and improvements? That
fairy."

"We want to expand. Launch a website."

"And I'm not the person to do this?" I asked, afraid I was about
to vomit étouffée. "The person who's been knocking them dead
all over the South?"

"You haven't looked at the exit surveys."

If this was a curveball, then it did its job. I didn't even swing as
it crossed the plate. And the wordless half-minute that followed,
during which I thought of several fruitless protests I could make
as someone manhandled cheap dishware in the kitchen, was mutu-
ally understood as my concession. At least she had waited until we

were finished eating, so I wouldn't have to receive the news with my hands mired in shellfish scum.

"This is so awful of you, Rachel."

"You made it awful. You're the one who made it awful."

She offered to drive me to her place for my toothbrush and shampoo, my shaving equipment. I declined. I wanted my toiletries to grow crusts of dust and germs on her vanity, to infect and ravage her the way she had infected and ravaged me.

And so — if I may leave out six weeks of moping, and the schemes of sabotage and defamation I considered, and a couple of reprehensible late-night phone calls to Jean, who is remarried — that's how I ended up at Johnson County High School, teaching three sections of AP English and two sections of expository writing. This is a big building, with hundreds of students whose names I'll never know, and I like it that way. I pee next to teachers with mystery names and mystery pasts. The male students, who are allowed by the administration to wear baseball caps inside the building, all look the same to me, and the girls all look frightened and yielding. Perhaps I exaggerate. A few students in my AP sections show flashes of courage, but they've propped it up with an idealism that is equal parts computer animation and cardboard. On Monday, Teresa Pohlmann, fixing her jet-black ponytail, told me I was wrong to describe the fly in Dickinson's poem as an image of despair and obliteration; it was, instead, an emblem of nature's caring touch in our final moment. God sends the fly to usher the dying soul into heaven, something like that. For once, it didn't seem my place to challenge such tender illusions. Teresa Pohlmann will believe in death soon enough.

Then there are the disillusioned kids, like Steven Casper. Steven slouches and doodles his way through third period, sketching vaginas and muscle cars in the margins of his notebook (there are no notes). I call his mother, and she seems preoccupied by something, maybe Judge Judy or Judge Brown or Judge Mathis. As far as I can discover, the worst blow Steven has suffered is that he's realized he won't be as rich as TV had promised him. But who knows?

Maybe he grew up under a tree in the woods where kids make their own houses and are their own parents; maybe he's learned that everyone is selling something all the time. I took him to the McDonald's across the street to discuss his academic progress, and we ended up having an hour-long conversation about Viking ship-construction as the kids in Playland beaned each other with plastic balls. How the lumber was cured, how the sails were sewn, how directional navigation was accomplished. I ate my deadly fries and listened to Steven. As children yelled and ducked beyond the glass, I imagined our hairy forebears in the prows of those proud vessels, those crafts of timber and hubris, daring the ocean swell in search of something they had never seen before.

Geoff Wyss's first novel, *Tiny Clubs*, will be published in 2006. His short stories have appeared in the *Chariton Review*, the *Seattle Review*, *Mid-American Review*, and *Northwest Review*. A native of Peoria, Illinois, he has lived in New Orleans for the last fifteen years, where he teaches high school.

ALLYS DIERKER

*M*eetings are the worst part of any job; academic meetings are the worst; and if a consultant is running the meeting, you're at least three steps removed from anything good and true. I spend meetings casually detesting the people who called them, doodling to appease my imp of the perverse, or assuming a look of sugary rapture and imagining the lives I might lead if I were a person who insisted on my full measure of human dignity. That's how this story started, as a mental walkabout during a meeting about . . . well, who knows. I doubt the consultants running it could have even said.

Keith Lee Morris

TIRED HEART

(from *New England Review*)

M y journey started in South Carolina, in what's called the
Low Country, along the coast. It would end in an old
Norwegian fishing village on the western shore of Puget Sound.
On my way I was supposed to stop at six locations, always on the
back roads, to pick up packages for a Mr. Griffin, who had called
me one night from New York. Mr. Griffin understood, he said,
that we intended to relocate, my wife and I. He understood that
she would fly to Seattle and then rent a car to take to the small
fishing village ahead of me, and that I would drive out with our
belongings in a U-Haul to meet her there. He understood that we
had sold our car to help pay for the move and that we didn't have
any plans to implement or any opportunities awaiting us once we
arrived. He offered me a pretty substantial sum of money to pick
up his packages, enough money to pay for the entire move and
then some, so that we'd be able to settle in comfortably and spend
some time determining how to get by. I would be paid in full once
I delivered the packages, which I would not be allowed to inspect,
to Mr. Griffin, who would meet me at the fishing village, at a lo-
cation that I would learn when I arrived. Mr. Griffin assured me
that he ran a legitimate business, and he did in fact send paperwork
to support this claim, along with a contract for me to sign. I was

satisfied with the arrangement. My wife knew nothing about it. I wanted the money to be a surprise.

So on the day I was scheduled to leave I drove across the Savannah River into Georgia and then through the small towns and the surrounding cotton fields. It was a dark day with heavy clouds and a steady rain, right at the height of the fall season, when the leaves are their most colorful. The cotton in the fields was ready for picking. The boles were plump like oversized snowflakes, very pretty in the gray light, and many of the fields had already been reduced to stubble, and at the edge of these fields the cotton stood in huge rectangular bales covered with tarps. The roadside was lined with white fluff blown from the trucks, gradually turning dirty in the exhaust and the rain. The U-Haul drove smoothly and was actually much more comfortable than I had expected. I wasn't thinking about how I would miss the South, about how this would be the last time I'd see the cotton fields, because that sort of thing never mattered so much to me. I wasn't the kind of man who spent a lot of time dwelling on the scenery, and I didn't care too much what kind of place I lived in. So I felt fine, rather happy driving along my way.

My first destination was just beyond a small town called Sardis, which had only one street and no pedestrians. The brick-faced buildings looked mostly empty, and the town hub seemed to be a convenience store where a black woman in a polka dot dress pumped gas and two men sat on the curb smoking cigarettes. The town's tallest structure was a storage elevator. My directions, which were very specific, said that I should drive 3.2 miles past this elevator and turn onto a dirt road to my left, into the middle of a wide cotton field. At the left edge of the field, approximately one tenth of a mile from the turnoff, I would find an oak tree draped with Spanish moss. From the base of this tree, I would step off, to the west, six rows of cotton. Between the sixth and seventh rows I would turn into the field, walk twenty paces, and find a package wrapped in brown paper.

It happened exactly that way. There was the package, rain water dripping from the cotton onto its surface. The paper wasn't ruined, though; it obviously hadn't been outside in the rain for long. I looked around the field, but there was no one out there to see, just what seemed like miles and miles of cotton, pretty and white. I picked one of the balls and rubbed it between my fingers. Back in the truck, I placed the package on the floorboard and the cotton on the dash. I checked my timetable, which, like the directions to the locations, was very specific. I had completed the first pickup three hours and twelve minutes early.

My next pickup was just south of Memphis. I drove on across Georgia in the afternoon, and Alabama, keeping to the back roads as I'd been told to do. I'd driven out the other side of the rain, and the sun was shining bright and clear, and a little mist rose off the wet surfaces of the road and the fields. I drove past collapsed barns and auto junkyards and trailers flying rebel flags and pastures with bony horses and acres that had been cleared for timber and dozens of brick country churches. At times, the branches of oak trees leaned over the roadway, brushing the top of the U-Haul. I thought of my wife in a plane on her way to Seattle, and then in her rental car on the way to the small fishing village. My greatest weakness in life for a long time had been that I was madly in love with my wife, and couldn't go very long without thinking of her. I was often a fool where she was concerned. She came from the sort of old Southern family that prided itself on once having been part of the leisure class, and she was used to having things done for her, getting her way. Even when I was on the right side of our many arguments, I forgave her quickly, never waiting for apologies. I was inclined to do virtually anything she asked. When she said, for instance, that she wanted to move away from the South, where we'd both lived all of our lives, to the Norwegian fishing village we'd visited on our honeymoon, which I suppose she thought was a more romantic, interesting place, I agreed. It meant subletting the apartment and giving up my job and starting over, but that was all right. As far as my job went, there was not much to say about it except that it was very routine and not at all difficult, and I was compensated fairly for the mediocre work I performed, meaning I didn't make all that much money.

Crossing the state line into Mississippi as night fell, the open windows sucking up the heavy air, I thought of my wife and how it would be when I arrived at the little fishing village, how I would surprise her with the news of my arrangement with Mr. Griffin, and how we would make love in a quaint hotel room all night and wake to the sound of foghorns, as we had done on our honeymoon. I also knew that it wouldn't happen that way, that instead she would have a number of complaints — she was tired, and it had taken me too long to get there, and she was bored with the quaint hotel room already, and the Norwegian fishing village wasn't all that she'd remembered it to be — and that my arguments would be feeble, and that we would sleep on opposite sides of the bed. But I loved my wife, and I pretended it wouldn't be like that. I loved her because she had pretty red hair that fell in an even line around her shoulders, and smooth pale skin, and because she was much smarter and funnier than I was, and because she could have had her pick of any number of men and had chosen me, perhaps because of my pliable nature.

In the Mississippi Delta there were almost no lights, but there were as many stars as I had ever seen out a windshield. Looking up at them I began to grow sleepy. It had been a long day. I thought I would pick up my package and check into a motel in Memphis. The broken yellow line of the road blurred at its edges. I watched it suck back toward my spinning wheels. To wake myself up I stopped at a convenience store in Batesville and bought a cup of burnt coffee and, back in the truck, tried to call my wife on her cell phone, because she'd asked me to keep her updated on my progress. But there was no answer.

Climbing back into the U-Haul, I looked at the directions for my next pickup. Just beyond a railroad crossing 1.7 miles past the first sign I'd see for the Tallahatchie River, I would take a right turn into the driveway of a white farmhouse. I would cut off the lights and walk down the gravel drive until I reached a white fence. I would proceed through the gate and across the pasture to a soybean field. I would walk between the seventh and eighth rows of beans to the left, all the way across the field, and I would find the package on the seat of an old tractor parked on the other side. This procedure seemed unnecessarily elaborate to me, and I couldn't remember having noticed it when I read over my instructions before I left. And when I arrived at the farmhouse and saw the lights blazing away inside, throwing a yellow glow over this little patch of the huge, dark Delta, I assumed that the farmer must have been waiting for my pickup. The clock on the dash of the truck cab showed 12:44. What else would a man who lived here be waiting up for until that hour? Alongside the driveway was a mailbox, and I thought of how much more reasonable it would have been to simply place the package inside it, or, if there were an arrangement between Mr. Griffin and the owner, how much easier it would have been to simply instruct me to ring the doorbell and ask for the package. But I parked in the driveway and cut off the lights, and while an old beagle barked at me from the fenced-in yard I walked down the gravel drive and swung open the white gate. I had forgotten to bring a flashlight, and I stumbled over the uneven ground of the pasture, which seemed to stretch on forever. Finally I could make out the bean field, and I could see that the bean field, too, went on for a considerable distance, and as I entered it and walked along the rows I began to worry about the time, and how late it would be when I arrived in Memphis, and how I would undoubtedly, now, be wasting my money on a room I could sleep in for only a few hours at best. Even in October there were crickets chirping across the Delta, and I listened to them and to my feet, because there was nothing else to listen to. The place was utterly lost in the night. Finally I came to the other edge of the field and there was the tractor, and there was the package, just as my directions had said. I trudged back all that long way and the dog barked outside again and the lights of the farmhouse were still on, and there was no indication that anyone had even noticed my presence there, the truck parked in the driveway. But I thought it would be prudent to get a little way down the road before I turned on the light in the truck cab and checked my next destination.

Stopped by the side of the road, sipping my coffee, I looked at my timetable. It had seemed easy enough to keep when I'd checked it out beforehand. But now I saw that my next stop was in Dubuque, Iowa, at 7:18 the next evening. The clock in the truck cab said it was now 1:12 AM. My road atlas showed a drive of at least eight hundred miles, and I wouldn't have the opportunity to drive on the interstate, if I wanted to stick to my instructions. But how would Mr. Griffin know if I didn't? What if I just slipped right onto I-55? That would give me time for four or five hours' sleep.

But as it turned out I slept only an hour, right there by the side of the road in the Delta. The night was warm enough that I had to roll down the windows, and mosquitoes whined in my ears, and the dying crickets whirred their anxious song.

Then I started driving again. I stuck to the back roads, as directed. I remembered that package in Georgia, how the rain had barely touched it, how I suspected someone might still be there watching me. And so I drove the winding roads along the river, often with the interstate in sight along the chalky bluffs, and at times I had to take other roads that led me out of my way, winding through the hills. I drove in a near daze past the cornfields in the autumn sun. I shifted around on the seat, and I exhaled loudly from time to time, and I thought of my wife, and for some reason I pictured her lying in bed in the quaint little hotel, playing the "Imagine Alice" game. Alice was the child we'd never been able to have. The doctors disagreed about the nature of our difficulties, but I had more or less accepted the blame, because I didn't like to argue. The "Imagine Alice" game involved nothing more than lying in bed and talking about the routine we would have after Alice was born, after I got over my problems, whatever they were, and helped my wife to conceive. I knew my wife played "Imagine Alice" even when I wasn't there.

Approaching Dubuque, I pulled into a gas station and checked my maps and my instructions. Again, I was frustrated at what seemed like the idiocy of the pickup arrangements. This time, Mr. Griffin had me retrieving the package at a rest area—*a rest area off the interstate!* And yet I wasn't allowed to use the interstate to get there. I was instructed to pull off my narrow two-lane road beneath a billboard advertising a local diner, and to proceed through *three consecutive cornfields* to reach the back side of the rest area, where I would crawl under the barbed wire fence, go to the nearest picnic shelter, and retrieve the package *from the roof of the shelter.* This seemed absurd to me. I had checked all the travel plans before signing the contract with Mr. Griffin, and I was sure that I had never signed my name to any agreement suggesting I climb on a roof. I wondered if, maybe, there were two sets of plans—maybe I had happened upon a provisional set of plans of some sort, for emergency situations, and the simpler, more reasonable set of plans was in the glove box or in my travel bag. I rifled through everything I had in the truck cab, and when that failed I threw open the gate to the U-Haul and checked through our boxes of important papers, thinking that maybe I had packed the real instructions away with other files. But no such luck. I sat there with my legs dangling over the trailer hitch, feeling defeated. The trip seemed long and hard, and I wasn't even halfway there. I had imagined a leisurely drive along pleasant back roads, a chance to take in some of the countryside, which I'd never really paid much attention to. My only worry had been figuring out how to explain to my wife why the journey was taking me so long. But now Mr. Griffin's ridiculous pickup arrangements were making it nearly impossible to keep to my timetable, which was awfully difficult to keep in the first place. I merely drove in a sort of frenzy, troubles and worries seeming to pile up on top of me there in the truck cab, so that I took no pleasure in the various sights, or even the songs on the radio. I tried calling my wife again, and again there was no answer. This time I left a message, saying that I would call again at noon the next day.

So then I humped along through the cornfields, and there were three barbed wire fences to crawl under total, not one, and I had to climb onto the roof of the shelter by dragging a picnic table over and placing a bench on top of it, while middle-aged women at the rest stop stared at me. But the package was there, as usual. I scanned the faces at the Coke machines and outside the restrooms, seeing if I could identify somehow the person who'd put the package up there in the first place. What would I have said? That Mr. Griffin was being unreasonable. That I wanted to talk to him about things. I walked rather shakily over to the front of the rest area and stood there at the top of a bluff while the sun disappeared, looking down at the Mississippi winding its way peacefully along in the purple light. There were boats on the river, a barge floating timber, a paddle wheeler with tourists aboard, lit from bow to stern with white lights. It was soothing to stand there in the cold wind, but I had to get back to my truck.

My next pickup was at 3:36 AM in the town of Worthington, Minnesota. The clock now read 7:32 PM. I had made my Dubuque pickup only by about five minutes. Again I hauled out the maps, and again I found that the schedule left me virtually no time at all for sleep, unless I wanted to ditch the back roads. I'd been driving for a day and a half on one hour's rest. Something had to be wrong; I had checked out the entire itinerary before signing the agreement, and everything had looked easy. I read down the list of my subsequent appointments: Newcastle, Wyoming, 3:13 AM, almost a full day after the next stop in Minnesota; Bonners Ferry, Idaho, 5:26 AM, more than twenty-four hours after I was due in Newcastle. That was easy enough—if I could just make it this one last time, just get to Minnesota without sleeping. But this same thing had happened before—it was always the *next* stop that seemed impossible, not the ones following. They only seemed impossible when it was time for me to go there. I had a thought—what if, when I left the truck to get the packages, the man who had left the packages was getting into the truck? What if, each time, he was substituting a new timetable? That was the only possible explanation. I was locking the truck each time I left it — the packages were just sitting there on the floor in plain view, after all, so I assumed I had to be careful — but it was definitely not beyond Mr. Griffin's capability to talk the truck rental outlet into issuing another key. But five more keys, one for each stop? Or was the same person following me? If so, why couldn't he just deliver the packages to the small Norwegian fishing village himself? But I was too tired to think. So I turned on the light in the truck cab, took my coffee cup from the dash, dipped my finger in the coffee, and very lightly dabbed a spot between the lines of type on the second page of my timetable. It made a perfect little stain, virtually unnoticeable to anyone who wasn't looking for it.

I thought of my wife again. There she was in the fishing village, reading a book out by a dock. She would hear the blast of a foghorn, and a chill would pass over her, and she would pull the sleeves of her sweater over her cold hands for a moment, and look up from the page, and shake her hair back from her eyes. Maybe she would think of me, driving my truck. Maybe she would wonder why she hadn't heard from me. Maybe her phone wasn't working. It seemed unfair that I couldn't be there already, that I hadn't had a chance to talk to her. I thought of the road I had to get back on. I thought of sleeping. I thought of how, if I could only drive on the interstate, I could take a nap in the truck cab and still make it to Minnesota in time. Who would know? Mr. Griffin in his office in New York? I turned off the light and stared down at my map, the spidery lines just visible, slightly translucent from the light that shined on the billboard. The truck cab was cold now. The numbers on the digital clock sent out a faint red glow. Everything — the trash I'd tossed on the passenger seat, the steadily growing pile of packages on the floorboard, the Styrofoam coffee cup in the holder, the T-shirts and socks I'd thrown around haphazardly, the cotton ball I'd placed on the dash — all of these things were as common to me now as my furniture back home, as familiar as my job, my town, my wife. It seemed like I'd lived in the truck cab for months instead of days, and the rest of the world — the night out there, the car lights going wide around me on the darkened road—felt a little threatening. For the first time I started to wonder if something had happened to my wife, if that was why I'd been unable to reach her. I had a hard time thinking of my wife, actually. I noticed that her image came to me indistinctly, that I couldn't quite capture the sound of her voice, and strangely enough that felt natural to me. I had the truck cab; that was mine. But letting that idea sink in made me apprehensive. What if I never made it to the small Norwegian fishing village? What if I really never saw my wife again? What if I were lost out here on the road somehow forever, scrambling over fields and onto roofs after Mr. Griffin's packages, what if the list of destinations simply went on and on and the highways never ended?

These thoughts startled me, and I cranked the engine and got the truck in gear. Right then I made a decision. I would drive on the interstate, agreement or no agreement. I would pull off at a rest area and get some sleep. My thoughts were getting jumbled—sleep was the only way to set them straight.

Soon I was on I-90 heading west, buzzing through the flat Midwestern night. I opened up the engine, laid my foot heavily on the pedal. I drove until my head began to nod, then pulled into a rest area, settled my head on a dirty T-shirt against the seat. When I woke the clock said 12:18. I'd slept two hours. Worthington, Minnesota, was 160 miles away. The rest area was mostly deserted, just a trucker wandering back from the restroom, a line of semis across the way, a few other cars spread out across the parking lot, people sleeping in them just like me. The truck cab was freezing. I blew on my hands, started up the engine, turned on the defrost. While the truck warmed up, I kept an eye on the truckers and the drivers of the other cars, seeing if anyone else was starting up, preparing to leave. When I pulled onto the freeway entrance ramp, I watched for headlights behind me.

Now I ran into serious trouble. I would make it to my stop in plenty of time, as long as there were no delays. But sleep had acted on me like a drug. For half an hour I was fine, but then the desire for more sleep hit me, and I was so overwhelmingly tired that the two remaining hours to Worthington became downright perilous. I drifted onto the rumble strips, crossed the center line. Trying as hard as I could to keep the speedometer up to seventy, I would feel nothing but the pressure of my foot on the accelerator, as if what energy my body had left was being channeled down my leg, and in response my eyes would close, my head would wobble as if my neck were no stronger than a rubber band. I turned the radio up until the speakers rattled, and I sang the songs I knew in a raging shout, and hummed the ones I didn't at such a volume that my teeth buzzed. I rolled down the window and stuck my head out periodically, into the icy wind. I slapped myself continually — my legs, my face — and I jerked my body around in the seat, trying to keep every part of myself moving at once. The lines on the road and the lights of the cars fanned out like ghosts, seeping past their own edges. I nearly wept when I discovered that the truck didn't have a cigarette lighter. It had occurred to me to burn my fingertips each time I felt my eyes begin to close. Instead I punched myself as hard as I could in the right ear, and that worked for a few minutes. I chanted to myself, moving my lips, *twenty thousand dollars, twenty thousand dollars* — that was the amount Mr. Griffin had agreed to. But then I was falling asleep again. My head fell forward and I slapped myself awake again in time to find myself headed straight for a dim figure at the side of the roadway. I jerked the wheel, and the figure disappeared. I looked in the rearview mirror and there was nothing. My heart, though, was awakened by the scare, and pumped blood where it needed to for several minutes. But then I started to doze off again, and each time I woke I was petrified by the thought that something — a creature, a person — had almost jumped in front of my headlights.

Finally, though, there was Worthington, and as I coasted down the exit ramp I was no longer sleepy at all. The town was nothing much — dusty streets and worn-out buildings, a shallow lake at its perimeter. I stopped in a little deserted park along the shore, and took note of the sign that said NO OVERNIGHT PARKING. It was a place I couldn't sleep, in other words, and I knew that I would want to sleep again when I had picked up the package, and I was determined to do so — this time, I intended to make sure my time-table wasn't changed.

To my surprise, Mr. Griffin's directions showed that I had come to the right place. I was instructed to stop right there at the little park by the lake. For a moment I felt almost lightheaded with my luck. Since I had arrived in Worthington more than a half-hour early, and I had already located the package, that meant an extra half-hour of sleep, or maybe even a chance to stop and eat at a place where I could sit down, have someone wait on me. But as I read on I found that the package was *in the water*. I would proceed to a stand of cottonwoods off to my right — I could see their shapes clearly in the moonlight — and standing under them I would look out over the water and see a buoy 150 feet away from shore. The package would be tied to the buoy. The directions did not go on from there to say what I was thinking — that Mr. Griffin was a son of a bitch. The directions just stopped, as if there were nothing unusual about asking a man to swim across an ice cold lake in the middle of the night.

But twenty thousand dollars was twenty thousand dollars, and once I had this package in hand I would be two-thirds of the way there. And according to the timetable the rest of the trip would be easy. This was it, the last real hurdle. So I lifted the gate on the back of the truck and rummaged through my duffel bag to find a pair of clean underwear and a shirt, and I placed them in the truck cab. I took off my shoes and socks and pants and left them in the truck as well, then I locked the truck and carried the keys with me. Looking around, I saw no cop car hidden behind bushes, no car that might have been following me, no one waiting to unlock the truck when I was gone. Still I watched the truck all the way to the cottonwoods, and I was upset to find that, down by the shore, I could no longer see the truck through the trees. The buoy was clearly visible, rocking up and down on gentle waves. The wind seemed to blow right through me, and I almost fooled myself into believing that the water would be a relief. It was not, of course.

My feet plunged through what felt like a skin of ice, and I could not commit myself to going further. And the thought came to me right then — it would be at this very moment, when I entered the water, that Mr. Griffin's spy would make his way to the truck. And so I was out of the water again, hustling up the bank in my underwear, emerging from the trees to find . . . nothing. A car whisked by quietly on the road beyond the parking lot, and I watched its lights round a bend. A tree branch snapped in the wind.

The water at the buoy was not over my head, and I stood chest deep untaping the package, which was wrapped in a plastic bag. The night was crystal clear, and I could see the reflections of stars dance on the water. I was colder than I could ever remember being, but despite that I stopped for a moment and held still. It was so quiet there that I could hear the water lapping at the bank far behind me. Then a train whistle sounded loud and clear across the water; it could have come to me from miles and miles, it could have been anywhere. I felt unusually calm — I wasn't angry, I didn't regret my ordeal. It wasn't embarrassing, to be a grown man out in this lake in his underwear, retrieving a package from a buoy. I felt purposeful, committed to seeing the whole thing through.

Back at the truck I toweled off in the cold air, changed into clean clothes, put on my jacket. I unwrapped the package from the plastic bag, saw that it was undamaged, tossed it on the floor with the other ones. They made a satisfying little pile, a sort of record of my progress and accomplishments. Then I settled in to check my timetable, feeling certain, for once, that it hadn't changed. And, yes, there was the light coffee stain right there on the second page. I was getting warm in the truck with the motor on and the heater running, and my heart beat easily. And so for a moment I doubted what I saw on the page in front of me.

The scheduled stop at Newcastle had been moved up almost half a day. I was now expected to arrive there at 4:32 the next afternoon. The clock in the truck cab said 3:31. I had estimated a trip along the back roads would take about eleven hours. One hour of sleep — that was all I could dare. One hour of sleep and then back on the road in the dark until the sun came up, when I would buy coffee and then more coffee and drive on through the morning past the barns and silos and cornfields and in and out of the dusty towns, the sky like a piece of blue china overhead, and then into the McDonald's drive-thru or a convenience store where I could grab a bite to eat, and then the afternoon that stretched out like an eternity, the part of the day I had come to dread most, when my eyes stayed at a half-squint and my mouth hung open and my head felt full of glue. I would arrive at Newcastle in the nick of time, and then what — another impossible stretch without sleep to pick up the last package in Idaho? For a minute that was all I could think of, just the torture.

Then I started to rebel. To hell with Mr. Griffin's rules, I would just take the interstate again. And more than that — I would sleep as long as I wanted to. I would get a motel room right there in Worthington, sleep until check-out time. I would stop for lunch at an actual restaurant, enjoy a leisurely meal. The package in Wyoming would just have to wait. If it was a matter of such great concern, Mr. Griffin's Wyoming spy could stay there and keep an eye out until I arrived. If, when I arrived at the end of my journey, Mr. Griffin refused to pay me, I would refuse to hand over the packages, simple as that.

But there hadn't been any spy here in Minnesota. I was staring at the same coffee-stained timetable, not a new one that had been substituted. The only explanation for this was that *the timetable had changed itself.* At that thought I felt my spirit of rebelliousness evaporate — it literally seemed to steam out my ears from my brain, and I could feel my body deflate with the loss of some necessary energy. My heart thumped, as if it were desperately trying to refill me, but I couldn't move, couldn't really even think. I felt alive only in the way a tree might feel alive, or a weed. My eyes were fixed on the timetable, expecting it to change before my very eyes maybe, and soon I believed it actually had. A section in bold print seemed to have appeared, something I hadn't seen before:

Violation of the terms of the contract entitles the contractor to reduce or eliminate payment to the assignee, according to the contractor's discretion. In addition, the contractor may seek retribution against the assignee as he deems fit and appropriate, whether said retribution should take the form of the assignation of tasks subsequent to those outlined in the original contract, or, in cases of particularly egregious violations, punitive measures not restricted by extant laws or statutes, which may be leveled against the assignee, or the property of the assignee, or persons legally bound to the assignee, according to the desires of the contractor.

I was close to tears then, there in the truck cab, thinking of my helplessness, thinking of the endlessness of Mr. Griffin's demands, how he would keep me there behind the wheel of my truck hunting down his idiotic packages until I died from exhaustion, or, if he preferred, seek retribution — that frightening word — against my poor wife, according to — that other awful word — his *desires*. But I did not have much time for crying.

Before I got back on the road, I threw open the gate of the U-Haul and rummaged through a box of my wife's things, pulling from it a black blouse I'd bought her for Christmas. Pressing the blouse to my face, I found that I could smell a trace of her perfume, and I closed my eyes and breathed. This was what I needed, something to comfort me as I drove the endless miles. I climbed back in the cab and placed the folded blouse on my lap, and two or three more times as I found a highway heading west I raised the blouse to my face and smelled my wife's perfume, though the scent was already fading.

I grew a little calmer. Mr. Griffin's warning had unsettled me, and for good reason. But as I drove along in the usual way, with nothing more out of the ordinary occurring, I began to feel the idleness of Mr. Griffin's threats. That one phrase, *not restricted by extant laws or statutes,* came back to me. Instead of frightening me, the phrase now seemed to indicate a measure of desperation, and I found myself laughing at Mr. Griffin as I sped along through the night. Surely he didn't expect me to believe that he was somehow above the law, that the normal rules didn't apply in his case, that he had been granted impunity to do whatever he liked. It was a ridiculous threat, an obviously transparent attempt to whip me into a panic, so that I would push myself harder to keep to his ludicrous timetable. Well, I would play along for a while. It was probably best to let Mr. Griffin think that he had succeeded.

For at least a hundred miles I turned these ideas around, and I felt better for them, but a tall figure crossed the road in the nighttime, or I imagined a tall figure, dressed in a long coat and brimmed hat, and while this figure passed by mere feet in front of the bumper my heart stopped and my hands froze to the wheel. I found that my body was absolutely rigid there in the cab, that I had locked up, couldn't move at all, but my eyes could move; they began to close involuntarily. And then there was a bend in the highway, and with a violent jerk my body started up again to make the turn. And then my body went on working by itself, out of fear, while my mind seemed to sleep. My body did what it had to to stay awake, the coffee and the slapping and the singing to late-night radio again.

And then I was past Mitchell, South Dakota, and I began to feel lost. I knew I was on the right road, but I would lift my wife's blouse off my lap, replace it with the map, and determine for the third or fourth time that I was on such and such a highway. My chest felt tight. Passing north of the Badlands along a highway notable only for its long stretches of barbed wire and the occasional eyes of field mice lit up along the road, I began to worry that my heart would stop. It would not be a heart attack, no great seizure and intense pain, just a simple stopping, as if my tired old heart had done all the work it intended to do in the world, had loved as well as could be reasonably expected and then some, and had nothing more to offer me or anyone else.

For long moments during that night I would feel that this was happening, that everything inside me had halted, and I waited for my eyes to close, for the truck to drift slowly off the pavement while I faded to my last unconsciousness. But each time my heart felt like conceding, fear — nothing more — would jolt me backward in my seat, and I would suck in air like a drowning man. I was afraid of dying, even though it seemed like the least complicated way out of my difficulties. I did not want, when push came to shove, for my life to end by the side of the road, in a U-Haul truck wrapped in barbed wire. And I did not want to die and leave my wife in the hands of Mr. Griffin, a man who took pleasure in cruelty, a man who had both the impulse and means to carry out unspeakable tortures, even if I doubted he would do so, upon this woman whom I loved beyond reason. I drove on.

But I had reached a point of nervous exhaustion. With the sun now well established in my side mirrors, and the barest chance of making my destination on time, my wits failed me. The road looked impossibly narrow, and each car that approached in the opposite lane seemed fated to collide with me. The needle on the speedometer kept drifting down, no matter how hard I tried to maintain a steady pressure on the pedal. Soon it stood at fifty, and yet the world seemed to whirl by at an impossibly dangerous speed. As I neared the Black Hills, I still had an hour to make my schedule. It was possible — possible if I pushed the truck far past the speed limit, if I ignored red lights and stop signs, barreled through tourist towns hoping not to hit any pedestrians. This was my plan.

But it was hopeless. The more I tried to hurry, the more my panic grew, until I could barely see the road in front of me at all, and my heart seemed to seize up every few moments, like an engine running without a piston or two. Finally I could not breathe or make my heart beat any more. I skidded the truck to a stop outside a convenience store. Somehow my legs carried me inside to the cooler, where I grabbed a pint of milk with a shaking hand. There were tears in my eyes as I approached the clerk, a teenager who looked shocked at my deranged appearance. My weakness had reached such a point that I intended to give up, to fall on my knees at the register and tell the boy to phone an ambulance and the police. Before I died on the way to the hospital I would tell my story, tell the police to alert the authorities in the small fishing village on Puget Sound, tell them to keep my wife from harm. But I couldn't do that. Calling the police would certainly constitute a "particularly egregious" violation. So I became confused, and stood there at the register in front of a line of customers, muttering the word *dying, dying*. I struggled to reach inside my pocket and my fingertips felt the rough surface of coins, but I could not seem to extract them, until finally my hand jerked upward and the coins spilled onto the floor and I began to sob. The boy behind the counter held up a hand, his face pale, his eyes fixed somewhere around my chest, and I wondered if my heart had exploded through my shirt. "I'll get it," he said. "Just take the milk."

Outside I sat in the gravel and tore open the top of the carton and poured the milk down my throat in a long stream, feeling it run down my neck onto the collar of my coat, until I succeeded in making myself swallow, and then my hand felt more controlled and I emptied the container in long gulps. I felt better, like I wasn't dying after all, and in a minute I was back on the road, pushing ahead to my next stop even though there was no longer any chance to make it on time.

I drove 1.3 miles past the high school football stadium in Newcastle, Wyoming, turned into the parking lot of an abandoned tractor dealership, located the Dumpster behind the building, slammed on the brakes and leaped down from the truck, and climbed into the empty Dumpster to find no package taped to the inside wall, no note, no anything. Wearily, I pulled myself back out and stood there in the gravel. The wind swept with a cold hiss across the dry Wyoming plains, and the sun was high and cold in the Wyoming afternoon sky, and a train that looked like it pulled a thousand boxcars wound its way east off in the distance. And there in the absence of anything I found a reservoir of hope. I was a man, after all, and I was still alive, and I had come all that way, made an almost superhuman effort to drive that truck across the country's narrow back roads in almost no time at all, and I could not be faulted. I grimaced into the bright sky and resolved to settle with Mr. Griffin in my own way. I would speed on to Puget Sound to offer my wife my protection. I realized that it was hours past the time when I had told my wife, on her voice mail, that I would call her again, but I also realized that there was no use in calling now. Mr. Griffin had cut off our communication — how else to explain my wife's failure to answer my calls? But it made no difference; I was close now, it was only a matter of time.

When I reached I-90 and pulled into the westbound lanes I had already devised my new strategy. Something had happened to the package in Newcastle. I had arrived too late, and someone had found it before me. Or it had been withheld by Mr. Griffin's drop-off party because I hadn't met the timetable. Either way, it was clear that Mr. Griffin had much at stake with the packages, and would still be expecting me to pick up the last one, which waited for me in an Idaho town not far from the Canadian border, still a good thirteen hours from now, according to the timetable. He would not make a move until then, because he would risk the loss of the last package. My plan was to take the interstate, which he would surely discover, by whatever means he had discovered it before. But he wouldn't know that I had no intention of picking up the package until I sped right past the turn-off to that little Idaho town, which lay seventy miles north of the interstate. A seventy-mile head start I would have, on whomever Mr. Griffin had sent to meet me. With the U-Haul humming along as fast as it could carry me I felt that heightened awareness peculiar to the best moments in life, those times when one feels slightly larger and more important than the other objects of the world. I churned straight on into the lowering sun, thinking pleasant thoughts of the fishing village and how we would live there happily. We had been there on vacation, and my wife had fallen in love with the fog that draped the hills in the morning and the miles of blackberry brambles lining the quiet country roads and the sound of foghorns over the water. Mr. Griffin seemed remote, as if I had not made a deal with him and he had not threatened me. But I had not slept in a long time. Toward sunset I began to grow so tired that the bare Montana hills seemed to bob before my eyes, rolling down and down and then popping up again in their proper places, as if I were watching a TV screen with a faulty vertical hold. There was no reason not to sleep, really, no reason not to pull over at the next rest area and fall asleep in the cool air next to a picnic table with the dreamy voices of families headed back and forth to the restrooms. I was no longer on a schedule. Nothing would matter until I passed the turn-off to that small northern Idaho town. But my foot held steady on the pedal, and at each opportunity to leave the interstate I found myself moving on.

Without intending to I began to play "Imagine Alice." Imagine Alice being born, the intimacy of the delivery room, holding my wife's hand, the sweat on her forehead, the smile on her face when it was all through and we held Alice close. Imagine Alice coming home, wrapped in warm blankets, to the little house we would have on a hill. Imagine Alice nursing, my wife holding her in a rocking chair on the porch. Imagine Alice going to school, how I would hold her hand going up a sidewalk while my wife sat in the car watching us, calling out last-minute instructions. Imagine Alice on her wedding day, as pretty as her mother.

It had grown dark. I was somewhere in Idaho. At the edge of sleep, I knew I had already passed the turn-off, had failed to notice it somehow. I jerked in the seat, and my hands made the motion of turning, as if I had decided I needed to turn. Then, strangely, I was not on the asphalt any longer, was tilted down into the ditch, and in what seemed a long tired motion, an exhausted and comfortable reclining, the truck turned onto its side as if it wanted to sleep as much as I did, as if it were a tired animal, tired of the incessant beat of its own old heart, and I pitched across the seat and came to rest.

I might have slept for days. I remember first the daylight, the feel of the packed dirt beneath my cheek, and a light rain. Sitting up, I looked across a field at a gravel pit, a huge truck rumbling and clanking. Turning, I found the interstate, a semi roaring past, its wind in my ears, mist hissing up from its tires. Not one of the drivers seemed to notice me there in the ditch, and I barely noticed myself. I merely watched the cars and trucks stream by in colorful waves, and listened to the hissing tires, which sounded oddly like radio static or the whir of electrical appliances. I thought of nothing—not my wife, not the small fishing village on Puget Sound, not Mr. Griffin and the task I'd failed to complete. My sleep had emptied all thoughts out of me.

It was some time, even, before I discovered that the U-Haul was missing. I remembered the crash, the slow and somewhat peaceful tipping of the truck onto its side, and the way I'd seemed almost to float downward to hit the passenger door. But there was no evidence of the crash anywhere. No tire tracks leading from the shoulder into the ditch, no broken glass, no trail left by a tow truck. I walked up and down the area several times, looking for clues, but to no avail. Not one head in any vehicle turned in my direction, not one person seemed curious about what I was up to. Without the truck heater to warm me, I was very cold, and I put my hands into my coat pockets. There I found my wife's black blouse, folded neatly, and the cotton ball. I checked my back pocket and my wallet was gone. I returned to the spot in which I'd slept, hoping to find the wallet there, but what I found instead, pressed flat to the earth where I had lain, was a note on a sheet of stationery. The letterhead read *Griffin Enterprises,* and the note consisted of one word, in bold black ink: WALK.

And so I got on the road again. This second journey would take much longer, and it would be much harder, even, than the first. For what lay ahead of me were the countless miles of ancient floodplain that made up eastern and central Washington, a stark landscape more like the surface of the moon than anything on Earth. What lay beyond that were the fog-shrouded Cascade Mountains, the huge fir trees leaning into the steep slopes rolling up the mountain peaks. Only after I crossed the mountains would I reach Puget Sound, and only after I crossed the Sound would I reach the fishing village, and all the time I would not know what

I'd find there. What lay ahead was the long, dead trek along the shoulder of the interstate. The crunch of gravel and the sift of volcanic ash beneath my shoes would become so familiar that I would dream it ever after in my sleep.

I obeyed Mr. Griffin's command; what other choice did I have? Not only could Mr. Griffin monitor my actions and my whereabouts, he could make large physical objects disappear. What other explanation for the truck? And in case I harbored any doubt, it soon began to seem as if *I* had disappeared as well. I was seemingly invisible to the drivers of the cars on the interstate. No one stopped for me. No one honked a horn. No head turned in my direction. I limped along my way—my right leg had been injured in the accident, and there was a painful twisting to my knee at every step—entirely unnoticed. I came to think of myself as a wandering spirit. And yet not wandering—my destination was always clear.

Since no one seemed at all interested in my plight, even on the first occasion when I became hungry I did not hesitate. I marched into a convenience store next to the off ramp, opened the door to the cooler and grabbed a soda. From one of the aisles I took a bag of chips and a package of beef jerky and stuffed them in my pockets. Walking out, I looked around, and only one customer appeared to notice—she seemed to have heard the rustling of a bag of chips, and was looking on the floor to see if it had fallen.

When I needed a place to sleep, I clambered into the back seats of unlocked cars, or huddled in the corners of service station restrooms or the stairwells of motels. I took whatever I wanted from the stores I passed along the way—food, a warm hat and a warm pair of gloves, cheap tourist items I thought would amuse my wife. In less than two weeks I covered over three hundred miles. I became familiar with the various carcasses of dead animals—the dogs, the cats, the skunks, the raccoons—and the detritus thrown from windows—cigarette butts and fast-food wrappers and dirty diapers and damaged CDs and ragged T-shirts and beer cans and old magazines. In one strange instance I found a gold wedding band just off the asphalt in the weeds, and a little farther ahead a corsage of some sort, but I could never understand the story of how the two were related, though I felt certain they were. I found a hockey stick and a gas mask and a letter from a girl to her mother. And all the time there was the icy, swirling wind kicked up by the semis. Once I reached the mountains there was the sigh of the evergreens, which I could only hear deep in the night, when fewer vehicles were passing.

And I grew stronger. In the end I walked by choice rather than compulsion. It would have been easy to slip into the cab of a semi parked at a rest area. The driver never would have known. But I understood that Mr. Griffin would know. I was not invisible to Mr. Griffin. And yet I felt that, even had I been able to avoid his scrutiny, I would have chosen to continue walking.

I thought of my wife now almost unceasingly, because the miles were monotonous and I needed a focal point. I played "Imagine Alice." And something began to take shape out of my new feeling of resolution — a new kind of relationship with my wife, a sense of possibility for the family we had always wanted. I thought of the months after we first met, how she had honestly seemed to feel passionate toward me, and I thought of how that passion had gone away, though I could not exactly remember the passage between the two feelings. We had passion, and then we didn't. But I began to see that my weakness had created her change of heart. By acceding to her wishes constantly, I had allowed her to become the worst part of herself, and for that she despised me. She selfishly tried to press her own advantage, and when she met no resistance there was nothing left for her but the selfishness and the accusations, and the accusations were really a sort of plea. She needed something to push against, and when she had it she would stop pushing. I felt confident, even, that our infertility would vanish with my newfound strength. I did not think at all, perhaps because avoidance of the thought seemed necessary for retaining my strength, about Mr. Griffin. Mr. Griffin I would deal with when the time came.

On an achingly cold day in November, I arrived on the western shore of Puget Sound via the Bainbridge Island ferry. I took some pleasure in violating the spirit, if not the letter, of Mr. Griffin's law, walking back and forth steadily along the deck while the ferry hummed across the water, the tourists and commuters ignoring me. From the ferry landing I walked a series of quiet country roads, the afternoon sunlight warming me a little. Finally I reached my destination, setting eyes once again on the quaint stores and restaurants and old wooden churches of the little Norwegian fishing village my wife had fallen in love with. And walking up the town's main street, looking out toward the sunlit water where the fishing boats swayed softly in their moorings, and seeing up ahead already, on a hill overlooking the Sound, the quaint hotel I had stayed at on my honeymoon, I thought of how I was only minutes away from seeing my wife again, and I had a clear picture of how it would be when I found her, how she would see me with a new sort of recognition. My legs felt strong and healthy, and my vision was sharp and clear. I carried the power of the journey I'd put behind me, those long weeks of the road and the weather, and I carried the power of my love for my wife. I felt full with this love to the point of bursting.

But as I began to climb the hill I came upon a little park, the waves lapping lazily on a sandy strip giving way to grass and picnic tables. On the closest table a woman lay with her legs spread wide, her red hair fanned out, and a man in a long coat and dark hat stood above her, the coat hiding his rhythmic movements, the hat pulled down to shield his face. My wife and Mr. Griffin, I knew.

I walked toward them, seeing only, for the moment, my wife's bare legs, the whiteness of them beneath her hiked-up skirt, the way her muscles responded to Mr. Griffin's pressure. Then I saw the blotchiness of her skin, the cold, and then her face, red and twisted tight, and the fogging of her breath. Her head turned in my direction, but she did not appear to see anything, her glazed eyes staring somewhere past me toward the buildings of the town.

Mr. Griffin kept up his steady rhythm, his face hidden behind the upturned coat collar, the brimmed hat. I could see nothing of him at all, and yet I knew him, and I knew what the two of them were doing—they were conceiving Alice.

I wanted to kill Mr. Griffin, grasp him in my hands and break him the way I knew I could now, but he seemed less than real to me, an insubstantial figure, an invisibility inside a coat. There was no mention of the packages, delivered or undelivered, and no mention of my payment. There was nothing from Mr. Griffin at all, not even a glance. There was no need for him to tell me that this was my punishment, this my failure, to see him taking his pleasure with my wife there on the shore of the little Norwegian fishing village. I could see now the lengths that he had gone to, the shady plan that he'd devised to take my place. But at the same time, something told me that he himself was nothing but a shadow. Mr. Griffin was not really there. It was only my wife and I, and if I could somehow make myself known to her, I would be the one there with her now.

My heart pumped hard into my limbs and into my head, and I knelt down on the ground and imagined Alice, imagined her harder than I ever had, imagined her as the culmination of the love I felt and that my wife would come to feel, the love we were on the verge of having together. From my coat pocket I took the few things I had collected along my way, and I held them tightly to my chest until I could feel the walls of my heart giving way, and I rose from my knees and stepped forward, closing my eyes to imagine everything better. Keeping my eyes shut, hearing my wife's breathing coming faster, I held my arms out in front of me, held out the life I'd made from those few lifeless items, a cotton ball and a black blouse, bumper stickers and key rings. "This is for you," I said, still walking forward. "Here's Alice. Do you see? She's right here in my hands."

Keith Lee Morris is the author of a novel (*The Greyhound God*) and a short story collection (*The Best Seats in the House and Other Stories*). His stories have appeared in such publications as *New England Review*, the *Georgia Review, Ninth Letter, Puerto Del Sol,* and the *Southern Review,* which recently awarded him the Eudora Welty Prize in Fiction. He teaches creative writing and literature at Clemson University, where he also serves as fiction editor of the *South Carolina Review.*

ANGELA MORRIS

I tend to think my stories through very thoroughly before I commit them to paper—a kind of internal mapping or blueprinting—and I wanted to see if I could break myself of the habit. I started writing a series of stories based on dreams (they now make up a collection tentatively titled Butterflies), *in which I would take some small part of an actual dream and try to work a narrative around it, letting the story go where it seemed to want to all by itself. Sometimes this worked, sometimes it didn't. "Tired Heart" was one of the happier accidents. It started with a dream in which, best I can recall, I was driving frantically over long distances and stopping at times to pick up mysterious objects by the side of the road for no apparent reason whatsoever. For the details of the narrator's trip, I need to thank my father—when I was a kid, his idea of vacation involved relentless and seemingly unending treks along the nation's byways, from which I learned a lot.*

Quinn Dalton

THE MUSIC YOU
NEVER HEAR

(from *One Story*)

Dobi came to help when Martha started dying. Martha had
been sick before, and Ned was used to what that looked
like, her eyes over-focused with pain and then medicine-blank. At
that time, her needs were simple — broth, painkillers, the TV kept
low. His daughters took care of most of it. They were grown and
married, with children of their own, but they took turns sitting
with her until Dobi came for the night, because he was still on the
road then, home only on weekends, his suitcase smelling of hot
pavement and hotel rooms.

Dobi was nineteen. She wasn't a nurse really, just a housekeeper
who was willing to sleep at white people's houses. You couldn't
find many white women willing to stay overnight, and the ones
who would took to stealing the drugs, a pill or two at a time. He
came home from one trip to find Martha sleeping on shit-smeared
sheets. Dobi had never let anything like that happen. She kept the
house smelling of Pine-Sol and starch. She had even graduated
from high school, not typical. Later she told him, when he asked
if she'd ever thought of leaving, that she'd wanted to go to nursing school, but the nearest one was two states away, and she was
the youngest and the only daughter, her brothers off married or

working, and so it was understood she would be the one to care for her parents.

In 1953, the town was hardly a town, but a cross formed by the river and the railroad tracks. Above the tracks were the few commercial streets and the Highlands neighborhood, where he and Martha had grown up and established their own household, and where their daughters lived, now, too. South of the river were a couple of mills and the docks; you could hear the hollow horns from Dobi's house, even with all the windows shut tight, he learned later.

Martha had taught French for twenty-six years and played the piano so well she could reproduce anything she heard without sheet music. She had few faults — a tendency to lose household items like bottle openers or garden gloves or even the occasional bill, and a habit of snacking in the middle of the night when she woke up to go to the bathroom, so she was always plump in the earlier years, though she ate hardly anything at meals. But he had enjoyed these things about her; they made her human, because in every other way she was so gentle and cultured and even-tempered, he had always felt a little beneath her. Not in such a way as to make him want to demean her, the way he'd seen other men put down their wives to remind them who was boss. He was simply mindful that she had come from a better family and in general had better manners and intellect than he. And she was tough — she had held off the disease more than once. But by the time Dobi started tending her, she had gotten tired, as anybody would, the skin of her face and arms slack, her chest a gray drape, her hair and nails yellowed from medication.

Years later, when the boy was old enough, Ned took him to other towns to see minor league baseball games in the summer. Nobody knew them there, and while Alfred was small nobody held them to the colored seating rules. Occasionally, some drunk would ask: *That your shoe-shine boy?* Ned pretended not to hear it, and Alfred, brown eyes shining up at him, did the same. The boy was a watcher, this was indisputable.

The outings continued until Alfred turned eight, and Dobi finally married. Until then, Ned had sent cash so it wouldn't show in his account. Mailing it meant he didn't have to hand it to her on his visits, and it wouldn't need to be acknowledged. It never was.

Dobi's house was a four-room shotgun on the edge of the Johnsons' four hundred acres that Dobi's father and, later, her brothers, sharecropped. Dobi's parents had the bedroom; Dobi and Alfred slept on a cot in the front room, or on the porch, depending on the weather. Ned had no idea how it had worked when her four brothers had still lived there; there weren't even that many chairs around the kitchen table.

When Ned brought ice cream on one of his first visits, they had to eat it right then because there was no freezer. Dobi served it in chipped, rose-patterned bowls. The gold on the rims had mostly flaked away. Dobi's parents ate shyly, smiling almost apologetically as they sipped the melting cream from their spoons. Dobi would not even look at him, but he could still enjoy the boy, happily stretching his mouth for each giant spoonful of vanilla. Dobi ate some, too, but with no expression on her face. Not rude or ungrateful, but as if she were eating alone and had no idea she was being watched.

He didn't think he was saving his soul, doing this. He just couldn't imagine how one could do it differently, in this world, where there were certain places one could sit or not sit, and yet there was also this pleasure in watching the boy's milk-coated pink mouth, his eyes closing and then opening wide with joy. He could take pleasure in this, in the coldness of his own tongue on a hot day, in seeing Dobi receive something from him, regardless of whether she'd wanted it.

She had been out of high school a year when she started caring for Martha. She fed and bathed her, emptied bedpans. One time,

Dobi found him standing with the laundry bucket open, staring at the soiled, clotted diapers. He'd caught an overnight train and hadn't slept. He'd entered the house quietly, knowing from the white flash of sheets on the backyard line that Dobi was there. His daughters left the washing to her. He told himself he was slipping in to make sure Dobi was acting right even when unsupervised, but in truth he had done it to avoid being confronted immediately with the bustling energy of someone who had come there to work. Martha had become someone's job, but, standing silently in the kitchen, he'd wanted to pretend for a moment that this wasn't the case, that she was only napping, and soon she would get up and finish potting plants and make him dinner.

Then he noticed the laundry bucket sitting at the end of the hall; Dobi had probably carried it from the bedroom and was planning to take it to the basement to wash. He heard her quietly talking to Martha. He could not discern the words, just the soothing, comforting tone of her voice — it could have been Martha, rocking one of their daughters to sleep. Overcome with this memory, he leaned without thinking to open the laundry bucket. The force of the smell dizzied him. Just then, Dobi stepped into the hall. Without a word, she picked up the bucket and carried it away, and he never saw it again.

He got used to seeing her, yet sometimes he was struck by her foreignness in his house. The house over time had become an extension of Martha: the pastel walls, the softly curved couches, the powder-gray carpeting, the quiet interrupted in their later years only by her piano playing, while she could still do it, and by the evening news. In contrast, Dobi moved like a pencil line through the rooms, dark and precise. Her short waist emphasized her long arms and legs and her small, high breasts. The skin on the backs of her arms and her collarbones shone, as if she'd rubbed in some kind of oil.

She lived there more than he did for two years; that was the truth. When he was on the road, he was a heartily laughing salesman of industrial tubing. He'd come home, sometimes after traveling all night, weak and silent with exhaustion — he couldn't do it much longer, he knew; it wasn't the adventure it had once been — and Dobi would fix him a meal and tell him things about Martha. Good things. "She sat up for two hours," Dobi would say. Or, "She fed herself half a cup of pudding." As if Martha was a friend accompanied to a movie, or shopping — not a dying woman whose pension paid for as much comfort as could be delivered. Dobi meant to be encouraging, he knew, but Martha's small victories were only a signal of smaller ones to come, until there were none.

The doctor prescribed morphine during the final weeks. He came and taught Dobi how to tie off the arm with a strip of rubber, slide in the needle. When Dobi left the room for a moment, the doctor turned to Ned. The pink skin around his eyes was puffed with fat. "We can send out a nurse," he said.

Ned looked at Martha, her eyes closed as if sealed now, her arm stretched over the folded lip of the sheets, palm up, as if testing the air for rain. "She's been with us two years," he said. "Martha's used to her." Strange, he thought, to talk about what Martha was used to — she hadn't spoken a word in over a year at that point.

One morning when he came home from traveling all night, Dobi made eggs and sausage and toast. It was when Dobi was staying six nights a week, even if one of his daughters could be there, too, and right after the morphine started — this was how he'd begun to measure time. She said something about Martha's medication, how she'd started giving two smaller doses rather than one large one and now Martha seemed more comfortable. He said, "You should study to be a nurse. You're smart enough, surely." He'd meant it as a compliment, but Dobi's calm face didn't seem to register any pleasure at his recognition of her intellect.

He wanted to say that he respected learning; after all, he'd offered to send both his daughters to college, and few girls from their town had had such an opportunity. "Well, their mother, being a teacher, insisted they go past high school even though we didn't have the money back then," he said. Nelda, the older one, had gotten her teacher's certificate, though she hadn't used it, getting married right after college to a salesman. She joked that she'd repeated her parents' lives, while Elizabeth had married right out of high school to an electrician. That had been the only time he remembered his daughters not getting along, because Elizabeth had wanted her best friend to be her maid of honor instead of Nelda. Maybe also because Elizabeth was younger and married first. He didn't know; it had blown over, and Nelda had been her maid of honor after all.

Dobi turned cold water on the hissing frying pan. "There's a school for nursing, but it's too far." She began scrubbing and said nothing else. So he asked how she got the name Dobi.

"That's not my given name, it's just short for Deborah," she said.

"Your mother's pet name for you?"

"What her boss lady called me. But it stuck," she said.

He rose from the table. He felt that whatever he said was wounding her, but he wasn't sure; he was just so tired, and dreading walking in to see Martha, and hating himself for dreading it. "How is she?" he asked, feeling foolish, as if there could be any change for the better.

"She's asleep," Dobi said.

"I bought you something," he said, suddenly, though he had not bought her anything at all. She didn't exist for him when he wasn't home, he realized. And when he thought of Martha, he didn't see her gray-faced in her bed, which had been their bed, but twenty, thirty years younger, dressing for church, leaning forward, settling her breasts into a brassiere.

Dobi took his plate. "You don't need to buy me anything, now."

"But I did. I bought it the last trip and forgot about it." He was surprised at how casually the lie came to him. "It's still in my suitcase." He picked it up from the foyer where he'd left it and carried

it down the hall to his room, which had been the girls' room. He
slept in the twin bed closest to the door, under a flowered spread,
when he was there. Dobi napped in the guest room, he supposed,
though he had never actually seen her asleep.

He put his suitcase on the twin bed next to the wall, opened it,
and walked quietly across the hall to Martha's room. He hoped
Dobi hadn't heard him, as she was still cleaning the kitchen. He
slowly closed the door behind him, leaving it cracked as it had been
when he'd come in, and waited for his eyes to adjust to the dark.
The brocade curtains were drawn, but a seam of light showed
along one side. Martha was propped on several pillows, her knees
propped, too, under the blanket. The bedside table was lined with
white cloths, on which rested brown glass bottles, a case of sy-
ringes, a special drinking glass with a top so it wouldn't spill.

He could barely discern the rise and fall of Martha's chest. The
bridge of her nose was the only smooth part of her face, the skin
white as bone. He leaned down to kiss it, and breathed in her medicine and talcum-powdered scent. Then he turned to the wardrobe, which had been her mother's, and drew from the bottom
shelf the hand-painted jewelry box he'd bought her in Germany
before the war.

He found the necklace in the purple velvet box with white satin
lining in which he'd first presented it to her, a few months before
they'd become engaged. It was a hair-thin gold chain with a single
pearl framed by two gold beads. He'd given it to her for Christmas,
and her delight had signaled he should take the next step. He'd always been a cautious man, a man who watched for cues from other
people, and he believed this was what had made him successful in
sales. He wasn't prematurely aggressive. People appreciated that.

He didn't realize he'd been looking for that necklace until he'd
seen the box. The chain rested light and cool as a line of water on
his knuckles. It would look completely different on Dobi. Instead
of receding so that only the faint outline of pearl shone at the
hollow of the throat, as it had on Martha, it would glitter against
Dobi's skin, the way her teeth seemed to glow behind her brown

lips. He worried then what might happen if one of his daughters saw her wearing it, but he decided he would just tell them in advance that it was his decision to give a gift from the family. They might be angry but they couldn't defy him.

Martha had told him once that she wanted to be buried in that necklace and with her simple gold wedding band. "You should pass the engagement ring on," she said, not specifying to which daughter, "or sell it. Or keep it. But the necklace was the promise, when we decided. Wasn't it?" she'd asked, and he'd nodded, of course, though he didn't clearly remember knowing he would marry her until after he'd given it to her.

Then she'd said something unexpected. They'd been married thirty years at that point. They were in their early fifties; she'd beaten back the first wave of the disease. He hadn't wanted to see her sick or in pain, but he did feel a last remaining veil had been peeled away, and in some way he knew her better, and he was grateful to have known her, even in her worst moments.

She said, "I don't know if there is a God. Maybe I'll just rot in the ground."

He looked at her, and perhaps she could read the alarm in his eyes at this casual questioning of her faith.

She put her hand on his. "Don't you ever wonder? Like the composer — who was it? — who said he was driven by a music he could never quite hear?"

God, for Ned, had been planted as firmly in the heavens as the yellow sun in a child's drawing. He could see God, or the idea of Him, hovering over his town like the deepest blue rim of atmosphere, the edges indefinable, but there. The idea that she might not see such a thing, or her own imagination's equivalent, terrified him for a moment. He felt it, looking at her quiet smile, unable to respond, thinking of the years they had sat in the same pew at First Methodist, and how he had taken comfort from that too, the ritual, the knowledge that they had done everything anyone would expect to receive God's mercy now.

The necklace still in his hand, he remembered this. He couldn't think of a substitute, couldn't spend too much time looking around or Dobi would know he had not told the truth. He had not realized until this moment that when Martha had asked him to bury her with the necklace, he had silently refused. If he outlived her, he would have to relinquish her. But he wouldn't give up anything else.

To keep it also seemed absurd, and it wasn't possible to give it to one daughter without causing calculations between them. He found an empty, newer velvet box and slid the chain into the card's two notches, so that it hung in a little *V.* He closed it with a muffled click, and Martha sighed in her sleep. He put away the jewelry box and closed the wardrobe and slipped quietly from the room.

Dobi was drying dishes when he came back into the kitchen.

When he handed it to her, she seemed surprised by the box more than what was inside it, he thought. She shook her head, confused.

"Go ahead," he said. He felt shaky, even giddy, as with the first time he'd given it.

Dobi opened the box, bent her head to look at the necklace. She touched the pearl with her fingertip. Then she looked up at him smiling, but it was an apologetic smile. "Mr. Dawson, I can't take this."

"I want you to have it."

"I think—" she stopped, took a breath. "Ms. Martha showed it to me once. I know what you mean to do, and I thank you, but it don't have to be that."

She had saved him. She could have rightly claimed offense, pointing both to his lie and to his disloyalty to his wife, but she didn't. She acted as if she hadn't heard what he'd said before about buying something just for her.

He bowed his head as she closed the box. He had bought it less than a mile away, at Stimson's Jewelers. He had kissed Martha after draping it gently around her bare collar bones. He was surprised, now, to realize that he was crying when Dobi put the box in his hand. The tears rolled down his nose and hit his leather loafers. He felt as if he could lie down on the linoleum, in the worn spot where they now stood. He felt as if he was seeing his life, his time on trains and in conference rooms, in leather chairs around dark wood tables, all designed to lend importance to meetings where numbers were debated and agreed upon, while his wife faded and his daughters lived their own lives. He'd been gone so much that he wasn't needed at all; they had gone on without him.

Dobi put her arms around him, and he was too grieved to be surprised. Maybe she made love to him to forgive him, there on the guest room bed, while Martha slept across the hall. Maybe, he thought later, had she been a few years older, she would've realized that there were plenty of sad old white men in the world, crying over their losses — wives, money, some perceived status — and that these old men would believe that, because they'd had more, they'd lost more than other people. She might have known how to comfort him without giving herself. He was sorry for it, sorry he had taken.

Later, after Dobi had dressed and left him sleeping, he'd found the velvet box on the counter where he'd set it. He'd slipped it back into the hand-painted jewelry box. He showered before kissing his wife goodnight.

Martha died two months later, and Dobi spent six nights a week at the house as usual until the final night, and during that time, they did not speak of what had happened. Ned attempted to apologize the next day, but Dobi had pretended not to hear him, and then had asked if he would go to the pharmacy for more morphine or call the doctor to have it delivered.

Dobi told him she was pregnant when she came to clean up after the funeral. It was winter, the rain distinguishable from the low gray sky only by its sound on the windows and bushes outside, quiet tapping.

He had offered her a job coming once a week to do laundry and clean. The way she'd answered him — those two simple words — without any further explanation, made it clear what this news should mean to him. And then he could see it, the way Martha's apron with the yellow ruffled edging puckered at her waist, the green-and-yellow flowers drawn tighter. Martha had made it from a faded bedsheet, doubling it so that the flowers on the inner ply showed through, shadows of the front pattern. The apron was as old as his daughters, maybe older. He had been standing in almost this exact spot in the kitchen, just home from work, when Martha had told him of her own first pregnancy, which had ended in miscarriage.

A collar of panic tightened around his throat. He wondered if Dobi's mother had known Dobi was pregnant when they'd come to the funeral home during visiting hours. He figured she'd had to have known, but when he searched his memory for any expression or gesture on her part that might have indicated it, he could remember nothing. He had barely paid attention to anything, letting his daughters handle all the arrangements, all the greetings.

He watched as Dobi placed two cardboard boxes on the kitchen table next to a laundry basket full of clothes pulled from Martha's dresser drawer. There were her slips, nightgowns, the pastel jersey tops that he hadn't seen in years. He pretended for a moment that he did not understand the reason she was telling him. "What will you do?" he asked, as one might ask any unmarried young woman who was "in trouble." He knew abortions could be had. Or perhaps she would give it up for adoption. Or perhaps she would miscarry, as Martha had the first time, and he felt a mean stab in his stomach for hoping it.

"What I been doing," she said. She was folding Martha's winter sweaters now. Why had she come back? he wondered. He assumed she was there to ask for money, an ongoing stipend. He would pay what she asked, he decided. "Staying down with my parents," she said then, as if to clarify what continuing in her previous life might mean. There was an edge to her voice that he had not heard before, the tone of a woman who had determined her future.

She turned away from him then, and crouched to retrieve a box of mothballs from under the sink, and he knew she didn't want him to ask anything more. She would finish that day and carry his wife's clothes to the Salvation Army when her father came in his truck to pick her up, and he would not see her again.

But now that it seemed clear she wouldn't ask him for anything, he wanted to express some kind of concern. "How do you feel?" he asked.

She rose to her feet again, mothball box in hand. "As good as can be," she said, turning to him, lips pressed into a line, and what he saw in her eyes was sadness and a kind of sympathy, which he did not understand, since it was her life that had been carved as clean as the table edge she leaned on.

But it was a small town. He heard from Clark the yard man first. Clark was white, retarded — you could see it in the open-mouthed slowness of his thought before words came, or when he poured gasoline in the mower, waiting until long after the container emptied to lift it from the spout. "People say a white man sired him," he said, his gaze sliding from Ned's face to his trembling fingers as he tore a match from a book, striking carefully to light his cigarette. Ned watched the slow progress in horrified silence. Clark raised his head again, blew out smoke. "But that nigger boy's as dark as his mama."

Ned had come out to pick up his paper. He squeezed the roll in his hand, the newsprint soft with late summer humidity. "Why are you telling me this?" He watched Clark's face carefully, trying to read the older man's twitching face as he dragged on his cigarette.

"She worked for you, is all," he said. "Thought you'd wanta know that's why she ain't showing up no more."

Ned thought the man was sincere. He hoped it. His heart squeezed in his ribs; every breath felt like a gasp. "She stopped coming here after Martha died."

Clark bowed his head again, nodding, and Ned was conscious of his pale ankles showing below the hem of his pajamas. "That's fine," he said, as Clark mumbled some form of apology for forgetting — his memory had never been good — and then he patted the man's sweaty shoulder, his own shoulders shaking. "That's all right," he said, before turning back to his silent house.

He did not sleep well when he wasn't on the road. His house seemed sealed off, breezeless that fall, even with all the windows open. His daughters invited him to meals, sending him home with casseroles, bread wrapped in wax paper. They never stayed long when they visited.

He began driving past Dobi's house in the early mornings, after he'd been awake for hours but the gray light was just beginning to reveal a slumping screen or the crazed pattern of sun-aged paint. He knew where she lived because he had taken her home on a couple of occasions if her father couldn't get out of the fields during harvest.

What made him finally stop his car was being seen. He'd come later than usual on a Saturday morning, driving slowly from the train station. An old woman sitting on her porch across the street from Dobi's house stopped her work, a knife poised over the white potato flesh in her hand. He felt her eyes on him as he parked next to a ditch and crossed the patchy yard to knock on the door.

He realized as Dobi opened the door that he had brought nothing for her. It seemed he should have brought something. It was the kind of thing Martha would have remembered, and his face burned, thinking of what Martha might do, knowing why he was there.

He tried to think of what to say as Dobi regarded him from the other side of the screen. By then, only the pines held any green, sunlight slanting almost white through bare branches, and, behind them, the yellow glare of field. Through the blur of screen mesh, her unmoving face looked like a photograph. Finally, she opened the door. "He's sleeping," she said. Her face was softer, her hair smoothed back into a bun at the nape of her neck instead of the girlish braids she'd worn the last time he'd seen her. It had been nearly a year. He thought she looked five years older but somehow more beautiful.

"I'm retiring this year," he said, just to have something to say as he sat in the arm chair Dobi had indicated. "Forty years in, nearly, and they told me it was time."

Dobi sat across from him on a bedsheet-covered couch, the pattern like one of Martha's aprons. He wondered for a moment if she'd kept anything. He had buried Martha in the pearl necklace and her wedding band after all. He had kept the engagement ring, and neither of his daughters had asked for it yet. He figured it was just a matter of time before they did — for that and the other jewelry still closed in the dark wardrobe.

Dobi asked after his family and he nodded. "They're fine. Elizabeth's pregnant with her third. Causing quite a stir." As soon as he heard himself, he wished he hadn't said anything about it. He wondered where Dobi's parents were — her father's truck was gone; he wouldn't have stopped otherwise. He imagined her mother in one of the dark back rooms, listening.

Dobi nodded. She straightened the tatted lace doily on the coffee table between them. Finally, she said, "People are going to ask why you're here." Her eyes flicked to meet his and for that moment she looked like the girl who had proved smart enough to be a nurse, quick and capable. Then she looked back to the doily, and it seemed she had nothing more to say to him, now that she had warned him.

He wanted to say that perhaps he'd long overestimated his life, his standing in town and in church, because these days he didn't feel as if he had much ground to lose. What would be the effect if people did know? His own daughters regarded him as a responsibility; his boss, younger than him, masked pity in statements of admiration for his years of service. Sometimes he looked at his hands to make sure he could still see them.

Then, in one of those darkened bedrooms, the boy cried out.

Dobi stood as her mother appeared in the hallway, holding the squirming child, who was wrapped in a blue blanket. "He's hungry," she said, and Dobi did not say a word as she took the boy from her mother and left the room, closing the door behind her.

Her mother nodded to him. It was a respectful nod, asking Dobi's leave, but also a good-bye. He realized, from her hands clasped at her waist, that she hoped he would not return, and as he replaced his hat and left, he felt sure he would not.

But he came back the following spring, when the boy was six months old. Alfred was babbling on his grandmother's lap when Dobi let him in. He chose a work day again, wanting to avoid the father.

For Christmas he had sent a toy truck made of red-painted metal, with a steering wheel that actually turned the rubber wheels. He'd never bought toys for his daughters; that had been Martha's department since she was around them more and could better assess what they wanted or needed.

If he'd had sons, he might have shopped for them on his travels. But dolls were dolls. The truck had thrilled him; he'd driven it on the living room carpet, carving narrow-gauge circles in the nap.

"What's this?" Nelda had asked, pointing at the carpet, when she came the following afternoon to dust and clean.

"Beats me," he'd said, turning from her gaze.

He packed the truck in a brown box with a twenty-dollar bill and mailed it from the next town, where no one would recognize the address. After that, he sent twenty a month. He didn't know what it cost to feed and clothe babies anymore. It was something.

The truck was perhaps what gained him an audience the following spring. He saw it on the mantel, gleaming, spotless, the morning Dobi let him in. Her mother was an older, smaller version of Dobi, branch-colored lines at the corners of her eyes, which were brown with a hint of yellow-green. She smiled at him and offered coffee.

"Yes, thank you," he said.

She handed the boy to Dobi, who reached for the truck on the mantel. "He likes it," Dobi said. She had two lines starting around her eyes, just like her mother.

He told her about his retirement party. "They held it at the VFW and gave me a plaque," he said. He laughed and shook his head. "Got it in my sock drawer now."

"You should hang it," Dobi said. She looked down at the boy, who was tugging on her collar. Then the boy twisted in Dobi's lap and leaned toward Ned, arm outstretched.

"He wants my pen," Ned said. He was still in the habit of slipping one in his shirt pocket before going out. He held out his hands. Dobi looked at them for an instant, as if not knowing what he was asking, but then she let him take the boy.

He had held Elizabeth's newborn girl a few days before. This had been what prompted him to come, that warm weight in his hands. The boy reached immediately for the pen. Dobi made a noise as if to stop him. "He won't hurt anything," Ned said. Clark had been right; the boy was as dark as his mother. But he had Ned's mouth. Having dragged the pen from Ned's pocket, he brought it, clutched in both fists, to his thin lips and grinned. Ned held the pen back from the child's mouth with one finger. "He's got two teeth," he said, and Dobi smiled proudly, her reserve slipping for a moment.

Her mother was just bringing the coffee when they both froze and turned toward a sound on the gravel road. It was a truck, slowing to pass Ned's parked car. Ned could not even tell its color through the breeze-shifted curtains, but when Dobi and her mother looked at each other, he knew who it had to be. Dobi reached for the child, saying he needed to be changed. Dobi's mother stood in the doorway to the kitchen, facing him, but he knew she wanted somewhere else to go, too. Ned decided he had no choice but stay right where he was. He burned his mouth taking too large a sip of his coffee as he heard the scrape of boots out front. He put down the coffee and stood when Dobi's father came in. He knew the man's Christian name of course; it was customary for a white man to address a colored man of any age as such, but Ned chose to say nothing more than "Afternoon." He did not smile or extend his hand; the normal niceties seemed at that moment more of an offense. He wondered if someone had alerted Dobi's father of his visit, or if the only preparation he'd had was seeing the car parked at the edge of the yard.

Dobi's father wore thick trousers and a jacket zipped to his throat. He held a pair of work gloves and a billed hat in one hand. He was taller than Ned, but narrower, and Ned realized Dobi had gotten her height from him. Dobi's father ducked his head, as if to make up for the difference in their height, and when he spoke to Ned, he looked only in his direction, not straight at him. "I was sorry to hear about Mrs. Dawson."

Ned looked at his polished dress shoes. Even in death, Martha had saved him. "I didn't deserve her."

"We don't know what we deserve." He switched the gloves and hat to his other hand, asked his wife for a couple of water jars. "I'll be outside," he said, nodding to Ned again, leaving the door cracked behind him. Dobi's mother was already clattering in the kitchen, then bustling past him with the jars. She came back in quickly, glancing toward the back rooms. If she had sat, Ned would have, too, but she remained standing.

"She gonna have a time with that baby," she said, as if to herself. Then she looked up at Ned, and said, as if to explain, "He never wants to sleep. Child's worried he might miss a single second."

He stayed away a while after that, but sent money every month and visited every six or so. He knew nothing would be said if he stopped. He had not been held accountable in any way. Not a word had been said to him, no rumors reported. But the thing he had not expected or feared happened. He loved the boy. He thought about him daily, wondered what he might be doing. On a visit the spring after Alfred turned three, he asked Dobi if he could take him fishing. She was cutting a dress of red calico. She had put on some weight, which she carried in her hips, like her mother. She looked up at him from the kitchen table, pins in her mouth, scissors in her hand. For a moment, he saw her fear, quick as the glint of metal in the afternoon sun as she stabbed straight pins into a cushion. She was afraid he would kill the boy. And there would be nothing to be done.

"Dobi," he said. "At night my knees ache so bad I dream I'm running on them. All I want is something to look forward to."

"You have your grandchildren," she said, scissors tight in her fist. She was right. He had five now, all girls. Would the boy have mattered to him if even one of his had been a boy? He'd stopped sending toys because, other than the truck, he never saw them on his visits. He wondered if it was because they didn't want to have to explain them, or didn't want to confirm anything that might be said about the boy's parentage.

"I'm his father," he said, coffee bitter in his throat. They looked at each other across the cut cloth, the color deepening to maroon in the lowering sun, the boy yelling outside, running across the yard with a pack of other children. What was said about his blue Buick, which he washed every Saturday, showing up on the edge of their front lawn once every few months? The boy turned, recognizing the car. He slowed, looking at the house, and then ran faster to catch up. His arms flashed as fast as the spokes of a turning wheel.

Dobi set the scissors on the table and told him when he could pick the boy up, speaking so quietly he could barely hear her.

Summers they went to baseball games in Pendleton or fishing. If it was too wet or cold, he took Alfred to one roadside diner where there was a sympathetic waitress. He always went in first to make sure she was there. The first time, with Alfred waiting in the car, he'd told her the boy was an orphan. It was a necessary lie, but it had pained him, and the waitress had misread it. Her face softened. "What a good Christian you are," she said, her eye following the line of his arm to his ring finger. He still wore his ring then. Her brows drew together in momentary disappointment. "It's through my church," he said, carried away. He always tipped well.

Once, during one of those diner visits, where the boy could eat up to six grilled cheese sandwiches in a sitting, Ned asked what he wanted to be when he grew up.

"A pilot," he'd said. He bit into his sandwich, his pressed fingertips white as the bread.

Ned watched the rain slide down the windows like grease. "You've got to do well in school for that," he'd said, and nothing more.

The boy always addressed him formally — "Mister" or "Sir." But on that occasion, he watched Ned sip his coffee, a question in his eyes. "Who are you?" he'd asked.

"Just an old man," Ned said.

"But who are you?" The boy was six then, and trying to put things together.

"You mean my name?" He said it, surprised.

The boy looked up at the stained ceiling and laughed. "I mean, are you my cousin?"

Ned looked down at his coffee. He could see his face reflected in the oily surface, as if far away. "Yes," he said. "Cousin and friend."

Then the boy laughed so hard Ned thought he might choke. But he was fine, and Ned laughed too, until a man in a booth across the room from them turned to look. He was a traveling salesman, Ned could tell from the thick valise on the opposite bench. Ned thought to ask him what he sold; he thought of sharing traveling stories, but then the man fixed a mean smile on Alfred, and Ned touched the boy's arm. Alfred became silent immediately, his laughter fading to blank watchfulness like a television unplugged, and Ned knew the boy understood more than he let on. He was sorry for it, but relieved, because he didn't want to explain.

When Dobi married, Ned knew he wouldn't see Alfred as much, maybe only rarely, but he was shocked to learn that they'd moved. Not just a few miles down the road, but to the next state in a fast-growing area, where the new husband had found a job in construction. It was Dobi's mother who had told him of the wedding plans when he'd stopped by to find only her there, canning in the steaming kitchen. He'd sent extra money that month, and a note saying congratulations. It was her father who informed him, when he came for a visit a month later, that they were gone.

"Where can I?" Ned began. "How should I?"

"Dobi asked me to say you don't need to send nothing," her father said mildly. He stared out past him, as if watching the horizon to gauge what weather might come.

His daughters helped him around the house for the next couple of years, then moved him to a nursing home when he fell and broke his hip. He had refused to use a cane even though his knees had gotten so stiff that he toppled easily. The facility had been built to look like an antebellum mansion. The residents were almost all black; the staff was divided — a few black doctors, white and black nurses and attendants. At first it had been a shock to find himself in such a mix, but he had assumed the role of jovial salesman among them — hearty hello's, polite "Yessir's" and "Yes ma'am's." In this twilight world where many of his fellow residents were simply waiting to die, the old divisions seemed to have fallen away.

He sat on a rocking chair on the porch each morning and read the paper, every word of it. Almost every day he thought of how for most of his life he'd barely had time to scan the headlines, and he often mentioned this to whomever happened to be nearby while he was reading. He knew he was repeating himself, but it was satisfying somehow, and so he gave into it. He could still drive, and he still had his mind, even if his repetition made people question his faculties. In some way he liked the faltering glances of his daughters when they visited on Sundays after church, bringing lunch with them. He was no longer something to be taken for granted. They watched him carefully, trying to detect some degree of decline. He appreciated the attention.

Collins was her new last name. He'd found this out not long after she'd left, but had not acted on it. Now that he was settled, and had time on his hands, he figured it was time.

He went to the library to find them. The place smelled of ink and glue and mold and reminded him of his school days. His boyhood seemed to be a memory belonging to someone else; something he might have read about.

The librarian set stacks of phone books in front of him to his left; on his right was the stack he'd finished with. He did not believe he was going to die soon, but he did not know how much longer he would be able to drive. He'd found that things you took for granted could be nipped away, and faster than you'd think. He'd thrown away his plaque, let his daughters divide his household. He kept a picture of his wife on his bedside table, his cane in the corner. He had nothing of Dobi or Alfred except the slip of paper with their address written in his hand in the library, the shaky script of an old man.

Then he studied maps, planning the best route. He decided not to call. He didn't want to be told not to come; he preferred to be turned away at the door, if it came to that, cane and all.

When the boy answered the door, they knew each other. He had that white man's mouth. Not full, but thin as a newscaster's, with a dip in the middle of his upper lip just like Ned's. The boy was taller than he was. He wore a red T-shirt and tight blue jeans; his hair, wavy, not kinky, rose in a dark cloud from his temples.

"How old are you, now, son?" Ned asked, smiling at their mutual recognition. He wasn't as nervous as he'd thought he'd be. He felt triumphant, actually. The old rhythms of the road had come back to him; the smell of bleach in motel sheets, the paper-wrapped cakes of soap. He felt clean, even after a day of driving with the windows down.

"Seventeen." The boy's face was long and angular, like his own, but his eyes and nose were Dobi's.

"You still in school?"

The boy stared hard at him. "Which school you mean?"

Ned didn't know what he was being asked. The boy could read his confusion. His smile was a sneer. "They gave the nigger school to the primary kids," he said. "But they're saying no breathing white person gonna let us in that high school."

He was an old man; he could feel it in the weight of his joints; the slowness of his mind. Years before, the salesman in him would have been ready with a friendly comment or joke to take the edge off the moment. *I'm your father,* he wanted to say. A father at fifty-eight, and then not a father. Not held as such, to his relief. A price for that, though, even so. "I didn't come here for a lesson, son," he said, a sudden rage thick in his throat.

The boy laughed at him. He laughed so hard he had to bend over, or made a show of doing so. But even in such contempt, he sounded joyful.

"Who's there?" Ned heard Dobi say. Then she was at the door, stepping around Alfred's still doubled form. Her hair was cut short and turned under at the edges, professional. She wore a suit jacket and skirt, and stood his height in her stocking feet. Even in the cloudy afternoon light, he could see in Dobi her mother's lines, her mother's skin. She was shaken, recognizing him, eyes tight in her sockets.

The boy stopped laughing. "Who are you, to come here?"

Ned leaned on his cane under that stare. He didn't have time, standing on that stoop, in that middle-class neighborhood with its reasonable rows of houses, to explain his regret. Or to admit that he didn't like a black man to look him in the eye, even his own son, and being completely honest would require such an admission, he knew. Or to say that he had tried to be a good man within the confines of his life, or to say that he even believed sometimes that he had been good. He could only look back at that stare, that firm, familiar mouth.

"Your mother," he said, finally. "She told me I would always be welcome." He tried to meet her eyes, to plead with her, but she turned away from him. He was saying a prayer now, not the truth. He could almost convince himself that at some point over the years, she had voiced an invitation. He believed he could hear it, even now, as he lowered himself painfully to his knees.

Quinn Dalton is the author of a novel, *High
Strung*, and a story collection, *Bulletproof Girl*.
Her stories have appeared in literary magazines
such as *Indiana Review,* the *Kenyon Review,* and
One Story and have been anthologized in *Where
Love Is Found: 24 Tales of Connection* and in the
forthcoming *Peculiar Pilgrims*. She was a 2002–
2003 recipient of a North Carolina Arts Council
fellowship. She lives in Greensboro with her
husband and two young daughters.

TRINA OLSON PHOTOGRAPHY

*U*sually *my ideas come from a daydreamed image, snippets of overheard
conversation, stories friends have told me, or something I've read or
seen on TV. But I can't think of the trigger for this story. I wrote most of it
one morning during a Christmas visit to my parents' house in Ohio and
finished it in the car as my husband drove us home. I don't like to travel with
my laptop if I can avoid it, so I just use a notebook. This story sat in the notebook for the better part of a year before I came back to it, revising as I typed.*

*I don't normally write historical fiction, and these are not typical charac-
ters for me. So I guess I felt the effort of being true to them more consciously
than I have with other stories. The moment when Martha compares her faith
to the composer who is driven by a music he could never quite hear—this is the
essence of the story for me. Faith—and salvation—are elusive, perhaps unat-
tainable, compared with the reality of how we live our lives.*

Chris Bachelder

BLUE KNIGHTS BOUNCED FROM CVD TOURNEY

(from *Backwards City Review*)

STARKE—It was perhaps a fitting end to a tumultuous and frustrating season for the Perlis High School boys' basketball team.

Friday night, in the first round of the Cedar Valley District Tournament, Perlis surrendered the game and its entire season—without firing a single shot.

Trailing Starke by a point with less than a minute to go, the Blue Knights had the ball but failed to attempt a shot before time expired, falling 64–63 to their cross-valley rivals.

"We just passed it and passed it," said Perlis coach Doug Way of the final 48 seconds. There must have been nine, ten, eleven passes there. Maybe more. I'll have to check the film. There was so much [frigging] passing. It was like a hot potato. I don't want it, you take it! Everybody touched it, but nobody wanted to step up and take that big shot. It's a thing now, a type of deal where I just want to throw up."

Perlis took a timeout with 48 seconds remaining, another timeout with 21 seconds remaining, and its third and final timeout with nine seconds left.

"Each time, we drew up a good play," said Way, whose daughter, Cassandra, was born in November without arms. "But I could see my guys were rattled, I could see the fear [in their faces and in their hearts]. These guys don't have any guts. They have two arms but it's a situation where they have no guts."

When the buzzer sounded, the ball was in the hands of Blue Knight senior captain Trevor Basham, who led the team in scoring with 19 points and whose mother and father sat in different sections of the gymnasium. "I got the ball with about four or five seconds left," said Basham, who sobbed inconsolably in the musty visitors' locker room after the game. "I was just scared to shoot. Just really scared. I kind of locked up. Then I tried to find someone to pass to, but it was too late."

"Winning is boring," said Clarence Block, my first editor, before he died alone at age 54 from a heart attack. "You want the story, go to the losers' locker room."

For most of the game, it looked like it was going to be the Blue Knights' night. Basham, whose father has been sleeping on a cot in the basement for about a year, scored 11 points in the third quarter and Perlis opened up a 59–46 lead with one quarter to go.

"[Golly Moses], I love that little girl of mine," said Way, rubbing away tears with the palm of his hand. "You can't tell me she's not perfect. To me, she's a perfect angel from Heaven."

Seldom-used reserve Nathan Kraft gave the Knights a spark off the bench by hitting two 3-pointers in the third quarter as Perlis improved on its six-point halftime lead. Kraft, a junior, has a funny-looking release, and both of his shots banked in hard off the glass. Many of the Starke students and parents jeered him and chanted "homo."

"It didn't really bother me," said Kraft, who does look like he might be gay. *I'm leaving this valley first chance I get,* he thought.

"Nathan should have started and he should have been playing the whole game," said Kraft's father, Nelson, after the game and pretty much after every game this season. "Way is an idiot. Way is a [frigged-up] idiot who couldn't coach a team of girls."

"Nelson, *please*," said Nelson's gaunt and mousy wife, Carol.

But Starke roared back in the final quarter behind the strong interior play of the Cedar Valley District MVP, Josh Stetson, a fundamentally sound and nicely proportioned center who scored 13 in the quarter and finished with game-high totals in both points (24) and rebounds (14).

"We had no answer for Stetson," Way said of the Bobcats' 6' 8" forward. "That kid is good. I always look for a reason to hate that guy and it's a deal where I can't find one. He seems like a nice kid and he's a heck of a player. But I have to say, our guys were cowardly on defense and the refs, Christ, don't even get me started on those [turds]."

Told that Stetson had set a CVD single-season scoring record with his performance, Basham said, "What do you want me to say? He's a stud. And he's a nice guy, too. I hear he's got a [turd]load of AP credit. News flash, Stetson is a model citizen. Next year, he'll be playing D-I ball while I'm on some intramural team at that mid-tier school I'll be lucky to get into with my test scores."

Told that he had snot in his nose from his crying jag, Basham said, "Oh, thank you."

With 6:34 remaining in the fourth quarter, Stetson tipped in a missed shot to break the CVD season scoring mark set by Perlis star Johnny Dill in 1978. Dill was not in attendance on Thursday. He lives in a trailer in the woods and rarely comes into town anymore. He makes dioramas, which are these little scenes in boxes.

"When I see people or when I get out into open spaces, my heart just starts racing and I feel like I'm going to pass out," said Dill in a rare interview conducted two years ago through an open window in his trailer. "I have my dogs and my dioramas. I do OK out here. You should go now."

Stetson then scored on Starke's next four possessions to pull the Bobcats to within four points at 61–57 with 3:43 remaining.

"I just want to thank my teammates and hopefully return to Starke after college and set up a car dealership," Stetson might have said to the throng of people surrounding him at the conclusion of the game.

The Blue Knights' second-leading scorer, sophomore guard Jeff

Lassiter, who came into the tournament averaging 15.6 points per game, missed four free throws down the stretch and finished with just two points on 1-for-7 shooting and six turnovers.

"Lassiter was sleepwalking out there," said Way, who has guided Perlis to three consecutive 11–13 seasons. "He was a nonfactor, completely out of it. You could stare into his eyes and you just knew it was a thing where he wasn't there. Off the record? It's [coochie], I guarantee it."

"I've been struggling," said Lassiter, who earlier in the week touched junior Stephanie Conley's bare breast beneath her department-store blouse while the couple made out on the couch at Stephanie's house after school. "Stephanie took off her bra and I couldn't believe it. Don't write this down. After I touched her [boob], everything was just different. Do you know what I mean? Like everything just changed. I can't explain it. I went home and my mom and sister and me all had dinner, and they were talking to me but it was like they were five miles away. The way it felt in my hand. God, it's just like nothing is the same now. Do you know what I mean?"

After two missed free throws by Lassiter, Starke guard J. R. Stein, a Jewish player, hit a 3-pointer with 2:30 left to pull to 61–60. The Starke fans, many of whom were laid off from the canning factory earlier this winter, began stomping on the metal bleachers, and I think many of us felt the ancient gymnasium would crumble to the ground, killing us all. There are things I want to tell my ex-wife. There are things she needs to know before I go to my grave, and I wrote some of them down on my stat sheet.

"This game is a big deal for us," said one unemployed factory worker. "We hate Perlis. We hate Perlis and everything it stands for."

The Blue Knights silenced the crowd momentarily when center Donny Weddle got away with a travel and then hit a 17-foot fade-away he had no business taking to give Perlis a 63–60 advantage.

"Obviously, that's a deal where that's not the shot we wanted in that situation," said Way. "That's a kid who has zero touch. But hell, at least he *shot* it. You can't score if you don't even shoot."

Weddle refused to talk to me or to the reporter from the *Starke Eagle* after the game. "No, we *lost,* grandma," he said into his cell phone, naked.

It may or may not have occurred to Donny, a senior, that he'll probably never play another game of organized basketball in his life. He'll gain weight and his feet will hurt all the time. He's a big guy. He'll have dreams at night, like I do, that he discovers that he somehow has one more year of high school basketball eligibility and he gets to put on the uniform again and play another season, but then he will wake up and see the fake varnished wood of his bedside table.

Stetson hit a pair of free throws to cut the lead to 63–62 with 2:02 left, and then 20 seconds later Lassiter turned the ball over on a double dribble.

"[Turd], I might have *triple* dribbled, if there's such a thing as that," said Lassiter, lying on the locker room bench and staring upward at the ceiling. None of today's players seem to wear a jockstrap, whereas when I played we all wore one.

"You try coaching kids who want to play basketball in *boxer shorts,*" said Way, who conjectured that Stetson wore a jockstrap.

"Tell me what it feels like to do it," Lassiter said, "I mean, if her left [boob] felt that good, I just can't even imagine. Tell me what it's like."

"No," I said. I wanted to tell him that any act he could imagine committing with Stephanie or any other person could be either lovely or grotesque, depending on the context, but I didn't say anything.

After Lassiter's turnover, the Starke fans were out of their minds, and it was pretty clear to everyone in the old gym that Perlis was going to lose to the Bobcats again.

"Sexuality is on a continuum," Kraft said. "It's not this either/or thing."

Starke guard Chuck Jasper hit a driving layup with 48 seconds left to give the Bobcats their first lead since early in the first quarter.

That set up the Blue Knights' final possession, which resulted in three timeouts, 13 passes, and, as I mentioned at the top, zero shots.

"You suck," said a Starke fan as the Perlis players left the floor. "You're a bunch of skirts."

Starke advances to play the winner of Cambria and Emmitt in the semifinals of the Cedar Valley District Tournament.

"So we don't play again?" Lassiter asked.

Outside, after the game, the night was so cold it hurt your throat to breathe. The team bus idled depressingly. I remembered the way it smelled inside, the rips in the seats, the bad sandwiches that someone's mother made with Miracle Whip instead of mayonnaise.

From what I could gather, most of the Starke kids were going to hang out in the Hardee's parking lot.

And now it's pretty clear that the cedars along the road back to Perlis are all dying.

"It's a disease," said Fred Owen, a county extension agent. "There's nothing we can do about it."

Chris Bachelder's most recent novel is *U.S.!* He is also the author of *Bear v. Shark* and *Lessons in Virtual Tour Photography* (an e-book). His stories and essays have appeared in *Harper's,* the *Oxford American,* the *Believer, McSweeney's, Mother Jones,* the *Mississippi Review,* and elsewhere. He grew up in Christiansburg, Virginia, and worked as a sportswriter for the *Roanoke Times* and the *Greensboro News and Record.* Bachelder recently joined the MFA faculty at the University of Massachusetts.

JENN HABEL

*F*or "Blue Knights," I began with form, as I generally do. I was inter- *ested to find out what kind of story could be told in the form of a news- paper article, or what might happen when a strong authorial voice broke through journalistic style, conventions, and standards of objectivity. I played sports in high school and later I covered a lot of games as a sportswriter. There is a glory and sadness to small-town high school athletics, and I suppose I wanted to create a reporter who refused to narrow his report of a basket- ball game to the game itself. I'd like to thank Gerry Canavan and the other editors at* Backwards City Review *for their enthusiastic interest in my work.*

Mary Helen Stefaniak

YOU LOVE THAT DOG

(from *Epoch*)

Mac left Jacksonville on Tuesday in a custom-painted Hummer destined for a dealership in Chattanooga — the first stop in a thousand-mile chain of trades and special deliveries that would bring him back to Jacksonville on Thursday, driving the fully loaded model of somebody's dreams. Lisa spent most of the time he was gone doing the same thing she did the last ten or twenty or a hundred times Mac went away, which was planning how to tell him it was over. She knew it was going to break his heart. Hers, too, in a way. Lisa respected Mac. She felt a fondness for him that seemed, at least at the beginning, like love. "It wasn't love," her friends at the college explained. "You were just grateful." MarySue and Shawndra in particular told Lisa that *they* believed Mac went out of town on purpose to give her a chance to enjoy the company of people her own age.

"Fella like Mac's been around plenty long enough to know the score," they said. "Because if he didn't, then how come he never asks you to ride along?"

Best not mix business with pleasure, is what Mac said. Half the time, he slept in the car en route. He did ask her to go on some short trips, though, like the time they delivered that limo to Brunswick, Georgia. He figured she'd never ridden in a limousine before. She told him he was right. Sitting in one at the curb when she was

194

in high school, just long enough for her date to puke a pool of red Kool-Aid and Everclear into the lap of her yellow prom dress, didn't count, she thought, so she didn't mention it. When she ran back into the house that night, her father had snorted, "Pretty short date." Except in age, Mac was nothing like her father.

Lisa's friends were dead wrong about her and Mac anyway. *He* was the grateful one. ("I'm your wife," she kept telling him, "you don't have to say *thank you* every time.") Mac's gratitude used to make Lisa feel powerful. Now, the only way she could endure sex with him was to pretend they were both somebody else. In her favorite fantasy, inspired by a tale in her World Lit book, a whole team of eunuchs—barefoot and perfect, like Ken dolls in bicycle shorts—prepared her for penetration by two or three rival kings, her job being to unite their kingdoms in a single heir. (She wondered, in fact, why some of those old kings and feuding princes hadn't thought of this themselves.) For a 230-pound guy pushing sixty, Mac did a pretty good job, Lisa had to admit, as king-plus-eunuchs.

That's what she was thinking about, waiting to make a left turn off Yulee Road onto Hwy 17, when she first saw the dogs. The bigger one, a black-and-white beagle-shepherd mix, was stretched out on its side under the gas station sign on the corner, its legs stiff, like a taxidermist's display, tipped over. A smaller dog, similar in markings, was sniffing at it. While Lisa watched, the smaller dog curled up and laid itself down next to the dead one's head. "Poor little thing," Lisa said out loud as a hole opened up in the traffic.

She tried to tell her friends about the dogs that morning, but they were more interested in why she couldn't go to lunch with them after class. There was a place they liked called The Neighbor's with a noontime Happy Hour.

"Mr. Mac won't let you?" asked Shawndra.

"Maybe she has some items to carry to the cleaners," said Mary-Sue.

Later, when Lisa pulled into the gas station on her way home from school, the dogs were still there at the base of the sign. The little one lifted its head as she got out of her car. It watched her unscrew the gas cap and take the nozzle from the pump. She stood with the nozzle in her tank for several minutes, watching the little dog get up and turn around and lie back down on the other side of its dead companion, before she realized that the numbers on the pump weren't moving. She tried squeezing the handle harder. Then she put the nozzle back.

Inside the station, Billy Sawyer was removing greeting cards from a sparsely stocked greeting-card rack. He was in his summer uniform: Carhartt coveralls cut knee-length and sleeveless. Billy looked over the top of the rack as the door opened and said, "Hey, there."

"Pump number one isn't working," Lisa told him.

He pointed to a greeting-card envelope taped to the glass door. From inside, Lisa read: NO GAS.

"Shoot," said Billy. "Y'all mind flipping that around again? Truck ain't come yet. Huge wreck on 95 outside Savannah, I heard. Lucky thing Mac don't come that way." Before she could say "Lucky thing," he went on. "Hey—could you all use some birthday cards? New baby? Sympathy? Roof leaked a good one," he said, holding the cards out to show her. "They're dry now. How about a quarter apiece? Big savings."

"No thanks."

"Free, then."

She turned to go, then stopped. "Billy," she said, "I suppose you've already seen the dead dog out by your sign?"

"Yep. Put her there. Somebody hit her and left her layin' in the road."

"There's a little dog, too, sitting by her."

"That's why I moved her out the road."

"Did you call the animal shelter or anything?"

"Up to County, you mean?" Billy looked out the window. A black car had pulled up to the pumps. A man got out. "They'd just put him down, mangy little dog like that—if they'd come out here at all. Prob'ly tell me to get out my rifle and take care of it myself."

Lisa and Billy watched the man put the nozzle into his black car, take it out, shake it, put it back in, smack the pump with the heel of his hand, and hang the nozzle up again. They could see the little dog peeking at the man over the concrete base of the sign.

"Maybe you oughta take him," Billy said. "Mac's lookin' for a dog, ain't he? I heard him say that dog of yours run off for the last time."

"She's back, though. She came home yesterday."

Mac's dog Susie had shown up last night during the eleven o'clock news. Lisa heard her whining on the porch. Her long blond coat was mud-spiked and full of burrs, and her left ear had a tear in it, black with dried blood.

"And he's forgive her?" Billy looked surprised.

"Mac's not home yet," Lisa said. "He's due tomorrow."

The door to the station opened, envelope flapping on the glass, and the man with the black car stuck his head inside.

"No gas," said Billy, "but we got ice cold Co-Cola." The door banged shut. Billy turned back to Lisa. "I know Mac. He said it was the last time, then he ain't gonna take that dog back."

"Of course he'll take her back." When Lisa came out to the porch last night, Susie had trembled with joy, her heavy tail thumping the floorboards. The dog was so glad to be home that she sat still while Lisa poured Mac's flea-and-tick formula all over her. Lisa had worked it in and toweled it off and locked Susie in the garage for the night, smelling like turpentine. "Mac loves that dog," she said.

Billy shook his head. He gazed out the fly-spotted plate-glass window, while the black car tore out of the station, raising dust, and the little dog dropped out of sight. "Now you take that little old dog out there," he said. "That's a loyal dog. That's a dog don't care if you're dead or alive, he'll stick with you." The salt-and-pepper stubble on Billy's chin and jowls glistened like sandpaper. "I've known Mac for a long time," he said.

Lisa knew it wasn't so much her and Mac getting married that got Billy's goat — "*Twenty-five years difference between 'em if there's a day!"* — it was the job she roped Mac into. Everybody knew Mac didn't need a job. Now here he was delivering fancy cars all over a seven-state area for Anderson Motors down in Jacksonville, where Lisa used to work, too, before she quit to go full-time at the college. To hear Billy talk, all she had to do for the past two years was take her little classes in the morning and spend the rest of her day lolling by the pool Mac put in the backyard for his first wife, who went and drowned in it. Mac told Lisa, "Don't pay no attention to Billy."

Lisa opened the door and let the heat pour in. Billy called, "Hey!" She turned around. He was holding up one of the wrinkled greeting cards.

"Here's one says, 'So long from all the gang!'"

Lisa waved a hand and went out. She kept her eyes away from the sign as she drove around the pumps. It didn't take her three minutes to get to her own driveway, a long, smooth lane of concrete that lead to a big redbrick colonial, tall white columns in front. "The whole nine yards," Mac said the first time he showed it to her. He had built it, free and clear, with part of his settlement from the railroad. The house sat on a two-acre lot surrounded by live oak and drooping vines. The near neighbors were small wooden bungalows and a few mobile homes.

Inside the house, the answering machine was blinking. The first message was from Mac. "Departin' Atlanta at 6 AM tomorrow. See you by lunchtime. Love, Mac." He hated talking to a machine. Anybody could be listening, he said. She told him if she had a cell phone he could reach her anywhere, he wouldn't have to leave a message, but he was afraid she'd get herself in a wreck, talking while she was driving.

The other message informed her that her drycleaning was ready for pickup anytime after seven. Lisa took a deep breath and punched in the number.

"Beach Road Cleaners."

"Scott," she said, urgently. "I can't get into town tonight."

The voice at the other end dropped to a whisper. "He's back?"

"Not yet. He says tomorrow noon."

"But you think he might show up early instead."

"No," Lisa said, "Mac doesn't play games like that."

There was silence at the other end. She had offended him. She never meant to. She never meant to buy so many clothes marked DRY CLEAN ONLY either.

"Scott?" she said. More silence, except for the squeaky start-up of the overhead rack at the cleaners. She pictured the clothes on hangers floating toward Scott in their plastic bags. In the dark, they always looked to her like ghosts waiting in line. She explained about Mac's dog Susie, how she had to get her cleaned up before Mac got home.

"You can't see me because you have to shampoo the dog?"

"You know it's the truth, Scott."

As soon as she hung up, Lisa changed into old jeans and one of Mac's T-shirts, which came down to her knees. She went outside with shampoo, old towels, Susie's metal comb and brush, and a pan of roast beef that Mac cooked on Monday. Lisa could hear the dog whining and barking in the garage, anxious little yips and yaps. She opened the door slowly, shouting, "Stay! Stay! Sit!" and sure enough Susie sat, in an agony of self-control, her tail sweeping the cool concrete slab of the garage floor. While Susie ate roast beef, Lisa tugged the metal comb through her coat from head to tail, careful of the torn ear. Then she dragged the plastic wading pool out on the grass. Watching the water bubble over the little mermaids on the bottom, Lisa said out loud to Susie, who was worrying the hose, "I never roped Mac into anything."

He had come into Anderson Motors to have the brakes done on his pickup, and while Lisa was filling out the paperwork, Mr. Anderson himself burst through the swinging doors into the service department, pulling at his hair. He had to get a Miata to Orlando by 6 PM, he said, and his driver was out sick! Mac said, "I'll do it." Mr. Anderson had looked at the cane hooked over the back of Mac's chair and asked, "Can you all drive a stick shift with that leg of yours?" Mac said, "Sure enough." Anderson narrowed his eyes like somebody in a movie. Mac poked an elbow toward Lisa. "This here young lady here can vouch for me, can't you?" Lisa, who'd met him ten minutes earlier, said to her own surprise, "Yes."

She still didn't know why she'd said it. Standing in the service bay, watching the Miata pull out into traffic, Mac's brand-new blue Anderson Motors cap visible inside, Lisa had felt light-headed, so certain was she that she would never see him again. She wondered if they would make her pay for the car. How many years would it take to come up with that much money? Toward closing time, she asked Mr. Anderson if he had heard from that man driving the Miata. Was he in Orlando by now? Mr. Anderson didn't even look up from the calculator on his desk. He said he hadn't heard anything, but Mac drove like an old lady so he wasn't worried yet. Only then did it dawn on Lisa that Mac and Mr. Anderson knew each other. They were local boys, had probably known each other since they were three. Lisa went to the ladies room and wept, mostly with relief.

The next day, she let Mac treat her to the Arctic Circle for lunch.

"You usually vouch for perfect strangers?" he asked her, grinning.

She played cool. "You've got an honest face," she said, which was true. Mac's face was tanned and craggy but round as a child's. It made him look younger than he turned out to be.

He asked her where she was from — north of here, he could tell that much. When she told him, he said, "So how does someone from Fon-doo-lack, Wiss-con-sin" — Lisa liked the way he made it sound like someplace she'd never heard of — "wind up in Jacksonville, Florida?"

By getting on the bus with two suitcases and no idea where she was getting off except that it would be far away from where she started, she said. She had written about the bus trip in composition class at the college, she told Mac. "We had to write a narrative about a life-changing experience."

"You had to write a what?"

"It just means a story," she said. "I wrote about looking out the window in every town trying to figure out if this was the place where I was meant to be." That last part was right out of what she wrote for class. It sounded phony to her now.

Mac seemed impressed. "And you got off in Jacksonville?"

"The bus broke down on Atlantic," she said, "right in front of the dealership. Everybody had to get off. The guys at Anderson were so nice, I couldn't believe it. They let us use the restrooms and the water cooler and the telephone." Lisa had stood by the phone for a while, when it was her turn, trying to think of somebody to call, but she didn't put that part in her paper. "They even said we should relax and watch the TV while we waited for another bus to pick us up. So I thought, heck, I was going to go to the manager's office and thank him, and I did, and he offered me a job." Lisa took a bite of her sandwich, chewed, and felt Mac looking at her, drinking her in. When she read her paper out loud in class, a woman about Mac's age asked her if she had on that there miniskirt when she went in to thank the manager. Everybody in her small group had laughed. "I don't know what I'm doing in college," she told Mac suddenly. "I'll never finish anyway, taking one course at a time."

"You should quit the job, then," Mac said, "and go to school all day."

"And how would I pay my bills—not to mention my tuition?"

"I'll pay it," he said. She laughed and said that she might be pretty free with the character references but she couldn't let a perfect stranger pay her tuition. Mac said, "Guess you'll have to get to know me then."

Lisa had looked at him across the small, wobbly table. The Anderson Motors cap was exactly the same color as his eyes. Her heart was beating a little faster than it should have been. She said, "So what would *you* write?"

Mac said, "I don't write," and for a moment Lisa thought he meant that he couldn't, but no, he had filled out all that paperwork. She persisted. "What if you had to?" she said. "If you had to pick the experience that changed your life the most. What would it be?"

"There were two," Mac said.

"You can only pick one."

Then it had to be when the train ran over his foot, he said, although it wasn't so much the train running over his foot as lying out there half the night after it happened that changed him. For one thing, it made the settlement much, much bigger. Gross negligence and all. And the delay made it harder to sew the foot back on, although things could have gone worse. It sure enough made you think, he said, lying out there in the dark. He had expected to be dead by morning.

Lisa tried to imagine what it would be like, flat on your back, staring at the stars, your foot on the other side of the tracks. "Did your whole life pass before your eyes?"

"Just fourth grade," said Mac.

She laughed. "Why fourth grade?"

"That was the year my mother died," he said. "I was trying to remember what she looked like. I figured I was going to see her pretty soon, and she sure wasn't going to recognize *me*."

To make him forget that she had laughed, Lisa asked him, "Can I see it?"

They went out to his truck and he put his foot on the seat, rolled up his jeans, rolled down his sock.

"There's metal in it," Mac told her. "For reinforcement. Not too pretty, eh?"

Frankenstein's foot. That's what it looked like. A scar like railroad tracks on a map, pinching the skin into a purple worm that wound around his ankle and up the inside of his leg. Lisa sat there on the bench seat next to his black sock and his Nike and thought that it was too bad she was finished with that composition class because she could feel a real life-changing experience coming at her. She heard herself say, "Can I touch it?"

Four months later, they were married.

One good thing: Susie loved a bath. She leaped into the water

before the pool was full, leaped out again, and shook herself, spray-
ing the yard and Lisa. She rolled on the grass in ecstasy while Lisa
lathered her up, and she stood against the rinsing force of the hose
like a figure on the prow of a ship weathering a storm. When it was
all over, she sat primly to be brushed and trimmed.

"For a dog that likes to run wild, you sure can be civilized if you
want to be," Lisa said. She pulled the brush through Susie's golden
coat and leaned over to take a closer look at her ear. It didn't look
too bad now that she was cleaned up, a half-inch tear scabbed over
and starting to heal. It was nothing, really, compared to other
times, people taking pot shots at her, setting traps. Susie had lost a
third of her tail last summer for trying to spend the night howling
under a doublewide out in the woods past Hodges. Another time,
somebody had poisoned her. Mac thought it was the fellow with
the emus, that maybe she had killed one of his baby birds. That
was a terrible time. Mac and Lisa had to keep Susie up all night,
walking and puking.

Susie nuzzled her wet head into Lisa's chest. The smell of tur-
pentine still clung to her coat, mingled now with coconut sham-
poo. "Whew," said Lisa. "You can't come in the house like that."
Susie lapped her long tongue across Lisa's cheek. "Cut that out!"
Lisa said. She scratched the dog's good ear and whispered into it,
"Save it for Mac."

That night, Lisa had barely fallen asleep when she woke up in
the dark and flung her arm into the empty space beside her. She
sat up straight in bed. The clock said 12:47. It took her a few seconds to distinguish the sound of the dog crying from the blood
pounding in her ears. "Oh Susie," Lisa said, falling back against
the pillows. "One more night in the garage is not going to kill
you." She stared at the ceiling, listening, and then threw off the
sheet and reached for the silky white robe Mac brought home for
her from Memphis last year. She padded on bare feet through the
family room to the garage.

"You big baby," Lisa scolded as she opened the garage door, but
instead of the crescendo of howls that she expected, there was only

the clicking of Susie's claws on the concrete. Lisa turned on the light and Susie sat, wriggling, hopeful, while the mournful howling continued outside, muffled by the concrete walls of the garage. Lisa patted the dog's head. "Poor Susie," she said. "And here I was blaming you." With the dog at her heels, she went to the windows in the overhead door and cupped her hands against the glass to look out. "If I open this door, you'll be gone for another week, chasing after whoever's out there making such a fuss — oh!"

Lisa stepped back from the door with her hand to her mouth. "It's that little dog," she said. She pictured him sitting by the corpse in the moonlight — although there was no moon tonight that she could see — howling the thin line of his sorrow into the sky. "Oh Susie, somebody's going to shoot that little dog if he keeps this up all night."

At three o'clock the little dog was still crying — a combination bark and howl, piercing and persistent and infinitely sad. For a while, Susie had taken up the chant in the garage, but she soon lost interest. Only the pure, sharp edge of real grief could keep up such keening. Lisa spent half the night expecting at any minute to hear the sound of a shot, followed by silence, but it never came. She buried her head under two pillows. In the morning, when the complaints of the crows woke her, she didn't understand the dread sitting like a heavy weight on her chest — had something happened? Was it Mac? Was she dreaming? Then she remembered the little dog. She feared the worst, but couldn't make herself go down to the station to see.

After she fed Susie, Lisa took a long shower and smoothed herself all over with the rose-scented lotion that Mac brought home from another overnight trip. ("You smell like my grandmother," Scott had said one time, and she hadn't used it since.) She took extra time with her hair, too, braiding it up while it was wet and then drying it to make blond waves cascade down her back like the picture on the barbershop wall that everybody called Venus on the Half Shell. (The first time Lisa wore her hair like that, Mac said, "I got me my own goddess.") She was lying by the pool in shorts and a halter, a magazine tented over her face, when Mac's pickup pulled into the driveway, well before noon. The gravel popping under his tires startled her. She sat up straight, and her magazine fluttered into the pool.

Mac lifted her right off her feet when he kissed her—he was a big man, but not fat like Billy Sawyer—the force of his embrace knocking the Anderson Motors cap right off his head. Then he stepped back and said, "Have I got a surprise for you!"

She resisted an impulse to smooth down his cowlicky hair. "I've got a surprise for you, too," she said. She was glad Susie hadn't started barking at the sound of his truck.

"Mine first," he said and led her by the hand to the driveway. He opened the passenger side of the pickup with a flourish. Lisa drew back. Curled on a ratty towel on the floor was the little black-and-white dog. At first it looked dead, but then the tail moved and the dog lifted its nose and whined weakly.

"I found him at the gas station," Mac said, lifting the dog out of the car and setting it on the grass. "Billy said he was there all night."

The little dog looked around. When Mac crouched to scratch its ears, the dog sat down on his foot. Lisa thought about what kind of vermin it must be full of after its vigil and the skin up and down the front of her body, every place where Mac had pressed against her, prickled and crawled. "It was about the saddest thing you ever saw," Mac was saying. His eyes were full of tenderness, looking at the little dog. "It would've broke your heart," he said.

She said, "What are you going to do with it?"

"Keep him." Mac patted the little dog's head.

"What if he doesn't get along with Susie?"

That's when Mac stood up and looked at Lisa, his whole round tan face darkening, as if a shade had pulled down over it. He said, "She came back?"

"Night before last. I gave her a bath already. She looks all right—cut on her ear but it's healing."

"Where is she?"

"In the garage."

Mac picked up the little dog and looked around as if he were deciding where to put it. "Maybe I'll just — put him back in the truck for now." Mac set the dog back on the towel and brushed his hands on his jeans. He took two steps toward the garage, hesitated, and came back to the pickup. He leaned into the cab, the little dog cowering in his shadow, and pulled his rifle out from under the front seat. It was a World War II carbine that he inherited from his uncle. He used it hunting deer and possum with Billy Sawyer. Mac always let Billy keep the game.

Lisa said, "What are you doing, Mac?"

He reached under the seat again for a clip. "I can't have a dog goes off for days, getting in fights and eating people's livestock — God knows what all." The clip snapped into place.

"Mac, you're not going to shoot her."

"If I don't take care of her, Lisa, somebody else will. People do terrible things to a stray. You know that." Mac's face had gone darker and tighter.

"You're talking yourself into this," Lisa said, but suddenly, even as she said it, she knew it wasn't true. Billy Sawyer was right. Mac had made up his mind over a week ago, when the dog ran away. For over a week he had known what he would do if Susie came home. Inside the house, the phone began to ring.

"I said if she ran off again, I wouldn't have any choice. You heard me say it, Lisa."

"But she . . . she was . . ." Lisa ran out of breath. She felt her heart racing. The phone stopped in the middle of a ring.

Mac straightened up with the gun under his arm and seemed to gather himself. He limped away across the lawn, leaving his cane behind, glancing at the mermaids when he passed the plastic pool. Susie must have heard or smelled him coming because a burst of joyous barking rose from inside the garage, and the overhead door banged in the doorframe. Mac was reaching for the handle to pull it up when Lisa cried out.

"Mac!"

He stopped, but he didn't turn around.

She said, "You love that dog."

The door went up and Susie came bounding out, jumping up on Mac, dancing around him, twisting and leaping and barking. Lisa watched them move back through the yard toward the woods, Mac dragging his foot, and the dog prancing beside him, racing ahead and falling back, running circles around him. As they approached the shadow of the trees, heat rose in waves behind them. Their shapes looked uncertain to her. Then the trees closed around them and they were gone.

Lisa remained standing by the pool, her hair floating around her bare shoulders. The air felt thick and hard to breathe. She watched her magazine float, warp, wrinkle and begin to sink in the pool, the woman on the cover smiling as she grew blurry and disappeared. In the house the phone started ringing again. It was still ringing when Lisa heard another noise. This one sounded like a car backfiring, or maybe Billy Sawyer taking care of a rattlesnake behind the station. It was loud enough to make her jump.

Mary Helen Stefaniak's first novel, *The Turk and My Mother,* received the 2005 John Gardner Book Award and was named a favorite book of 2004 by the *Chicago Tribune.* Her first book, *Self Storage and Other Stories,* received the Wisconsin Library Association's 1998 Banta Award. She is a graduate of the Iowa Writers' Workshop and a contributing editor for the *Iowa Review.* Her mother is from Georgia, and her grandmother's maiden name was Califf, but her novel-in-progress—*The Cailiffs of Baghdad, Georgia*—is 100 percent fiction, in case anybody wants to know. This is her second appearance in *New Stories from the South.* She teaches at Creighton University in Omaha.

ANDREW MARINKOVICH

*M*y mother, my sister, my daughter, and I were visiting the relatives near Milledgeville, Georgia, when we saw a dead dog at a gas station on the corner, a smaller but nearly identical dog sitting tragically beside it. Another time, somebody told us a story about shooting his dog because he couldn't keep her from wandering off and getting into trouble. His wife of forty years or more said, "I told him, you can't shoot that dog. You love that dog." The minute she said it, I was struck by what it would be like to find out that your husband would shoot a creature he loved if he couldn't stop her from wandering. A year or so later, I was getting ready for a swim at the university where I teach, awash in the voices of young women and the banging of locker doors, when the story started telling itself to me, in bits and pieces, in flashes of scene. I missed my swim, shivering on a bench in my suit and towel, writing it all down.

Daniel Wallace

JUSTICE

(from *The Georgia Review*)

It was his only spoken rule, but every other rule arose from this one, as if he had devised the final perfect test of character and resolve: *the last of everything was his.* It was so simple: whatever you wanted was fine as long as what you wanted wasn't the last of whatever it was. Because if you took the last one, that was it, you were done for. You knew the rule and when you broke it there were no second chances. When the last one was gone, it was gone forever. So how could there *be* a second chance?

It didn't matter what it was the last of, either. The last cookie, the last paper towel, the last clean glass, the last respectable sip of apple juice from the bottom of the jar. The last of everything, of anything, was his.

He kept an inventory of last things in a special place in his mind. When he came home from work, his hand scratching the tarnished key into the golden lock, he paused briefly, thinking—not of any one last thing in particular, but preparing himself, gathering himself together for the event of his homecoming, a routine which included an awareness of the family's resources, and how close each item was to running out.

Had he no children, this issue of last things may never have come up in his life, but the harsh reality was that he had children, two of them, so there it was. His wife wasn't much help in this regard either. She had been easier to train, of course — she was always very considerate. But the children were harder. It was their needs — hunger, for instance, or thirst — which sometimes compelled them to take the last of something, even knowing what would happen if they did.

He thought of what they might have taken as he walked, unheralded, into his own home. His children no longer greeted him as they did in their youth with their excited screams and yells, jumping on his back and hugging his legs, and this was just as well; he couldn't take it. Honestly, the last thing he needed after returning home from his job — he managed a repack operation for a large grocery chain — were two balls of fire and energy tackling him in the hallway. Jill and Thomas didn't do that now. They were almost teenagers, and most of their energy was used up outside of the home. Except for occasional fits of manic desperation or wild elation, both seemed willing to orbit pointlessly in their own private solar systems. And he let them. His wife was an office manager, and was often kept there late. She might not be home for hours, and when she got home the last thing she wanted to do was talk: talking is what she had been doing all day. So nobody spoke much in this family, and he thought perhaps this had something to do with him.

Sadness brushed past him like a shadow, and a great stillness embraced him in the small, dim hallway. Then, tilting his head to one side, he heard the muffled sounds of music thumping behind a closed bedroom door. That would be Thomas; Jill was probably napping. He shook his head and sighed, and braced himself for the beginning of another night at home.

Being a father was harder than he ever imagined it would be. It was so difficult for him to remember that his children were human beings, *people,* like him, and that he in fact was once a child himself. They grew and changed, and what seemed appropriate one day wasn't the next, and if he had to buy another pair of shoes he thought he would scream. He tried to hang in there, as the kids said, or as kids at some point in time had said, and yet he worried he went too easy on them. He let them get away with things. He let them get away with almost anything, in fact, except—well, they knew where he drew the line.

They knew. He walked into the kitchen first, took his coat off, and hung it from one of the table chairs. He could see that they had been in here eating—which, in and of itself, was fine. He wasn't against them eating. They'd left their crumby plates on the counter beside the sink. Bread, cheese, almonds, cookies. This was no problem. There were plenty of all those things in the apartment; he remembered his wife shopping for them only yesterday . . . and yet he had to check to make sure. So he checked.

Okay then, fine.

Although they were getting low on bread. They were getting *very* low on bread.

But bread was tricky.

A *sandwich* was composed of two slices of bread. One slice of bread was meaningless as bread unless you were going to make *toast*. So when did you get to the last of the bread—when there was one slice left or two? A conundrum.

He had figured it out like this: it depended on the time of day. In the morning, one slice was last; in the afternoon or evening, two. This seemed clear enough. But somehow the concept was lost on Thomas and Jill and even his wife: he couldn't count the number of times he'd come home from work to find one slice of bread in the plastic, as if there was anything he could do with one slice of bread. The complexity of the issue, however, made punishment unacceptable, so he dealt with it as best he could: on the occasions there was only one slice of bread left in the evenings, and he wanted a sandwich, he cut the single slice in two, and the sandwich he had was very small.

He opened the refrigerator. There was just enough apple juice left in it for one full glass. He poured it, and drank a sip, and then regarded the empty jar with a tired gaze. He had thought of the juice situation once, earlier that day, at work, and knew there was a chance that it would be gone by the time he got home. The idea that this might happen made his heart race briefly, as though he or someone close to him were in real danger. Because worse for him than the actual taking was the fear that something *might* be taken; and as the supply of a certain thing diminished the fear increased. Returning home to find a sufficient quantity of the thing didn't actually please him, though; it merely allowed him to transfer his fear to something else.

He poured the juice back into the bottle, and put the bottle back into the refrigerator. There was still one good serving left.

He would drink it later.

The telephone rang once, and stopped. He didn't bother to answer it anymore. Invariably it was for either Jill or Thomas; his phone calls consisted of donation requests, magazine subscription and credit card offers. But his kids were popular, apparently. They had phones in their own rooms, and recently they had even begun arguing for separate lines — their own personal phone numbers! This is the sort of request he wouldn't even dignify with an answer. He would just look at them and shake his head and go back to whatever it was he was doing, pretending as best he could that, at this particular moment, they didn't exist.

It was dark outside now. The fluorescent kitchen light hummed and trembled. He stood in the middle of the kitchen, illuminated like something on display. He should tell the kids he was home, he thought, but first — his wife having yet to arrive — he wanted to check on things.

Oh, yes, it was that time again! Time to check on things. He leaned into the refrigerator, closely studying its contents. He opened the cabinets. He looked in the bathroom, at the toilet paper and the soap. He checked to see how many spare light bulbs were left, how many clean towels. He opened the medicine cabinet and removed a plastic bag in which two small cotton balls nestled. He shook the aspirin bottle. He looked everywhere he looked every evening, and found that there was something left of everything — *not a lot* — but something, and this made him wary and a bit sad, because he knew this situation couldn't last much longer: soon, they were going to get down to last things, very last things, and the situation could easily become intolerable.

In his own bedroom he removed the spare change from his pocket, and dropped it with a dull jingle on the dresser. A picture of his wife beamed sweetly at him. She was not a particularly attractive woman, though he believed she had many fine features. Her eyes were small and her cheeks made her look something like a squirrel, and her hair was thin and sparse, as if she had undergone some kind of chemotherapy, which she hadn't. But she had a beautiful smile — her teeth were almost perfect — and her legs, though it was on a rare day when he saw them, were long and smooth and elegant as any he had seen on television or in the movies. She hid them beneath long skirts and pants suits, and never made an effort to show them to him, and in all fairness to her, he never asked for the view. But the thought that these legs dwelled in his own home and that he saw them no more than did a man who lived a hundred miles away hit him with all the power of its severe bleakness, and seemed in that moment (it had been a long day) to embody so much about his life and what he had made of it that he began to cry. No sobbing, just a couple of lonely tears rolling down his sad, white cheek. Enough for a tissue, though. He turned and reached for one in the box he kept on his bedside table.

But there were none. As he was reaching for the box he realized that it was empty, and yet his hand kept reaching until he touched it. *Empty.* It hadn't been empty this morning; he remembered quite clearly the puff of white peering from the plastic. So someone had used it. Someone had taken the last tissue from the box, and now the box was empty.

So.

He walked stiffly through the hallway to the kids' rooms and rapped with a sharp urgency on their doors, three times.

"I want to see both of you out here," he said. *"Now."*

He waited for them in the living room. He had his back to them when they came in, and when he turned he was holding the empty tissue box in his hands.

Jill and Thomas looked at each other—not conspiratorially, but with a deep empathy. Thomas was a tall, thin, awkward boy, and Jill, only eleven, had yet to lose the baby fat that rounded all her edges. Both had short brown hair and green eyes and—with their small noses and big round cheeks—looked more like their mother than their dad.

"Don't. Say. A word," he told them, though neither seemed about to speak. "Not a word until I'm done. I'm really upset and disappointed right now. Just very upset. And I think you know why. I don't ask for much—at least, I don't think I do. I have but one rule—*one.*"

He shook his head. He didn't have to tell them what the rule was. All he had to do was hold up the empty box of tissues for their inspection.

"Who did this?" he said. "Who?"

Reluctantly—and at the same time with a kind of tired insolence—Thomas raised his hand. Jill gazed over at him, as the distance between them suddenly seemed much greater, and he shrugged his shoulders.

"You, Thomas?"

Thomas nodded.

"You know what this means, don't you?" he said.

This time Jill and Thomas couldn't even look at each other. They just stared into their own laps in bleak silence. Thomas sighed.

"That's right," his father said sadly. "I'm going to have to kill you."

Thomas shook his head slowly, and shivered once, as though overtaken by a chill. He tried to swallow but found he couldn't: he'd lost every ounce of wetness in his mouth. He'd dried up. He felt that swirling feeling in his head, which made him dizzy. But it was always like this and it would pass. He knew it would pass.

"Well?" his father said.

"Well *what?*" Thomas whispered, managing just to take a quick sullen glimpse at his father. His father, on the contrary, never broke his gaze.

"How is this going to happen then?" his father said.

"What do you mean, *how?*"

"How is it you want to die?"

"So you're giving me a choice."

His father didn't like his tone and conveyed that feeling with a harsh stare. "Within reason," he said.

"Well, I haven't really thought about it," Thomas said quickly, a note of sarcasm rising in his voice.

"Well, I have," his father said evenly. "I've had to. What comes from being the dad."

He rubbed his face and felt his shoulders sag as he seemed to feel, all at once, the sum of all his responsibilities as husband, father, primary wage earner, son of two deceased parents — *and now this,* his shoulders seemed to say to him. There were not enough hours in the day.

"I have," he said again. "And I suggest you do the same."

He looked at his daughter, who appeared frozen there.

"You can go, Jill," he said.

But Jill didn't move. She stayed cross-legged on the floor a few feet away from her brother.

"Don't you have homework?" her father said. *"Something?"*

"A little," she said. "But it can wait."

He looked at her. "You know, I can encourage you to do these things," he said. "Like homework. Like cleaning your room. But ultimately, it's your responsibility."

"I just have some reading to do in humanities," she said softly, as though she were talking in church. "It won't take long."

Satisfied with this explanation, he nodded, and looked again at the empty box of tissues he was holding. Beyond the soft plastic dual strips of plastic the darkness of the box inside seemed positively haunting, and vast. How many hundreds of tissues had it once held? How is it that Thomas was destined to take the very last? He loved his son; he didn't want to hurt him. But being a father meant making the hard decisions. It meant being as good as your word. Thomas would lose all respect for him if he backed down now, when it was most important that he show resolve. He had a rule; it had been broken; this was the consequence. It was as simple — and difficult — as that.

"Well?" he said, looking at his son.

All this time, Thomas had been breathing deeply, and at varying speeds. One minute you could hear him pull the air in slowly and with vast effort, and the next shallow and fast. Jill reached out tentatively and touched the edge of his knee, and this seemed to calm him for a moment. He almost smiled.

"Thomas," his father said.

"Its not *fair*," Thomas said.

"What?"

"I said it's not —"

"I heard what you said," his father told him. "I just can't believe what I'm hearing. You don't think the rule is fair? Wow. Why is this the first I've heard of it? And who said rules are fair? They're just *rules*. And rules have consequences."

"Not the rule," Thomas said. "I mean tonight. What happened with the tissues."

"Oh?"

"Tissues should be different. You don't know it's the last tissue until you pull it out. You can't *tell* with tissues. Whether it's the first or the last, it looks just the same, and when there wasn't another, I —"

He stopped, and looked at his father, whose expression of mild contempt hadn't changed.

"I tried to stick it back in," he said. "I tried to fold it and place it in there so it looked the same, like new. But it's impossible."

His father tried a smile on, but it didn't quite take. "I get it. I hear you. But I can't make exceptions, Thomas," he said. "You have to understand. If I make an exception with this I'll have to make an exception the next time, and the next and the next. It doesn't work that way."

"But this is *different*."

"I don't think so."

But perhaps it was different, in a way. The same thing had happened to him in his own life: he had taken the last tissue without knowing it was going to be the last. It happens. It happens, but of course, the rule didn't apply to him. And at any rate, exceptions were impossible. For in a sense, it could be argued that every instance of *every* last thing was different. What if it had been milk in question this time — just a bit of it at the bottom of the container — and Thomas had been playing soccer and was especially thirsty and poured it without thinking? What's the difference, really? You can't see exactly how much milk is left. If Thomas took it, he'd still have to kill him. He'd still have to kill him because that was the rule, *even though an argument could be made to the contrary.*

Finally, he sat down on the couch, the empty box of tissues resting in his lap, cradled on either side with his hands, his face grim now with the thought of the task before him.

"I never wanted this to happen," he said. "Believe me, Thomas, you wouldn't want to be in my shoes now."

"No," he said, "I guess I wouldn't. Would you want to be in mine?"

But then he looked at his son's feet and realized he wasn't wearing shoes, and that neither was Jill: he was the only one wearing shoes here. Black shoes, heavy shoes. For some reason, the fact that he was wearing shoes when the others weren't embodied for him the difference between the world he lived in and the world of his children: they might as well have come from a different species for all they knew and understood of the other. There was no way Thomas — who basically didn't have to wear shoes if he didn't want to — could understand his father's plight. Having a son die is bad enough, but having to *kill* him — that was an excruciating thing for a father to go through. And then there were the practical consequences: how to do it cleanly and painlessly, for instance, how to dispose of the body, et cetera. There were so many things to take into consideration . . .

"No, I can't do it!" his father said suddenly, crumpling the tender box of tissues in his hands. "Theory is one thing, but practice is entirely another. I can't kill you, Thomas."

Thomas' face brightened a bit at his father's announcement, and he looked at his sister hopefully. But only for a moment.

"You're going to have to do it," his father said.

"What?"

"You're going to have to kill yourself. It's the only way."

Thomas' shoulders fell. "Give me the gun, then," he said, hand extended, his patience with his father's antics clearly at an end. "Or the knife. Whatever it is. Let's get this over with."

"Mom's pills," Jill suggested. "That might be the easiest."

The quietest and cleanest as well, his father thought.

"So — it's decided," he said after a moment, the tips of his lips curling to a point. He stood, somewhat excitedly, and looked at his watch: time was passing. "I'll get the pills. Be right back!"

But just as he was leaving the living room the apartment door opened, and his wife walked in. She was a tall, strong woman in a long skirted suit; she breezed into the apartment with a custodial air, looking left and right to see what might or might not be out of place. Clearly aware of having walked into a scene in progress, she stopped cold, and the others did too, and for a moment it was as if they had been frozen in amber. Mom, dad, sister, brother — the whole family. Everyone looked at her. And then everyone looked at the box she held in her hands.

"Tissues," she said into the stillness. "We were running low, right?"

"Right," her husband said.

And as if those were the magic words which broke the evil spell, the children stood and ran to her, and hugged her, as if days had passed since they last saw each other, instead of just this morning, at breakfast.

"So. What's all this?" she said, looking at them, then over her shoulder at her husband, who stood there, somewhat deflated, and watched.

"Nothing," he said. "We were just . . . talking."

"Talking," she said, as if she didn't quite believe him. "I guess that's good. We don't talk enough around here."

But if Thomas and Jill agreed, they didn't say so. They simply held onto her, tight, as if the three of them were about to float away together, off to a strange and foreign land.

Then, in the next moment, everyone seemed to disappear. The kids scattered. Doors slammed. Music pumped through the walls. And without so much as a glance behind her his wife went into the bedroom, where, he knew, she began to change into something more comfortable. Seizing on this opportunity, and emboldened by his forays into the heart of his desire, he loped quickly after her, hoping at least to catch one small glimpse of her fine, sculpted calves, and a peek at a patch of her lovely, white thighs.

Daniel Wallace is the author of three novels and numerous short stories. He lives in Chapel Hill, North Carolina, with his wife and son.

ROBYN TOWNEY

*I*t's hard to put my finger on a specific impulse
or desire that justifies or explains a story's existence, and I try not to think about it. It may simply
come down to the lucky pair of underwear I was
wearing at the time, or the way I part my hair, or
the perfect cup of coffee I had that morning, but
I honestly don't know. This story, for instance, is about a man I've never
known, about a family I only imagined. I do know that the first sentence of
the story is the first sentence I wrote, and the next sentence followed its dim
trail, and the next the same, each moving the story along until there was
nowhere left to go. It's a dark story, I think, but I had a lot of fun writing it.

FILL IN THE BLANK

(from *Epoch*)

1. If I were a bird, I'd be a _____.

Nighthawk, she writes. Not a hawk at all, but a gray-and-white bird ticked like a mattress. Nighthawks nested every spring on the edge of the driveway at home in shallow cups made of grass, twigs, gravel. When Garland approached, the parent birds danced away from the chicks, dragging an open wing. *Look at me! Take me!*

2. If I were a word, I'd be _____.

Surmise, because all of life was uncertain. Nothing to do with surprise, except for the rhyme, which you kept on hearing, like feeling your hat on your head after you've removed it.

3. If I were an object, I'd be a _____.

Without hesitation. Garland writes *ring.* Round and perfect, like the pattern of the quilt her mother had made, World-without-End. Interlocking rings that slipped in and out of each other. She'd be a ring pavéd with rubies, like the ruby slippers of her namesake, Judy Garland. And to match the stud in her navel, which was set in a gold circlet like a tiny pulltab. Sometimes she imagined tugging it until she turned inside out — intestines, heart, lungs blooming from her belly like slick flowers.

In fact, Garland McKenney, aged twenty, believes that she will be struck down at a young age, like her mother, who died of a stroke at twenty-six while watching *Laugh In*. So inured is Garland to this belief that she hasn't the faintest awareness of it. She only knows she is hungry — for food, for sex, for risk — for life.

Not long after Garland arrived in New York City, she stopped telling people the name of her hometown. Instead, she simply said "Florida," and let them picture tourists gleaming with suntan oil and gold chains on the beaches of the south. The state might as well have ended at Disney World for all they knew about north Florida and a town like Sweetheart.

She'd noticed Kroner's Physical Therapy while temping at a brownstone next door. From her office window on the third floor, she watched people limp in and out, including her boss, who had a sprained back. Garland had once delivered a contract to her while she lay under hot packs in a treatment room. She had used the bathroom and noticed the closet with the door ajar and the purses hanging there like ripe fruit on a tree. That's when the idea first occurred to her.

Would anyone at Kroner's remember her from that one brief visit? Her hair had been long and brown then; now it was red and short, with dreadlocks accumulating like dust bunnies on either side of her face. The semi-homeless look, her roommate Lynda called it. She'd met Lynda at a laundromat. On the day Garland moved into Lynda's tenement apartment on the Lower East Side, the two had celebrated by having their tongues pierced.

"All we need is an Ace bandage," Garland told Lynda one evening soon after. She wedged two pillows under her head on their shabby couch. "Beyond that, we'll play it by ear. We're just going to be using their bathroom."

"I don't think it's going to work," Lynda said. "This is New York. Why should they let two complete strangers use the john?"

Garland thought for a moment. "You have a point."

They decided to smoke a joint. Garland liked company when she got stoned. Alone, she became homesick. She never yearned

for the people in Sweetheart, only the place — the kingfishers crying as they swooped along the Sweetheart River, the crystal-blue
eyes of deer bunched together at night like a chandelier above the
levee in the backyard.

Lynda examined a strand of her streaky blonde hair. "Have you
ever done anything like this before?"

Garland couldn't decide how much to tell. She wanted Lynda to
have confidence in her plan, but she didn't want her to think she
was a hardened criminal. "Let's just say I've broken the law more
than once. What about you?"

"Me too," Lynda giggled. "I've crossed the street on red. And
I've shoplifted." She frowned. "A lot."

They compared what they'd shoplifted. Then Lynda asked,
"What else have you done?"

Garland's mind sorted through her transgressions: *Underage
girl buys beer at Piggly Wiggly. Teen grows marijuana in 4-H field.
Juvenile defaces courthouse bathroom.*

"Come on," Lynda wheedled. "I thought we were sisters."

"We are, we are." Garland trusted Lynda. Lynda was generous,
lent Garland clothes, money, jewelry, and makeup. Most of all,
Lynda was affectionate in a way Garland had never encountered
and found irresistible. Though Lynda was straight and had a boyfriend named Greg upstate, she held Garland's hand when they
shopped, and put her arm around her on the street. When they
watched TV together, she'd rest her head on Garland's shoulder.
She was a tall, fleshy girl who kissed women as well as men on the
mouth — wet kisses that were innocent and completely genuine.
People felt loved by Lynda. Once, early on, Garland had caught
herself mimicking Lynda's free and easy ways, and it had embarrassed her to realize how much she admired her new friend. She
would have to wait until she lived somewhere else before she could
adopt Lynda's charms as her own. "Did you grow up in Europe or
something?" Garland suddenly asked. She had seen people kissing
like that in European films. Lynda was born in Pennsylvania.

"Me? Europe? Get out!" Lynda inhaled. "This is good weed.

Come on," she pressed through held breath, "tell me what crimes you've committed."

Garland told Lynda everything except the reason she had left Sweetheart—that she had burned down Wilbur Sanders's fish camp. While she talked, the two of them collected their perfumes onto a tray and took turns smelling them.

"Normal teenage stuff. But you got caught. I wonder why," Lynda said.

"I'd have to attribute it to native stupidity. Oh, and the expert guidance of my teachers and parent. Such shining examples of assholehood." The high school counselor had been wrong: She hadn't gotten caught to get attention since there were virtually no consequences, not even unpleasant ones. None of it had mattered. "Listen, I've got an idea." Garland sniffed from a squat bottle of L'Air du Temps. "I'll go to Kroner's wearing the Ace bandage by myself a day or so beforehand and ask about physical therapy. Then we'll come back and do it."

"Yeah, then we'll clean them out," Lynda added.

After that, they referred to the plan as a cleaning job, as if they were merely afterhour maids. Neither of them ever said the word *robbery.*

Seized by an idea, Lynda bolted straight up. "We could buy an old car with the money, get out of the City on weekends." She sank back into the couch. "Or we could take a trip. I've never been to Mexico."

"We could." Slumped against Lynda on the couch in a cloud of sumptuous aromas, Garland felt closer to her roommate than she had to anyone in a long time. But should she confide to Lynda her worry about being recognized? Lynda might veto the whole plan.

As if Lynda could read her mind, she said, "Since you're going there twice, maybe you should wear a disguise."

Garland raised the mirrored tray to her face. Hazel eyes, a broad snub nose, and a delicate mouth met her gaze. "This *is* a disguise. I just need dark glasses and a hat."

4. If wishes were rabbits, disappointments would be: a) lions b) hat boxes c) frogs d) rabbit-skin coats.

Garland had been subjected to all sorts of tests in her life — SATs, PSATs, an IQ test in seventh grade — but never one with such a bizarre question. Irrelevant, too: She didn't waste her time wishing for things. Her father, Eastman, wasn't the fairy godmother type. He'd granted only one wish in her life: Judy, the massive pit bull mix he rescued from the Tupelo County Animal Shelter for Garland's eleventh birthday. Eighty-five pounds of chest with jaws like a bear trap, Judy was a sweet-tempered animal fond of crushing apples in a single chomp. She'd never bitten anyone, but Wilbur was leery of her. Garland had always brought Judy along on their trysts. When she became a dogwalker in New York, Garland decided to specialize in large, problem dogs that other walkers rejected — Dobermans, pit bulls, shepherds, the big unruly mutts. Garland adored the dogs she walked; she was proud of reforming the recalcitrant barkers and nippers. Taking a cue from Lynda, whenever she encountered clients walking their own dogs on the weekends, she'd kiss the dogs smack on the muzzle. The owners seemed mildly embarrassed by this outpouring of affection. She knew they pitied her for being one of those single women who had replaced people with animals, but they trusted her completely.

The idea of a rabbit-skin coat outraged her.

Later that week, Garland showed Lynda pictures of Wilbur, calling him her ex-flame. She didn't mention he was the Tupelo County sheriff.

"Manly." Lynda touched the photo with her finger. "Nice torso."

"He's got really good legs, too, and a butt from heaven."

"I didn't know they gave out butts in heaven."

They were lying on their backs at opposite ends of the sofa, the soles of their feet pressed together. Lynda raised up to pass Garland a joint. She held Garland's wrist for a moment, eyeing her green fingernails. "Cool polish," she whistled. "You're such a girlie girl."

"It's from eating all that Southern fried chicken."

"So why'd you break up with him?"

What Garland had loved most about Wilbur was that he desired her in a way that compelled him to take chances. He was completely at the mercy of this profound lust — or was it love? — for her. For Wilbur, the affair with Garland was the equivalent of cheating on the whole town. "Oh, he lied to me sometimes," she told Lynda now. "And we always had to sneak around to be together."

"Why?"

"He was married. When I got angry at him, he was afraid I'd tell his wife or blab it." It hadn't occurred to Garland to use Wilbur's wife against him, but after he mentioned it, she realized how much power it gave her.

"God," Lynda said, closing her eyes. "You can't have a relationship if you can't get mad."

"Is this one of your yoga positions?" Garland asked, aware of pressure coming from the soles of Lynda's bare feet.

"Yoga isn't done in pairs, you idiot," Lynda laughed. "You know, I'd kill Greg if we were married and he had a girlfriend. That's why I never want to get married. I'd be such a bitch."

"Really?" Garland had always admired the way Lynda managed Greg. Nothing rattled her. "You're usually so relaxed about Greg."

"Oh, I am. Because we're not married."

"But you love him enough to marry him, don't you? What difference would a piece of paper make?"

"Worlds of difference, my dear," Lynda said. "Worlds."

5. When I'm angry, I: a) tell people off b) break things c) cry d) go to the mall.

As a kid, when Garland was upset she found solace in the family photo albums. Because she didn't remember her mother, who died when she was six, she'd spent hours poring over the professional portraits from the Sears in Tallahassee and candid snapshots captioned by her parents: *Baby Garland at 22 mo. . . . Lorelei and*

Garland go swimming at Wakulla Springs, 5/2/87. Often, Lorelei and Garland wore identical mother-daughter outfits that Lorelei had sewn. She tried to love her mother then, but felt instead like a spy memorizing someone else's past.

Whenever Garland got into trouble, Eastman would invoke his dead wife, doubly aggrieved because she wasn't there to share his frustration. "My poor Lorelei," he'd say piously, hanging his head so his chin touched the second button on his shirt. "I'm glad she never lived to suffer this heartache." And, "If your mother wasn't already dead, this surely would kill her" — as if Garland's only role in life was to be the daughter of a dead woman.

Garland pitied her mother for dying young, but anyone could see that the real tragedy was Garland's: to be raised by Eastman McKenney, the most boring, humorless man on earth. The Human Dust Bowl. Mr. Zero — that's what his students called him when he taught math, before he became principal. Twenty years in high school had damaged him in peculiar ways. His daily life consisted of an inflexible collection of habits. He rose every day at 6:45, put on one of four suits, drank a cup of coffee, ate a bowl of grits into which he'd stirred two dabs of butter and a raw egg, then drove to work. Garland often had the sensation she was hearing his voice through a P.A. system. He behaved identically to everyone, as if he'd misplaced his private life.

6. When I go to a party, I usually: a) talk with people I know b) talk with strangers c) observe people d) leave as soon as I can for one reason or another.

The only parties Garland knew much about were the private kind she and Wilbur had had. In most other recollections, they are sitting around in their underwear.

The following Tuesday afternoon, with Lynda stationed at the corner, Garland rang the bell of Kroner's Physical Therapy, her arm snugged in an Ace bandage. She was clad in black, wearing sunglasses. Both girls had decided Garland's hair was too unusual, so she'd covered it with a knit cap.

She was buzzed through two electric doors to the waiting room. A plump middle-aged receptionist talking on the phone motioned her to take a seat.

The room was dirty, with beige walls that hadn't been painted in an ice age and red carpeting so discolored by dark oily patches that Garland itched just contemplating it. The motley assortment of furniture might have been salvaged from the street. She and Lynda had filled their apartment with such discards. Curb foraging, Lynda called it. If Garland had truly needed physical therapy, she wouldn't trust this place. A cheapskate — Mr. Kroner? — was interested in separating people from their money first and foremost.

The receptionist hung up the phone. "How can I help you?"

"I've got tennis elbow, though I don't play. I thought I'd stop by, check out my insurance, maybe take the two-cent tour."

"Of course," the woman said. "My name is Grace."

"Virginia," Garland replied, shaking hands. "I work in the neighborhood."

"Where?"

"I just . . . baby-sit," she fluffed. "I'm in school. You know, college."

"Let me show you the office." Grace pushed back her chair and squeezed past a dented filing cabinet. "What insurance do you have?"

"Cigna." Was that the name she'd seen on the subway ads?

"We take Cigna. I think you get twelve visits."

Garland followed Grace down a narrow hallway with four numbered rooms opening off it. In one, a patient lay under bulky towel packs. At the end of the hallway was a bathroom and next to it the closet with the door ajar that she'd noticed on her earlier visit. At least six pocketbooks hung on hooks. Garland marked the spot on the mental map she was sketching. The hallway ended at a thin curtain, which Grace rattled aside on metal hooks to reveal a measly exercise room with a NordicTrack, treadmill, and universal machine. The room was dingy, with a naked overhead bulb and a small ground-level window. No back door, Garland noted.

"Would you like to make an appointment? I can start processing the paperwork," Grace said as they returned to the waiting area. She handed Garland a business card.

"I'm seeing the doctor in a few days to pick up my prescription. I'll stop by after that."

Outside, Garland spotted Lynda slouching at the corner, paging through *Vogue*. They hurried to the subway. "Way cool," Lynda said, nestling her head on Garland's shoulder as Garland told her everything.

7. If my father were a food, he'd be: a) an omelet b) a Popsicle c) a steak d) cherry pie.
She blacks out the choices and substitutes *celery*.

8. If my mother were a food, she'd be: a) meatloaf b) wine c) macaroni and cheese d) fish filet.
Even though most food is dead and my mother is dead, this is not relevant.

A baby on the floor of Kroner's waiting room was crawling across the stained red rug toward his mother, who was chatting on a cell phone. It made Garland sick to see the baby's nice clean body against the hairy, soiled floor. The baby put his fist in his mouth.

"Oh, hi," said Grace. "You're back."

"I'm ready to make my appointments."

Friday was a good day for a robbery, Garland reasoned, because people were distracted. The caution with which they had armed themselves on Monday had thinned to an impatience for the weekend to arrive.

Lynda and Garland had smoked a little dope to smooth them out before taking the train uptown. Dressed in the same black outfit as before, Garland was feeling confident. Lynda, also in black, wore reflective sunglasses. Garland knew that behind them, Lynda's eyes brimmed with excitement. Each girl carried an empty tote.

"This is my friend," Garland said. "Lorraine, Grace."

"Hello," Lynda said. She turned and whispered to Garland as Grace placed a clipboard and pen on the desk.

"Would you mind if I used the ladies' room first?" Garland asked. "If *we* used the restroom?"

Grace cast a sharp appraising glance at the two young women. "It's at the end of the hall. Remember?"

Garland hooked pinkies with Lynda, the familiar thrill of trespass surging through her body as they traversed the hall. The layout matched the map she'd drawn for Lynda. She could hear muffled voices behind two doors. The other two were open, revealing reclining figures engulfed in darkness. But there was a fifth door at the end of the corridor where she remembered none. A plate on it said *Office*. How had she missed it?

They reached the bathroom. Beyond the curtain of the exercise room something metallic thunkety-thunked.

"Turns out I really do have to pee," Lynda muttered, entering the bathroom.

As before, the closet door stood open. Garland snatched a purse from a hook and quickly niched the wallet. She slipped it into her tote, then proceeded to the next purse and a third. Lynda emerged, her face eager.

"Check the coat pockets," Garland whispered, then closed the bathroom door behind her. Two of them standing at the closet might arouse suspicion.

Garland looked at her watch. How long since they'd left Grace? She'd meant to note the time. She used the toilet, washed her hands, yanked a paper towel from the dispenser, and checked her watch again: Twenty-two seconds had elapsed. She walked out of the bathroom.

Lynda wasn't there.

A pile of coats littered the closet floor. She resisted the urge to hang them up.

A noise caught her attention. She stepped into the hallway. Nothing. She peeked around the curtain of the exercise room. An elderly man was working weights on pulleys. He grunted and closed his eyes. He hadn't seen her.

Perhaps Grace had summoned Lynda to the front. Garland craned her neck, but she was at the wrong angle to see the reception area. I am going to kill Lynda, she thought.

An egg timer buzzed in one of the rooms. The OFFICE door swung open to reveal a lanky man with a pencil wedged behind his ear and a chart in his hand. Garland froze, a shower of icy needles bombarding her spine and chest. Pretending to retrieve something from the floor, she nudged the closet door shut. When she stood back up, the man was staring at her. "Can I help you?" Surprise and annoyance tinged his voice.

"Yes. Well, no. I'm just signing up for treatment." The voice sounded like pre–New York Garland, her old Cracker drawl bubbling up through her fear. "Grace let me use the john before I did my paperwork."

The egg timer continued to gnaw at the air.

"I'll get Mrs. Millstein off her electric stim," he shouted. A muffled female voice thanked him.

She hated this guy for making her feel like a school kid caught in the hall without a bathroom pass. She hated his crappy furniture and snot-colored walls. He was probably the son of a bitch who didn't care if babies had to crawl on filthy rugs.

"I'll see you around then," he said in a friendlier tone. "Oh, I'm Hank Kroner." He had a smooth face, and trim body. About thirty-five, Garland guessed.

"Virginia." As Garland took his hand, she imagined the tote bag swinging forward of its own volition, dumping the stolen cache at his feet. She tried to hold his gaze, but he turned and strode into Room 3, chatting airily as the door clicked shut behind him.

The office door opened again, and Lynda burst through it. "Jackpot!" she squealed, her voice breaking. "Big jackpot!"

"Shut *up!*" Garland hissed.

Another buzzer sounded, and Grace appeared in the hallway, startled to see the two women there. A question formed on her face, but the buzzer prevented her from asking it. "I'm coming, Mr. Marx," she called, disappearing behind a door.

In the reception room, they stepped around the baby, who was now sitting upright, trying to wedge both fists in his mouth, his blue romper webbed with red lint. They bustled through the inner and outer doors, down the brownstone steps to the cold, sunny street. The abrupt change of light reminded Garland of leaving the Saturday matinee as a child, that moment she was spilled back into the daylight and realized, always with amazement, that the movie was the false world and this featureless, encompassing brightness the real one.

9. When my employer drops $100 under my desk, I decide to: a) return it immediately b) treat everyone in the office to lunch c) return it later d) spend it at the mall.

The money totaled $2,200, which they divided equally. Lynda had found $1,410 in a strong box under Kroner's desk, where she had dived when he walked in. "My body felt like it was on fire," she told Garland. She catalogued every rivet of pleasure and fear she'd experienced while hunched on the floor. "I can't believe I did it. It was so totally cool. We're going to have some good shit to reminisce about when we're old and gray."

"Yep." Garland squared her stack of cash. "It'll always be a bond between us." Now she understood that Lynda had come along not for twenty minutes of being thrillingly alive, but to fashion an adventure to paste into her memory book. She did it so she could say she had done it, so she could hark back to the experience, like looking at vacation pictures. She'd bet anything it was Lynda's first and last big excitement, while Garland might move on to bigger, riskier—she censored the thought. "Hey, do you know why Kroner had that stash hidden in his office?"

Lynda looked at her blankly.

"He's skimming, pocketing cash off the top to avoid paying tax on it. No wonder he can't afford decent carpeting." She'd learned about skimming from Wilbur, who claimed everyone in business did it.

Lynda said, "When my friend Roger, the night manager at Starbucks, did that, they called it theft, but if you own your own business, it's skimming. It doesn't even sound illegal. It sounds like water-skiing." She dropped her money into a silk jewelry pouch. "The working class really does get screwed."

Garland punched her on the arm. "You're a regular Robin Hood."

"Do you want these?" Lynda pushed a pile of pleasantly misshapen wallets toward Garland. Without knowing what she would do with them, Garland dumped them into her dresser drawer.

On Sunday, Garland braved the tourists in SoHo to buy shoes at Tootsie Plohound—red leather pumps with round heels shaped like upside-down lighthouses. Back home she posed the pair stepping jauntily forward on her bureau so she could admire them from her bed.

She tossed the wallets onto her mother's World-without-End quilt. She discarded all the bits of paper and scissored the credit cards to a jagged heap. Her attention shifted to what remained: IDs and photos.

She arranged the pictures on the bed into family groupings, spinning stories out loud about them the way she used to play with paper dolls. Fancily-dressed children encircled a blue Christmas tree; a bar-mitzvah boy posed solemnly with his prayer shawl and yarmulke. Among the bouquets of faces, she identified the progenitors, their countenances like pressed corsages. She named them Shields, Hornstein, Ventadour. There were elders from Kansas, and European cousins thrice-removed wearing woolen jackets still faintly aromatic with naphthalene. Now the quilt resembled the family album that Lorelei had hoped to fill. Here were the paternal aunts and uncles, there the maternal. Here was the daughter who joined the Air Force, the distant cousin on Eastman's side who'd be released from prison in six years, the twin nieces she'd never met on Lorelei's side who owned a dress shop in Atlanta.

Was it her imagination, or was Lynda acting funny? Though Lynda had described the robbery to Greg on the phone, when he visited a week later, she forbade Garland to discuss it, claiming that it made her feel creepy.

"Creepy?" Garland echoed. She cut a BLT in half. The three of them were preparing lunch in the tiny kitchen.

"It makes me nervous."

"You weren't nervous when we did it. I was the one who nearly peed in my pants when Kroner walked out of his office."

Greg laughed.

"Stop it! You're talking about it," Lynda said.

Garland had complied. The rest of that day, Greg and Lynda stayed in the bedroom, even for dinner. They spent Sunday at the Central Park Zoo, a place the three of them had frequented in the past. Greg told her that he and Lynda needed some time by themselves.

Greg left at dawn on Monday. That afternoon, after work, Garland bought the ingredients for spaghetti with meatballs, Lynda's favorite. While she cooked, Lynda remained in her bedroom. She was unusually quiet during dinner.

"Is anything the matter?" Garland finally asked. It was just a formality — obviously something was terribly wrong.

"Nope."

"You're acting strange."

"No I'm not." Lynda had wound so much pasta on her fork that it looked like a cone of cotton candy.

"You are. Have I done something to make you mad at me?"

Sighing, Lynda set the fork down. She regarded Garland, her face so sad it looked as if it would melt. "I feel guilty about what we did." Tears began to trickle down her cheeks.

Garland moved to Lynda's side of the table and did what she imagined Lynda would do: She draped her arms around her friend's neck and kissed her on the cheek. "Don't cry, sweetie. It's okay." She pushed back the hair on Lynda's forehead. "Everything's over and you're safe."

"No, I'm not," Lynda blubbered. "We could still get caught. I feel horrible, even if you don't."

"I think we should discuss this and then you'll see that everything is all right. Let's calm down. Let's smoke a little, okay?"

Lynda agreed, sitting at the table like a zombie while Garland rolled a joint. They smoked in silence, waiting for the drug to work.

They piled the dirty dishes in the sink and moved to the living room, to opposite ends of the sofa. They'd planned to paint the living room walls apricot, but they were still a crazed eggshell.

"Every time I see you it reminds me. I know I shouldn't blame you, but it was your idea," Lynda told Garland.

"But you gladly participated."

Lynda hugged a throw pillow to her chest. "But now I regret it. We might have stolen money intended to feed a child."

"Don't be melodramatic. Nobody's life changes because their pocket gets picked."

"You don't know that."

"None of the wallets even had enough money for a month's rent. Remember, most of it was Kroner's. And he's a crook."

Lynda stared at her lap. "I think we're very different people."

Garland's breath caught in her chest. She knew what "different" meant—that you weren't a person at all. "Actually, I think we have a lot in common."

"I don't think we have the same values," Lynda said.

It felt like a breakup in the making, like when her tenth grade boyfriend called her immature and took back his friendship ring. Garland's face felt hot. The next thing Lynda would say was that she didn't want to hang out together anymore.

Instead, Lynda clasped her hands behind her head. "I've decided to give my share of the money to Habitat for Humanity," she announced. "Maybe you should do the same."

"You've got to be kidding. What about the car?"

"We don't need a car."

"Duh! That's obvious. We both knew we'd just buy crap with the money." Garland tossed a pillow onto the floor and kicked it. Something shifted in Garland, as when an animal realizes the stick its owner is holding is intended for its head. She heard her own voice rise. "Now I think we *should* buy a car, to ease your conscience. We should buy a car and take poor kids for rides, what do you say?" That was weak. "You're so judgmental," Garland stumbled. "I thought you were special, but you're so ordinary. You're just like everyone else."

"Exactly," Lynda said. "You're the one who's weird."

10. Flower is to seed as _____ is to teenager: a) education b) adult c) loneliness d) school.

Lynda wrote the check for Habitat for Humanity in front of Garland, sealing the envelope with a kiss, muttering something Garland didn't want to hear.

In the next week, when they food-shopped, Lynda used a separate cart. On the street, instead of holding hands, she skipped ahead or hung back, pretending to look at something on a tree or in the gutter. Garland wasn't fooled. In fact, she was touched by these awkward deceptions. The only thing Garland deeply regretted was that she and Lynda weren't getting along. She decided to wait until this rough patch in their friendship smoothed itself out.

A few days later, Lynda invited Garland into her room while she was packing for a long weekend upstate with Greg. "I know you think I'm giving you the cold shoulder," Lynda said, sitting down on the bed next to Garland.

"You're treating me like I have the plague," Garland whispered, suddenly on the verge of tears.

"I'm not trying to." Lynda put her arm around Garland, lightly. "It's just happening. I can't help myself. And I know I'm just as guilty as you."

Garland had never known anyone to speak so honestly.

"I'm so sorry," Lynda said. "I know it sucks for you."

It was as if a giant hand had reached down and seized Lynda, leaving her dangling just out of reach. All Garland could do was watch as Lynda twisted and turned, struggling to free herself.

Lynda resumed packing, throwing underwear into her bag. "Do you want me to go with you to the Greyhound terminal?" Garland offered. It was nearly midnight, and a light sleet was falling. Lynda would be traveling most of the night.

"No, that isn't necessary."

"I'll bet you wish you had that car now."

Lynda zipped up her suitcase. "How can you joke about it?"

"Aw, come on, Lynda. I'm not allowed to make jokes now?"

"I guess not." Lynda frowned with regret, then turned and looked straight at Garland. "What I really wish is that I could confess, take my medicine, and be done with it."

"Don't say that, okay?" Garland could feel the blood draining out of her face. "Not even as a joke. It really freaks me out."

"I'm sorry." Lynda walked toward the front door with Garland following. She donned her coat in silence.

"I'm sorry, too, okay?" Garland's tears welled up at last. "But I can't undo it. You're just going to have to forgive yourself." *And me,* she wanted to add, but didn't. She wanted to comfort Lynda and have Lynda comfort her in return. She wanted them to dissolve into laughter and fall into each other's laps the way they used to. Instead Lynda bustled down the narrow hallway, mumbled good-bye, and slammed the door without once turning around.

Three days later, Greg and Lynda phoned. Greg explained that he'd be spending more time in the city, staying in the apartment with Lynda. In mild, hollow voices the two of them asked Garland to find a new place to live. Though Garland knew this was a lie intended to spare everyone's feelings and avoid a scene, she couldn't muster even an iota of rage. She felt crushed.

Because she hadn't bought anything but the shoes with the robbery money, Garland had no difficulty producing the security deposit and last month's rent for a studio sublet in the less trendy Murray Hill section. By now, Garland figured, Lynda probably had a new roommate to hold hands and snuggle with.

Garland's view of New York from the eighteenth floor reduced the city to a more manageable grid devoid of individual faces. A mirrored alcove next to her bedroom glittered with designer lipsticks and nail polish boosted from the best department stores. She had added three Rottweilers to her daily roster and begun boarding canines in her apartment at exorbitant prices. Her roommates were all dogs, she joked to herself. New York was starting to feel like home.

One evening two months later, Garland recognized Lynda's number flashing on her caller ID. They hadn't spoken since Garland moved out. What good could come from speaking now?

"Hello, Lynda," she said, snatching up the receiver on the last ring.

"Caller ID, huh? Or are you psychic?"

"Both. What are you up to?"

"Oh, the usual. What about you?"

"Yeah, the usual." Garland waited, letting the chilly silence accumulate, like snow.

Finally, her voice shaking, Lynda said, "I have something to tell you." Words that always heralded tragedy — a traffic accident, dying parent, pregnancy?

Garland waited again.

"I'm going to the police tomorrow." Lynda's voice dropped. "To confess. I just wanted to give you a heads-up."

Garland felt woozy.

"I don't expect you to understand, but it hurts me. Every day I feel worse and worse. I'm sick to my stomach, I can't eat, I can't sleep. I've got to get some relief."

"Have you considered Valium?"

"Can you ever be serious?"

"I am serious. Come on, Lynda, please don't rat me out." She hated the pleading tone in her voice.

"Garland, listen, I have a lawyer, and he says if we confess together, we'll get probation. He's willing to represent both of us."

"I thought we were straight on this. I mean, shit, I moved out like you wanted."

"I'll go crazy if I don't do it. I already feel crazy."

"Have you ever heard of the concept of loyalty?" She had believed that Lynda loved her, that Lynda understood her.

"I'm sorry. I don't blame you anymore. I've been seeing a shrink, and now the lawyer. It's tomorrow at ten thirty. Please come."

Garland's mind felt like the room in the Edgar Allan Poe story where the walls begin to contract. She couldn't breathe. "What's the lawyer's name and address?" She grabbed a ballpoint pen and scrawled the information on her forearm. "I'll think it over," she mumbled, and hung up.

Garland sat without moving for a long time, her breathing deep and slow, as if she were nodding off. Her juvenile records in Sweetheart had been sealed; they couldn't be used against her. Wilbur had never reported the arson for fear of being compromised himself. After all, she was a minor at the time. His angry face surfaced in her memory, red as a boiled crab.

Garland had started breaking rules at such a young age that she couldn't recall if she had ever felt the urge to confess. She didn't think so. Lynda, however, stewing in her apartment, was another case altogether. The urge to confess had erupted and spread like a bodily contagion.

Mr. Michelson was a white-haired man with watery blue eyes and a kindly expression. He greeted the two young women warmly, directing them to thick leather chairs angled casually toward his desk. The office had a homey look that probably translated to a high bill. Garland hoped Mr. Michelson would accept a postdated check. She had $230 to her name, not counting credit cards.

She listened as he summarized what had happened, how Lynda had phoned him, crying. He stressed how pleased he was that she had come forward, and now Garland. First-timers, he said, worried about two things: getting caught and being forgiven. Confession was the remedy for both. In the end, the girls would be happy with their decision. His voice was even and reassuring. He'd arranged a brief interview with the captain at the local precinct where they would be booked.

Garland had not realized how much she had missed Lynda until she saw her in the lawyer's waiting room. Lynda had stood and embraced her, then quickly returned to *Entertainment Weekly*. She had still not spoken to Garland, and now she avoided looking at her. Gone for good, Garland thought with a pang. In the past, Garland had always felt justified when she made other people suffer. Now, she wondered: Did her regret for losing Lynda count as genuine remorse, or was it more selfishness?

They would be arrested, photographed, fingerprinted, and then sent home. The police captain, he said, was a sympathetic guy with kids of his own.

Lynda had been sniffling from the first moment, but Garland remained dry-eyed. As the lawyer talked, she realized that she was beginning to feel better, as if she had eaten a solid meal and was now settling down to a good video. It seemed impossible, considering that he was now discussing bail bonds. She felt . . . optimistic, that was the word. As if she were anticipating something beyond the punishment. But what?

Since they were pleading guilty, there would be no jury. "That's good," the lawyer continued. "I hate to rely on juries. Some of them are prejudiced toward single young women. If you came into court with a baby stroller, that would be one thing. But you girls . . ." He smiled at each of them in turn. "You look like you're having too much fun. A jury might imagine lying awake at three in the morning, worried out of their skulls about you."

Garland said, "You mean we look like troublemakers?"

"If you dress the way I tell you, no one will take you for a troublemaker."

"Are we dressed all right now, for the police station?" Lynda asked.

"You're fine," the lawyer said. "Do you have any other questions?"

Garland felt sorry for Lynda, already worried about dressing respectably. Undoubtedly, this was a girl who would never jaywalk again. Garland, on the other hand, was feeling less frightened. The calm that had surfaced moments before now settled around her like a soft, old blanket. "What's actually going to happen to us?" she asked.

"You're first offenders, so the law will go easy on you." He explained that they'd be sentenced and then, most likely, given probation for a couple of years, assigned community service or counseling or both. He planned to talk about their character and to have respectable adults seated at his table who could be mistaken for their caring, tax-paying parents. They'd have to allocute to the crime, to tell the details. That would be the most humiliating part, he said. That was where the actual confession came in.

Lynda burst into tears at the mention of confession. Mr. Michelson whisked out a Kleenex, passed it to her, and continued. "You should think of community service as a job you can never be absent from. If you are, they can throw you in jail."

"I'm not really scared," Garland blurted. "I guess I feel relieved."

"But you're the one who didn't want to do this," Lynda objected angrily through her tissue. "You should be glad that I called you."

Garland knew that Lynda expected gratitude, that she had a right to it, but she could not bring herself to thank her.

•••

Garland had rarely asked herself why she kept breaking rules. When she did wonder, when she closed her eyes and concentrated, she had always envisioned the same thing: herself in a car, careening along a curving mountain road. In this waking dream, the robbery or graffiti or arson was neither her destination nor the place she was hurrying from. No, it was another tap on the gas pedal.

But now that she had been caught, the girl in the fast car paused ever so slightly to look back and glimpsed the wreckage in her wake: Lynda weeping, endlessly weeping, a crowd of indistinct others congregated behind her.

Four months later, in a trial that took less than twenty minutes, they were sentenced to community service. Garland, the admitted instigator, was also ordered to attend counseling, where each week the feeling of being caught reasserted itself, producing an odd joy. You might have thought she had fallen in love.

In early May, the parks of New York City bulged with people. Especially noticeable were those whom illness or age had confined all winter—the elderly with walkers; those gone bald and fragile from chemotherapy; people rolling by in wheelchairs. The parks ran with torrents of baby squirrels and children pursued by shouting nannies. Frisbees and baseballs soared over the paths and promenades through air tinted lime green by the new spring canopy of leaves.

Garland sat on a bench beneath tall sycamores contemplating faces from every continent. She'd once told Lynda that the only things alike in Sweetheart and New York were the sky and the asphalt. The faces of Sweethearts were sunburned and etched with deep lines from a life lived out of doors on tractors, in boats and backyards. New Yorkers' faces were blander, blanker, more like masks. Subway faces, Lynda used to call them.

11. Which of these doesn't belong? a) tomato b) baseball bat c) ball d) pie.

Garland imagines herself twirling tomatoes and baseball bats, eating a pie stuffed with a ball. No, not shape or color. Cannot all be eaten? Cannot all be thrown?

"Our time is up," the counselor announced. The voice was firm but kind, with a sustain like an organ note.

Garland leaned back in her chair and dreamily placed the number two pencil on top of the test booklet. She knew there were no right answers on a test like this.

———————

Enid Shomer's stories have appeared in the *New Yorker,* the *Virginia Quarterly Review, Prairie Schooner, Shenandoah,* and elsewhere. *Imaginary Men* won the Iowa Prize and the LSU/Southern Review prize, both awarded to the best first collection by an American. A story from *Modern Maturity* was included in the 1998 edition of *New Stories from the South. Tourist Season and Other Stories* is coming in spring 2007, followed by her first novel.

LEVENT TUNCER

*I*n 1998, while receiving physical therapy in Manhattan following a back operation, I overheard a therapist describing a burglary. The boldness and simplicity of the crime fascinated me. I didn't much like the place where I was getting my therapy (I chose it because it was a five-minute walk away), so I was happy for it to be burgled in my story! Its shabby interior and greedy owner slid right into place in the fictional therapy practice. I already had a character from another story who was capable of such a gutsy crime, and I had been wanting to find out what happened to her next. Like me, Garland McKenney hails from Florida. But she is younger, one of the thousands of dreamers who inundate New York City every year.

Luke Whisnant

HOW TO BUILD A HOUSE

(from *Arts & Letters*)

A cap is the first thing you need, preferably a primary color, emblazoned with the logo of a tool company or a lumber-yard—Snap-on, DeWalt, Remo, Plum Creek, Georgia-Pacific—or a common brand of beer or perhaps a hot sauce—Tabasco, Texas Pete, Hot Cock Vietnam. Avoid mauve or chartreuse caps featuring yacht club names or internet service provider logos. Note also that although its correct name is "cap," no one calls it "cap"; here, in the circles you move in, it is a "hat." The second thing you will need is a truck, preferably a Ford, Chevy, or Dodge. A Japanese truck counts, but not much.

Draw every stick of lumber, every brick, every nail, every strip of aluminum flashing, every bead of glue on a tongue-in-groove panel of plywood; draw in hyper-realistic enlarged detail; draw in colored pencils with coded colors for each material and construction sequence. Draw draw draw. Tell yourself: *If you can draw it, you can build it.* Delay breaking ground until you have finished the drawings, all of the drawings. Keep drawing long enough and you might not have to build it.

Get back to nature. Find a waterfront building site on a beautiful tea-colored river eleven miles from the closest town, forty-two miles from a secular bookstore or an iced latte, two counties away from the nearest daily newspaper, a site where the display screen of your cell phone blinks NO SERVICE AVAILABLE. Drive a few stakes under the cypress trees and string some line. Start digging. A few weeks after you've finished the foundation, get married to a local woman with two teenagers. Your two favorite rooms in the house — your study and your music room — are now morphed in an instant into teenage bedrooms. You stand where your built-in bird's-eye maple desk was going to be and look out over the tea-colored river and you think *surfboards, stuffed animals, Britney Spears posters.*

The last time your wife ventured out to help you on the house you took her up on the roof with a 3000-count plastic bucket of button-cap nails and three rolls of 30-pound roofing felt; the two of you rolled out the long black strips of felt, overlapping the seams and nailing them down every six inches. Your wife, squatting on the hot roof with Little Tap-Tap, says the nails' orange plastic heads on the black tar paper remind her of Halloween, as if these precise rows of nails were cute little pumpkins lined up like soldiers. You watch her bend a nail, pull it out and toss it over her shoulder, start another one and bend it, start a third and smack it sideways so that it ricochets off into the woods; Easy, you tell her, these are expensive. She reproaches you by hammering in the next dozen perfectly. You got it now, you say, but she just gives you a look. You turn for another handful of nails and accidentally kick the 3000-count bucket with the side of your workboot and watch it tilt and tip and spew two thousand nine hundred and sixty-seven nails across the ridge and down the steep plywood sheathing, a rushing flood of airborne orange nails headed over the eve, a stormburst of orange raindrops pelting your backyard.

When you can't stand the sawdust and dirt on your plywood subfloor another single day, get in your Japanese truck and make a special trip to Beldon's Welding and Hardware to buy a broom.

There is a very pretty young woman in Beldon's who can distinguish at a glance a half-inch lag screw from a five-eights-inch lag screw, who coifs her brown hair in a loose swirl held in place with a couple of 16-penny nails, who wears bluejean shorts and tennis shoes and a chartreuse Beldon's Welding T-shirt and has brown arms and legs in the dead of winter and level brown eyes, and just for fun you have a desultory crush on her and think of her as your Secret Girlfriend. You always contrive to check out when she is manning the rickety old cash register, and today she looks at you holding this broom, an ordinary black-handled yellow-strawed broom made right here in our beloved homestate, and she turns her mouth down further and her eyes dance as she says, "Goin' to do some sweepin'?" and you say yes, wondering why she finds that so god-damned funny, and she looks at the broom again and can barely contain herself and that's when you realize that men in this county don't sweep, or more accurately, they don't sweep with this kind of broom; you should have gotten a push-broom, a janitor's broom; but instead, by mistake, you're buying a woman's broom, and you might as well be buying a tube of lipstick or a box of Tampons. She takes your money and hands you your change and turns away with her face scrunched up and says "Enjoy your sweepin'," and you can't do a thing but say that you will.

Don't take your hat off inside, even if you're inside a church. Leave it on.

When it is 97 degrees and 80 percent humidity with a heat index of 101 at 5:00 PM, and you have spent all day digging postholes for 4x4 pressure-treated posts, rough wet wood soaked in arsenic and copper chromate, hallucinogenic fumes of toxicity wafting off them in the staggering heat, and you are choking on concrete dust as you lift and tear and dump the 80-lb. bags of Redi-Mix, just add water, and with the side of a hoe you are churning buckets of muddy riverwater into the choking powder until it's a bubbling slurry you can hardly heave and pour toward the posthole, and when you have tried unsuccessfully for the fourth time to lift and set plumb a 12-foot post into the wet concrete, and the two snarky teenagers who will share this house with you are, one, at the beach surfing and two, back in town lying in bed in the air conditioning watching music videos, then there is nothing you can do except go inside the house you are building for them and stand in the teenagers' rooms, first one and then the other, and spit on their floors.

Jeffery is an idiot, and the reason you know this is because (a) Mr. Hollowell says "I knowed him all my life, and that boy ain't right," and (b) out of nowhere he materializes one afternoon—Jeffery Skittlethorpe, a grownup high school dropout skidding across your muddy yard on a tiny trick-bike—to introduce himself and offer his help building the house, and when you ask him how much he would charge he squints at the white noon sky and then stares at his tattered blue bowling shoes and then looks up at you to gauge your expression and then says "Not much" and you ask him "How much" and a little uncertainly he says "How 'bout two dollars an hour?"

Invent goofy names for everything and give them a sardonic twist when saying them aloud. For example, at a used tool shop you find an ancient sledgehammer that some previous owner has painted pink, perhaps to forestall theft (who would want a pink sledgehammer?). Buy this thing and call it Big Pink and lisp a bit when asking your wife to hand it to you. You have four other hammers at the building site, so you name each of them: Wafflehead, Steely Dan, Cherry, Little Tap-Tap. In the evocative shadows that dapple the plywood subfloor you artistically arrange these four with Big Pink and a rubber mallet called Condom and take several photos from different angles: your hammer arsenal. In this manner you avoid working on the house.

Call an electrician a few months before groundbreaking and ask him to put in a temporary power pole so you can run the necessary tools to cut and drill wood, mix cement and mortar, and maybe play a radio for a bit of diversion. Ask yourself what he really means when he wonders on your answering machine if you're seriously framing the house yourself. Call him back and get his voicemail. Play phone tag for a few weeks. Look in the mirror one morning and say *Fuck it, I'll just build the whole goddamn thing with 14-volt rechargeable hand tools.* When the battery on your rechargeable circular saw gives out after two hours, reach for your Dad's old snaggle-toothed handsaw and pretend you're Amish.

The word *house* comes from the Old English *hus,* derived from the Indo-European *(s)keus,* a word which means "to cover or conceal from the sky." The word *board* is related to the Old French *bord,* the side of a ship, and derives ultimately from the Indo-European *bher,* meaning "to cut." The word *window* is a compound from the Old Norse *vindruga, vindr,* "wind," and *auga,* an eye: *window,* literally an eye for the wind. Now close the dictionary and go buy some nails.

Go into Beldon's Welding and Hardware, stroll the rows of farm implements, tractor hitches and feed bags and irrigation-system replacement valves, dusty iron and steel and aluminum things you cannot discern the purpose of; say "hey" to your Secret Girlfriend behind the counter, feel stupid when she doesn't reply, doesn't nod, just waits, gazing with her brown impassive eyes; tell her that for the lally columns holding up the second story of the house you're building you need two 6x6 quarter-inch steel plates cut and sized and drilled out just so and does she think somebody there can do that for you, and she says with her down-turned mouth, "Well, *yeah,* this is a *welding* shop, you know," and you stand there and think, *It is? I thought it was an idiot shop,* but you don't say it, and all the men sitting around the drink cooler eating their Nabs and swigging Co-Colas look down at the tiled floor grinning and won't meet your eyes because they're idiots, all those idiots sitting around an idiot shop.

• • •

For some reason all your life you have loved it when instead of "an idiot," people say *"a idiot,"* as in "I don't know what got into that boy; I reckon he's just a idiot." So when 85-year-old arthritic Mr. Hollowell from next door climbs out of his gleaming black-and-turquoise Dodge Dakota and hobbles over to the property line and shouts to you the same exact sentence he shouts every single day, *You're comin' along real good now, ain'tcha?,* you nod and smile and wave and think to yourself that he may be a idiot. "That man useta be mean as a snake," Jeffery told you once, "but ever since he lost his health he's been right nice to me."

A four-foot blacksnake lives under your lumber pile; you saw him one day when lifting the last sheet of plywood. Leave him alone.

You see a black house in a magazine and read an interview with the owner; he says his neighbors hate his house and he doesn't care. Stop framing your house — tell yourself the roof can wait and you're sick of pounding nails and need a break — and paint your exterior walls black. Sing "I see a red door and I want to paint it black" over and over again while slapping your brush against the cedar siding. Think *The neighbors will hate this,* and laugh. Think of names for your house: The Black Box, The Death Star.

There is no plot to the house, no sequence of causally related events. There is no order, no logical development. It yields no secrets to deconstruction. If there ever was a meaning to it, you can no longer express it. You build. All you are doing is creating an object distinct from the objects around it.

Laying brick is a stressful occupation, so for comic relief the local brickmasons take to driving by for a look at your concrete block foundation.

You go into Beldon's hoping to impress your Secret Girlfriend by asking for a carbide tooth blade for a reciprocating saw, and they tell you she isn't working there anymore, that she eloped over the weekend, that her daddy is fit to be tied 'cause he's way too young to be a grandpa and he's swearing on a stack of Bibles to shoot his new son-in-law on sight, and that the reciprocating saw blades are over there, by the C-clamps. You get rung up and bagged by Miss Myrtle, a palsied old woman who smells like cats. You spend the afternoon hacking out window holes with your new saw — ragged ugly slots in the plywood sheathing, empty eye sockets for a bitter wind.

One drowsy day sweet with the scent of swamp magnolias in bloom, your wife and her kids surprise you by toting a picnic out to the house site, where with cries of delight they admire all you've done and ask how long it will be before they can move in, a question you cannot bear to answer honestly. Your wife sets down her wicker basket, lets down her lovely hair, spreads a yellow blanket on the riverbank, and feeds you hummus, olives, tomatoes, and bread; the kids get boloney sandwiches and Cheese Doodles. You eat fresh strawberries for desert and toss the tops in the river and watch black-and-green turtles float up and nudge them with their snouts as sunset paints your black house orange and pink.

One day you count the months backward and realize you have been working on the house for almost two years. A little later it strikes you that you have been thinking about the house, imagining it, trying to will it into existence, for the past decade. Then you remember that as a child, you would put yourself to sleep each night designing a house in your head: a big house with lots of secret spaces, trick doors and hidden alcoves, walk-in fireplaces and spiral stairs. You find that you can't remember a time when you weren't building a house, and then, with despair, you realize too that you will always be building a house, you will never finish the house, that the house is your life: never quite what you wanted, always a work in progress, a collaboration at times but for the most part solo. One nail, one board, one window, one door at a time.

Luke Whisnant is the author of the novel
Watching TV with the Red Chinese; Street, a chap-
book of poems; and the story collection *Down in
the Flood.* His stories have been published in the
United States in *Esquire, Grand Street, Arts &*
Letters, the *Dos Passos Review,* and other publications, and internationally in *Frank* (France) and
Revista Neo (Portugal). Since 1982 he has taught
creative writing and literature at East Carolina
University in Greenville, North Carolina. This is
his third appearance in *New Stories from the South.*

O ne blazing July day with the heat index at 110, I was out at the house
    site installing double top-plates and throwing things and cussing a lot
because nothing was going right, and I disgustedly started making a mental
list of all the things I'd screwed up on this house and what I should have done
instead. The list was in imperative mood and naturally phrased in second
person, because I was talking to myself: "The next time you build a house,
subcontract the foundation, you damn idiot." After a while I realized I was
writing. Stories sneak up on me like that. I start making mental lists or notes
about this or that and eventually I realize I'm not really thinking, I'm writing, and it's time to get to the keyboard. In this case, I thought I was writing
a creative nonfiction piece, but when I started putting words to paper I fell
into my natural mode of lying, so most of the story is imagined.

I set myself three formal restrictions when I was drafting: (1) retain the
"you" point of view of the original mental list; (2) write exactly twenty separate sections (Why twenty? Why? I don't know); and (3) make each section
one paragraph long, no longer. Doubtless this is a bizarre way to write a
story, but I tend to bore myself if I don't set up a puzzle to solve.

And as usual, I didn't know what I was writing about, really, until I had
my "ah-ha" moment in the middle of the third draft. Being "child-free" by
choice my whole life, I was surprised to see that the emotional movement in
the story is toward acceptance of children as a natural part of things. Kids
show up in your world whether you're ready for them or not, and by the end
of the story, the narrator has accepted this essential fact of life.

THE CURRENCY OF LOVE

(from *Epoch*)

I rent a car at the Atlanta airport and set out through rural Georgia. Range Memorial is a small hospital, the kind nobody really goes to anymore if they can help it. But my mother'd rather die than deal with anything that goes on in Atlanta, medical or otherwise.

"It's a little test," she explains when she calls me. She has filed this procedure under the general heading *female trouble*, about which she knows quite a bit in the larger sense, but very little medically speaking. But there was no talking Mother into seeking treatment elsewhere than Range. She's partial to the familiar. My mother believes that all hospitals are essentially the same. All universities, the same. All county governments, police departments, public schools, the same. Institutions are of little or no interest to her. She makes no distinctions among them. This outlook has streamlined her life. Kept her from ever having to travel more than fifty miles from home to conduct the business of her life. Although twice she's gone on a vacation with her senior citizen group at church, once to Canada, once to Mexico. Both times she came back saying, "People are the same everywhere. People are people."

I don't believe that, which is the reason I moved away from Range before I was twenty-one.

I was surprised my mother called me to come. It seems she'd

have called one of my sisters who lives nearer. But they have husbands and children, which my mother translates into having *real* lives. Whereas I simply have a job and a live-in boyfriend — neither of which my mother is impressed with. Normally if she calls me to come to Georgia it's because she has a crop of poison ivy overtaking her yard and she wants me to pull it up. My claim to family fame is that I'm the only daughter not allergic to poison ivy. A less sensitive sort of person. Although that's not completely true. In recent years I've started to break out just like anybody else and have to get a shot to stop it, but it's just that it doesn't bother me that much — the itching or the needle.

I like pulling weeds. Poison ivy, poison oak, poison sumac — I'll yank it up by the roots. I'm fearless in this way. I'll pull anything that looks remotely weedlike — and face the consequences. That's how much I like the idea of a weed-free yard. The pursuit of it gives me satisfaction that's hard to explain. So I don't want to give the idea that my mother is abusing me, asking me to weed out her poison ivy. She believes I have the gift for it. I appreciate her faith in me.

I get to Range Memorial Hospital right on schedule and find my way to surgery. Sure enough, there's my mother lying on a gurney, draped in white sheets. A lady from her church is with her. I recognize her, but can't remember her name. She hugs me when I come in and then my mother reintroduces us — she the good Christian woman, Oswalla, me the *divorced* daughter who my mother explains, *is an English professor.* "She's read cover to cover just about everything there is," Mother says, "except maybe the Bible." Her brows furrow. I've been here barely thirty seconds, and already my mother is disappointed in me.

What my mother says is partly true. I have not read the Bible to her satisfaction. If I had I'd be free to abandon all other literature, which my mother insists is just the tawdry stuff of the secular world. My mother keeps telling me the Bible is a library in itself and if I would just read it and believe it then I would never have to bother reading anything else. This has been her approach to literacy. She insists it has served her beautifully. It has also saved her enormous amounts of time. Although none of us is sure just what exactly she's saving all that time for.

"How's the patient doing?" I ask Oswalla.

"Your mama is a strong woman," Oswalla says. She kisses my mother's cheek, leaves her a scripture written out on a personalized card and goes home to make her husband some lunch.

As soon as she leaves my mother says, "Poor Oswalla. Her husband is bad to drink. He used to be principal at Range High School when integration hit. He had a mess on his hands."

I smile at my mother, the way she still thinks of integration as something that hit — like a tornado or a hurricane. I sort of know what she means. Right now, nearly everybody we see in pre-op is black. "It's the new Georgia," my mother always says whenever she makes a racial observation. It's a saying she picked up from my ex-husband, Randy.

"For years everybody in Range was mad at Oswalla's husband," my mother says. "No one man could deal with all the ignorance he was dealing with. It would have tried Jesus hisself."

"Too bad," I say. I don't really know these people.

"Oswalla is a living testimony," Mother says. She tugs at the sheet folded over her. "Is it cold in here? I got the shivers."

"It's probably nerves." I pull a blanket up over her, tucking her feet in.

"My doctor is older than I am," Mother says. "That's one thing."

I'm not sure of the point she's making.

"I guess it's better than having a teenage doctor. What do teenagers know about old ladies?"

"What do old men know about old ladies?" I say.

She laughs. "Oswalla's been with her husband forty years, come hell or high water."

"That's nice," I say. I don't know if she's suggesting that that's the course of action I should have taken with my first husband, Randy. Forty years of hell and high water. Or if she's thinking about Daddy.

"Usually life is easier on a pretty woman," Mother says. "Oswalla's so pretty."

"She is," I say. "She doesn't look like somebody who's lived a hard life."

"She's spirit-filled," Mother says. "That's why." She sighs like she's going to sleep.

It occurs to me that my mother is a beautiful woman too, her white hair against the white pillow, her clean face and small dark eyes that she keeps closed. She has good bones. That's how she once described herself—a woman with good bones. Now they want to take a sample of flesh to see if her breasts are as good as her bones.

It's odd to be in a hospital with my mother. She's not the hospital type. My mother has the sort of faith that reduces every worry to just a pleasant annoyance, like making out the grocery list or overcharging her Sears credit card. It's a good sort of faith that insists every problem is a small one. My mother raised my sisters and me never to be sick. We had the standard cramps and bled on the bedsheets until they couldn't take any more bleach and had to be thrown out. The pain was so bad sometimes she'd give us sips of whiskey with honey. But that was not being sick, that was being *women.* Zana was allergic to seafood and puffed into a pink ball that time down at Panama City. Leena broke her arm when she fell off the Homecoming float in her strapless dress. Otherwise our range of illness growing up was little more than the common cold—or in the case of my sisters, the dreaded poison ivy. This was because Mother had faith—and we knew it. She rebuked Satan every time we sneezed or slipped or vomited. It seemed like it worked. At least on us. Daddy—he was another story.

"I want to get this over with," Mother says. "Some old man going at my breast with a knife."

"Try not to think of it like that," I say. I wonder if she's been watching too much TV.

An orderly comes by our open-curtained cubicle. "Hey, honey," he says to my mother. He's a fat white boy, gay as the day is long.

He makes himself busy tucking Mother's blanket. "You aren't getting too chilly, are you?"

"This is my daughter. She flew to Atlanta and drove over to be with me today."

"Sweet," he says. "Kids don't have time for their Mamas these days. Don't have to work here long to see that. I get my heart broke twenty times a day—the things I see around here."

"This is Roland," Mother says to me. "I had him in Sunday school."

"Hey, Roland." I smile and we shake hands. I wonder if my mother doesn't know that Roland is gay—or if today, under these particular circumstances—she doesn't care.

"Your mama is a sweet lady. She knows her Bible," he says.

"She does," I say.

Roland looks at me and I know that he knows I know. And yes, my mother, his former Sunday school teacher, also knows. But we will all rise above this situation—the fact that Roland suffers from what my mother would call an alternative lifestyle that is an abomination to God.

"Roland is taking mighty good care of me," Mother says. "He's a sweet boy."

"Ooooohhh," he laughs, "don't go spreading that around. You're gonna get me fired."

When he leaves my mother says, "He was raised by his mother. She did the best she could."

Besides Roland nearly all the nurses are black women. This has changed since I was a kid. When Leena fell off the float and we brought her to the emergency room all the doctors and nurses were white and nearly all the patients. They had a special room for sick black people off to the side. It was where we imagined they stitched together colored men who had sliced each other to pieces with razors and knives. Back then it seemed that colored women struggled through their births and deaths at home—where they lived their secret lives out of view of white folks like us. Only the guy sweeping up the blood and germs was black. It's different now. My mother is the only white patient in sight. Next to her is an old black man so quiet it occurs to me that he might be dead. Then an old black woman whose breasts will not stay inside her gown. Twice I have seen a nurse go by and try to tuck them in, but they always came loose again.

Some of the black nurses are sweet. They come by and take Mother's blood pressure. They hold her hand. She says, "This is my daughter. She flew to Atlanta. Drove over to be with me."

"Idn't that nice?" they say. "It won't be too long now. We a little bit behind."

But some of the nurses are mean and have smart mouths nobody likes. They talk too loud and move too slow and have bad attitudes. I'm sorry to say this, but it's true. I do not want the mean nurses to come near my mother. I'm afraid they might give her the feeling she's not in good hands. Because they give me that feeling. This is not good to say, but some of these mad nurses act like they think things going *wrong* is the natural order, like in their own lives things go wrong all the time, so now they think *wrong* is normal. I don't want them around my mother with any sharp instruments in their hands. I don't want them manning the controls of any life-and-death machinery. They're just too mad. I don't see how they made it through nurse school as mad as they are.

We wait forever.

The old man in the next cubicle finally gets rolled into the operating room. He's all alone and I feel like I want to kiss his cheek before they roll him away. Just in case. Naturally he gets a mean nurse who acts like his lying there dying is a huge inconvenience to her — like she has a phone call to make or she brought macaroni and cheese for lunch — and needs to get to it while it's still hot. The old man is not on her mind though. I see that. I smile at him, but it's my mother who reaches out as his gurney goes by and grabs his hand, saying, "Good luck in there."

He looks at her all glassy-eyed. "Thank you, M'am," he says. The mean nurse stops rolling his bed and just stands there looking closely at her fingernails. They are painted lavender with little decals glued on them.

"What you having done?" Mother asks. This is not right, of course, to ask him his personal business. He doesn't even know us.

"Prostate," he says.

"Oh," Mother thinks a second, then adds, "I'm having a biopsy too."

He nods and closes his eyes. And the mean nurse rolls him on down the hall. When they get to the operating room Mother says, "Black people have taken over the hospital."

"Seems like it," I say. I don't want to dwell on it today, under the circumstances.

"You didn't want to go to Atlanta," I remind her.

"In Atlanta all anybody is is a number and an insurance payment," Mother says. "I believe you could die while they're busy jotting down your insurance digits. Your sister nearly delivered her baby in the waiting room over there."

The black nurses are eating lunch at the desk. They have good-smelling food they brought from home—greens and cornbread, fried okra and tomatoes. One has spaghetti and meatballs from the hospital cafeteria. I listen to them talk and I think they know I'm listening. The nice ones talk in nice voices and the mean ones talk loud and bossy or else sit sullen and eat with a look on their faces like they are contemplating murdering somebody. I just hope they can wait until they get off work.

When Roland finally comes to get Mother she's sleeping sound. "If I ran this hospital I'd fire some of the people around here," I say.

"You and me both," he grinned.

"Part of what you're paying a nurse for is a good attitude," I say. "How hard is it to be nice?"

"It helps if you know what you're doing too—medically speaking," he says.

I kiss Mother's cheek. She looks exhausted from so much waiting. "I'll be here when you come out," I say. "Everything is going to be fine."

The doctor appears then. "Sorry for the delay," he says. "Had complications we weren't expecting." He shakes my hand. Mother's right. He's old as the hills. He's fat too. Fatter than Roland. He looks unprofessional in his green scrubs. His hair is too long for a man his age. It's like nobody has bothered to tell him it's past time to retire and he's been too busy to notice.

"We'll take good care of your mother," the doctor tells me.

"Thank you," I say, but a chill goes over me and I realize I don't believe him at all.

I go upstairs to call Gill. He's my boyfriend. He's divorced and has a daughter who hates me. Luckily she lives in New Jersey with her mother, although I tell Gill that if we could spend more time together I think I could win her over. I could try at least. This way she only comes for short, hostile visits where Gill tries to buy her as much stuff as he can. He says sadly that money is the currency of their love. I tell him that's sick. Then the next thing you know I'm buying her a fistful of CDs or four pairs of shoes she doesn't need because she can't make up her mind which pair she likes best. I buy her things so she will see that I also understand the currency of her love. I picture her taking all the loot home to New Jersey and showing her mother how she fared on the visit.

I think we're going about Lyndie all wrong — parenting her — but Gill says I don't have any children so I don't really know what it's like these days. I've seen him break down and cry when he puts her on the plane home — all her packages in tow — back to her mother. I would not be against buying love if I believed it could really be bought. But I know it can't. I know it. I wouldn't be divorced now if money was really the currency of love.

Gill is a lawyer. He's from up North, New Jersey too. Two reasons my mother doesn't like him much. When he comes to Georgia with me he acts odd. He doesn't understand anything here. I cannot be explaining and apologizing for a place that defies explanation and apology. I just wish he could grasp that.

I call and tell Gill that Mother is in surgery. He tells me he has sent her flowers—they should already have arrived. I imagine one of the mean nurses making off with the flowers, taking them home and setting them on her coffee table, or taking them out to the cemetery and putting them on her own mother's well-kept grave.

"It was nice of you," I tell him, "to send flowers." I don't tell him there's no sign of them so far because I don't want Gill to think he's wasted his money. He makes a good living, but he's got alimony and child support payments—and pretty soon he'll want to buy Lyndie a car too for her sixteenth birthday. Then there will be college tuition and all. So he worries about money sometimes. We split the rent fifty-fifty. He pays his bills and I pay mine. We're equals in that way. Neither one of us owes the other one anything. Not in a monetary sense.

"You sound funny," Gill says. "You okay?"

"It's my accent," I say. "It flares up when I'm down here."

"I love you," Gill says.

"I love you too," I say.

"You don't sound right," Gill says again. "You sure everything is okay?"

"I'm the only white person in the waiting room," I whisper. "Mother is probably the only white patient in the hospital."

"I don't get it," Gill says. "This is a minor procedure? Right?"

"That's what they say."

"It'll be okay," Gill says. "Don't worry."

The waiting room is large and dumpy. It is theoretically air-conditioned, but you'd never know it today. It looks like a meeting just let out, church maybe, since it's mostly women and children. Some look worried, some look tired, some are sitting in a corner laughing at something—for a moment I think it might be me, the only white person. But I'm not funny.

I go inside the waiting room and sit down in one of the empty chairs. I sort through some raggedy magazines thinking I'll read while I wait. All eyes are on me. The room gets quiet. The laughing lets up. I have contaminated the comfort zone. It's something white people do all the time in Range. I try to smile. I notice a *Southern Living* magazine. It has a basket of colored leaves on the cover—not a good sign since outside right now you could fry eggs on the hoods of cars. I flip through the magazine. It makes me want to plant something—immediately. People around me pick up where they left off. Kids roll toy cars over the furniture making them crash and spin. An old man sleeps beside his granddaughter. The women resume their conversations. I listen half-heartedly. Meanwhile my mother is downstairs being tended to by a sharp knife.

"Who you got in here?" I look up to see a woman my age. She's standing up, drinking a Coke. She has a nametag on her Wal-Mart smock, but I can't read it.

"My mother," I say.

"How bad is she?" the woman asks.

"It's a biopsy," I say. "Routine."

"I bet she be alright," the woman says, "if nothing don't go wrong."

"What about you?" I ask.

"My grandmama's down there," she points toward ICU. "They don't believe she gon make it."

"Sorry," I say.

The woman points to a family of women at the center of the room. "They got kin brought in by ambulance. Been here all night."

"What happened?" I ask.

"Car went off the road," a large woman in a pantsuit says. She has a professional look about her and her daughters do too. It's that Spellman sort of look which really stands out in Range. "They think the driver fell asleep. The car went across the median and slammed into a van full of people coming home from church. My uncle was killed."

"That's awful," I say.

"We've about prayed ourselves sick," a third woman says.

"My name is Vergie," the woman drinking the Coke says. "That's my cousin Mary over there."

I introduce myself and nod hello. It looks like some of the children belong to Mary.

"They letting somebody see my grandmama every thirty minutes," Vergie explains. "We taking turns. She's alone in her head. Grandmama don't know her own name — or none of ours. But we can't let her go out and nobody be with her," Vergie says. "You from here?"

"Not anymore. I live in Virginia now."

"Too bad," she laughs. "You missing out on the high life around here."

I smile.

"Where your mama stay?"

"She's out on Ballard Mill Road."

"I live right there at the turn-off," Vergie says. "It used to be just a few houses. But they got a neighborhood out there now. New houses. It's mixed out there."

"Mixed?" Mary says. "That means maybe two white families out there."

"I'm not talking about that trailer park, Mary," Vergie says. "The neighborhood. We got white and colored out there. Don't lie to the woman."

Mary rolls her eyes at me. The woman with the daughters shakes her head. "Vergie goes with a white man," she says. "Seems like she wants everybody to know that."

"It ain't nothing to be ashamed of," Vergie says.

My mind is roaming like a searchlight, trying to land on something to say. In my childhood I never saw a black woman with a white man. I was raised to believe no such combination ever happened — well, maybe in Atlanta, but not in Range County.

"You get much hassle going around with a white man?" I ask.

"Lord no," Vergie says. "White men been sneaking around the neighborhood going after black women all my life."

I am a little bit too interested in this, and it shows. I look at Mary. She nods her head, "Lord, yes. White men love black women."

"I see lots of mixed couples in Virginia," I say. "But I've never seen it around here."

"Well, open up your eyes, honey. This world is rolling over down here."

"That's good," I say. "It's about time."

"You ever go with a black man?" Vergie asks me. She sits down in a chair across from me and one of the children comes and sits on her lap.

"In college," I say. "In Virginia."

"You like it?" she asks.

"It was a long time ago," I say. "It was sort of dangerous back then."

"Used to be a white woman get caught with a black man some-body liable to get shot," a church woman speaks up.

"Shoot," Vergie is unraveling one of the child's braids while she sucks on the Coke can. "Y'all some dinosaurs," she laughs.

"They don't have the KKK around here anymore?" I ask. This is what I miss — right here — the way when it goes right, that South-ern women will tell their lives. Honest to God. The way they don't shy from the truth once they get started toward it. The way they will tell a total stranger the sort of truth they have to lie to their own loved ones about.

"They still here," the professional says. "More things change, more they stay the same."

"The Klan is the old timers," Mary says. "They've mostly died out. You got skinheads now. They're the ones you got to watch out for."

"I got skinheads at my school," the girl says whose granddaddy is asleep next to her with his mouth open. "They're not all in spe-cial ed, either. They mostly talk. They wear those flags and tattoo themselves like Nazis, but they the same white trash always been around here."

"The woman don't want to hear you talk about white trash," Vergie says to the girl.

"I don't mean nothing by it."

I look at the girl talking. She's about Lyndie's age. She has the same ripe look to her, like she's ready to bust loose in this life, like she's a damp firecracker but when she dries out a little—then look out—the fire hazard she will be.

I always wanted to be a mother. Now it looks like Lyndie might be my only shot at it. If things were better between Lyndie and me, Gill and I would probably already be married. I'm usually great with kids, my nieces and nephews love me to death, but Lyndie—she's a child I just can't connect with. Lord knows I've tried. Gill says I try too hard—that that's the problem. But it's just because I know it can happen—it has too. I have to keep believing in order to stay with Gill. Otherwise I'd have given up and gotten out a long time ago. Lyndie has made it clear she doesn't want a stepmother. And to tell the truth the idea of dealing with Lyndie the rest of my life—the holidays, the vacations, the family dinners—you know, it's made me think twice about ever marrying Gill. I never pictured myself as the wicked stepmother.

My mother says there is nothing wrong with Lyndie that half a dozen spankings when she was a child couldn't have corrected. This makes Gill defensive. It's true he's never said *No* to Lyndie in her life. He's one of those *Yes* daddies that gets kicked in the teeth on a regular basis. But it's a little too late for the get-tough approach now. I think that's why Lyndie hates me. I'm like the living, breathing *No* she's managed to avoid all her life. I'm just a big *No* waiting to happen. I hate thinking of myself that way. *No* personified.

Gill doesn't believe in spanking. He tells my mother, "What are you supposed to do when the court tells you that your only child—who you love more than anything—is going to be raised by the one person on earth who hates and despises you? Think about it. I have to do the best I can with the scraps of time I get—trying to undo the bad-guy image my ex-wife is so devoted to. You try bringing up a kid like that." It struck me at the time he said this—*I don't think I want to.*

In crazy moments I wish I'd had kids with my first husband. I know it would probably have been one mistake on top of another, but at least I'd have something to show for it—besides a lot of wasted time. Sometimes I tell Gill, *let's get married now, have a baby now, before it's too late. Before we stop wanting to. I tell him maybe a baby brother or sister will be just the thing to turn Lyndie around. I say it will be good for her to realize she is not the center of the universe, that she doesn't run the world—despite the way we all treat her. It might be a relief to her.* But Gill is not the type to just take charge and barge ahead. He analyzes situations. Tries to avoid making another wrong move. He *is* a lawyer after all. I don't think he'll do anything until Lyndie grants him permission. So in a way I've got a fifteen-year-old making the major decisions in my life. I can get depressed thinking about it.

"You got any kids?" I ask Vergie.

"My kids live with their grandmother."

"Oh," I say, banging my head against the Range stereotype.

"I got boys. They hard to manage."

"Teenagers?" I ask.

She nods.

"My boyfriend has a teenage daughter," I say. "She lives with her mother."

"A child got to live with who can do the best by them. My boys live good with my mama. They help her out too. My job don't allow me to look out for them like they need."

"Do they like your boyfriend?" I ask. "The white guy?"

"Naw," she says. "They against him. Don't want nothing to do with him. The thing is I hear them at my mama's house calling up those white girls. They think that's different, I guess."

"Your boys don't hate Van because he's white," Laticia says. Laticia is the woman in the nice suit. She looks like she drops a lot of cash in Atlanta. "They hate him because he's sorry."

"He's good to me," Vergie says. "He treats me nice."

"He can't keep a job," Mary says.

"They jealous of me," Vergie smiles. "You can see that."

"Vergie got a big imagination," Mary says.

"You think Laticia is big?" Vergie asks me.

"Excuse me?" I say.

"Don't ask her that," Laticia says. "She don't need to say if I'm big or not. I know I'm big."

"White men love Laticia," Vergie says.

"Hush up," Laticia says. "Look at all these kids listening to you talk."

"See? I'm skinny," Vergie says. "I eat like everybody else but I just don't put on no weight. My mama used to worry because I wouldn't gain. Look here," she shows her leg, "I got these skinny ole legs. I had them all my life."

"Don't nobody care how skinny you are," Laticia says.

Vergie snapped the barrette on her niece's perfect braid and kissed her head and put her down on the floor. She looks at me then, "You got a boyfriend, right?"

"Gill," I say.

"He like women big or small?"

"Sort of middle-sized, I guess. He likes me."

"So about your size? That's what he likes?"

"Well, his daughter is a pretty big girl. Plump, you know. Like Gill's sister."

"People act like white men are so crazy about skinny women, right?"

"I guess so," I say. "Seems like everybody is always on a diet."

"White men love Laticia over there. Look at her. She's big and damn if white men don't fall all over themselves getting after her. She can cook good. And she likes to eat too."

"I'm not big from eating," Laticia says. "I'm big boned. Thick. All the women in my family are thick. I don't eat near what Vergie eats."

"Shoot," Vergie says.

This conversation is making me nervous so I'm relieved when the front door swings open and slams up against the wall making a racket. We turn to see a man walk in as if he'd been summoned up by the nature of our conversation. He's tall and muscular. White. Mean looking. His head is shaved slick and beaded with sweat and he has a row of gold hoops in one ear. He's wearing jeans and boots and a faded T-shirt with a confederate flag on it. Damn. His arms are decorated with tattoos that gave them a bruised, needle-tracked appearance. He looks like the kind of guy who'd scare the hell out of you in a dark alley — or maybe even in a hospital waiting room. We all look him over, then look at each other and raise our eyebrows. The room is silent except for the kids zooming toy cars around, making them crash off the edge of the end tables.

"Look what the cat dragged in," Vergie says to me under her breath.

"You know him?" I whisper.

"Hell no," she says. "He looks like he ain't been out of prison a good fifteen minutes."

The man walks over and slumps into a chair next to where Mary is sitting. *He is big for his size,* as they say down here. He sits slouched with his legs sprawled out in front of him taking up the walking-by space, his elbows slung out over the chair arms and his head thrown back like he's planning to get a little shut-eye. Mary scoots over in her seat and grabs one of the little boys by the arm and directs him with her eyes to play with his toy cars far away from the man. The little boy doesn't object or ask why. He knows.

I realize it's crazy but I can practically feel the evil coming off this guy. He opens his eyes and looks around at the rest of us. It is the coldest stare I've ever seen, the kind those serial killers have. Serial killers are almost always white, right? I'm getting the creeps. I'm hoping he doesn't have a weapon on him. I'm wondering what he's doing at the hospital. If he's here to visit somebody, then he ought to go visit him and be done with it. Maybe he's just trying to get out of the god-awful heat. Or maybe he has a sick crime in mind and he's biding his time.

He makes me think of boys I went to high school with. It was clear back then that certain boys were furious about something, just fuming on the inside—and as much as you would love to know what it was—you were also scared to death to find out. We used to call them *hoods* back then and we meant it as a sort of compliment. It's possible to compliment people and look down on them at the same time. Hoods didn't play sports or attend school with any enthusiasm. They liked to fight mostly. They liked to work on beat-up cars and race them around county roads. It seemed like they were excited about the possibility of dying violent, meaningless deaths. They kept their hair long and greasy, pegged their jeans, and were not afraid to go to jail. In fact, hoods allowed for a stay of incarceration in their overall life plan, which usually had them punching a clock at the textile mill on and off all their lives. These were the boys of preference in high school. Girls like me liked to see if we could find a hidden spot of decency inside their decadence. A soul underneath all the sin. Sweetness stirred into their bitter, nasty ways.

What hoods liked to do most though was harass black people. Not the black kids at school that they joked with and took showers with in gym and messed with with a friendly sort of animosity. More likely strangers they came across walking down a dark road late at night. Or some guy whose car had stalled out. Or a couple of guys they thought they outnumbered and could outrun. It was as near to a team sport as most of them ever came. A hit-and-run sort of game involving baseball bats, firecrackers, spray paint, matches—and later on, even guns. Nobody ever accused hoods of not knowing how to have their own sort of good time.

When I met my first husband, Randy, he was pretty much a hood. For a while it looked like he was destined to become the skinheaded guy sitting across from me. His specialty back in high school was picking on people. Consequently nobody gave him much trouble. He was not the sort of guy you wanted to get crossways with. His meanness was just irresistible to me. His bad reputation was like a magnet where I was concerned. I got my heart set on him going to church with my family, wearing a necktie, bowing his head and praying for redemption. I dreamed of being powerful enough to bring him to his repentant knees. But I could never make him do it. Ever. So I finally just gave up and married him instead.

How was I to know that later on he would decide to move to Atlanta, start his own construction company and become totally respectable — and Republican? He's built houses for two of my sisters. Big houses. Nice. They're always telling me how much Randy's changed. But nobody knows that better than I do. Which is one of the reasons we ended up divorced.

Last time I came to Georgia to deal with my mother's poison ivy she invited Randy to drive over for supper. Like me, he has never remarried either. Mother insists it's because he still loves me, although I tell her maybe he can't find anybody who'll have him. "You've got more to work with with Randy than you ever will with Gill," she said. "Look what Randy's done with hisself. And he wants kids too."

"I don't love Randy," I said.

"Well, I don't see why not," my mother said. "I don't see a thing wrong with him."

I look at Vergie. She raises her eyebrows in mock horror. The skinheaded guy wears work boots and has a diamond stud in his left nostril. He isn't what you'd call unattractive in the purely physical sense. It's his aura that's so off-putting, the confederate flag wrinkling across his stomach, the wet spots where he's sweat right through the glory of the confederacy into this very moment. The somber face, glistening pink scalp, his see-nothing, see-nobody eyes that scan us all in an unfriendly way, before he rolls his head back and closes his beady eyes. There's a bulge in his pocket — a gun maybe, a roll of stolen money, some drugs he'll sell or snort later.

I think of my mother, anesthetized and trusting, downstairs in surgery. It suddenly seems wrong that surgery should be performed in the basement of a building. It doesn't inspire confidence.

Surgery should be performed on the top floor of a hospital. Closer to God.

We sit in such silence that the waiting room seems even hotter than before. My feet are so sweaty I slip my shoes off. I'm digging through my purse for a hair clip when a loud bell rings. I jump. Vergie lets out a little yelp. The big guy slaps at his bulging pocket. He sticks out his leg and fishes for his cell phone. All eyes are fixed on him. "Yeah?" he barks into the phone.

It makes me want to call Gill. Across from me the big guy is folded over mumbling into the phone, "Yeah, Yeah." I don't want to watch him rub his hand over his sweaty, pink scalp. I don't want to watch him bounce his knee up and down as he talks. I slip my shoes on and go to the phone in the hall and dial Gill's office. There's no answer, so I call our home number. No answer there either. I don't know what I want to say to him really. It is more like I want him to say something to me and I'm calling to give him that opportunity. On rare occasions Gill can come through like that, say just the thing I need to hear.

When I give up and walk back to the waiting room it feels like walking into an oven. All around the people are cooking in the heat. All faces sullen, all bare skin gleaming with perspiration. I have sweat rings on my blouse too. The big guy has put his cell phone away and given up on his nap. He's righted himself and is hunched over a *Field and Stream* magazine. He is the kind of person who reminds you what all is wrong with this world. He does it silently too. Hatred is funny that way — how unspoken it often goes, but not undetected. He hates. It's a feeling you get around a person like him. It's eerie. Maybe he was raised by his parents to be a hater, maybe he learned it while he was doing time in prison, or maybe his name just randomly showed up on a Nazi-style mailing list and — as a guy who mostly got overdue bills and evictions notices — he really appreciated being notified of his superiority.

I sit down next to Vergie. She's tapping her fingernail on the arm of her chair, like a nervous woodpecker. It's because of the hate coming off the big guy. It has a smell to it.

"Who you called?" Vergie asks me.

"My boyfriend," I say. "He wasn't there."

She nods like she isn't surprised, like she could have told me the man wasn't going to answer and saved me the trouble of the call. She shook her head like maybe she felt sorry for me—hoping like I was that a man—any man—would answer my call when I needed him.

Two little black girls push the front door wide open. They look about six or seven years old. I check my watch to see if school is out already. The girls have braids everywhere with colored barrettes on each one. They're wearing shorts sets and jelly shoes. Sisters, I think. They race down the hall toward the waiting room, too loud and happy for an antiseptic hospital full of the injured and dying. The girls peer around the room where we sit. "In here," the taller girl says.

The big guy looks at them and slams his *Field and Stream* down on the end table. The girls bound into the room like eager puppies and run right to him. The smaller girl climbs up into the big guy's lap, "Hey," she says. The other girl leans against his leg.

"Where's your Mama?" the big guy asks.

"She's coming," the taller girl says.

The big guy stands up and takes the girls' hands.

"Mama said you'll get us a cold drink," the girls say.

"Is that right?" he says.

We all watch the trio walk across the waiting room. A pretty black woman with a reddish weave in her hair comes in the door then. She smiles at the big guy, a look of relief coming over her. "You got off work?"

"I told you I'd be here," he says.

She hugs his neck then.

"I ain't gon let you down," he says. "Have a little faith, why don't you."

The woman nods at him like she might cry.

"Let's go," he puts his arm around the woman. "The kids are

thirsty." They follow the arrow pointing to the cafeteria. We crane our necks watching them disappear down the hall.

"Damn," Vergie says.

"You see those children jump on that white man?" Mary says.

"I done seen it all now," Vergie says.

"Me too," I say.

My mother is still groggy when Roland pushs her wheelchair out to where I have pulled the car around. "She did real good," he tells me. "Didn't give me no trouble."

We get Mother into the car and she pats Roland's plump hand, "This dope has got me swimmy-headed," she says.

"You gon sleep good tonight," Roland promises.

I hold my mother's hand all the way home, driving one-handed, not wanting to let go. She's precious to me in her postsurgical stupor, like she's caught in a dream she can't be waked from.

At home, I help her up the steps into the house. We get her in her nightgown and into bed. She shows me the bandage on her breast, a big bandage for what is supposed to be "a couple of stitches." I make some hot tea and prop her up on pillows and flip through the TV channels until we find *Murder, She Wrote,* her favorite. "I like a show where an old person is the smart one," she told me once. Before the show is half over my mother is asleep. She's sweet and peaceful. I'm grateful for the chance to be needed so I sit with my mother until Jessica solves the murder, then I turn the TV off and call my sisters to give them a report on how Mother's doing. After I go home to Virginia they'll take turns coming to see about her. She'll really like that.

I call Gill because I want to tell him what happened today. How wrong Vergie and I were about the big guy. "It's wonderful to be wrong, Gill," I plan to say. "It's so good to know how wrong you can be." But Gill is distracted when I get him on the phone. His ex-wife has called him about Lyndie. It seems she's trying to get Lyndie signed up for a weight-loss camp this summer and Lyndie is refusing to go. Gill's ex-wife wants him to come to New Jersey and try to talk some sense to Lyndie, explain to her that everything a mother does is for her child's own good. Gill is leaving first thing in the morning to drive up there. He doesn't care if Lyndie goes to the stupid camp or not—but he's happy because his ex-wife is calling on him to be something more in Lyndie's life than the guy who sends the checks. "This might be the breakthrough I've been needing," Gill says. "This might be my chance." I hear the excitement and fear in his voice. It doesn't seem like the time to discuss the joys of being wrong. "Good luck," I tell Gill.

I don't know why, but when I hang up I look through my mother's address book that she keeps beside the phone. There it is. Randy's Atlanta phone number. My mother has copied down his home, office, and pager number from the business card she has paperclipped to this page in the address book. I wonder if he knows what a high opinion my mother has of him. I bet he feels the same way about her. He'd probably be interested to know that she's had a recent biopsy. He might be concerned enough to send a card. Maybe he'd also be interested to know what happened to me today. That Vergie and I both experienced the power and the glory of being dead wrong. And what a beautiful thing being wrong can be. Maybe he'll say, "It's the new Georgia, honey. I been trying to tell you."

I haven't talked to Randy since he came to dinner at my mother's invitation, but I dial his number. I have no idea what I'll say. It crosses my mind that he might hang up on me, but for some reason I don't think he will. I used to believe there weren't many surprises left. But tonight I'm feeling like maybe I've been wrong about that too. Maybe surprises are all there are.

Nanci Kincaid has published four novels, *Crossing Blood, Balls, Verbena,* and *As Hot As It Was You Ought to Thank Me,* and one collection of stories, *Pretending the Bed Is a Raft,* the title story of which was adapted to film in *My Life Without Me* (Pedro Almodovar). She has received a NEA grant and a Bunting Fellowship. She is presently working on a second collection of stories and reworking a novel-in-progress set in the Alabama women's prison. She divides her time between San Jose, California, and Honolulu, Hawaii.

THE HONOLULU ADVERTISER

*T*his story began to hatch on a visit to see my mother when she was having a minor medical procedure in a less-than-cutting-edge facility. I was nervous, because the threat of "something going wrong" was such a persistent undercurrent there, and everybody seemed to accept deadly consequences as the unhidden cost of modern medicine. Many of the hospital observations and characters in the story were lifted from the events of that day, others were tampered with significantly or purely invented. The skinhead guy was real, though. His girlfriend and her daughters were real too. So was Vergie, by another name. And Roland. But Randy, the ex-husband, was mostly borrowed—and insistent on his place in this story. And Gil, the live-in boyfriend, and his daughter, Lyndie, were composites born of laments of my friend who recently married a man with a young, highly resistant daughter whom she believes can never be won over, really. She reports getting the best results when heavy doses of cash, credit cards, and shopping sprees are stirred into her otherwise unwelcome and clearly substandard love offerings. She hopes in time to be proven wrong about this "currency of love," of course. I think nearly everyone in the story longs to be wrong about something— whether alert to the longing or not. I love the idea that being wrong can be one of the best things that can ever happen to a person—much more satisfying than just being right again or being sure.

R. T. Smith

TASTES LIKE CHICKEN

(from *Louisiana Literature*)

All these here behind the screen wire—look out!—are your eastern diamondbacks, *Crotalus horridus,* which are your most popular native snake, and as you see a little testy by nature. They've got the color pattern like Indian wampum or an hourglass, and those silver-looking noisemakers on the tail give 'em a musical impact, nodamean? Can't read the age by it, like some folks think, though. They'll not slough skin on any man's regular schedule. Woman's neither. Whoa back now. That's Darth, and the palish one twined with him is Michael for that Jackson freak on TV. Over there giving us the hard eye is Hillary. They all sense we're here through the infrared plan and some have to make their strike, but they're used to people, mostly. Still, you can't predict 'em. They can always marvel me, and everything they inspire I write down like their secretary. It's what you might call my passion, the scribbling. Some day, luck comes for me, I'll make a book and make a killing, downpay me a condo in some paradise. Jesse Turley's the name.

As for all these lazy boys dozing in the red crates, they are your copperheads, also indigenous to our Blue Ridge, which are more shy but prone to hide at the wrong place in the woods where you'll reach your hand every time. Truly. See the yellow tail tip? They favor your old sawdust piles and wild blueberry shrubs. The smell,

I think. They have given me some near misses. Speaking of smell, a kingsnake in the area tells a copperhead "make yourself scarce," and they skedaddle. You have to love a kingsnake. Not mean, these copper rascals, but serious poison, even the younguns. Let me stir em. See those fangs? They fold up when the mouth is shut but pop out to needle in the hemotoxins and serotoxins and all those other strange aminos. Miracle, if you ask me, like the way a snake's jaw'll unhinge so he can swallow a rat or frog or even a kittycat. You just missed feeding. Females, I expect, are the worst. Mother instinct, maybe. Science don't know. You'd have to ask a permanently married man.

And this hermit over here is my only timber rattler, so I call him Herm. Big shakers on the end almost like a pine cone. He could be over a dozen winters old. Six foot long if he's a inch. That black back half like dipped in tar, that's his family sign. Herm's got a story. Guess he was sunning on the railroad bed when the Charleston freight passed. Stunned, I reckon. He was an easy acquisition, truly. He was nearly demised. I brought him home in my bare hands. His kind, now, has the tendency to sull back and not eat. I've seen a many of 'em starve, but Herm has the old-time life will, for sure. I wouldn't sell him for gold nor rubies. It's like we're a couple old brothers running this outfit without another human hand.

I mostly catch 'em when Orion's up and they're dreaming under rocks. Groundhog holes and old fox dens or just a karst pocket in the dark. They's always two holes to the den, and I slop some gasoline in the one, then snag them with a pincer on a pole when they rouse and make a sluggish run for clear air. Don't use the well-known forked locust stick 'cause I need to lift 'em into the sack, which you probably guessed is a step toward your heavy-duty aluminum trash can. You get a bin weighty with them rascals, all snarled up—man, they can hiss some. Like a ladies' auxiliary gossip party at the Moose. Truly. That's women.

Course, my wife didn't take to the whole exhibition. She's farm raised and don't see them as nothing but trouble. "A deadly animal is not entertainment," she'd say. Fussy as a pullet, she was. Being in the Navy so long, I got to missing all the land critters from ticks to jennets. Coulda been anything, but snakes kind of came to me, as I was handy with 'em when a boy. I had some store pets — parakeets, kitties, a canary — but they didn't satisfy. In the Philippines I saw my first snake zoo, kraits and mambas and everything, right down to a bitty harmless gardenhose green. Out there on the Pacific, I'd dream of setting up a rattlesnake ranch for tourism just like this. Imagine. I schemed someday to marry till forever and settle in as a sort of ringmaster. I wrote down all my plans for years and read up what I could cheffing down there in the galley with the skillets and pans and barrels. Thinking of snake dens I'd pour water off the spaghetti and watch it tangle like a bunch of honest Injun albino vipers sharing a dark space in winter.

Buchanan's where I hail from, over toward Roanoke, little dying town off the path but perched over the James like a picture book. Blacksnakes was my favorite when I's a boy, Kings and ringnecks, racers and corn snakes, but the Peaks of Otter park was full of coppers, and once I got the surprise of my life from a jumbo copperhead under the push mower when I tried to yank-start it cold in April. That's another story, and you can bet I've got it spelled out in a notebook somewhere here. Mostly copperheads I yarn up. Plenty of time for that these days, batching it, nodamean?

I used to drive on down to Georgia and Alabama, where they'd have the famous roundups. The wind bloweth where it listeth, the saved are prone to say. I'd take my notebooks and story pens, compete at harvesting with the locals on behalf of Kiwanis and my own wallet. Prizes for the longest, the heaviest, oldest, most. Deep Dixie is a snaker's paradise, nodamean?, and I've got some brassy trophies to show for my labors. Those were mighty fine times, the rodeos, for bluegrass and dancing. They'd carry on all weekend. Lots of bourbon turned to pure yee-haw and morning piss, buddy. Even had a beauty pageant in a one-hearse town called Opp. My wife herself was a beauty when young — sparrow-color eyes and hair long as a willow — but she went sallow and skinny.

Worry, probably, putting up with me long as she did. My collection of slithers and all my windy stories. I promise you, though, they're mostly safe in the cages. Now I do my daily double check. That was her first ultimatum—at least twice a day, every inch of cage wire and frame, every possible escape. I was sure not a one would ever be a threat to us.

Course, there's more than a little money in the merchant game. Roadside restaurants way off yonder in the north and even overseas love to serve them up. Rattler fingers. Serpent on a stick. Reptile jerky. Probably sliver 'em into an omelet or pot pie. Being a former galley slave, I can just imagine. Usually they deep fry them, though, and you gnaw off the meat. It's mostly spine, truly, but a good eggy batter makes you think you've latched onto a genuine delicate delight. Pepper, some Texas Pete. Odd to the Yankees as grits, I guess. Exotic. It's the batter makes the taste familiar and not like snacking on evil. Some people will say snakes are evil.

Roving around to those festivals and reptile rallies, I thought myself part of the export world, a man with a profit mission, and Verna, she'd stay here and run the stand, hang out the flags and tapestries, hose down the yard art. She'd get lonely since Feather finished school and moved to Staunton. She's a tooth hygiene worker, Feather is.

Anyway, most folks stop for the fireworks—Black Cat, Ting No, Wild Jack, Pirate—till a gnome (with a g) strikes their fancy or wind-flapping textiles of the faux Cherokee persuasion. A bird bath might grab 'em then or blue Buddha or even a polymer bear. They're native too, old bruins, and I have seen more than one buffeting at the trash, but you can't collect them on account of the law. Once a she-mama tried to scramble into my car on the Parkway near Afton, but the rangers frown on picking up hitcher bears. Stone angels, pixies, and nativity shepherds, though, I can move them all year.

Now, your wild goose in many postures is the present popular favorite. Dreamlike, nodamean? We only see them mostly way yonder up there, majesticlike, sky-riding in formation like a ploughshare. Unless we shotgun them into a limp dinner. Myself, I've never taken to the hunt. I'd rather wave when they pass and write them into a fable or some such, a goose gospel, I guess. What if animals have souls?

Yard ornaments was always okay with my better half and all these rebel caps, off-color bumper stickers, and souvenir whatnots. No family battles. Come to snakes, though, Verna was a yellow-dog skeptic. "Virginia is for lovers," she'd say, pointing to the bumper sticker display. "Snake ranchers need not apply."

Here's the real deal. I know you know about milking fangs for the medical antitox, but the Holiness Church has run rife up here, hiding out in the coves and gaps, I spect, and they put faith in signs and wonders, tongue speaking and rolling about like they swallowed an Isaiah ember. Them firebrand congregations — End-Timers and New Lights — and I won't say a congregation's place name for legal reasons, but you've heard of the ones up to Jolo on *Sixty Minutes* — they almost always want a box of snakes to test their spirits on. The Word, they say, is their shield.

Even the best won't hardly last out a year. The brethren do what they can to rile 'em, kick the crate, yell down at 'em, shake the floor with their godly dance. Guitars, too, the Telstar Gospel. They call it Signs Following. They say they get anointed. They say they are proving the Sacred Lord's Victory over free-range devils. Then they haul 'em out and speak directly to the creatures, snakes wrapping around their arms, crawling over their heads and shoulders. It ain't legal. Poison ones, I mean. Truly. The copperhead and moccasins, rattlers especial, all the pit vipers. Rattlers are the best, spearpoint with eyes on one end, tambourine on the other. It's like they're baptized members just lapsed since the Eden incident. I hear the true anointed like them in Raphine'll pitch jumbo timbers about and even try to get cobras and corals and such. Plain crazy. They sing-say scripture in the eyes of a snake, but now and again a saved soul gets bit. Comes a swelling, retching and thirst. Myself, I'm more wary of the coppers, who will lure you and look so lovely, calling to your touch. That's the Eden trick. Hypnosis, like the way they charm a bird.

Talk about some writing. I've got all the handling stories, but second hand, nodamean? The faithful don't lay on ice but use blessed palms to try for healing, and prayers too. Some say it's just a jolt and then a bliss. Brother Horton swears by eating a bucket of sauerkraut to fight the venoms. Lily Briscoe says she washes in coal oil if one fangs her. Come over here to buy replacements, you can see the swole up or dead places on their wrists and palms and fingers. Grown man usually makes it if he's caught on a limb. Neck or face or any place on a child—goner. Not even Sister Sharon can save their bacon, and she's said to have the touch. Preacher Bannister himself is always trying to coax me over—now I've slipped and said a name—but I was Saved five times in my country's service until I was officially immune. What all that's got to do with Jesus is way outa my range. They will tell you, though, the crowned and born over, that more folks die from lightning in our country than snakebite every year. Divorce, I've heard, has also taken its share. Do you notice how those twice born don't hanker to be weaned?

Anyway, when I got wind of the high demand, I thought I'd make the market here, close by my native ground, catching the devil's animal and trading in them. Verna was not keen for it an eensey bit, nodamean? Not from the start. It's like the way I'm telling this. Stories. She thought it foolish I'd ramble on with customers like I do, but hell, I'm colorful, the local genuine article, don't you reckon? Maybe that's too much, but on four different destroyers, I have seen the world so far as it touches salt water. A good story or a voyage is like a snake for suspense, nodamean?

Now for myself, I believe in due respect, and I know how to catch a viper behind the head, squeeze his neck and keep the tail from lashing about with my other hand. Been me in the First Garden, I wouldn't gone all swoony just because the creepy thing could talk. We'd had snake chili and cut the tree down, lived forever on long meat and peaches.

I milk them into jars I keep sterile in a warming cabinet. Send the goodies to Roanoke clinics in a six-pack cooler. Licensed — up there in that frame. Pursuing my chosen field, I'm close to danger, but I take precautions. I'm no daredevil. I won't have but one out at a time, and I won't let them holies handle their purchases here in the shop. They point them out, and I pincer the choice ones — the elect, I guess — with my three-foot gizmo, drop one by one in the box. They wanna be geeks or corpses, it's their own business, but not on the premises. Nothing crazy in me. And I keep their secret from the police. A little hush money, cold-blooded cash, and it's all off the books. Nobody asks. Retirement nest egg. Rainy day.

Verna, she didn't see it that way, and she thought even having them in the pens was foolish. What if one gets out? What if one comes snapping after us? Women, nodamean? There at the end, she was so arguey, I started calling her the Rib in my secret diary, my private version of the Word.

We did a brisk business from the get-go, but she hated the smell, which is like a mild reek. Everybody has his own description, but I'd say rotten cukes is close, the juice simmering with summer. Still, it's life.

It like to give me the giggles, selling those big velvets of Elvis, the ark, suffer the children with a lamb, Last Supper, also Gandalf and Nemo, but inside charging a buck to visit Jesse's Last Chance Hall of Reptiles. It had to be all snakes, like the Indiana Jones movie, nodamean? So they was writhy in the holding pens, waiting to get their day in church, and passerbys would see the sign and pay to watch them doing mostly nothing. I'd sell some star shells and whirligig sparklers, Big Blast and Roman candles. Verna said it had to be a sin, stooping to the lowest nominator.

Fella come in here from New York, he claimed, though the accent was wrong. Empire State he said. "Let me see what you got." We had a full house, and it knocked him silent. "How'd you get so many?" he wanted to know. "Do you eBay? Do you breed 'em?" I had to laugh and answer back, "Stranger, we let 'em do that themselves." Ain't that a holy hoot?

One time, I fried up a diamondback was so faded nobody saw fit to take it off my hands, not even discount. Wallflower, nodamean? I hate to think the creatures are stuck in this place more than temporary. I worry about being the host of Limbo. Sometimes, though, I will flat-out kill the overstock, skin them for the saddle-shaped cross bands and distribute to leather crafters, the folk art trade. Belts and boots, hat bands and guitar straps. I'd pickle the heads as paperweights, keep the rattles to make keychains and other geegaws. That evening of the supper secret I was careful to spiral cut all the tender meat free of backbone and laced the batter mix good with cane sugar like a hush puppy. Verna, she ate hearty, said I was always a better cook than her or Feather. Want to bad enough, I guess you can fool anybody, nodimsayin? Tastes like chicken. Truly.

This geezer comes in here once, big Panama hat and one of them Rolliflex watches with a rusted-out Cadillac hissing on my gravel. He says I'm so good at painting pictures with my words. Says, "Fella you should write down this shit. You got the gift." Them notebooks on the shelf behind me, every color you can put a name to, binders spiral as a snake vine, that's my brainwork, my library of stories. I was way ahead of the game. I started them somewhere off Australia. Not all snake tales, but I do have some special ones I made up with a Tarzan-like jungle man who has a pet python. No Jane around, though. Gist of it, all Tonga's — that's his name, my savage man — all Tonga's other pets keep disappearing, and he thinks the snake is sick too, count of it won't ever take the rats he usually gives it. Turns out, well, you can guess. Python is just real sleepy, all fat and smiling and sassy. Whole time, Geezer keeps snapping his watchband and grinning.

That old guy was having some fun at my expense, asking more detail information about poison and if they lay eggs, if a self-defense shocker on a bite will cure it. He was deep-eyed and deep country, and I made out the scars on his gnarly hands. I didn't let on, you see, but I knew him for a handler.

Once I get moving on a new yarn, I'll set at the linoleum table there and cursive my words for hours, like vines all looping. We live in the back. I do. All night sometimes, the writing. Missed the Super Bowl once just plotting out a detective mystery I never did figure how to finish. It had a villain type dosing kinfolk with venom. Verna said back then, "Put me in one," but she was not the story type, a dry country woman. And a temper. I couldn't trust how she'd react if I even tried to describe her. She had that streaky hair, crow and gray, and a face that was good only in a smile, which was more and more rare. The snakes I reckon. Nossir, not the story kind.

She's long gone, of course, and I don't do much cooking. Not worth the grease to chef for one, so I like to slip on down to the Pedal Car Café at Berky's, grab some grub and listen to the truckers hassle with their dispatchers over the booth phones. Or pocket phones, lately. Now it's mostly cells, which seems wrong-headed, the booth phones just hanging there useless, no words flowing through the cords. Dead snakes, a man like me would say. Most everything is changing.

The Berky's crew still brews up a great mug of mud, though, and I sweeten it with Equal in the blue-sky packages. Black eyes and niblets, corn muffins, some mighty fine steak and gravy — make you wanna smack your mama and kiss a clown, nodamean? Kiss a snake might be too far, like that Roy guy out in Las Vegas. Born stupid in my book. Tigers. You got to keep to the borders of good sense. It wasn't an idiot invented the cage.

Diamondback got loose, of course, slipped free one night when Verna was gabbin' at me. I was tending to the feeding, when I don't need distraction with those live mice scrabbling in the box. She got me flustered, and I couldn't get back my stride. Cage cleaning, I set him in what I reckoned a safe container, and he nosed up the wicker lid of the basket. All she wrote, so to speak. He thought he was a cobra, maybe, but he was really my other timber rattler I called Timbuktu. I been there. Anyway, that was when the horrificant music commenced, Verna's high pitch like a skyrocket.

You never seen a woman dash about like that. And climb. She got up there, high rack of that star shell display frame with the sparkler sign on top yelling it was over, I was headed to hell and she was going to Richmond. Crazy snake was whipping about on the floor, addled, scared, looking for shelter. It was touch and go, but I snagged him in my catching instrument and whacked him at the neck with the hatchet. Tail flipping one way, head going the other, biting air. A waste, but I was hoping extreme rescue would settle her down. George and the dragon, nodamean? Dream on, Jesse, dream on.

I followed her about, making my plea and promises I couldn't keep. In the bedroom, she was stuffing her frillies into a zip-up bag. "I don't know what I'll do without you," I said.

"Write something," she says. "Make something up. You're good with words."

I knew what she meant, but even your best artist needs to get mused and worked up. Verna gone, I'm starting to yearn out for stimulation. The snakes do not make a whole life. Need to sing a new tune, find a new direction. I hear scuttlebutt the New Lights up to Raphine are planning a brush arbor wedding this weekend. Lots of lemonade and catch-as-can eats, a big spread, even if you place no faith in those dusty vows people swap. That Preacher Bannister, though, says he has a passel of satinback rattlers never before been handled, wild things just ripe for the Glory and the stroke of a hallowed hand. He's been working on me to get in the Word, to witness the Son of Man in action and watch believers bathing in serpents and not being bit for the Hand of the Lord hovers over. I might just go down and see that for myself.

"And copperheads," he said, "I promise—copperheads a pluplenty."

Canaries. Now that would have been smarter from the start.

R. T. Smith's fiction has appeared in the *Southern Review*, the *Virginia Quarterly Review*, *The Pushcart Prize XXX*, *Best American Short Stories*, *Best American Mystery Stories*, and two previous volumes of *New Stories from the South*. His second collection of stories, *Uke Rivers Delivers*, will be published in the fall of 2006. Smith edits *Shenandoah* for Washington and Lee University and lives in Rockbridge County, Virginia, with his wife, the poet Sarah Kennedy. In 2005 he served as Phillips Family Distinguished Professor of Rhetoric at Virginia Military Institute.

UKE RIVERS

I have a healthy respect for pit vipers and an unhealthy interest in them. Probably something to do with the Eden story. When I lived in Alabama, I used to attend the Rattlesnake Roundups in Opp, and I surprised a few sunning diamondbacks in the Priesters' woods outside Opelika, but now my primary contact with reptiles involves visiting a World's Largest Rattlesnake out on the Lee Highway at a yard sculpture and fireworks shack. It's deceased, stuffed, and wall-mounted, but still an impressive specimen. I don't know much about the fellow who runs the place, except that he has a terrific sense of humor, but I started inventing another snake wrangler to sit in for him, and as soon as I began to hear my character's voice, he seemed to be asking for living snakes around him and a bad habit to fill the slow hours. I decided to let him write. In cursive, like the snakes.

Ben Fountain

BRIEF ENCOUNTERS WITH CHE GUEVARA

(from *Shenandoah*)

1. Love and the Revolution

When I was six my father became president of a college in Virginia, a small, well-endowed Episcopal school to which generations of wealthy Southern families had sent their sons, and which, though it had admitted women since the early fifties, still very much expressed that ripe, combustible blend of sentimentality and viciousness so vital to the traditions of the monied Southern male. We lived in the president's mansion on campus, a massive Greek Revival structure in the old plantation style, with columns towering along the broad front porch, a sweeping central staircase fit for royalty, and high-ceilinged formal rooms whose hardwood floors had the acoustic qualities of a bowling alley. School tradition required my parents to host receptions for the faculty several times a year, and it was at these gatherings—peeking with my sisters from the top of the stairs at first, then later as a fringe participant, serving punch with the help in my coat and tie—that I became aware of my attraction to Mona Broun. Mrs. Broun was a faculty wife, a trim, petite woman in her early thirties who I confused for a time with the actress Natalie Wood. She had the same wholesome looks as the famous movie star, the same well-scrubbed, faintly exotic sex appeal, along with fawn-colored hair worn loose and soft, this at a time — the mid-sixties — when women's hairdos, in the South at least, resembled heavily shellacked constructions of meringue. But it was her eyes that got our attention from the top of the stairs, intense brown eyes with rich, lustrous tones like shots of bourbon or maple syrup, framed by sharp, exaggeratedly arched eyebrows like the spines of enraged or terrified cats.

"She looks surprised," said one of my sisters.

"She's holding her breath," said another sister.

"She hates her husband," said my oldest and wisest sister.

As the youngest, and the only boy, I was expected to say nothing, but an opera went off in my head whenever I saw Mrs. Broun. That opera, of course, was the sound of sex, and the news that she hated her husband gave me a secret thrill, though "hate" was probably too strong a word — by then the Brouns had likely burned through enough high drama to have exhausted all the more flamboyant emotions. Some years before, in the very early sixties, they'd lived in Cuba as part of an academic exchange, one of the last before diplomatic relations were broken. Either inspired by the revolution, or sick of her husband, or both — maybe she'd met the dashing Che and had already become entangled — Mrs. Broun remained in Cuba when her husband left. Her defection was a news sensation for a couple of weeks, a Cold War scandal of the human interest sort and a public humiliation for Dr. Broun, who returned to campus more abstracted and aloof than ever. He took up his old position in the Sociology Department and refused to speak to the press; when Mrs. Broun abruptly rejoined him several years later, she, too, maintained a wall of silence, resuming the life of a conventional faculty wife with no more fuss than if she'd spent a long weekend at the beach. Given material like that, the community had no choice but to glut itself with gossip. She'd been brainwashed, people said, or she was a spy, or had been switched out in Havana for a surgically altered double, but the steamiest and most persistent rumors concerned the affair she'd allegedly had with Ernesto "Che" Guevara, the famous revolutionary.

According to the orthodoxy of the times, Che was high in

our pantheon of national enemies, but for me he was a clue, a key player in some essential human mystery that linked us both to Mrs. Broun and therefore to one another. In any case, I was consumed; at faculty receptions I couldn't take my eyes off her. I watched her eat, her graceful juggling of purse and plate and how she'd tap her ears from time to time to make sure that her earrings were still in place. I studied her clothes, the high heels and snug-fitting suits, the sleek bulge of her bottom underneath her skirt. She rarely spoke, preferring instead to be a poised and careful listener, though even when she seemed at her most engaged there was an air of distraction or restlessness about her, as if she sensed someone standing too close to her shoulder, an intimate, vaguely hostile presence to whom she would momentarily turn. I know now that this was her tragic aura following her around, though at the time I had only the coarsest sense that she would never be happy again. Certainly *I* couldn't make her happy, and that, for me, was part of the tragedy.

The fact that she ended up exactly where she started, as a faculty wife at a small, conservative Southern college, strikes me now as the sort of peculiarly specific hell that life has a way of devising for us. I remember my alarm on hearing the news that Che had been killed—what were we going to say to Mrs. Broun? It didn't occur to me that people could act as if nothing had happened, but when I saw her at the Christmas party later that year she looked absolutely the same. She moved about the room as she always did, saying little, eating less, seeming to blink about once every ten minutes. I kept trying to make passionate eye contact with her, to convey some urgent message of solidarity or love, but my best chance came when she approached the table for a cup of punch. I was trembling as I filled the cup and reverently passed it to her, and as the punch changed hands her eyes met mine. She froze, staring at me as if I'd just that moment materialized, and the next instant she seemed to know everything; she understood, at the very least, what I wanted to say, because little lightning strikes started going off behind her eyes. I think she would have slapped me if I'd opened my mouth. She was that ruthless, that jealous of her epic shame and grief, and no brat was going to taint the great love of her life by talking of things he knew nothing about.

I was desperate to speak to her, but that look stopped me cold. She scared me so badly that I remember thinking that I didn't want to fall in love with anyone, ever, not if that's what it could do to you.

2. Death in Bolivia

When I was twenty I dropped out of college and got a minimum-wage job delivering office furniture. At the time I was living in the Northeast, in a cold, dirty, technically bankrupt city where dozens of random murders occurred every night, but my main concern was finding work of the sort that would allow me to stop thinking for a while, which seemed advisable after a near-sleepless sophomore year during which I fell prey to certain compulsive behaviors, such as trying to read everything Ezra Pound had ever written. So I got a job with a discount office-furniture company, found a cheap apartment in a high-crime neighborhood, and started taking the bus to work every morning. It was a lonely, orbitless time in my life; I had few friends, and was too bottled-up to talk to women, but delivering furniture had its satisfactions. You could double-park all over the city, for one thing, and I liked lifting stuff and riding around in the truck, and the other guys in delivery didn't mind me too much. I think they knew instinctively what they had on their hands—stressed-out white boy whose life had jumped the tracks—but my troubles must have looked pretty puny to them. My first day they sent me out with Clifton Weems, an older black man with a barrel chest and a mangled, arthritic way of walking. After a couple of hours of brooding he turned to me and said: "Hey kid, you know what?"

"No, what."

"You turn sideways when your woman's shooting at you, you cut her target more'n half."

They thought I was funny with my goofy formal manners, the

way I automatically called the older guys "sir" until they yelled at me to stop. During the day I hauled furniture and took a fair amount of guff; at night I listened to gunfire barking up and down my street and had conflicted, homesick dreams about the South. I'd come to this place of my own free will, following a perfectly honorable subset of the Southern tradition by going north for school, but somehow I'd managed to make an exile of myself. "Good luck," my father said when I called to say I was dropping out. By then he was president of a bigger, even more prestigious college. "Come see us when you feel like getting serious again."

Life became very basic. Work, food, sleep; as long as I rolled my body out of bed in the morning everything else just seemed to happen by itself. One day I was out on deliveries with Luis Batista and Clifton, sitting in the peon's middle seat while Luis surfed the truck through six lanes of traffic. Clifton relaxed on my other side with his arm out the window, humming into the early spring breeze. We heard something shift in the back of the truck, then glass shattering. Clifton reached over and turned up the radio.

"Hey," he said, leaning back in his seat, "you know Gustavo's the guy who killed Che Guevara?"

"You're kidding," I said, instantly reeling with nostalgia; it was like opening an old steamer trunk full of mothballs. "You mean Che Guevara the guerrilla?"

"No, man, Che Guevara the nightclub singer. Who the hell do you think I mean?"

"I—"

"You're surprised I know about Che? You think I'm just an ignorant *nee-gro,* doncha boy."

"No, Clifton, I just—"

"Shit, man, I knew Malcolm X. I used to hang with Adam Clayton Powell, Jr., all the time, you dig? I was right in the middle of all that sixties shit."

I couldn't tell if Clifton was razzing me or really mad, so I shut up. Luis glanced at us and casually shifted gears.

"Yeah," he said, "I heard that about Gus."

"You think it's true?" Clifton asked.

"Sure, why not. He was in the Army down there. He's a pretty tough guy."

"You ever ask him?"

"Fuck no, man, you don't talk about stuff that happened down there." Luis was Chilean, a former soldier himself; it seemed a vaguely sinister coincidence that all the Latins in delivery were ex-military men.

"Dude ought to write a book, make himself some money."

"No." Luis was adamant. "No books. He'd just bring a lot of grief down on himself."

They were talking about Gustavo Torres, a taciturn Bolivian whose flat Indian features and long mournful nose gave his face the moral authority of a death mask. Gus exhibited behaviors that were baffling to most North Americans — modesty, reserve and courtesy, to name a few — and transmitted with every gesture an urbane self-assurance that made me think of the best class of movie gamblers. He had a wife and kids in Bolivia and a string of stylish lady friends here in the city, along with a Monte Carlo that he garaged at unimaginable expense. Nobody knew how he managed to live so well on a workingman's wages, which only added to the Gustavo mystique.

Of course I asked him about Che; the question burned inside me like a lit fuse. The next time we went out on deliveries together I gathered my nerve.

"Ah, Gus," I began, "I don't mean to bug you or anything, but there's these rumors going around about you, and I was just wondering—"

He brought his hand down on the dashboard, *slap,* then raised it as if taking an oath. "The rumors are true," he declared.

"We're talking about Che, right?"

He flinched like I'd thrown acid in his face. "Che Guevara, of course. The *revolucionario.*"

"I don't mean to pry," I said by way of invitation.

"That's good," he said curtly, eyes fixed on the street. "You shouldn't be too curious about these things."

"Okay," I agreed, and then I told him about Mrs. Broun and her alleged affair with Che, because it made me feel good — more authentic and grounded, and less homesick, I suppose — to talk about Che. Gus just grunted, but a couple of days later he came up to me in the stockroom.

"It is true," he said in a low voice. "About that lady you knew, and Che. There was an affair."

"Yeah?"

"*Yes.*" Gustavo's English was all tight corners and crisp edges. "She lived in *La Habana* for two years; he kept her in an apartment in the Old City. It's a miracle she got out with her life, you know."

"How did you — "

"Yes, well," he said with a tidy cough. "I just thought you'd want to know."

So that was the end of it, I thought, and I filed it away until a couple of weeks later, when a bunch of us went out drinking after work, to the sort of serious, no-frills neighborhood bar where the walls sweat tears of nicotine and the waitresses have the grizzled look of ex-child brides. I had three quick ones, drinking too fast as usual; I looked up halfway through beer number four to find Gustavo watching me with imploding eyes.

"It is like the Pietá," he intoned. When Gus drank his face planed off like weathered drywall, and his nose seemed more commanding and ancient than ever.

"Say what?"

"The portrait of Che in death, his body lying on the table. Have you seen it?"

Of course I'd seen it, the famous Freddy Trigo image of Che laid out on a stretcher after his slipshod execution — it's one of the iconic photographs of the twentieth century. Che's eyes are open in the picture, fixed on some distant point, and his lips are parted in a sleepy half-smile. The tousled hair and beard give him a Christ-like look; his naked torso, pitted here and there with bulletholes, seems to emanate light. In the hushed, satin tones of that black-and-white image Che's body has an aura of distilled transcendence.

"I've seen it," I answered, trying to match Gus's gravitas.

"The Pietá," he repeated, "it's so beautiful the way his eyes gaze past the camera. He seems so calm and forgiving, so much at peace. Yet for anyone who was there that day, that photo is like a curse."

"Hunh," I murmured, afraid of spooking him, but I didn't need to worry. Gustavo was speaking from some deep confessional booth within himself.

"Jesus could not have been the Christ without his Judas, correct? And someone had to play the Judas for Che, too, for Che the man to be transformed into Che the martyr. But that goddamn photo, man, it drives me crazy. We were only trying to prove that Che was dead. Those were our orders that day: send us proof that Che is dead! So we looked for the best light, we took off his shirt to show his wounds, we had the nurse trim his beard and comb back his hair. We only wanted to take a decent photo that day—who could have known we were making the new Pietá?"

While we drank he described the military operation for me, how his unit—most of them Indians—had harassed and tracked the guerrillas for weeks, finally cornering the survivors in the Churo Gorge. They captured Che after a firefight and marched him into the tiny village of La Higuera, where they locked him in the schoolhouse overnight. When the order came the next day to execute him, the junior officers drew lots to determine who would do the shooting. "I talked to him early that morning," Gus said. "I brought him a cup of coffee, and we chatted for a minute. I told him I was the guy who'd tracked him all this time through the mountains. Che was a human wreck by then—he was starving and sick, his feet were a bloody mess, and his asthma was like a snake crawling up and down his throat. But still fighting—that son of a bitch was still fighting his war. He just stared at me for a minute, and then he said, 'Look around you, Lieutenant. Look at this village—what do you see? There's no doctor, no running water, no electricity, no decent road. They have nothing; the lives of these people are shit. So all that time you were trying to kill me, brother, did you ever stop to think what this war is about?'"

"It's a conversation I have sometimes in my dreams," Gus went on. "We're in the schoolhouse there in La Higuera, and he's sitting on the floor in his filthy clothes, his feet sticking out in their bloody rags. But he's already dead! His skin is a pale blue color, and his shirt is torn and bloody where the bullets went in. We talk for a while, and he says he's not angry with me. I ask him if it hurts very much to be dead, and he says, 'No, not very much.' And then I get up the nerve to ask him about heaven and hell, whether they're real, and where exactly he is in all that. He always smiles a little when I ask him that, and then he says, 'You know, Gustavo, it's a very interesting thing I've learned here: I had no idea God and the Devil live so close together. They're neighbors, in fact; their houses are right beside each other, and sometimes when they're sitting around with nothing to do they play cards, just as a way to pass the time. But they never wager money—what good is money to them? No, it's only souls they're interested in, the souls of all these sinners running around the earth. It's us they bet on when they sit down to cards.'"

"'So what about me?' I ask him then. 'Have they ever bet on me?'"

"'Of course,' he says, but when I ask him who won, the Devil or God, he never answers. He just sits there staring at me."

3. Comrades-in-Arms

In my early thirties I began making trips to the beleaguered island nation of Haiti. With the recent fall of the Duvalier regime it struck me as an interesting place to be, and I had credentialed, more or less credible reasons for going—to write articles and, hopefully, a book—but my true motives seemed to have more to do with being Southern, and white, and having a natural affinity for the quagmire of race. By this time I had a beautiful wife and two wonderful children, a loving family which I'd done nothing special to deserve, but I'd leave them for weeks at a time to go messing around a place that was perpetually on the verge of devouring itself. After several trips I met a young Haitian, a doctor, with whom I became friends. Ponce was rather Che-like himself, an intense, good-looking, often disheveled mulatto who practiced near one of the downtown slums and treated most of his patients for free. Because he made so little money, he had to live with his wife and their two sons in a cramped, buggy apartment in the middle of Port-au-Prince, a few rooms carved out of an ancient gingerbread mansion that must have been quite grand in its time but now looked more like a pile of moldering elephant bones. He insisted that I stay there when I came to Port-au-Prince, and often I did, though with some misgivings. The apartment had no running water, for one thing, and it was always crammed with friends and poor relations and mysterious strangers whose connection I never could figure out. They just arrived, hung around for a couple of days, and moved on; I got the impression this was how a lot of them lived.

It was by staying at Ponce's apartment that I met an elderly Haitian who claimed to have been comrades-in-arms with Che. Laurent was a tall, spry, ebullient old man with jaundice-yellow eyes and ebony skin that glistened in the heat of the small apartment, and I suppose there's no point in withholding the fact that he was quite insane. He'd turn up several times a week, usually in the mornings for a cup of coffee; in his *guayabera* and slacks and white patent-leather loafers, carrying his zippered portfolio under one arm, he looked every inch the tropical man of affairs, but as soon as he opened his mouth you wanted to run for the doors.

"I have an appointment with Mandela this morning," he might say, shrewdly tapping the portfolio he was never without. Another day it might be Thatcher or Mitterand, or he might be going to the Palace to confer with President Aristide. The thing is, if you listened to him long enough, his delusions began to take on a plausible air. For most of his life he'd flirted around the edges of power, ever since he'd been a captain in the Haitian Army and launched an early, failed coup against Papa Doc. He could talk quite rationally about politics and history, and there was a gamesmanship to his madness, a playful self-aware quality, that kept us guessing as to how seriously he took himself.

He liked taunting the *blans,* the foreigners, best of all. If there were journalists at the apartment—and often there were, since Ponce spoke English and lived near the Holiday Inn—Laurent would shake their hands and solemnly declare, "I am the lidder of the Haitian pipple!" Which was absurd, of course, but with time I found myself adjusting to the notion that, madness aside, Laurent would have made as decent a president as anyone could hope for. He spoke five languages, held degrees in business and economics, and boasted a distinguished, if brief, military career, and over the course of his harrowing thirty-year exile he'd kept body and soul together on four different continents. But Cuba had been his first stop, where he had offered his protean talents to the freshly anointed Minister of Industry, El Che. "We recognized at once that we were brothers," Laurent told anyone who would listen. "He put me in charge of the office of Bureau of Statistics, and often I would accompany him as he traveled about the country inspecting projects of industrialization. We talked about so many things in our time together—about his life, about philosophy, about my dream of liberating Haiti, which he fully supported. 'Laurent,' he asked me on one occasion, 'what is the first priority of government? What is the first thing you would do if you were president of Haiti?'"

"'Education,' I said at once, 'I would build schools, Comandante Guevara. To raise the awareness of the people.'"

"'Good answer,' he said, 'but wrong. Before schools, before medicine, before anything, there must be security. Security is the precondition for all other advances.' Therefore," Laurent continued, raising his voice to an imaginary crowd of thousands, "when

I am elected president, the security of the nation will be my number one priority!"

"Don't laugh when he talks like that," Ponce told me later. "Don't ever laugh when a Haitian tells you he's going to be president, because it might happen. And if it does he won't forget that you laughed at him."

Ponce was right, of course—as proof we had the elections of several years before, when only a fluke of history kept Laurent from high office. After thirty years in exile he had returned shortly after Baby Doc's fall and declared himself a candidate for the Senate, one of a pack of hopefuls vying for the three Senate seats from Port-au-Prince. He ran a lucid if little-noticed campaign until the final week, when Duvalierist diehards launched a terrorist blitz that threatened to doom the elections. Amid the all-too-familiar scenario of lies, international hand-wringing, and a rising body count, Laurent caused a sensation by appearing on TV and announcing that he was going to dance for peace. "All Haitians should dance!" he cried wherever he went, breaking into a hot, hip-swiveling shuffle that brought cheers from an instantly smitten electorate. "Let's dance instead of fight, all Haitians should dance!" Election day turned out to be a disaster, with death squads running wild all over the country, but before voting was cancelled observers in Port-au-Prince reported that huge numbers of people were marking their ballots for "the guy who danced."

It was scary to think how close he'd come to real power, though the idea was good for some vengeful laughs, too, because the sane politicians had made such a mess of things. But as for poor Laurent, he'd missed his chance; now he spent his days dropping in on friends and battering them with stories about his time with Che. At the Bay of Pigs he'd commanded a detachment of militia, putting his life on the line for the Revolution; he'd also been at Che's side in the humiliating aftermath of the missile crisis, when angry Cuban crowds had chanted "Khrushchev, you faggot!" There in the small, sweltering apartment without running water Laurent would describe Che's brilliant mind, his Herculean work habits, his love of practical jokes, and the curse of his asthma, the stories piling one on top of another until we lapsed into a sort of historical trance. Then the old man would catch himself and glance at his watch.

"*Bon*," he'd say, taking a last slurp of coffee, "please excuse me, I'm due for my appointment now," and off he'd go to meet Carter or Yeltsin or whoever was on the agenda that day, dismissing us with a wave of his empty portfolio.

4. The Consoling Voice

Throughout my thirties I kept going to Haiti, convinced that I'd found ground zero for all the stupidity, waste, and horror inflicted on the hemisphere since Columbus and the Spaniards set up shop. Meanwhile Ponce, as part of his duties for a national medical commission, made several trips to Cuba, returning with tapes of Che's speeches that he'd play in the evenings on a cheap boom box, Che's voice ringing through the old gingerbread mansion with the propulsive resonance of hammered sheet metal.

As he rose in prestige and prominence, Ponce began to neglect his wife, a beautiful woman with piercing anthracite eyes and skin the color of brandied chocolate. She came from a poor family, but she was direct and strong-willed, and had a quick, intuitive mind that put my college degree to shame. She and Ponce had met shortly after the Aristide coup, when a ruthless military regime took control of the country; their romance had flourished amid the heady atmosphere of brutal repression and messianic resistance, but the adrenalin rush of those days was long gone. Now they spent most of their time together arguing about money. There was never enough, of course, and they spent too much, and the debts were piling up, and so forth, and watching them fight I began to think that Marx, who was so wrong about so many things, had been right about money's relentless genius for invading every aspect of human life.

Not the most practical man when it came to finance, Ponce dealt with the problem by running around on his wife, and he described his erotic adventures to me in an urgent, hissing whisper that sounded like the air leaking out of their love. He told me everything; to her he denied everything, though what he was doing was pretty obvious. "I'm going out to get some Cokes!" he'd yell, and then be gone for three hours. So she and I would sit in the dark at the kitchen table, drinking rum without Coke and talking into the night while her family snored on mattresses scattered around the room.

"*Je suis une femme deçue,*" she told me, I'm a disappointed woman. She knew her position was tenuous; even though Ponce introduced her around as his wife, they'd never actually married, and along with her lack of legal standing she had no money, no family means, no education to speak of. Things lacked clarity, she said. "I don't know what I'm doing anymore." She kept returning to a dreamlike story about a resistance group that she and some friends had formed shortly after the coup. At first it was all *bloff,* just meetings and talk, but then a *blan* turned up and started teaching them things. How to use a gun, how to make a bomb. How to plan an ambush. How to disappear.

"Who was this guy?" I asked.

She shrugged. "Just a man, a *blan.* An American."

"Was he military? CIA?"

Another shrug.

"Where did you meet?"

"In Carrefour," she said vaguely, "at a friend's house. At night."

It sounded like a fantasy to me, a crude form of wish fulfillment; on the other hand there was the .38 she always carried in her purse, with which she seemed as casually proficient as your average American housewife with her cell phone. So maybe I was the one dreaming, living the fantasy. When I asked what happened to the group she said, "I quit. I got scared." One night the *blan* gave them a stack of Aristide posters and told them to blanket the neighborhood. They split into teams of two and slipped out the door with their sheaves of posters and pots of wallpaper glue, and within minutes she and her partner were picked up by attachés. She would have been shot if this boy hadn't convinced the attachés that she was a stranger, just a girl who happened along and stopped to talk. So the attachés told her to go, get lost; the next morning her partner's body was found in a sewer on Grande Rue. A few days later she met Ponce and moved in with him, in a different part of town where she wasn't known.

"He saved my life," she said. "He got me out of there." When I was alone with either of them, they spoke tenderly of one another; when they were together they couldn't stop arguing, and eventually Ponce threw some clothes in a suitcase and moved out. He gave her some money now and then, but it was never enough, and whenever I was in Haiti I'd go by to see her and bring a little cash if I was able. Sometimes when I arrived for one of my visits Che's speeches would be playing on the boom box. It surprised me at first, because she didn't understand the words any more than I did, but then I realized that the sound alone was enough, that the tense, florid arabesques of Che's Spanish served her much the same way as a torch song. This was the record she chose to play in her solitude, the music that spoke all the longing and truth and hurt that we couldn't talk about in ordinary conversation. Those secrets we keep, even when they aren't so secret. When I asked, half-joking, if she was learning Spanish, she just laughed and turned away.

5. *Seremos Como El Che!*

"Be like Che!" Fidel urged his countrymen on the day he announced *El Comandante*'s death. Thirty years later Che's unmarked grave was discovered at last, bringing an end to one of the Cold War's more potent mysteries. For eighteen months a team of forensics experts had poked holes in the airstrip near Vallegrande, Bolivia, searching for the famous revolutionary's remains; I followed the story with guarded interest from 3,000 miles away, wary of attaching yet more personal baggage to the subject. For decades Che's enemies had kept his shameful grave a secret, fearful of creating a shrine and rallying point for the militant left, but once he was found it seemed that everyone wanted him for themselves. The Bolivian government lobbied to keep him in Vallegrande, where he was sure to generate millions in tourist dollars. The Argentines, their savage "dirty war" safely in the past, laid claim to him as a native son. The Cubans, who had ignored Che's pleas for help in his last desperate days, insisted on their rights as his adopted countrymen and spiritual brothers.

The Cubans got him, though not without some ugly bickering. I continued to follow the story in the newspapers, goaded by the notion that I had some sort of stake in the outcome. In any event, the discovery and subsequent reinterment of Che's remains inspired a spasm of worldwide reflection on the Guevara legacy. Dozens of new books were published, and old ones reissued. Thousands of sordid CIA documents came to light. Fidel made a lot of interminable speeches, while tidal waves of Che merchandise swamped the world's free markets. The global revolution prophesied by Che had yet to come to pass, though he would surely find the reasons just as compelling as ever. Poverty, injustice, oppression, suffering, these remain the basic conditions of life on most of the planet—whatever else has changed since his death, this hasn't, but as life becomes more pleasurable and affluent for the rest of us, the poor seem more remote than ever, their appeal to our humanity even fainter.

I'm in my forties now, halfway to heaven, as they say—the years are going faster, gathering speed. Recently it occurred to me that I've spent a lot of energy and many years trying to learn a very few basic things, which may be nothing more than crude opinions anyway. There's so little in the world we can be sure of, and maybe it's that lack, that flaw or deficiency, if you will, that drives our strongest compulsions. The last time I visited Haiti, Ponce was harried and overworked as usual, embittered by the terrible working conditions. "I'm like a jet pilot without a plane!" he cried. There were more sick people than ever, and fewer doctors to cure them; what was left of the Haitian professional class was bailing out, liquidating their assets and heading for the U.S.

"Not me," Ponce declared. "I'm staying. Everybody says I'm crazy, but I'm staying." I told him I wanted to see Laurent, to get his thoughts on the final chapter in the Che story—it might be an interesting historical exercise, I said, though secretly I was hoping for some sign or clue that always seemed to be hovering just beyond my reach. Because his health had declined considerably, Laurent rarely left his home these days, but Ponce knew where he lived, and so one hot, sleepy Sunday afternoon we bought some sweets and rum to present as gifts and drove over to his house. Laurent lived in the old Salomon quarter near the center of town, close enough to the Palace that he could still, if proximity counted for anything, sustain his dream of ruling the country some day. Ponce got lost in the tangle of eighteenth-century streets, made some random turns, swore, seemed to find his way again. Bands of sunlight and shadow tiger-striped the narrow streets; the old houses had the slumped, encrusted look of shipwrecks lying at the bottom of the sea. After some more addled swearing and driving around, Ponce pulled up in front of a crumbling wood-frame cottage. The sorry state of the house, the piles of trash in the yard, seemed to belie the fundamental human urge to cope. Two teams of wild-looking boys were playing soccer in the street, the match swirling around us as we climbed from the car.

"I'm sure he's home," Ponce said as we crossed the street. "He hardly ever leaves his house anymore."

The afternoon light had a coppery, brackish tint. The dry weeds seemed to explode at the touch of our feet. "He might not recognize us," Ponce warned as we crossed the yard. "He's pretty senile, but maybe the rum will get us in." We stepped from the sun into the cavelike shadows of the porch, careful to edge around the rotten floorboards. We knocked on the door, waited, and knocked again. I turned and watched the street for a minute, the shrieking boys absorbed in their game of soccer, the slow procession of Sunday passers-by The wall of sunlight tracking the porch's shadowline seemed as smooth and final as a marble slab.

"Is he sick?" Ponce wondered out loud. "My God, has he died?"

We knocked again, and we called, then we walked along the porch tapping all the windows, trying to rouse some sign of life from the house. He could be sleeping, we told each other, or maybe his hearing was gone, or maybe he was confused and couldn't find the door. So we kept knocking, though we knew after a while it was useless. And yet we stayed, we knocked and called until we made fools of ourselves, but no one ever answered within.

———————

Ben Fountain grew up in eastern North Carolina and now lives in Dallas with his wife and their two children. He is the author of the collection *Brief Encounters with Che Guevara* (2006). His short fiction has appeared in *Harper's,* the *Paris Review, Zoetrope: All-Story, Southwest Review,* and elsewhere, and he has received a Pushcart Prize, an O. Henry Award, and other honors. He is working on a novel set in Dallas, scheduled for publication in 2007.

LILIANA CASTILLO

*H*ow do you come at a figure like Che? The only way I could see myself trying it with any hope of success was obliquely. By degrees. I'd picked up various stories about or having to do with Che along the way, some my own, some others', and while none of them alone seemed likely to get me where I wanted to go, maybe a handful of them together could carry me part of the way. So that's how I wrote it, as five stories, five fragments. Breaking it down seemed like the only way of making it whole.

N. M. Kelby

JUBILATION, FLORIDA

(from *One Story*)

It's not a good idea; Nordan and Sara both know it. Both are over forty. Both love their spouses. Both are drunk. Both naked — and not thin. Both wonder if the other is lying when they say, nearly simultaneously, "I've never done this before."

And they're friends — or think they are. It's difficult to tell. They were total strangers before they checked into adjoining hotel rooms in Jubilation, a planned community featuring Key West–styled homes in sherbet colors with white picket fences. The resort is Gingerbread Victorian, with a permit-only beach where the sand is raked into traditional Zen patterns three times a day. There are no homeless people in Jubilation. No tattoo shops. There's nothing sordid, or dangerous. You can't even walk down the side streets unless you have security clearance; surveillance cameras are every-where. It's not the kind of place you'd have an affair in.

But here they are, naked — and a little cold. It's off-season.

"Two things before we go any further," Nordan says — all busi-ness, all courage, all confidence. In the moonlight, his goose bumps are disconcerting; make him look a little like a plucked turkey.

"I want to be clear. My wife is so great, I don't even have a pool because I'm afraid she'd run off with the pool guy. Mary Anne is the most glorious control freak on Earth. Kicked my ass into

303

shape. I have to warn you, if she finds out about this, she'll hunt you down like a feral dog and chew your heart out."

Sara is unfazed. Doesn't even blink. "That's a given," she says. "More bourbon?" She pours the last of it before he can answer. Nordan takes a mouthful, swallows it so fast he coughs.

An alarmed look passes over Sara's face. "We don't have to do this."

"No. I want you. I want to."

"So, what's the second thing?"

"The second thing is that I would never leave my wife. For all her goofy shit, she's fierce. Not many women like that anymore."

Sara is relieved. She takes a sip from Nordan's glass, looks at him closely—the plucked skin, the pleading eyes, the 'What the Hell am I doing?' look on his face. She has no idea how she's going to explain this to her therapist.

"Okay," she says. "There are two things you should know."

"Fair enough."

"First, my husband is the kindest, most gentle man I have ever met. I clearly don't deserve him. He's like a surfing, golfing St. Francis of Assisi. If *he* ever finds out, he may want to kill you, but he's so kind-hearted, and not very well organized, so he couldn't pull it off. I'd have to do it. I'm kind of his 'go-to' guy. Just thought you should know."

"Noted. The second thing?"

"Well, afterwards, I'm planning to burn your body and sprinkle your ashes on my roses."

"Makes sense."

"Absolutely. Bone marrow is a superior fertilizer, plus I've kind of gotten used to you hanging around—so, it would be the best of both worlds," she says, then corrects. "Well, for me of course. You'd be mulch."

It is at this moment that Nordan realizes why people should not talk before having sex.

"Okay," he says. "That's—" He is fumbling for just the right word, one that won't ruin whatever shreds of desire that remain.

He decides on "sweet," and she smiles, which unfortunately encourages him so he just keeps on talking. "Yep. That's sort of sweet. Twisted, but slightly endearing."

Sara looks so beautiful standing there in front of him, like a freaking Botticelli, so it makes him nervous. Her skin reminds him of vanilla ice cream, not the no-fat crap, but the expensive stuff with 27 percent saturated fat—the Lipitor stuff. He'd like to tell her that, but already has, and doesn't want to repeat himself. Might ruin the moment. So he tries to remember a poem by James Dickey about adultery. Something about not being able to die in this room, about having this moment only, stealing a little bit more life from life. Nordan would like to remember this poem because he knows it would be the perfect thing to say, but he's had so much bourbon all he can manage is, "Quoth the raven, 'Nevermore.'"

Sara looks confused. Nordan's mood turns frantic, hopes she isn't having second thoughts. "Nevermore," he says again, as if trying to make a point. Better to bluff, he thinks, than look like an idiot.

"Great," Sara says. *What am I doing with this idiot?*

Nordan can feel her think this. He shrugs, looks a little sheepish, and slaps himself on the forehead—and that changes everything. Suddenly, it's clear to Sara that this man has crawled into her brain, pitched a tent, and, somehow, is a part of her now. It's too late to turn back, so she takes the glass out of his hand and pulls him into her arms.

"Maybe we can stop talking now," she whispers, throaty, and before he can say anything else, she kisses him. Open mouth. Greedy. He shudders with pleasure, fear. They both do, actually.

Neither is quite sure how they got to this point.

Sara and Nordan are supposed to be on a retreat. They've both won this year's Bennington Foundation Leadership Award, along with twenty-two others. It's a very prestigious award. There's no application process, nomination only. Leaders from both the arts and sciences are chosen every year.

Nordan was honored because he's a consultant who teaches poetry to business executives from Fortune 500 companies. He once told Ed Bradley on *60 Minutes* that poetry in the workplace humanizes and makes change. "It's the ultimate form of revolution," he said and then called it a 'slick gig,' and drove off in his Maserati. The piece was titled "Corporate America's Abby Hoffman."

Sara's award was given because she'd written a memoir about her own personal search for grace. It was elegant and heartfelt and more or less true.

Sara is one of *those* women. Big-boned. Bleached blonde. Seems taller than she is. She'd been a police beat reporter for the CNN affiliate in Twin Cities for nearly twenty years. She'd been shot at while covering drug raids. Beaten up at a race riot. She once went undercover at a strip joint and knows that pasties hurt if you pull them off too quickly.

When Sara turned forty she wasn't interested in a monthly regime of Botox, as the news director suggested, so she left television to write a memoir. Her agent cautioned her that she'd need a new angle, something fresh.

"Maybe you could join a convent or something."

So she did. Sara was between husbands at the time, her second had just left, so living with cloistered nuns seemed to make a lot of sense. "I'll spend a lot less on makeup," she told her friends. The book proposal created a bidding war between publishers and brought a high-six figure contract. But once the check was cashed, reality set in. All that kneeling, and not speaking, and averting one's eyes drove Sara crazy after three weeks, so she left—but wrote the book anyway.

"They've taken a vow of silence," she told her agent. "It's not like they'll tell anyone."

Cloistered was a *New York Times* bestseller for a week. That was in 2000, the same year she married Mike—who is ten years younger, takes in stray animals, volunteers at soup kitchens, and has no marketable job skills. Sara hasn't written a thing since. She and

Mike are just about out of money, but that's okay. The Leadership Award provides a guaranteed income of $100,000 a year, for two years. Which is good for Nordan, too. He recently came to the rude discovery that he's fallen out of fashion, and is now forced to teach at a community college.

So Nordan and Sara have come to Jubilation to get the check, although the foundation president would not describe the situation so indelicately. According to the website, every year, before the money is given out, award recipients are brought together at resorts around the country and, for fourteen days, they take part in networking sessions with titles like "How to Unleash Your Inner Leader."

"It is our desire to create a think-tank atmosphere," the foundation director is quoted as saying. "When you make it easy for leaders to cross-pollinate, their communities will benefit tenfold."

Sara and Nordan are pretty sure this is not the kind of cross-pollination the director had in mind.

"Well," Nordan says.

"Well," Sara echoes.

Outside, a seagull squawks.

When they were first introduced, Nordan told Sara he was the biggest egomaniac she would ever meet. He meant it as a joke, but he is. And she knows it. And yet, here they are — Sara standing at the edge of the bed watching Nordan watch her. Her lips are now bruised from his. Her breasts, full and round.

"Just like those little cheese wheels," Nordan says. "The ones in red wax. Gouda, is it?"

Sara guesses that's a compliment, but it's difficult to tell. She's lactose intolerant. "Sure," she says. She'd like to say something more, something to compliment him, but she knows of no cheese product that Nordan reminds her of, and he's told her repeatedly that he hates compliments.

"I'm a realist," he said. "There were two years in college when I was handsome. The baby fat had dropped away and I played

NCAA basketball with a full head of hair that wasn't implanted from somewhere else. Now, I'm one hot fudge sundae away from morphing into Jabba the Hut."

Nordan is clearly a man who likes his dairy.

Sara finds it hard to believe Nordan is completely unaware that he is still handsome, still has an athlete's grace. His body may have grown thick with age, but it's powerful and muscular. His broad chest is covered with golden hair, like fleece. He reminds her of a lion. Sara's never seen anything quite like Nordan. Her husband Mike is smooth and nearly hairless, like a boy. Nordan is sweaty, unwieldy and passionate. He shudders when she touches him, which is a little unnerving. It makes her wonder if he's been in prison for the last seven years instead of a suburb in Connecticut.

Of course, she thinks, soccer moms and guards both carry whistles. Lights out by nine PM. This is why she doesn't live in the suburbs.

Still, when Nordan lifts her into his arms and kisses her, she is lost in it. It feels as if they are skydiving through each other's lives.

"This is such a bad idea," he says.

"You're right," she says.

But they don't stop.

For the past two weeks, Nordan and Sara have spent every night drinking and watching the sun set in what could only be described as a boozy filibuster haze. They never seemed to stop talking. They talked about the NBA, the NFL, rock and roll, Japanese baseball teams, his career, his dreams, his ambitions, his wife's obsessive love of Lilly Pulitzer resort wear ("She's wearing pink flamingos in Connecticut, for chrissake."), and his uncle, a five-hundred-pound circus clown with narcolepsy.

Sara recounted minute details of her first, second, and current marriage. Funny stories, nothing too sad. It seemed like an endless cocktail party, but every now and then one or the other would say, "Shit, I can't believe I'm telling you this. I've never told anybody this."

And then they'd both stop talking.

On day six, Sara confessed that when she was seven years old, she actually believed she could grow up to be a superhero. She was laughing when she told Nordan she'd climbed onto the roof of her family's double-wide trailer with a bed sheet wrapped around her neck and jumped, breaking her right leg.

She expected Nordan to laugh too, but he was quiet.

"It's a true story. I swear," she said. "What kind of an egomaniac believes they're a superhero?"

Nordan cleared his throat. "In my case," he said. "It was a garage. I was eight. It was my sister's blanket and my left foot."

Sara looked concerned. "Shit," she said. "Did you ever wonder why we're on this porch? You and I? It's not some sort of destiny thing, is it? I'd hate that. I don't even read my horoscope."

Nordan thought about it a minute, then shook his head. "Naw. We're here because we're poseurs. We have to stick together." Then he poured her another bourbon.

That's when Sara decided she liked Nordan. Yet, in all those drunken nights, she never imagined having sex with him, even though they had adjoining rooms. Then, on night thirteen, things changed.

It began rather innocently. Sara fell asleep in her wicker chair while Nordan was rambling on about steroids and batting averages. So he picked her up in his massive arms and carried her into her room—and she's not exactly a small woman. "Time for bed, Slugger," he said and placed her gently on top of the sheets. He brushed her hair out of her eyes and covered her with a blanket. Then kissed her forehead. "Sweet dreams," he said.

The noble gentleness of the gesture, the quiet innocence of it, stunned her. Who is this guy, really? She suddenly wanted to find out. So, the next night, their last night together, Sara called for a 'no-bullshit zone.'

"Tell me about Seth," she said. Seth is Nordan's only child, from his first marriage. He just turned fourteen. "You said his birthday was last Saturday, right? What's he like?"

Nordan looked surprised. "I can't believe I mentioned Seth, let alone his birthday. But, Hell, you know me; I don't listen to a word I say—"

"Shut up then and tell me about him."

"What's to tell? Seth's my kid. A real slacker like his old man. When he comes to visit, we hide out together in the basement and watch ESPN. I bitch about the Lakers. He pisses about the Timberwolves. It's pretty great."

"Do you see him a lot?"

"Every other Christmas. Every other summer."

"Is that hard?"

"It just is. How about you? Your kids?"

"Just one," she said. "Hannah. She died a long time ago."

Nordan wasn't expecting that at all. "Jesus. How old?"

"Six days."

"How long ago?"

"Fourteen years."

"That's horrible."

"It just is. Hannah suffocated in her crib. The mattress was too soft. I didn't know."

Nordan reached over to take Sara's hand, but she moved it away.

"I'm fine. It was a long time ago."

What Sara didn't say was that she could have saved Hannah. She heard her baby fussing, but didn't get up to check on her. She was too tired. So Hannah died. Right in the next room. Hannah with her perfect fingers and buttermilk skin. Her Buddha eyes. And it was Sara's fault. But she didn't have to tell Nordan any of this because he heard it in her voice—all the details she couldn't speak—and that scared him. So they sat in silence and watched the moon slip in and out of the clouds. They rocked back and forth. The chairs creaked. After a time Nordan said, "Your daughter and my son would have been about the same age."

"Sorry I brought it up."

"No, it's good. I just realized that they could have dated. Man, that would be something, or what? Your kid would speak five languages and mine would show her how to dye her hair rainbow colors with Jell-O. Wouldn't that be something?"

Sara didn't know what to say. She never thought of Hannah as a young girl, or dating. But as soon as Nordan said it, she did. She imagined evenings spent with Nordan, driving around in her Jeep, looking for their kids in tattoo shops, or behind the bleachers at football games.

"It would be something," she said and laughed and leaned over and kissed Nordan on the cheek.

"Thanks," he said gratefully, just as he had earlier at dinner when she had handed him her piece of key lime pie, which she remembered, at the last minute, contains sweetened condensed milk.

"You're all right," he said then.

"I'm lactose intolerant."

"Well, you're all right, too."

And then she laughed.

And hours later, when she kissed him out of gratitude for this vision of Hannah, he said it again. "You're all right." Then kissed her back, quickly. "Bruised as Hell, just like me, but all right."

And then she unbuttoned her shirt.

That's how it all began. Nordan carried her into his room and placed her on his bed. They undressed in silence. They tried to make small talk, but much of it revolved around dairy products. And now, three hours later, somewhere around two AM, after speaking about Gouda cheese at great length, Nordan finally finds his courage, runs his teeth along her neck, her breasts.

Sara feels her skin bruise under them, feels him grow hard against her leg.

Nordan's thoughts bounce like tennis balls. *It'll be great. Nobody will get hurt. It's only sex. No big deal. Game. Set. Match.*

Love.

He stops, again. Shudders. Then holds her so tightly she can barely breathe. For some reason, he's suddenly afraid to let go.

"What's wrong?"

"Shh."

"You okay?"

"Give me a minute, I'll be fine."

His breath is rapid, and for the first time in a long time Nordan feels afraid. He has no idea why. When the moment finally passes, he lets her fall out of his arms. "That was weird," he says, his voice hoarse. "I just had this feeling like there's a storm raging around us, and I didn't even know it was raining."

The moment feels airless.

"I better go," Sara says and stands. "I have an early plane to catch."

"Right."

Nordan picks up her bra from the floor and looks at it for a moment. "We still friends?"

"Sure."

The word feels brittle. Nordan catches her arm. "Look, I don't know what the Hell's going on but when you touch me, I don't hate it. I always hate to be touched —"

"I have to go."

"I'm talking too much again, aren't I?"

"It's an early flight."

"Okay. Here's the deal," he says, then stops. Takes a deep breath. "I get you. And underneath all my bullshit, you get me too."

And it's true. Sara knows it. So she runs. She runs out onto the porch and out the screen door and onto the perfectly groomed Zen-themed beach.

And Nordan follows her.

And they're both naked.

And it's April.

And the air temperature is sixty-nine degrees, with a light chop off the Gulf.

Nordan and Sara are still a little drunk, and working off adrenaline, so they aren't thinking about any of this. Nor are they thinking about the CAUTION, NO SWIMMING sign they pass, nor that it's nesting season for sea turtles.

And most of all, they aren't thinking about the fact that the

Red Cross suggests that the optimal temperature for Gulf water is about 80 degrees. Colder than that, and you risk hypothermia. Or maybe Nordan and Sara don't know that. Either way, it doesn't matter. It's 72 degrees when Sara dives in, and Nordan blindly follows. Once wet, it's quite clear that the Red Cross knows exactly what they are talking about.

"Shit!" they both scream.

Nordan lunges for Sara out of a primal need—for warmth, mostly—and pulls her close to his hairy body. He's panting hard from the cold and feels his heart beat in his teeth when he asks, "Would it be better if I told you I just wanted to 'do' you? I could say that."

Sara laughs and a cloud moves away from the moon. The night shimmers. "Look, sea turtles," she says and points to the beach.

There are five, perhaps six, it's difficult to tell. They are lumbering mountains, some as big as Nordan, maybe 200 pounds or more. A few swim in the waters nearby, mating. They are graceful as they circle each other, but nearly drown as they try to mount.

"They're worse than us," Nordan says.

"Shh," Sara laughs.

The hotel lobby, and also the beach, has signs that warn guests not to swim at night and not to make any noise or use flashlights when walking the shore. Sea turtles are endangered.

ANY DISRUPTION OF THEIR MATING COULD HAVE SERIOUS LONG-TERM IMPLICATIONS, the signs state in large red letters. Nordan suddenly remembers that, and wonders what the "implications" are, and who should be more worried about them—the turtles or swimmers. He pulls Sara closer, and watches. The turtles are terrifying and beautiful, uncaring as gods.

"They live to be one hundred years old," Sara whispers, "and come to the same spot every year to mate."

Apparently, they've not heard of Club Med, Nordan thinks, but remembers a verse from "Song of Songs" and says, "I will arise now and go about the city in the streets and seek whom my soul loveth."

Sara kisses his cheek. "I love you," she says simply.

The words sound so sweet, a horrible panicked look crosses Nordan's face.

"Calm down," Sara says. "I love you like pie. Like key lime pie."

"But you're lactose intolerant."

"That's the breaks."

And so he kisses her hard. And she, him.

And for a long time they hold each other and watch the turtles and their awkward dance. They watch until their fingers go numb, then their feet, then hands, then legs. They watch until they can't feel a thing.

N. M. Kelby is the author of *Whale Season, Theater of the Stars,* and *In the Company of Angels.* "Jubilation, Florida," has been featured twice on NPR'S "Selected Shorts."

STEVEN E. KELBY

*J*ubilation, Florida" *was written on a bet. At least, that's the way I remember it. There is some disagreement on this point. In fact, the writer who bet me now denies the entire incident. Says it didn't happen. I remember it clearly. I'm pretty sure that he said I couldn't be a great writer until I wrote a story about sex. I'm pretty sure I blushed. I'm pretty sure he gave me grief for blushing. I'm pretty sure that I wrote it to spite him. He now says he doesn't remember any of this. Of course, there was bourbon involved.*

APPENDIX

A list of the magazines currently consulted for *New Stories from the South: The Year's Best, 2006,* with addresses, subscription rates, and editors.

American Literary Review
P.O. Box 311307
University of North Texas
Denton, TX 76203-1307
Semiannually, $10
John Tait

The Antioch Review
P.O. Box 148
Yellow Springs, OH 45387-0148
Quarterly, $40
Robert S. Fogarty

Apalachee Review
P.O. Box 10469
Tallahassee, FL 32302
Semiannually, $15
Laura Newton

Appalachian Heritage
CPO 2166
Berea, KY 40404
Quarterly, $18
George Brosi

Arkansas Review
P.O. Box 1890
Arkansas State University
State University, AR 72467
Triannually, $20
Tom Williams

Arts & Letters
Campus Box 89
Georgia College & State University
Milledgeville, GA 31061-0490
Semiannually, $15
Martin Lammon

Atlanta
260 W. Peachtree St.
Suite 300
Atlanta, GA 30303
Monthly, $14.95
Rebecca Burns

The Atlantic Monthly
77 N. Washington St.
Boston, MA 02114
Monthly, $19.50
C. Michael Curtis

Backwards City Review
P.O. Box 41317
Greensboro, NC 27404-1317
Semiannually, $12

Bayou
Department of English
University of New Orleans
Lakefront
New Orleans, LA 70148
Semiannually, $10
Joanna Leake

Bellevue Literary Review
Department of Medicine
New York University School of
   Medicine
550 1st Avenue, OBV-612
New York, NY 10016
Semiannually, $12
Ronna Weinberg

Black Warrior Review
University of Alabama
P.O. Box 862936
Tuscaloosa, AL 35486
Semiannually, $14
Fiction Editor

Boulevard
6614 Clayton Road, PMB 325
Richmond Heights, MO 63117
Triannually, $15
Richard Burgin

The Carolina Quarterly
Greenlaw Hall CB# 3520
University of North Carolina
Chapel Hill, NC 27599-3520
Triannually, $18
Fiction Editor

The Chariton Review
Brigham Young University
English Department
4198 JFSB
Provo, UT 84602
Semiannually, $9
Jim Barnes

The Chattahoochee Review
Georgia Perimeter College
2101 Womack Road
Dunwoody, GA 30338-4497
Quarterly, $16
Lawrence Hetrick

Cimarron Review
205 Morrill Hall
Oklahoma State University
Stillwater, OK 74078-4069
Quarterly, $24
E. P. Walkiewicz

The Cincinnati Review
Department of English and
   Comparative Literature
University of Cincinnati
P.O. Box 210069
Cincinnati, OH 45221-0069
Semiannually, $15
Brock Clarke

Colorado Review
Dept. of English
Colorado State University
Fort Collins, CO 80523
Triannually, $24
Stephanie G'Schwind

Columbia
415 Dodge Hall
2960 Broadway
Columbia University
New York, NY 10027-6902
Semiannually, $15
Fiction Editor

Confrontation
English Department
C.W. Post of L.I.U.
Brookville, NY 11548
Semiannually, $10
Martin Tucker

Conjunctions
21 East 10th Street
New York, NY 10003
Semiannually, $18
Bradford Morrow

Crazyhorse
Department of English
College of Charleston
66 George St.
Charleston, SC 29424
Semiannually, $15
Anthony Varallo

Denver Quarterly
University of Denver
Denver, CO 80208
Quarterly, $20
Bin Ramke

The Distillery
Motlow State Comm. College
P.O. Box 8500
Lynchburg, TN 37352-8500
Semiannually, $15
Dawn Copeland

Epoch
251 Goldwin Smith Hall
Cornell University
Ithaca, NY 14853-3201
Triannually, $11
Michael Koch

Fiction
c/o English Department
City College of New York
New York, NY 10031
Quarterly, $38
Mark J. Mirsky

Five Points
Georgia State University
P.O. Box 3999
Atlanta, GA 30302-3999
Triannually, $20
Megan Sexton

Four
Box 323
Spelman College

350 Spelman Lane
Atlanta, GA 30314
Yearly
Ariele Elise Le Grand

The Frostproof Review
P.O. Box 21013
Columbus, OH 43221
Semiannually, $15
Kyle Minor

Fugue
200 Brink Hall
University of Idaho
P.O. Box 441102
Moscow, ID 83844-1102
Semiannually, $14
Marcia Kmetz

The Georgia Review
Gilbert Hall
University of Georgia
Athens, GA 30602-9009
Quarterly, $24
T. R. Hummer

The Gettysburg Review
Gettysburg College
Gettysburg, PA 17325-1491
Quarterly, $24
Peter Stitt

Glimmer Train Stories
1211 NW Glissan St., Suite 207
Portland, OR 97209-3054
Quarterly, $36
Susan Burmeister-Brown
    and Linda B. Swanson-Davies

Granta
1755 Broadway
5th Floor
New York, NY 10019-3780
Quarterly, $37
Ian Jack

The Greensboro Review
English Department
134 McIver Bldg.
University of North Carolina
P.O. Box 26170
Greensboro, NC 27412
Semiannually, $10
Jim Clark

Gulf Coast
Department of English
University of Houston
Houston, TX 77204-3013
Semiannually, $14
Mark Doty

Harper's Magazine
666 Broadway, 11th Floor
New York, NY 10012
Monthly, $18
Ben Metcalf

Harpur Palate
English Department
Binghamton University
P.O. Box 6000
Binghamton, NY 13902-6000
Semiannually, $16
Letitia Moffitt and Silas Zobel

Hobart
submit@hobartpulp.com
Biannually, $10
Aaron Burch

The Idaho Review
Boise State University
Department of English
1910 University Drive
Boise, ID 83725
Annually, $10.95
Mitch Wieland

Image
3307 Third Ave., W.

Seattle, WA 98119
Quarterly, $39.95
Gregory Wolfe

Indiana Review
Ballantine Hall 465
Indiana University
1020 Kirkwood Drive
Bloomington, IN 47405-7103
Semiannually, $12
Will Boast

The Iowa Review
308 EPB
University of Iowa
Iowa City, IA 52242-1408
Triannually, $24
David Hamilton

The Journal
Ohio State University
Department of English
164 W. 17th Avenue
Columbus, OH 43210
Semiannually, $12
Kathy Fagan and Michelle Herman

Kalliope
Florida Community College–
    Jacksonville
South Campus
11901 Beach Blvd.
Jacksonville, FL 32246
Triannually, $20
Mary Sue Koeppel

The Kenyon Review
Kenyon College Walton House
Gambier, OH 43022
Triannually, $30
David H. Lynn

The Literary Review
Fairleigh Dickinson University
285 Madison Avenue

Madison, NJ 07940
Quarterly, $18
René Steinke

Long Story
18 Eaton Street
Lawrence, MA 01843
Annually, $7
R. P. Burnham

Louisiana Literature
SLU-10792
Southeastern Louisiana
    University
Hammond, LA 70402
Semiannually, $12
Jack Bedell

The Louisville Review
Spalding University
851 South 4th Street
Louisville, KY 40203
Semiannually, $14
Sena Jeter Naslund

Mid-American Review
Department of English
Bowling Green State University
Bowling Green, OH 43403
Semiannually, $12
Karen Craigo and Michael
    Czyzniejewski

Mississippi Review
University of Southern
    Mississippi
Box 5144
Hattiesburg, MS 39406-5144
Semiannually, $15
Frederick Barthelme

The Missouri Review
1507 Hillcrest Hall
University of Missouri
Columbia, MO 65211

Triannually, $24
Speer Morgan

New Delta Review
English Department
15 Allen Hall
Louisiana State University
Baton Rouge, LA 70803-5001
Semiannually, $12
Ashley Berthelot and Robert Bloom

New England Review
Middlebury College
Middlebury, VT 05753
Quarterly, $25
Stephen Donadio

New Letters
University of Missouri at Kansas
    City
5101 Rockhill Road
Kansas City, MO 64110
Quarterly, $22
Robert Stewart

New Millennium Writings
P.O. Box 2463
Knoxville, TN 37901
Annually, $12.95
Don Williams

New Orleans Review
P.O. Box 195
Loyola University
New Orleans, LA 70118
Semiannually, $12
Christopher Chambers, Editor

The New Yorker
4 Times Square
New York, NY 10036
Weekly, $47
Deborah Treisman, Fiction
    Editor

Nimrod International Journal
University of Tulsa
600 South College
Tulsa, OK 74104
Semiannually, $17.50
Francine Ringold

Ninth Letter
Dept. of English
University of Illinois
608 South Wright Street
Urbana, IL 61801
Biannually, $19.95
Philip Graham

The North American Review
University of Northern Iowa
1222 W. 27th Street
Cedar Falls, IA 50614-0516
Six times a year, $22
Grant Tracey

North Carolina Literary Review
English Department
2201 Bate Building
East Carolina University
Greenville, NC 27858-4353
Annually, $10
Margaret Bauer

Northwest Review
369 PLC
University of Oregon
Eugene, OR 97403
Triannually, $22
John Witte

One Story
www.one-story.com
Monthly, $21
Hannah Tinti

Ontario Review
9 Honey Brook Drive
Princeton, NJ 08540

Semiannually, $16
Raymond J. Smith

Open City
270 Lafayette Street
Suite 1412
New York, NY 10012
Triannually, $30
Thomas Beller

Other Voices
University of Illinois at Chicago
Department of English (M/C 162)
601 S. Morgan Street
Chicago, IL 60607-7120
Quarterly, $26
Lois Hauselman

The Oxford American
201 Donaghey Avenue, Main 107
Conway, AR 72035
Quarterly, $24.95
Marc Smirnoff

The Paris Review
62 White Street
New York, NY 10013
Quarterly, $40
Philip Gourevitch

Parting Gifts
March Street Press
3413 Wilshire Drive
Greensboro, NC 27408
Semiannually, $12
Robert Bixby

Passages North
Dept. of English
Northern Michigan University
1401 Presque Isle Ave.
Marquette, MI 49855
Annually, $13
Kate Myers Hanson

Pembroke Magazine
UNC-P, Box 1510
Pembroke, NC 28372-1510
Annually, $8
Shelby Stephenson

Pindeldyboz
23-55 38th Street
Astoria, NY 11105
Annually, $12
Whitney Pastoree

Pleiades
Department of English and
   Philosophy
Central Missouri State University
Warrensburg, MO 64093
Semiannually, $12
Susan Steinberg

Ploughshares
Emerson College
120 Boylston St.
Boston, MA 02116-4624
Triannually, $24
Don Lee

PMS
Univ. of Alabama at Birmingham
Department of English
HB 217, 900 S. 13th Street
1530 3rd Ave., S.
Birmingham, AL 35294-1260
Annually, $7
Linda Frost

Post Road Magazine
853 Broadway, Suite 1516
Box 85
New York, NY 10003
Semiannually, $18
Rebecca Boyd

Prairie Schooner
201 Andrews Hall
University of Nebraska
Lincoln, NE 68588-0334
Quarterly, $26
Hilda Raz

Puerto del Sol
Box 30001, Department 3E
New Mexico State University
Las Cruces, NM 88003-9984
Semiannually, $10
Kevin McIlvoy

Quarterly West
Univ. of Utah
255 S. Central Campus Drive
Dept. of English
LNCO 3500
Salt Lake City, UT 84112-9109
Semiannually, $14
Jenny Colville

The Rambler
P.O. Box 5070
Chapel Hill, NC 27514-5001
Six issues/year, $19.95
Dave Korzon

River City
Department of English
University of Memphis
Memphis, TN 38152-6176
Semiannually, $12
Keith McElmurry

River Styx
634 North Grand Blvd.
12th Floor
St. Louis, MO 63103
Triannually, $20
Richard Newman

Salamander
Suffolk Univ. English Dept.
41 Temple St.
Boston, MA 02114-4280
Semiannually, $12
Catherine Parnell

Santa Monica Review
Santa Monica College
1900 Pico Boulevard
Santa Monica, CA 90405
Semiannually, $12
Andrew Tonkovich

The Sewanee Review
735 University Avenue
Sewanee, TN 37383-1000
Quarterly, $24
George Core

Shenandoah
Washington and Lee University
Mattingly House
Lexington, VA 24450
Quarterly, $22
R. T. Smith

The South Carolina Review
Center for Electronic and Digital
    Publishing
Clemson University
Strode Tower, Box 340522
Clemson, SC 29634
Semiannually, $25
Wayne Chapman

South Dakota Review
Box 111
University Exchange
University of South Dakota
Vermillion, SD 57069
Quarterly, $30
John R. Milton

Southern Exposure
P.O. Box 531
Durham, NC 27702
Quarterly, $24
Chris Kromm

Southern Humanities Review
9088 Haley Center
Auburn University
Auburn, AL 36849
Quarterly, $15
Dan R. Latimer and Virginia M.
    Kouidis

The Southern Review
43 Allen Hall
Louisiana State University
Baton Rouge, LA 70803-5005
Quarterly, $25
Bret Lott

Southwest Review
307 Fondren Library West
Box 750374
Southern Methodist University
Dallas, TX 75275
Quarterly, $24
Willard Spiegelman

Sou'wester
Department of English
Southern Illinois University at
    Edwardsville
Edwardsville, IL 62026-1438
Semiannually, $12
Allison Funk and Geoff Schmidt

StoryQuarterly
online submissions only:
www.storyquarterly.com
Annually, $10
M.M.M. Hayes

Swink
244 5th Avenue, #2722
New York, NY 10001
Semiannually, $16
Leelaila Strogov

Tampa Review
University of Tampa
401 W. Kennedy Boulevard
Tampa, FL 33606-1490
Semiannually, $15
Richard Mathews

Texas Review
English Department Box 2146
Sam Houston State University
Huntsville, TX 77341-2146
Semiannually, $20
Paul Ruffin

The Threepenny Review
P.O. Box 9131
Berkeley, CA 94709
Quarterly, $25
Wendy Lesser

Timber Creek Review
8969 UNC-G Station
Greensboro, NC 27413
Quarterly, $16
John M. Freiermuth

Tin House
P.O. Box 10500
Portland, OR 97296-0500
Quarterly, $29.90
Rob Spillman

TriQuarterly
Northwestern University
629 Noyes St.
Evanston, IL 60208
Triannually, $24
Susan Firestone Hahn

The Virginia Quarterly Review
One West Range
P.O. Box 400223
Charlottesville, VA 22904-4223
Quarterly, $25
Ted Genoways

West Branch
Bucknell Hall
Bucknell University
Lewisburg, PA 17837
Semiannually, $10
Ron Mohring

Willow Springs
705 West First Avenue
Spokane, WA 99201-3909
Semiannually, $13
Brian Maxwell, Josh Wiley

Yemassee
Department of English
University of South Carolina
Columbia, SC 29208
Semiannually, $15
Fiction Editor

Zoetrope: All-Story
The Sentinel Building
916 Kearny Street
San Francisco, CA 94133
Quarterly, $19.95
Michael Ray

ZYZZYVA
P.O. Box 590069
San Francisco, CA 94159-0069
Triannually, varies
Howard Junker

PREVIOUS VOLUMES

Copies of previous volumes of *New Stories from the South* can be ordered through your local bookstore or by calling the Sales Department at Algonquin Books of Chapel Hill. Multiple copies for classroom adoptions are available at a special discount. For information, please call 919-967-0108.

NEW STORIES FROM THE SOUTH: THE YEAR'S BEST, 1986

Max Apple, BRIDGING

Madison Smartt Bell, TRIPTYCH 2

Mary Ward Brown, TONGUES OF FLAME

Suzanne Brown, COMMUNION

James Lee Burke, THE CONVICT

Ron Carlson, AIR

Doug Crowell, SAYS VELMA

Leon V. Driskell, MARTHA JEAN

Elizabeth Harris, THE WORLD RECORD HOLDER

Mary Hood, SOMETHING GOOD FOR GINNIE

David Huddle, SUMMER OF THE MAGIC SHOW

Gloria Norris, HOLDING ON

Kurt Rheinheimer, UMPIRE

W. A. Smith, DELIVERY

Wallace Whatley, SOMETHING TO LOSE

Luke Whisnant, WALLWORK

Sylvia Wilkinson, CHICKEN SIMON

New Stories from the South: The Year's Best, 1987

James Gordon Bennett, DEPENDENTS

Robert Boswell, EDWARD AND JILL

Rosanne Caggeshall, PETER THE ROCK

John William Corrington, HEROIC MEASURES/VITAL SIGNS

Vicki Covington, MAGNOLIA

Andre Dubus, DRESSED LIKE SUMMER LEAVES

Mary Hood, AFTER MOORE

Trudy Lewis, VINCRISTINE

Lewis Nordan, SUGAR, THE EUNUCHS, AND BIG G. B.

Peggy Payne, THE PURE IN HEART

Bob Shacochis, WHERE PELHAM FELL

Lee Smith, LIFE ON THE MOON

Marly Swick, HEART

Robert Love Taylor, LADY OF SPAIN

Luke Whisnant, ACROSS FROM THE MOTOHEADS

New Stories from the South: The Year's Best, 1988

Ellen Akins, GEORGE BAILEY FISHING

Rick Bass, THE WATCH

Richard Bausch, THE MAN WHO KNEW BELLE STAR

Larry Brown, FACING THE MUSIC

Pam Durban, BELONGING

John Rolfe Gardiner, GAME FARM

Jim Hall, GAS

Charlotte Holmes, METROPOLITAN

Nanci Kincaid, LIKE THE OLD WOLF IN ALL THOSE WOLF STORIES

Barbara Kingsolver, ROSE-JOHNNY

Trudy Lewis, HALF MEASURES

Jill McCorkle, FIRST UNION BLUES

Mark Richard, HAPPINESS OF THE GARDEN VARIETY

Sunny Rogers, THE CRUMB

Annette Sanford, LIMITED ACCESS

Eve Shelnutt, VOICE

New Stories from the South: The Year's Best, 1989

Rick Bass, WILD HORSES

Madison Smartt Bell, CUSTOMS OF THE COUNTRY

James Gordon Bennett, PACIFIC THEATER

Larry Brown, SAMARITANS

Mary Ward Brown, IT WASN'T ALL DANCING

Kelly Cherry, WHERE SHE WAS

David Huddle, PLAYING

Sandy Huss, COUPON FOR BLOOD

Frank Manley, THE RAIN OF TERROR

Bobbie Ann Mason, WISH

Lewis Nordan, A HANK OF HAIR, A PIECE OF BONE

Kurt Rheinheimer, HOMES

Mark Richard, STRAYS

Annette Sanford, SIX WHITE HORSES

Paula Sharp, HOT SPRINGS

New Stories from the South: The Year's Best, 1990

New Stories from the South: The Year's Best, 1991

Nanci Kincaid, THIS IS NOT THE PICTURE SHOW

Bobbie Ann Mason, WITH JAZZ

Jill McCorkle, WAITING FOR HARD TIMES TO END

Robert Morgan, POINSETT'S BRIDGE

Reynolds Price, HIS FINAL MOTHER

Mark Richard, THE BIRDS FOR CHRISTMAS

Susan Starr Richards, THE SCREENED PORCH

Lee Smith, INTENSIVE CARE

Peter Taylor, COUSIN AUBREY

NEW STORIES FROM THE SOUTH: THE YEAR'S BEST, 1992

Alison Baker, CLEARWATER AND LATISSIMUS

Larry Brown, A ROADSIDE RESURRECTION

Mary Ward Brown, A NEW LIFE

James Lee Burke, TEXAS CITY, 1947

Robert Olen Butler, A GOOD SCENT FROM A STRANGE MOUNTAIN

Nanci Kincaid, A STURDY PAIR OF SHOES THAT FIT GOOD

Patricia Lear, AFTER MEMPHIS

Dan Leone, YOU HAVE CHOSEN CAKE

Reginald McKnight, QUITTING SMOKING

Karen Minton, LIKE HANDS ON A CAVE WALL

Elizabeth Seydel Morgan, ECONOMICS

Robert Morgan, DEATH CROWN

Susan Perabo, EXPLAINING DEATH TO THE DOG

Padgett Powell, THE WINNOWING OF MRS. SCHUPING

Lee Smith, THE BUBBA STORIES

Peter Taylor, THE WITCH OF OWL MOUNTAIN SPRINGS

Abraham Verghese, LILACS

NEW STORIES FROM THE SOUTH: THE YEAR'S BEST, 1993

Richard Bausch, EVENING

Pinckney Benedict, BOUNTY

Wendell Berry, A JONQUIL FOR MARY PENN

Robert Olen Butler, PREPARATION

Lee Merrill Byrd, MAJOR SIX POCKETS

Kevin Calder, NAME ME THIS RIVER

Tony Earley, CHARLOTTE

Paula K. Gover, WHITE BOYS AND RIVER GIRLS

David Huddle, TROUBLE AT THE HOME OFFICE

Barbara Hudson, SELLING WHISKERS

Elizabeth Hunnewell, FAMILY PLANNING

Dennis Loy Johnson, RESCUING ED

Edward P. Jones, MARIE

Wayne Karlin, PRISONERS

Dan Leone, SPINACH

Jill McCorkle, MAN WATCHER

Annette Sanford, HELENS AND ROSES

Peter Taylor, THE WAITING ROOM

NEW STORIES FROM THE SOUTH: THE YEAR'S BEST, 1994

Frederick Barthelme, RETREAT

Richard Bausch, AREN'T YOU HAPPY FOR ME?

Ethan Canin, THE PALACE THIEF

Kathleen Cushman, LUXURY

Tony Earley, THE PROPHET FROM JUPITER

Pamela Erbe, SWEET TOOTH

Barry Hannah, NICODEMUS BLUFF

Nanci Kincaid, PRETENDING THE BED WAS A RAFT

Nancy Krusoe, LANDSCAPE AND DREAM

Robert Morgan, DARK CORNER

Reynolds Price, DEEDS OF LIGHT

Leon Rooke, THE HEART MUST FROM ITS BREAKING

John Sayles, PEELING

George Singleton, OUTLAW HEAD & TAIL

Melanie Sumner, MY OTHER LIFE

Robert Love Taylor, MY MOTHER'S SHOES

NEW STORIES FROM THE SOUTH: THE YEAR'S BEST, 1995

R. Sebastian Bennett, RIDING WITH THE DOCTOR

Wendy Brenner, I AM THE BEAR

James Lee Burke, WATER PEOPLE

Robert Olen Butler, BOY BORN WITH TATTOO OF ELVIS

Ken Craven, PAYING ATTENTION

Tim Gautreaux, THE BUG MAN

Ellen Gilchrist, THE STUCCO HOUSE

Scott Gould, BASES

Barry Hannah, DRUMMER DOWN

MMM Hayes, FIXING LU

Hillary Hebert, LADIES OF THE MARBLE HEARTH

Jesse Lee Kercheval, GRAVITY

NEW STORIES FROM THE SOUTH: THE YEAR'S BEST, 1996

NEW STORIES FROM THE SOUTH: THE YEAR'S BEST, 1997

Dwight Allen, THE GREEN SUIT

Edward Allen, ASHES NORTH

Robert Olen Butler, HELP ME FIND MY SPACEMAN LOVER

Janice Daugharty, ALONG A WIDER RIVER

Ellen Douglas, JULIA AND NELLIE

Pam Durban, GRAVITY

Charles East, PAVANE FOR A DEAD PRINCESS

Rhian Margaret Ellis, EVERY BUILDING WANTS TO FALL

Tim Gautreaux, LITTLE FROGS IN A DITCH

Elizabeth Gilbert, THE FINEST WIFE

Lucy Hochman, SIMPLER COMPONENTS

Beauvais McCaddon, THE HALF-PINT

Dale Ray Phillips, CORPORAL LOVE

Patricia Elam Ruff, THE TAXI RIDE

Lee Smith, NATIVE DAUGHTER

Judy Troy, RAMONE

Marc Vassallo, AFTER THE OPERA

Brad Vice, MOJO FARMER

NEW STORIES FROM THE SOUTH: THE YEAR'S BEST, 1998

PREFACE *by Padgett Powell*

Frederick Barthelme, THE LESSON

Wendy Brenner, NIPPLE

Stephen Dixon, THE POET

Tony Earley, BRIDGE

Scott Ely, TALK RADIO

Tim Gautreaux, SORRY BLOOD

Michael Gills, WHERE WORDS GO

John Holman, RITA'S MYSTERY

Stephen Marion, NAKED AS TANYA

Jennifer Moses, GIRLS LIKE YOU

Padgett Powell, ALIENS OF AFFECTION

Sara Powers, THE BAKER'S WIFE

Mark Richard, MEMORIAL DAY

Nancy Richard, THE ORDER OF THINGS

Josh Russell, YELLOW JACK

Annette Sanford, IN THE LITTLE HUNKY RIVER

Enid Shomer, THE OTHER MOTHER

George Singleton, THESE PEOPLE ARE US

Molly Best Tinsley, THE ONLY WAY TO RIDE

NEW STORIES FROM THE SOUTH: THE YEAR'S BEST, 1999

PREFACE *by Tony Earley*

Andrew Alexander, LITTLE BITTY PRETTY ONE

Richard Bausch, MISSY

Pinckney Benedict, MIRACLE BOY

Wendy Brenner, THE HUMAN SIDE OF INSTRUMENTAL
    TRANSCOMMUNICATION

Laura Payne Butler, BOOKER T'S COMING HOME

Mary Clyde, KRISTA HAD A TREBLE CLEF ROSE

Janice Daugharty, NAME OF LOVE

Rick DeMarinis, BORROWED HEARTS

Tony Earley, QUILL

Clyde Edgerton, LUNCH AT THE PICADILLY

Michael Erard, BEYOND THE POINT

NEW STORIES FROM THE SOUTH: THE YEAR'S BEST, 2000

Margo Rabb, HOW TO TELL A STORY

Karen Sagstetter, THE THING WITH WILLIE

Mary Helen Stefaniak, A NOTE TO BIOGRAPHERS REGARDING FAMOUS
    AUTHOR FLANNERY O'CONNOR

Melanie Sumner, GOOD-HEARTED WOMAN

NEW STORIES FROM THE SOUTH: THE YEAR'S BEST, 2001

PREFACE *by Lee Smith*

John Barth, THE REST OF YOUR LIFE

Madison Smartt Bell, TWO LIVES

Marshall Boswell, IN BETWEEN THINGS

Carrie Brown, FATHER JUDGE RUN

Stephen Coyne, HUNTING COUNTRY

Moira Crone, WHERE WHAT GETS INTO PEOPLE COMES FROM

William Gay, THE PAPERHANGER

Jim Grimsley, JESUS IS SENDING YOU THIS MESSAGE

Ingrid Hill, JOLIE-GRAY

Christie Hodgen, THE HERO OF LONELINESS

Nicola Mason, THE WHIMSIED WORLD

Edith Pearlman, SKIN DEEP

Kurt Rheinheimer, SHOES

Jane R. Shippen, I AM NOT LIKE NUÑEZ

George Singleton, PUBLIC RELATIONS

Robert Love Taylor, PINK MIRACLE IN EAST TENNESSEE

James Ellis Thomas, THE SATURDAY MORNING CAR WASH CLUB

Elizabeth Tippens, MAKE A WISH

Linda Wendling, INAPPROPRIATE BABIES

New Stories from the South: The Year's Best, 2002

New Stories from the South: The Year's Best, 2003

NEW STORIES FROM THE SOUTH: THE YEAR'S BEST, 2004

NEW STORIES FROM THE SOUTH: THE YEAR'S BEST, 2005